STARS UNCHARTED

S. K. DUNSTALL

ACE
NEW YORK

ACE
Published by Berkley
An imprint of Penguin Random House LLC
375 Hudson Street, New York, New York 10014

Library of Congress Cataloging-in-Publication Data

Names: Dunstall, S. K., author.
Title: Stars uncharted / S. K. Dunstall.
Description: First edition. | New York : Ace, August 2018.
Identifiers: LCCN 2017052595 | ISBN 9780399587627 |
ISBN 9780399587634 (ebook)
Subjects: LCSH: Science fiction.
Classification: LCC PR9619.4.D866 S73 2018 | DDC 823/.92—dc23
LC record available at https://lccn.loc.gov/2017052595

First Edition: August 2018

Printed in the United States of America
1   3   5   7   9   10   8   6   4   2

Cover art by John Harris
Cover design by Judith Lagerman
Book design by Kelly Lipovich

To our mother, Della Dunstall. We've named the most precious element in the galaxy after you. You deserve it.

We miss you, Mum. May your afterlife be filled with lots of love, travel, and adventure.

1

NIKA RIK TERRI

The first thing Nika noticed about the man who buzzed the studio bell was his scar. A deep purple line that started at the top center of his lip and went upward in a diagonal slash across his right eye and into his hairline. She zoomed in on the eyeball. A wound like that should have destroyed the eye, but his right eye was real, and tracked as well as the left.

Why hadn't they fixed the scar when they'd fixed the eye?

She glanced at the clock at the bottom of the screen. 00:07. Midnight. Way too late for her studio to be open. Way too late for anyone to demand service—no matter how badly they were scarred, especially not for a scar that old.

"Come back tomorrow," she told him.

"Nika Rik Terri?" Red drops sprayed out of his mouth onto the camera lens above the doorbell. "I need your help."

Once Nika wouldn't have known what the red-brown spots were, but that had been before Alejandro.

Her eyes moved to his collar, to the now-familiar obsidian bird-of-prey pin there. An Eaglehawk Company man. She couldn't tell him to go away. She quashed the quick adrenaline flutter, sighed, and buzzed him in. "Move directly into the room on the left, and try not to bleed on the floor as you go."

She collected a bucket and bleach as she went down to meet him. Blood was hard to get rid of. She didn't want the health inspectors on her back.

But first, she had to stanch the bleeding and get her new customer under a machine.

Saving people's lives hadn't been what Nika had planned to do with her career. Not until Alejandro had walked into her life and brought his scummy friends with him.

The smaller room had glass walls she could wash down easily. Reinforced, because some of the people who came in were prone to violence. On the back of the glass she'd painted scenes of the dappled purple-and-rust trees of the Lower Sierras, with their distinctive radioactive rocks that glowed in the same colorway. One wall for each season—wet, dry, and reactive. The fourth wall, the one with the door, blended the wet and reactive seasons so seamlessly you couldn't tell where one season started and the other ended.

Most people thought only of the stunning visual impact it gave the room.

Nika saw practicality. Good camouflage for any blood that might have spilled.

The tiled floor emulated the phosphorous purples and rusts of the Lower Sierran radioactive rocks.

A work of art, according to respected media site *Popular Art*. A galactic treasure. She could have charged people to see it.

Overpowering, in Nika's opinion, but it did what it was required to do.

According to *Popular Art*, the only thing that spoiled the view was the big black box in the center of the room. The Songyan gen-emod machine. To Nika, the Songyan was the most beautiful thing there. State-of-the-art, built to her specifications. There was only one machine better, and that was in her main studio next door.

There wasn't any blood on the floor of the foyer, and most of the blood on her visitor's jacket and hands had dried. The bleeding was internal, then. That was bad. Still, this man had known to come here, so he'd been sent by Alejandro's boss, who could help her dispose of a dead body if she needed to.

She collected bandages and a pressure seal from the main store. "Where are you wounded?"

"You don't look like Rik Terri."

Nika stifled a sigh. "I'm a body modder. I change my appearance every season." This season it was a small, straight nose, deep black eyes, porcelain skin with a tint of gold and a soft glow to prevent the color from looking ghoulish, a boyish figure with almost no bust, and short-cropped spiky black-and-blond hair. She'd had it two days now. "Where are you wounded?"

He indicated his stomach, which was dressed, but blood seeped through the bandages.

She in turn indicated the Songyan. *Popular Art* had called it a big black box, but it was actually two boxes, one hip-high from the floor, topped with a soft table to lie on. The other descended from the roof. The machine did everything from a full-body analysis all the way down to complete cellular regeneration.

"Lie back and I'll take a look. Put your clothes there." She indicated the sterilizing unit beside the Songyan.

He was a tall man, with good bone structure under the terrifying scar. She could see that he kept himself in shape, and she took a moment to appreciate the aesthetics. This body she could do wonders with.

His hair was thin. Balding even. But she had designed a new plug-in to deal with that. She could give him luxuriant hair of any color. Purple? No. Too fashionable. A more natural color. Blue-black with blue highlights.

And blue eyes to go with it. Ultramarine, flecked with silver.

She pondered the combinations as she removed the dressing and let the scanner check his internal organs. A knife wound.

Once upon a time she wouldn't have recognized the distinctive lacerations left by a knife.

"You've blood in your lungs." Not much—yet—but each breath rattled out with a wheezing bubbling that she didn't need the machine to hear. "You're still bleeding internally. If I don't fix it, you'll drown."

Or die from internal hemorrhaging. Or loss of blood.

"Wait." He held out a bloodied hand to grip her arm. His grip was stronger than it had any right to be, especially given how much blood was floating free around his innards. "You are Nika Rik Terri?"

Technically, she was Nika James now, but that was her secret. "What do you think?"

"You built the exchanger."

She froze. The exchanger was also her secret.

One of her customers—formerly male—had wanted to be female. The customer was happy with her new look, but Nika wasn't. Her client still walked with a heavy, masculine tread. Nika had come up with a plan to retrain her memory of walking by strengthening the synaptic link between short-term and long-term memories, so that the newer memories of walking were the ones she retained.

She'd used the same technique, with success, on other clients. It had worked well, until the day Nika had been short of the alloy that helped create the memory net, and had used the wildly expensive transuride—dellarine—instead.

Luckily, she'd tried it out on Alejandro, not a client, because the net hadn't worked. Well, it had, but not the way it was meant to. The pure metal had transferred the brainwaves through the gene-mod machine across to him, temporarily putting her thoughts and memories into Alejandro's body, and vice versa.

Damn Alejandro. He was the only person who had known about the exchanger. This man could only have learned about it from him.

"No."

His grip tightened. "You built an exchanger."

She tried to pull away. Couldn't.

She ignored the panicked racing of her heart. She could deal with this.

"It was an accidental by-product of something else I built. It's untested." Although she and Alejandro had played around with it. Not to mention, it had been the final crack in a relationship she was fast becoming concerned about, and the excuse she used when she had finally tried to kick him out. Alejandro had loved that blasted exchanger.

She told him she'd destroyed it. But she hadn't, of course.

"Look." She deliberately changed the subject. "I can fix that scar for you while you're under."

The grip on her arm tightened. She thought she'd pass out from the pain of it. Skanky-smelling drops of red-brown sprayed her face. "Leave my scar alone."

"All right." Some people were like that. Proud of their physical deformities. "Let's get you under the machine."

She pulled her arm back again. This time he let her break free.

Something hard pressed into her stomach. She looked down.

It was a weapon.

"The exchanger," the scarred stranger said.

Nika should never have accepted help from Eaglehawk Company, back when she realized Alejandro would never let her go. *This* was what happened. She forced her breathing to slow. "I destroyed it."

She should have taken him into the main studio. There were more things there she could use to defend herself.

"If you destroyed it I have no reason to keep you alive."

Nika stepped back. "You really should let me put you under. You'll die from internal bleeding otherwise."

"I estimate I have four hours before it becomes debilitating."

Nika would put it more at two, but she didn't argue.

"I have time to get to a hospital and have it fixed." He smiled. His scar twisted the smile and turned it into a leer. Blood rimmed each tooth. "What I can't do is get it fixed and do the job I have been paid to do at the same time." His voice hardened. "I always deliver on my contracts."

"Don't ask" had been Nika's policy ever since Alejandro's boss had started sending his people to her to be fixed. But a job, plus an exchanger, didn't add up to anything good.

She hated surrendering her body to this. She didn't trust any of them. Not since Alejandro. Not knowing how her body might be used.

"You want to borrow my body so you can go and do this job." Probably a murder. They were the sort of people Alejandro worked with.

"While you fix mine."

She forced her voice to be calm. "It seems to me all the benefits go your way. What do I get out of it?"

"How about your life?"

That was a given, although she rather doubted it would be part of the bargain. Anyone who pulled a weapon on her and wanted to use the exchanger was unlikely to leave her alive.

She still had her escape-from-Alejandro plans in place, though she'd never had to use them. But she couldn't escape while this man was conscious.

"I don't do this sort of thing for nothing. It's a hundred thousand credits if you want to use the exchanger. I want payment up front."

She held up the scanner. For a moment, she thought he would haggle. He had better not. She'd charge ten times that for the use of the exchanger if it were legal. And that was without her body being one of those exchanged.

He finally took the scanner, allowed it to read his iris and fingerprints, and accepted the charge.

She couldn't stop her smile, and hoped he interpreted it as relief.

Her scanner was something she'd invented herself after one too many dodgy dealings from Alejandro's friends. Scarface didn't know it, but now she had a record of the details the biometric scanner required for identification. She'd fix that when she fixed his body. This was the last time he'd be able to use that account. Not until he got access to a first-class hacker.

It also gave his name. Tamati Woden.

Ice slid between her shoulder blades. Alejandro and his friends had talked about Tamati "Scarface" Woden. No wonder he didn't want her to fix the scar. It was his trademark. Rumor was that Tamati's scarred face was the last thing you saw before you died.

And you did die. Tamati Woden left no witnesses. He'd once killed a high-ranking executive from Brown Combine and murdered the witnesses while they stood. Two of the witnesses ran. Tamati had tracked them down and murdered them, too.

There was no question. Tamati would kill her after he'd finished his job.

She hid her shaking hands. "Come into the main studio. The exchanger is built into the large machine."

He followed her in.

Her back itched.

"On the bed," she said.

"Exchanger first."

It was a good idea to be on the bed for that, too, but she didn't argue, just pulled the headsets out. "You might want to lie down."

He didn't.

Bastard. It was his body she would inhabit, and *she* didn't want to be standing up when the change happened. She knew how disorienting it was. Still, if he wanted to be contrary, so would she. She placed the tiny nodes around Tamati's head—one on either side of his forehead, one behind each ear, one at the top of his spine—and checked that the connections were stable.

She repeated the process on herself, and didn't warn him about the dizziness or the disorientation he would experience. Or how strange a tall man like him would find it in a shorter body like hers.

She'd get her body back bruised. The first time she'd swapped with Alejandro he'd bumped into a lot of things because he hadn't taken into account her curves. After a while he'd gotten used to them, come to like them rather too much. So much so that she'd offered to give him his own, which had led to their second-last major fight.

This time her curves were smaller, but it didn't take much to misjudge.

She set the connections. "Ready?" And she flipped the switch before Tamati could get out the "Wait" he'd started to say.

A flash of blue, white, then gold. There was the usual moment of disorientation where her brain interpreted things at a different height and in a different color than what she was used to. The room smelled strongly of blood. His body's blood. Her blood now. Then the pain centers kicked in and she dropped the weapon Tamati had been holding to clutch at her stomach as she realized how much she hurt.

Her thoughts were fuzzy.

"How many painkillers have you had?" It was a wonder he could walk, let alone talk.

Tamati dived for the weapon, misjudged the distance, and planted himself nose-first into the floor.

He stood up, weapon in hand, stepped back, and waved the weapon in her face.

Nika ignored him. She concentrated instead on the slow, steady movements she needed to make until this body became familiar to her. Everything was obscured by the haze of painkillers Tamati had taken. How had he gripped her arm like he had? She felt leaden and heavy.

Tamati waved the weapon under her nose, unsteady, but enough in control that it could kill her. "Fix my injury while I am away. I'll be back in two hours."

"It will take four hours to fix the knife wound. You've lost a lot of blood." A genemod machine was fast on the basics, like repairing damaged bodies. It was only when you tried to change a body that it took time.

"Don't try killing my body in the interim." He leaned close. "I know that when one of us dies, the other returns to his own body. That's how it works, isn't it?"

Nika nodded mutely. That was the theory, although she'd never tested it. Otherwise, the bodies automatically swapped back after twenty-four hours.

A bigger worry was that Tamati would consider her body dispensable, and let her be killed on his job.

He'd get a nasty shock if he did, for she'd take a long time to die. Long enough for him to think the bodies weren't going to change back.

Nika was paranoid Alejandro might almost-kill her one day. Just for fun. That he'd do something to her body while he was in it—like maybe put a noose around her neck and jump off somewhere high. He'd be fine, because once she was dead, he'd return to his own body. He'd then cut her down and put her into the genemod machine. If he didn't time it right, she'd be brain-dead.

Hence her own last modification but one. To push extra oxygen to her brain when her body started to shut down. It gave her fifteen minutes before any brain damage started, and another fifteen before she was irreparable.

She hadn't tested that, either.

"I have taken precautions," Tamati said. "If I don't get out of here alive, you won't either."

"You can be sure I'll do my utmost to keep you alive." The comment was heartfelt.

He smiled the twisted-leer smile with Nika's face. Even when he didn't have a scar he twisted his mouth the same way. "I am glad we understand each other." He brought his weapon down on her home link, smashing it. "No calling anyone."

"You didn't have to do that. Who am I going to call with your voice and your face?"

"The police, maybe."

Who, if they knew Eaglehawk was involved, would run fast the other way.

"Remember, our bodies switch back after twenty-four hours."

"Won't be a problem. I'll be back long before." Tamati waited for her to connect herself into the regen unit. "I want to be sure you're under before I go."

She set the timer for four minutes instead of four hours, and prayed he wouldn't notice the difference. Any longer and it would be too dangerous to come out of it before full repairs had been done.

The last thing she remembered before the machine knocked her out was her own face looming over her, saying in her own voice, "Don't think you can double-cross me."

When Nika regained consciousness the room was quiet. For a moment, she lay in the haze of the painkillers Tamati had taken and wanted to go back to sleep.

She forced herself off the machine.

She hurt in every single place she could hurt, and her brain kept going *hurry, hurry*, reminding her she hadn't stopped the internal bleeding. He would die if she didn't stay on the machine.

She felt dirty in this body she hadn't asked for, and the sight of Tamati's longer fingers touching the controls on her machine, mimicking the moves her hands normally made, turned her stomach.

Four minutes had drained enough liquid out of her lungs so she was no longer in danger of imminent drowning, although she imagined she could feel new blood pooling in, even now. She was also weak from loss of blood. She hooked herself up to a portable plasma supply and waited precious minutes until the feed had finished. She didn't have long, but there was no point dying before she was done.

Tamati hadn't wasted any time leaving for his job, but he'd still stopped to lock every door that was coded to her own DNA—iris and fingerprint. There was no way she'd get out before he came back.

That was fine. She didn't want out. She wanted to stay alive. Tamati would keep her body alive until they switched back, at least.

She hoped.

All she had to do was keep this one alive for that long.

Someone like Alejandro, or Alejandro's boss, would have kept her alive and come back to use the exchanger, again, and again. Not Tamati. Not with his reputation. He'd tidy up after the job.

What could she do to increase her chances of living through the next day?

She swallowed the bile—or was it blood—that rose at the thought of Tamati, in her body, waiting to kill her.

If she could keep him in the genemod machine for more than a day, and his—her—body outside for twenty-four hours, she'd be back in her own body before he came out of the machine.

Nika laughed, although it hurt. One advantage of having had an abusive boyfriend was that you were paranoid about him getting back in to hurt you. She had locks—double, triple, quadruple—on everything. Cleverly hidden from her clients, but still there. Manual locks that would take time and effort to break through.

She'd be gone before he got out.

Maybe she could get a little revenge at the same time. Redesign his body. Make him unrecognizable as Tamati Woden. That might scuttle future job prospects. Yes. She'd do that. A full-body redesign would take days in the machine, give her more time to escape.

She didn't have time to create a new look from scratch, so she picked through her old designs, heavy-headed from the pain-killers.

Sex change? No. Tamati was the sort who'd adapt. He'd proba-bly find it useful in his profession.

The scar was a given. She programmed that in. Consider it gone.

Iris and fingerprint change as well. When she had finished, he wouldn't be able to touch anything he'd secured with biometrics. If he was as paranoid as she expected him to be, he wouldn't have another way in to his own personal system, because he'd expect someone to hack it.

She kept the data, carefully ensuring that her off-site backups recorded every detail of his DNA, his irises, his fingerprints, toe-prints, and everything else about him. A blood sample. Hair and skin.

She had to stop. She was getting weaker. She'd have to put him under soon.

What else could she do?

What would an assassin hate the most?

To be noticed.

She laughed again, and foul-smelling drops of brownish-red liquid sprayed onto the screen. If you were an assassin, you didn't want to be seen. Although how Tamati managed that with his scar she had no idea. Probably covered it with a nuplas face when he went out on jobs.

She'd had a client once who'd been allergic to nuplas. It had taken weeks to work out what had caused the allergy. A tiny marker on the end of the MC1R gene. She programmed the marker in. If Tamati tried to disguise his face with nuplas he'd break out in a painful rash that would take weeks to clear and itch like mad all the time he had it. Standard painkillers—even nerveseal—made the rash worse.

She flicked through her templates, looking for the one she'd designed for Alejandro. Back when she'd first been smitten by him.

She'd worked on it ever since, perfecting it over time. Yes. That one. It was fitting, really. Passing Alejandro's new body over to someone else signaled the end of this period of her life.

She hesitated. This truly was the end. The end of Alejandro. The end of Alejandro's boss. The end of Nika Rik Terri.

She'd thought she was ready. She wasn't.

She turned back to the design, Tamati's strong fingers shaking. She couldn't stop the shake.

It was a simple design, deceptively natural except for the deep cobalt green of the eyes and the thick, luxurious hair that picked up the metallic sheen of polished copper, along with a touch of the tarnished green patina of hydrated copper chloride, which would become more noticeable as his hair became damp. Wet, it would be totally green.

The patina had taken her years to perfect.

Deep-set green eyes, copper hair. Delicate, unblemished skin that carried a hint of the copper. Square jaw. Strong mouth, soft lips. Aquiline nose that looked as if it would be too large but wasn't. Noses continued to grow over the years. If he wanted to continue to look his best he'd need to come back in two to three years and have some shaved off.

He wouldn't, of course.

A pity she didn't have time to build something in so that he couldn't leer as he smiled. He'd still do that. It was an ingrained habit.

This man was going to turn heads wherever he went.

What else?

Nika's first and only boss, Hannah Tan, had specialized in DNA changes. She'd been passionate about them. "No one knows how to do them anymore," she had said. "Not like the golden days when artists like Gino Giwari were at their peak."

Hannah had lived and breathed DNA changes, and for five years Nika had too.

"I am the best," Hannah had told Nika often. "But Gino Giwari, he was . . . he was God. He could do anything."

Nika had learned everything she could about Gino Giwari. There was plenty to learn. He hadn't been a modest man. He'd published extensively and documented many of the changes he had made.

Over time she had come to believe that while Giwari had been more than capable of successfully changing someone's DNA, he hadn't been an artist, he'd been a technician. His changes were always in the same places. It got so that all Nika had to do was read a sequence of DNA and she could recognize Giwari's work.

In fact, the thing he should have been famous for, which had been buried under years of posturing about DNA changes, was his pioneering use of transurides in body modding. Nika was using it now, to give her skin its ethereal glow.

Giwari's DNA techniques had never taken off. Nika had reproduced some of them, but always with problems. And DNA modified that deeply didn't take well to future mods.

Drops of blood spattered onto the screen. A little tweak of the DNA, Giwari-style, and Tamati would always have trouble with genemod machines.

A perfect design for an assassin who liked to go unnoticed except when he did his kills, and a nasty surprise next time he was injured.

She set up the life support. Her calculations told her it would take twelve days.

She set the safeties.

Alejandro's meddling had taught her early that she had to build in safeties. Especially after they had started using the exchanger and she'd come back to her own body once to find that while he'd been in her body he'd redesigned it to add twenty millimeters to her bust and to remove the same from her waist. After that she'd made good and sure he couldn't touch what she'd set up. The controls were memory-based. Nothing Alejandro could use by forcing her body to the scanner. No biometrics, no prints, no DNA. Pure memory.

Once Tamati's body went into the box, nothing would let him out until the process was complete.

It was done. She triggered the locks, including the manual locks—old-fashioned bolts that you had to pull back, and chains—that stopped anyone coming into the shop but could be opened from inside. And you didn't need DNA to do it.

The exchanger had been their final fight. After she'd dumped him, he'd come back again, and again. It had terrified her that he might get into her shop while she was in the machine. He knew just enough to do major damage.

When Tamati came around he'd get out.

He just wouldn't get in beforehand.

She tubed up, and immersed herself in the mutrient bath.

2

JOSUNE ARRIOLA

The *Hassim* was three days late. At first, Josune had only been worried because every day's delay increased the chances of discovery. If she had known how paranoid Captain Hammond Roystan was about trackers on his precious ship, *The Road to the Goberlings*, she'd have found another way to keep in touch with the *Hassim*. Would even have risked a coded message.

Now she was just worried.

Captain Feyodor had been waiting for her signal. She should be here by now.

"You going to do some work around here?" Carlos demanded, and Josune dragged her attention back to the gear she was curing. She spared a wistful thought for the *Hassim*'s workshop, whose molder cured as it built. The gear she had just built would have been harder than tempered steel when it came out of the molder, instead of her having to cure it for an hour afterward.

"Both ends, Josune. Do it evenly. I don't want a gear breaking in nullspace."

"Teach your grandmother, Carlos." But Josune obediently switched the gear around so the heat lamp could work on the other end. Carlos might be unqualified, but he was a natural engineer, and he certainly knew his way around a molder. So did Josune, but she had spent years studying ship engineering. Those qualifications didn't show on the certificate she'd handed Roystan when she'd applied for this job. That certificate said she was a junior technician who'd gained all her experience on an old cargo runner named the *Breadbasket*, which had worked out on the rim.

Carlos watched her. "For a newbie, you're good at this."

"I had a lot of practice. The *Breadbasket* kept breaking down."

"Thought you claimed it had the best engine in the sector."

She had to be careful, remember what she'd said. "That's because I was on it."

Roystan hadn't been able to check her credentials with her supposed former captain. The *Breadbasket* had fallen afoul of a cattle ship. The reason Josune hadn't been with her crew? She'd been in jail, drunk and disorderly, when they'd shipped out. She was supposed to meet them at their next port. At least, that was what she'd told Roystan.

Roystan had taken her on because he needed an extra general hand. Josune being an engineer was a bonus. But he'd given her a stern warning. "Get drunk here and we won't bail you out. Don't expect to join us at the next port, either."

"You young people," Carlos said. "Always think you know everything."

She'd lied about her age too; said she was twenty-five. She'd spent time in a machine to make herself look ten years younger than she was. The hardest part was trying to act like a twenty-five-year-old.

She shouldn't have to lie much longer. But the *Hassim* was late.

They gathered as a group for the evening meal. Roystan switched the boards from the bridge to the display in the crew room so they could eat together. Over time, the crew room on *The Road* had been modified so much that it had become a secondary bridge. If they'd been able to connect the pilot controls and the calibrator to the crew room, Josune was convinced no one would ever step onto the main bridge except for maintenance.

There were seven crew. Josune and Roystan. General hand and

de facto engineer Carlos. Chef and cargo master Jacques, who'd spent the six weeks Josune had been on board cooking and talking to his kitchen appliances. The longest time he spent in cargo was when choosing what to cook for dinner. There was plenty of cargo space set aside for food.

Cargo assistant Pol did most of the cargo work, with the help of two other general hands, Guardian and Qiang. Guardian doubled as the second pilot. Josune didn't know what Qiang's second role was, but as she was the only one allowed to carry a blaster, she assumed Qiang was the ship heavy.

She touched her hand to the welcoming hardness of the sparker strapped to her stomach. It made her uneasy to walk around on a ship unarmed. Roystan and his crew might think they were safe here so deep in the legal zone, but Josune knew from experience that when a company wanted something, the legal zone was no barrier. The Justice Department—paid by the companies to maintain the legal zone—turned a blind eye to what the companies did, and sometimes actively helped them. Weapons were occasionally necessary.

Eating together was a ritual Roystan insisted on. At first Josune had thought it strange, but she had to admit, they solved a lot of problems over the dinner table.

Captain Feyodor would hate it. She ate alone in her room, working at the same time. Josune had lost count of the times one or another of the *Hassim*'s crew had brought a cold, congealed dinner back to the galley because Feyodor had forgotten to eat. But then, they hadn't had anyone like Jacques to cook for them either.

Tonight, dinner was a white root vegetable in an exotic green cream sauce, with reconstituted rainbow chard on the side.

Josune closed her eyes and savored the smooth spices on her tongue. "This is so good, Jacques." She would miss Jacques's cooking.

"Of course it's good. I cooked it."

She wouldn't miss the arrogant certainty that he was the best chef in the galaxy.

Pol and Qiang had their heads together, doing sums.

"Easy," Pol said, "and we can still have a four-day layover at Atalante." She looked up.

Captain Roystan shook his head. "We've been over this before, Pol. I'm not taking on extra work."

"It's not your decision. Shared profit, remember."

Josune took a piece of spicy flatbread and stayed quiet. She was paid crew on this ship, not part of the profit share. This argument didn't concern her.

"If you don't like it, take your share and go. I have final say on what we carry, and where."

"We spend a third of our time on rec leave. Spending credits we don't have. We waste our ship capacity. We—"

The ship rocked. Proximity alarms blared.

A ship. Coming out of nullspace close by. Too close.

The emergency jets fired automatically, providing a counterforce to the oncoming ship, using the other ship's speed to push their own ship back, so that the two ships traveled parallel.

Roystan and Guardian ran for the bridge.

The rest of them watched it on the screen.

"Why doesn't the bastard slow down?" Jacques demanded, as *The Road* fired jets again. This time the burst was longer, more controlled. Josune could tell from the burn that Roystan was at the controls, not Guardian.

Josune had seen pilotless ships before. "There's no one at the helm."

Otherwise the pilot would be frantically firing his own jets to put as much distance as possible between the two ships. And answering his calls, for Roystan was hailing him.

"Dead ship," Carlos said, softly beside her. Around the table, the crew sucked in breaths of anticipation.

"Don't start counting your credits," Josune said. "The pilot might have had a heart attack. The engines might have gone down. There'll be people on there, for sure."

"One can hope." Carlos moved over to the screen feed and flicked through the external cameras to get a good image of the ship. "Let's see what our treasure might be."

Josune put a hand to her mouth as the view of the ship magnified. She recognized it.

Roystan must have identified the ship's beacon then, for he changed his message. "*Hassim*, are you receiving us? Please respond."

The *Hassim* still wasn't talking to them half an hour later, when Guardian and Roystan finally had the two ships drifting together at the same speed and distance.

"*Hassim*." Pol's voice was hushed. "Do you know what that ship is?"

Roystan ignored her. "Four of us will go across." He unlocked the weapons cupboard. "Me, Guardian, Qiang, and Josune. The *Hassim* crew won't have deserted their ship, not without a fight."

"Josune's not in the profit share," Pol said. "Why should she go across?"

"Because she's an engineer," Roystan said. "If they're in trouble, that's probably what they need."

"Why not send Carlos, then?"

"Because Carlos is *our* engineer and we can't afford to lose him." Roystan handed out weapons. A blaster for Guardian, a stunner for himself. Qiang had a blaster. "Don't forget, this could be a trap."

He hesitated at Josune.

"Stunner." She didn't want to kill her own crew accidentally. Plus, she had a sparker strapped under her shirt. Not that she planned on telling him that. She certainly didn't intend to use it, not unless her crewmates were alive and needed help.

"A trap?" Pol asked. "This far into the legal zone?"

"It will be a trap if we don't get over there soon," Guardian said. "Every second we delay means someone else might take our prize."

Salvage law had come into being to keep the spaceways clean, for nothing was more dangerous than space debris colliding with a ship, or a ship hitting debris as it came out of nullspace. Salvage law gave the finders the right to sell the ship and everything on it—provided all the crew were dead. A ship like the *Hassim* would draw a lot of salvage hunters.

Josune shivered.

"Let's go," Roystan said. "Be wary."

Josune expected trouble.

Captain Feyodor hadn't yet contacted her. She'd had time. If there was anyone alive on that ship, they wouldn't be *Hassim* crew. And they would be waiting for them.

As soon as the airlock opened, Josune fired.

Two men in business suits went down, one of them spraying blaster fire up and over their heads as he fell.

If she'd been any slower the boarding party would be dead.

Guardian, from behind her, yelped as the blaster of the third man caught him.

Roystan's stunner hummed at her ear. Close enough to make the hair on her head crackle as the beam passed over her shoulder. The third man went down, his blaster also spraying the walls, thankfully wide of the airlock.

There were spare panels in cargo. They could repair the damage.

Josune stepped out cautiously, stunner ready.

"They'll be watching from the bridge," Roystan said. "They'll send reinforcements."

Not likely. The *Hassim* wasn't an easy ship to hack the controls on. She'd helped make it that way. The chances of someone external getting the ship's cameras to work were remote.

There'd been a fight at the airlock. Five people dead. Three strangers, all in business suits, plus Reba from cargo, and Deepak, Josune's own second engineer. He'd been a good second.

The *Hassim* carried a crew of twenty. By necessity—and experience—they could all fight. Reba and Deepak were unlikely to have been downed by just three people. There'd be more. A lot more.

Roystan swallowed hard as he turned away. "Walk carefully, people."

"Internal or external?" Qiang wondered.

Josune looked at her.

"This is the *Hassim*. Wouldn't put it past the crew to mutiny."

She had to bite down hard to stop the angry denial and knew her jaw showed white.

"External," Roystan said. "That's a company outfit."

Company clothes were a uniform, of sorts. The attackers all wore suits. Different colors, to be sure, but they were still suits. Deepak's casual coveralls were outlandish beside them. Cargo master Reba wore suits herself on occasion. She spent time with company representatives. Today she was in her nonsuit mode. Sweats, which had soaked up the rapidly drying blood beneath her. Bloodstains spattered the hallway behind her. She'd been stabbed elsewhere but had still run here to make a last stand with Deepak.

Josune silently picked up Reba's sparker. Small, like her own. And one of the blasters from the dead company men. The charge was full. She put her stunner away and settled the blaster in its place.

"Could still be crewmates," Qiang said.

Roystan pointed to the body Josune had taken the blaster from. "That is not one of the *Hassim* crew. The *Hassim* last took on new crew ten years ago."

In the time between identifying the ship and them getting here, Josune hadn't seen Roystan check any records. How did he know how often the *Hassim*'s crew had changed? Had he recognized her? She hoped her modded body was good enough to fool him.

Roystan moved across to check Guardian's injury. "You'll be fine. We'll dress it when we get home, which will be enough until we get you to a genemod machine."

Josune made for the passageway that led toward the bridge. Roystan motioned her to wait.

Behind them, Qiang inspected the suits on the dead company people. "Nice suits. I'd work for a company that paid well enough to afford these."

"You'd work for anyone who pays you," Guardian said. "All of them at the same time."

Roystan shushed them. He was listening, waiting to see if anyone was about to attack.

Josune had the codes. She could have logged in through her implant and seen what was happening on the whole ship. Except if she turned it on, the telltale brightness under her eyelid would give her away, and she hadn't mentioned that particular mod before. It wasn't something she'd have been able to afford on the *Breadbasket*.

She waited, the longest five minutes of her life, until Roystan waved them on.

They found another body halfway down the passageway. Indira Walken, one of the *Hassim*'s general hands. Kristopher Gunn, another general hand, outside the rec room. Josune was glad to see thrice that number in suits. The crew had made the invaders fight for their prize, at least.

There were ten bodies in the rec room. Tied together in a circle, facing inward. Someone had gone around the outside of the circle with a blaster, so their backs were charred but their faces untouched. All of them dead. All of them crew.

The bodies were starting to smell. They'd been dead a while. How many company people would it take to do that to the *Hassim*'s crew, who were prepared for boarders?

Someone would pay for this.

"Tied them together, then executed them," Qiang said.

Roystan gulped, then bolted.

"He has such a weak stomach." Guardian looked green himself. He clapped Josune on the back with his good hand. "You're all right, Josune. You're one of us. Stronger stomach."

It was a nightmare Josune was never going to wake from.

They moved on cautiously.

Josune's shoulders itched.

More than once she was tempted to access the system, because surely giving oneself away was smarter than allowing yourself to be killed.

They passed a link node.

She didn't have to give herself away. "I'll see if I can log in."

"Won't work," Roystan said. "The *Hassim* codes are the best you can buy. You won't crack it. It's our only advantage. You can bet the company are trying to hack it, too."

How did Roystan know so much about the *Hassim*?

"Why were they waiting for us at the airlock, then?" Qiang asked.

"They heard us coming. They'd have felt our shuttle locking onto the outside of a ship."

"I still want to try," Josune said. "I'm good." But Roystan was right. There was no way a young engineer from an old rim ship could break into the *Hassim*'s system. A pity he knew that. Otherwise she could have pretended she had cracked the codes.

Did it matter now? She was on her own ship.

"Down," Roystan yelled, and the heat of a blaster whooshed down the passage.

Josune used the cover of the blaster heat to blink on her implant as she dropped. Five blinks turned it on.

She checked the heat patterns. She didn't need to know who they were fighting, just where the fighters were.

Two warm bodies at the junction of the passage. Another around the corner. Five more heat signatures on the bridge, and three at the airlock. They should have killed the ones at the airlock.

One of the warm bodies at the junction moved. Josune fired as he edged around the corner. She took out part of the passage as well, but she scored.

The other two heat signals started moving away from them. They moved fast.

Josune jumped to her feet. Took off after them. Pounded into the passageway as they turned the next corner. She kept running.

"Wait," Roystan said, but he followed.

The company men were heading for the bridge. "Close Sector 3A doors," Josune whispered, and hoped Roystan was far enough behind not to hear.

The sector doors closed smoothly in front of the company men.

Josune rounded that corner. She fired at the man on the left.

He went down. The other man went down seconds after, stunned by Roystan.

"Thanks." She had to hold herself back from using the blaster to kill the man Roystan had stunned. These people had killed her crewmates. None of them warranted a stunner. They all deserved blasters, as painful and as deadly as those they had inflicted on the *Hassim*'s crew.

"You're very good at this."

"*Breadbasket.* Lots of practice."

Roystan looked at her, but all he said was, "You might want to turn that thing in your eye off before the others get here."

Busted. How much did he know? She touched her finger to her lid and applied the gentle pressure that was the signal to turn off.

"Five heat signals on the bridge. That's all I can see."

"Impressive bionics." But Roystan didn't say anything else.

Qiang and Guardian thundered up then.

"Crazy woman," Qiang said. "You could have got us killed. If that's how you fought on your ship, no wonder the cattle ships got her."

Close to the bridge Roystan stepped up beside her. "Can you tell where they are?" he asked softly.

He was shielding her from the other two. She blinked fast, five times, and touched her finger to her eyelid as soon as she had the heat signals. "Two at the center console, one behind the secondary panel at the far left end, two either side of the door, waiting for us." She kept it soft, for Roystan's ears alone.

She rethought the signals she'd seen. Whoever was inside had locked the door. She blinked again and unlocked the doors. Touched off again. It would give them a few extra seconds, because the people inside would expect them to have to work at the lock. They'd know whoever entered would be enemy. No doubt they'd already tried unsuccessfully to contact their own people at the airlock. Josune knew it wasn't her own crew, for they would have recognized her and said something. At least, she hoped they would. They'd only seen her new body once, the afternoon she'd left for *The Road*. They knew she'd shoot if they didn't identify themselves. Any of them would have. It wasn't the first time the *Hassim* had been attacked.

"Right." Roystan looked at Qiang and Guardian. "We'll sweep the room as we enter. Josune and I will fire close to the door. Josune left, me right. Qiang, you take the far end. Start from the left and sweep across to the right. Guardian? Do you have any aim with that left hand?"

Guardian shrugged.

"Aim for the center panel. There'll be someone there. Keep moving. Don't make yourselves an easy target. And don't either of you shoot us by mistake."

Roystan looked to be around Josune's natural age. He'd spent at least fifteen years running a cargo route well inside the legal zone—Josune had checked before she'd come on board. Where had he got his fighting experience?

Roystan opened the door. They went in firing.

The two men at the door went down. A pity Roystan only had a stunner. They'd have to worry about the company men recovering. And they were all men. Which cut down the number of companies it might be, but that still left a lot it could be.

Guardian's aim was short. Roystan pushed him out of the way. Josune left that fight to him and turned to the two men at the main console.

They'd been working at the panel and had to scramble for weapons. Qiang finished one, Josune the other. Satisfactorily dead, unlike the company man flat on the floor at the secondary panels. Another body to worry about when the stun wore off.

Josune looked around.

Bodies lay everywhere. The rest of the crew. Along with—she counted—eight dead company men. And two not-so-dead, whom they'd have to dispose of somehow.

"Underestimated the *Hassim* crew, at a guess." Roystan sounded sad. "It wouldn't be the first time a company has done that."

It was certainly the first time a company had bested the crew, though.

Josune moved over to where Captain Feyodor sprawled, as ungainly in death as she had been in life. She'd fallen against the main console, her palm flat against the nullspacer button, her body twisted awkwardly over the top of it.

"May your Afterlife be as adventurous as this life."

Roystan looked at her sharply.

"It's a saying we have on my world." It wasn't; they'd said it on Feyodor's world. "Don't you say that for the dead?"

Captain Feyodor would have said it for all her crew. Josune would say it as well.

Roystan shook his head and looked down at the captain's body. "Last thing she did was nullspace. I'm guessing she did it to escape whoever was attacking her. A random jump, to give her and her crew a chance. The company would have had a ship back there, waiting to board her."

Except it hadn't been a random jump. Tears blurred Josune's view. She was glad Roystan pushed the body aside and hunched over the controls so he didn't see her face. The jump had saved her ship, but it hadn't saved her crew. She breathed in deeply and breathed out through her mouth to hide her shuddering sigh.

"Lucky she jumped into our space," Qiang said.

Josune checked the boards, discreetly whispering the codes to her implant to open the cameras. "They got into the security system." She pulled it up. Basic access, which was all the company would have managed.

Roystan rotated through the cameras. "Can't see the cabins. No one is in the passageways."

There were cameras in the cabins, but they were coded to Feyodor and Josune alone. You needed cameras on a spaceship, because if anything went wrong—say an air breach—you needed to see inside every compartment, but that didn't mean you should spy on people.

Roystan turned back to the crew on the floor. Counted them. "Five here, ten back there. Two at the airlock. Two on the way." He looked around. "There's one missing."

How did Roystan know so much about the *Hassim*'s crew?

"Probably still in his bunk," Qiang said. "Waiting for the fight to be over."

Not on the *Hassim*.

Their communicators pinged. A group call.

"Is anyone alive over there?" Pol demanded. "Is it our salvage?"

"I'll check the cabins." Josune walked away numbly, blindly, hardly hearing Roystan's "Wait. Go in pairs."

To Pol and everyone here, this ship was money. Good money, for this was the *Hassim*. Josune's friends were dead. Her home would be picked over by these scavengers. Unless Josune claimed the ship as her right.

She could do it. She had all the codes. The others would think she was stealing their salvage. Except, perhaps, Roystan.

Did she want the ship? She'd never be able to forget the dead everywhere.

Guardian caught up to her. "It's all right. Nothing to be ashamed of. Dead people aren't something you see every day."

"And you do?" Josune didn't look at him. She had probably seen more dead bodies than Roystan's crew combined. But this was different. This was personal.

"A lot of us came from the rim," he said, and she had to remind herself about the *Breadbasket*. "That doesn't mean you get used to the bodies. Even if we pretend to."

In the six weeks she'd been on *The Road*, she'd spoken to Guardian three times outside of their dinner conversations. Once to ask him where supply cupboard three was, and twice to say, "Excuse me," as she came up behind him in one of the narrower passageways.

"Thank you, Guardian."

His smile was a self-conscious twist of the mouth. "Just don't show any weakness around Pol or Qiang. They'll both use it."

"Thank you," she said again.

Their search of the cabins produced no one.

"I don't like it. They're a crew member down." Roystan frowned at Josune as if he suspected something.

"Who cares?" Pol had joined them on the *Hassim*. "Can we get to the important part? Claiming this ship as our salvage."

If Josune was ever going to claim the ship as hers, the time was now, but Pol had a blaster, and greed in her eyes. She'd use the weapon if she had to.

Josune stayed silent.

"Let's not make the claim right away."

"Roystan. You know what ship this is."

"Precisely. As soon as anyone knows it's here, and salvage, every fortune hunter in the galaxy will come. It will be a bloodbath."

"This far inside the legal zone?"

"Even this far." Roystan refused to be swayed by Pol's entreaty. Or by any of the other crew siding with her. "Not until we have everything we want from the ship. Not until we're ready to sell it."

"The bodies need disposal," Josune said. No one but her was going to send her friends off. "What do we do about these?" She indicated their prisoners. They'd bound them in quicktape from engineering and brought them to the bridge where they could keep an eye on them. The company men had since come around.

"Lifeboats," Roystan said.

"This is our ship," one of the prisoners snarled. "We'll take you through the courts for theft."

Josune thought he might be in charge.

Inside the legal zone, the companies had a formal agreement and a court they all contributed to and abided by—which was why it was called the legal zone in the first place.

Roystan laughed, and crawled under the panel. "If it truly were your ship we'd give it to you. But this is the *Hassim*. Everyone knows her crew. Josune?"

She jumped, thinking he knew who she was. Then she realized what he wanted. She unhooked the portable toolkit from her belt and handed it down to him. Roystan was after the ship's memory.

Everything that happened on ship went through that memory. Every keystroke, every spoken command, every change of course, every resource used. With that memory they'd have a full record of where the *Hassim* had been, and every interaction on ship. Even Josune's. Somewhere in there they would hear Captain Feyodor ordering Josune to find Hammond Roystan. Would hear every ping from Josune's marker.

It didn't matter. By the time they hacked the memory, Josune would be gone.

The company man said, "We've already staked our claim."

Roystan's laugh echoed in the chamber he'd opened. "Was that before or after Captain Feyodor jumped through nullspace?"

"What if they did register the ship?" Pol asked.

Roystan grunted, and worked something loose. Josune watched. He'd pulled a memory out before.

"They didn't."

The company man smiled. "It's our word against yours in the courts."

Josune didn't see Pol raise her blaster, but suddenly the room smelled of more burned bodies, and the company men were smoking.

Roystan bumped his head coming fast out from under the panel. It was the only sound.

"Now they won't say anything," Pol said.

A screw dropped behind Roystan. It made a tiny *plink* on the floor.

"You ever murder anyone in cold blood again, Pol, and you're off my ship. This is your only warning."

Roystan lay back to get at the panel again. Josune saw that his hands were shaking.

"I'll start the disposal process," Josune said, and walked out. She didn't say a word to Pol.

Qiang and Guardian came to help her.

"I hate this part." Qiang started to drag one of the company bodies across to where Josune was straightening Deepak.

"Don't." She knew she'd made it too sharp. "Let's do two groups. Put the company people into a different pile."

"But that'll take another rocket."

She didn't care. "Separate piles."

"I'm not wasting credits on extra rockets."

"It's not your credits or rockets to start with. You wouldn't have them without this ship."

Guardian put up his good hand to stop them. "We can put them together at the end."

Not if Josune could prevent it.

When Reba and Deepak were straight and fastened together, Josune grabbed the trolley from the store and went to collect the others. It was only as she was loading Captain Feyodor onto the trolley that she thought they might ask how she had found it.

They didn't.

When she was done, she touched each of them and whispered Captain Feyodor's "May your Afterlife be as adventurous as this life" to each of them.

Guardian and Qiang moved aside so she could do the same thing to the company people. She didn't want to, but they'd think that strange. She studied the bodies while she thought about how to get out of it.

Half the men wore black birds pinned to their collar. A bird of prey, wings wide, talons stretched out to attack. She knelt to study one more closely. A company pin, although she'd never seen this design before. As soon as she tracked down which company it belonged to, she'd know who she had to destroy.

"How long does it take to say a prayer?" Qiang demanded.

Josune pulled the pin off each man as she whispered, "May you get the Afterlife you deserve," and didn't think either of them noticed the change.

Roystan backed up Josune's decision to split the two groups. "One rocket won't make much difference to the profits," he told Qiang. "This is the *Hassim*, after all."

Or an extra four rockets in the end. Roystan sent each sorry human parcel swiftly and surely heading for the nearest sun. Josune was grateful for the mercy.

Reaction was starting to set in, and she wasn't sure if she imagined Roystan's bow and the quiet murmur of "You were an admirable foe, Taki Feyodor. May your Afterlife be more satisfying than this life."

She didn't imagine the avarice that set in after that—although she was almost too numb to think—with Qiang and Pol going through the cabins to see what valuables they could find. She wanted to scream at them, use the sparker under her jacket to keep them away from other people's private belongings.

Maybe Roystan knew she was almost at the breaking point, for he looked at her. "Go back to the ship, Josune. You too, Guardian. Send Carlos over. He can claim what he wants for the engines. Send Jacques over, too. He can claim any cargo he wants."

"Sure." She didn't look back. Her old life was dead.

Josune examined the pins as soon as she was back on *The Road*. No obvious electronics, but that could be hidden. The black metal was an enameled platinum-transuranic alloy. Very expensive, not something a company would hand out to every employee.

An elite group, then. She scanned one and sent it through the link to find out which company it was. No result. That was unusual.

She clutched the tiny pin in her hand. It was her only link with her past life.

This and the marker she'd secreted in engineering so the *Hassim* could track her.

The marker was useless now. Feyodor would never track her again, and it would be one more black mark against her if Roystan discovered it.

Josune retrieved the marker, tossed the tiny device into the recycler, and stood watching long after it had turned to ashes. Like her life. Nothing but ashes.

She spent the rest of the shift mindlessly working through the tasks on Carlos's work-to-do list. Crossing each item off after she'd done it. Deliberately not thinking about the disaster that had happened.

She did as she was bid from her end as Roystan lashed the two ships together. Even admired his technique. He used a classic Endian truss. You couldn't link two ships more securely than that.

The shuttle was loaded, and she heard the minor jets fire as the calibrator compensated for the extra weight.

She stayed in engineering as Guardian went down to greet the crew, and watched their return on the screen. It didn't need the close-up to see what Pol was thinking.

She watched Jacques and Qiang unload.

"Empty." Pol was loud and angry in the silence of the cessation of the shuttle engines.

"Doesn't look empty to me," Jacques said.

"What do you mean, empty?" Guardian demanded.

"There's nothing," Carlos said.

No treasure, he meant. The *Hassim* was an exploration ship, and people expected her to be stocked to the top of her holds with her discoveries. Down in engineering, Josune smiled grimly to herself. Why would it be? If you were exploring, you needed supplies. Food, spare parts, raw materials. And empty cargo holds.

Jacques was morose. "The food is useless. Most of it's from Pisces III. What did they eat?"

The *Hassim* hadn't been anywhere near Pisces III for months. Feyodor must have gone there after she'd left Josune and stocked up for a long trip. What had she found?

Roystan rubbed his eyes. He looked exhausted. They all looked exhausted. "If you don't like it, Jacques, we'll sell it off."

Pol stepped up to them. Josune couldn't see what she did, but Jacques stepped back fast. "We're not wasting good credits on food when there's plenty to spare. It's the only thing the damned ship did have. You'll take it, and be grateful."

Jacques turned away. "Roystan gets indigestion with food from Pisces III."

"We don't."

"Enough," Roystan said. "We're all tired. We're exhausted, and I'd kill for some of your spicy flatbread, Jacques. Let's get this stuff unloaded so we can eat."

Even Josune's mouth watered.

Roystan looked around. "Where's Josune?"

"Holed up in engineering," Jacques said. "Can't take the bodies."

"There's no bodies here," Qiang said. "She's trying to get out of helping."

"Give her space." Guardian scratched at his newly dressed arm. "She's not used to bodies."

"She was happy enough to create them," Qiang said. "She killed more than the rest of us put together."

Josune turned off the feed. She didn't plan on staying on *The Road*. But first, she had to discover what Captain Feyodor had wanted Roystan for.

She was on her knees in front of the engine she was disassembling, staring at nothing, when Roystan stopped in front of her. She jumped. He'd moved so quietly she hadn't seen him arrive.

Roystan squatted down beside her. She heard his knees creak, understood the wince that went with it. "You're off this ship at the next port."

She'd been expecting that. Hadn't expected feeling like he'd stabbed her in the gut, or the tightening of her throat. She didn't want to leave.

She was being stupid. She had nowhere to go, that was all.

She blinked twice, forced herself to stop. Nodded.

"I'll pay you a month's wages." A pause. "It's a pity. We could have . . . You were good crew. And your bioware saved our lives, but I can't endanger my crew."

"Thank you." She went back to cleaning the part she'd been working on, not trusting herself to say more. She'd miss Roystan, with his crooked smile and his insistence on them eating together. The way you could sit and work beside him in a companionable silence.

She'd only known him six weeks.

The silence stretched. "Which company are you with?" Roystan asked eventually.

It was a natural assumption. Few people outside the companies could afford the bionics she had behind her eye.

"Not a company." She owed him that honesty. "Private." If you could call ship crew private.

"Mods like yours cost company-type credits."

Josune shook her head. "I'm an explorer."

"An explorer!" He sighed. "And here you are."

"Here I am." If he was kicking her off at the next stop, she had to use the time she had. "Why did Captain Feyodor want to talk to you?"

Roystan's gaze locked on hers. He had hazel eyes. Gray, flecked with green and gold and brown. She couldn't look away. "You know the problem with modern-day explorers?"

"What?"

"They're too busy following others. Not prepared to do the work themselves. Don't follow Taki Feyodor, Josune. Go make your own finds. Don't take someone else's seconds."

Roystan hadn't realized who she was, even with her question. Which was good, because he'd force her to claim the *Hassim* if he knew, and Pol would kill her if she tried. She could kill Pol first, but did she really want the *Hassim* now?

"Feyodor never found the big one."

"There's more than one big one, Josune. What we get out of the *Hassim* memory will make us all rich."

There was only one big one for her. "Captain Feyodor had a dream." So had she, and no matter what Roystan said, she would follow that dream.

Roystan shook his head.

Jacques's voice came over the ship address system, and Josune was more glad than she expected to be for the interruption. "This spicy flatbread is coming out of the oven in two minutes and fifteen seconds."

Josune set a stass field over the parts and stood up. A stass field prevented parts moving when a ship jolted unexpectedly. But *The Road* wasn't a ship that jolted unexpectedly. Not often. Not like the *Hassim*, which got attacked a lot.

Had been attacked a lot.

"We can't let Jacques's food go cold." She knew her voice wasn't steady.

Roystan stood up too, although he made more work of it. He needed time in a machine, but it wasn't her business to tell him that.

3

NIKA RIK TERRI

When Nika came back into her own body—exactly twenty-four hours after she had left it—she found she was wedged between a drainpipe and the wall on the ledge above the second floor at the back of her studio. The ledge was wet. It had been raining.

Tamati had known about the twenty-four-hour limit. He wanted her dead—he'd been going to kill her anyway, and would be doubly determined after he found she'd locked him out—but he wouldn't want to kill himself accidentally. Therefore, she'd be safe until she tried to move.

How had he even gotten up here?

The smell of frying glee-fish from the restaurant across the road and two doors down was strong in the air. Nika breathed in the familiar smell of it. Her smells, translated by a brain that recognized them. A door opened; sounds spilled out and were silenced as the door closed again. Kafismoke spiraled up.

Undercook Amarri often ducked out for a few puffs.

Nika peered down and almost lost her breath. How was she going to get down?

"Hey. Amarri."

Amarri didn't look up. A moment later the noise from the shop kitchen spilled out again, and Amarri was gone.

She lay back and waited for the queasiness to pass. Amarri would be out again later for another puff. Meantime, she could wait. She still had eleven days.

Provided she didn't freeze to death first. Or it didn't start to rain again.

The restaurant stayed open till 3:00 A.M. Plenty of time for Amarri to duck out another five times. Unless they'd had a quiet night, in which case they'd all be gone by one. Maybe they'd gone already.

And she had to be sure she didn't fall asleep in the meantime and fall off the ledge. She could tell from the lethargy of her body and the way her eyes wanted to close that Tamati had been awake the whole twenty-four hours.

She pushed herself in tighter behind the drainpipe. If she accidentally fell asleep, she didn't want to fall.

She pushed too far. The drainpipe gave way. She grabbed at it, for there was nothing else to hang on to. The bracket that held the pipe and roof guttering in place broke free. It tumbled to the ground, bouncing as it hit. Nika pushed back, digging her heels into the ledge. There was nothing to grip, nothing to stop her from sliding. The pipe, no longer connected to anything solid above her, moved—slowly—away from where it had been anchored.

For a moment, her weight provided a counterbalance, but there was nothing to hold her there.

She started to slide. She would go over the edge, no matter what. She grabbed at the pipe. She could slide down it, as long as she didn't lose her hold. If she let go, she'd hit the ground the same way the bracket had. Except *she* wouldn't bounce.

She wrapped one leg around the pipe. The pipe moved away from the ledge. She clung as she lost contact with the only solid piece of the building she could feel, and prayed desperately to any gods listening.

The pipe seesawed. She hit the wall behind her and wrapped her other leg around the pipe. It swayed the other way.

Her hands burned as she clung, slid, clung, and slid again.

The pipe itself was smooth, but whatever had been holding it against the wall was sharp and cutting. Her expensive white nen-silk trousers were no protection at all; they shredded instantly, leaving the inside of her legs open to scrape the surface. Her hands fared no better.

The pipe crashed against the wall on the other side of the street.

It stopped her downward momentum.

She dropped the last body length to the ground, feet first. The guttering and pipe fell to the ground behind her.

Amarri came out at the crash.

"Nika. What in all hells?"

She stood up, wincing. Nothing was broken, but her hands and the inside of her legs were a mess. Her heart thudded with the adrenaline spike.

"You look like shit. In your brand-new body and all."

"I feel it, too. Don't touch me," she said as Amarri came over to help her up. She couldn't think for the pain. "Have you got any nerveseal?"

They were a food shop. They'd have it in their first-aid kit for burns.

"Sure, but you're going to need more than we've got. Can't you—" He looked back at her own shop.

"Just for my hands."

Amarri came back with the nerveseal. Snorri, the head cook and owner, came with him, plus another staff member Nika didn't know. Snorri's staff was forever changing.

"You need us to carry you into your shop?" Snorri asked. He was a big man.

Nika shook her head. "No. I need—" The numbing spray on her hands made the pain of her legs three times as bad. "I can't go . . . Do you have any more nerveseal?"

"It's not cheap, Nika."

"Sorry. I—"

She needed a regen. She needed it now. "Can you call me an aircar?"

Snorri spat and looked over at Nika's shop. "*He's* back. You should go to the police."

A lot of good that was going to do. The first police officer Nika had called about Alejandro had taken a ten-thousand-credit bribe and "lost" her complaint. The second one had been beaten to a pulp. It had taken Nika six weeks to reconstruct his body. Detective Sanray still hated her for it.

"I've sorted him," Nika said, though they meant Alejandro and she meant Tamati. "I'm leaving now. You should pretend you never saw me. And keep away from my shop, Snorri. He's bound to be a little bit mad."

She'd be long gone, but the neighbors would have to put up with whatever Tamati did.

"Good for you." Snorri finally called her aircar.

She went to the docks, because she knew the respectable places would call her injury in. On the way, she stopped at a vending machine and picked up a pair of cheap coveralls—at least Tamati hadn't destroyed her credit—and pulled them on to hide the damage to her legs. A rust-brown pair, slightly large, but they hid most of the residual bleeding.

She chose a genemod studio, rather than a medical one. Someone would tell Tamati she'd been injured. The time he wasted looking through the hospitals could only be to her benefit.

Because he would come looking for her.

Nika walked out of the first four studios she tried. She wanted to come out of the process alive.

Was she setting her standards too high? A woman on the run couldn't afford to be choosy. And the nerveseal was starting to wear off.

In the fifth—and last—shop the proprietor met her with a blaster to her face. "We don't want people like you here."

He was about her age, tall and lanky, with red-gold hair almost the color she'd dialed up for Tamati. Nika hoped it wasn't a bad omen. The weapon trembled in his hand.

"I thought any business was good business." She kept a wary eye on the blaster. Nervous people were trigger-happy people.

"But you're not here for business, are you."

"As a matter of fact, I am."

She limped over to look at his machine and hoped he wouldn't shoot her in the back. A basic model Netanyu 3501, thirty-five years old at least, maybe up to fifty. An antique in cosmetic modeling terms. Still, it had been a good model, and it had a lot of regenerative functions built in. Not like now, where you had to buy them as add-ons.

The shelves alongside were tidy and dusted. Each jar of plasma was clean and neatly labeled, although some of the labels had faded with time. She frowned at two side-by-side. Who put naolic acid and mutrient next to each other? That was asking for trouble.

"When was the last time you had this serviced?"

"I know who you are." His voice shook as badly as his hands did. "No deal. Get out."

Something had him spooked, and it wasn't her. He hadn't noticed her hands. Or maybe he had, and that was what this was all about. "I'm not whoever you're expecting."

His voice went up an octave. "What makes you think I'm expecting someone?"

"Maybe because you held a gun to my head the moment I walked in the door." The shrillness made him sound young. How old was he really? Nika looked around for the certification papers that all modders had to display prominently in the shop. Certifications were dated, and cosmetic and gene remodeling was a career you entered when you were young and thought you could make a difference.

The certificate was shiny and new. He'd graduated six weeks ago.

Nika looked at him again and revised her estimate of his age down by at least fifteen years. "You made yourself look older."

He'd done a passable job of it, too. It was his actions that made him young, not his looks.

She moved closer to check out the work. "Did you do it yourself?"

He waved the blaster at her. "I'll fire this."

She held up a raw hand for him to see. "Customer."

She could almost see the neurons firing as he looked at them.

"Sorry." He flushed and put the weapon behind the counter, out of sight, hunching in on himself as he did so.

She looked at the certificate again to find his name. "Snowshoe? Snowshoe Bertram."

He sighed. "It's Bertram Snowshoe. They got it the wrong way around at the academy and couldn't fix it."

Information was shared electronically. Names should be impossible to muck up, but Nika knew as well as anyone how badly a machine could screw up when something went wrong. And how hard it was to fix once it was wrong.

"Most people call me Snow."

"Well, Snow. I want some work done."

"You need a medical center, not a modder." He reached out to take her hands and didn't flinch away, which was promising for his career. He would see a lot worse—if he survived his penchant for greeting prospective customers with a weapon.

She moved away. "I know what I need, and I want to program the machine."

He looked down momentarily, then up. His lashes were long and the same copper as his hair. Most modders darkened the lashes. His hair was probably natural. "I program my machine."

She approved. "I want to watch you set it up, then."

He hesitated.

"For goodness' sakes, Snow. It's not spaceship science."

"I know that. It's not—"

She waited.

Finally, he blurted, "It's just buckets of plasma. It's not very pretty, that's all."

They taught you at the academy to retain the mystique, but this sounded like experience. He'd probably shown some of his friends, who'd been disappointed that behind the glamour it *was* nothing but buckets of plasma.

"It's *art*, Snow. It's the end result that matters. Even a canyon carver uses a drill and explosive." She didn't have time to sit here debating philosophy with a kid. She wanted to get fixed. She wanted off planet. The more time she wasted, the less time she would have to hide. "Can we do the job now, please? I'll pay up front."

The shop bell chimed.

"And I'm first." She'd drop him in a vat of his own plasma if he tried to service this next customer before he serviced her.

She recognized the man who entered. Nervous bile rose into her throat.

Banjo. The thug Alejandro had hired to beat up Detective Sanray. The reason she couldn't go to the police anymore.

No wonder Snow had been on edge.

"Customers, Bertram. You haven't paid your dues, remember." Banjo had a deep voice. Strong and bass. Liquid chocolate. It didn't go with his occupation.

Nika moved closer to the naolic acid.

"You know the arrangement. I keep the area safe for you. For a fee. Otherwise who knows what might happen to you?" He glanced at Nika. "Or your clients."

"You should go," Snow told Nika, and cast an anguished glance at the counter underneath which he'd left his weapon.

It wouldn't have helped. Nika could have told him that.

Banjo flexed his fingers, pulling at the knuckles until the joints cracked.

"You shouldn't do that." Snow kept one eye on Banjo even as he flapped at Nika as if he could flap her out the door. "Later in life you'll regret it."

Later in life he could go to a good modder who'd fix it for him.

Nika unscrewed the lid on the naolic acid, trying not to be obvious about it. She was clumsy with her damaged hands. The pressure of turning the lid made her wince.

"You really should go." Snow looked at the jar Nika was trying to open and made a moue of distress. "Don't touch—"

"Yes, you should go," Banjo agreed. "This next bit won't be pretty." He stepped aside to let her out the door.

"I need some work done." Nika held out her hands. The nerve-seal had totally worn off now. All she could feel was the pain in her hands and her legs, and if she didn't get some work done soon she might scream.

"Please, just go," Snow said.

Banjo shrugged and turned back to Snow. "Well, I'm a busy man. Lots of people to beat up today. Let's get this over with."

Snow ran for the counter, and his blaster.

Banjo snatched it out of his hand before he could fire. "Carrying weapons around. Naughty. And dangerous." He used it to hit Snow across the face. Once, twice, three times.

"Excuse me." Nika raised her voice above the sound of the blunt object hitting flesh. "Excuse me." Louder still. She hefted the jar of acid and hoped her hands weren't too numb to hold it.

Banjo turned to look at her.

She tossed the acid into his face.

"What the?" He ran toward her. Then the acid started to work. He howled and scrubbed desperately at his face to wipe the acid off.

"Quick." Nika turned to Snow. "The mutrient. Open the jar." She couldn't feel her hands. "Now."

Blood from the short beating ran down his face, a cut on his cheek so deep it would need work. He stumbled forward, shaking his head. Droplets of blood flew out.

She hated cleaning up blood.

She grabbed clumsily at the jar of mutrient. "Hurry."

Banjo lurched toward the sound of her voice, his high-pitched keening adding an edge to the urgency.

"We should escape while we can."

"Unscrew this blasted jar." Once Banjo wiped the acid off, the mutrient would be useless.

Some of her urgency must have got through. Snow twisted the lid. Mutrient slopped over and turned pink from the blood on his hands. "Can we go now?"

As soon as the lid was off, Nika threw the mutrient into Banjo's face.

The mutrient in contact with the acid started to bubble.

Banjo dropped to the floor, keening.

"And that," Nika told Snow, "is why you never store naolic acid and mutrient next to each other." She looked at her hands. She wasn't going to be able to do this next bit. "Put some gloves on. We need to stabilize it before it eats his face away."

"Who are you?"

"Gloves on," she said sharply. "If you don't act fast the damage will be irreversible." They were modders. They fixed skin problems, not created them. "Every second you waste eats away at his eyeballs. He'll be blind in another minute."

Snow snapped his gloves on fast, although he was shaking hard enough to make it more of a chore than it should have been.

"Right. Saline solution." She hoped he had some made up.

He pointed to a twenty-liter container. It had a tap, thank gods.

"Add a handful of dendrian salts."

"I can't afford dendrian salts."

She looked at what he had. Picked out Arrat crystals and aluminum salts and dumped them in. "Drag him across, so his face is under the tap. By the feet," she added as he made for the shoulders. "Do everything you can to avoid touching that stuff."

He was young, and strong. As soon as Banjo was under the tap, Nika turned it on.

Banjo finally stopped screaming.

Snow wiped blood from his face. "What now?"

"Basic stabilizing gel. You do have that, don't you?" It, too, was expensive, but it was a staple in any good modder's workshop.

He flushed. "Yes."

"Good. Cover his face with it. As thickly as you can without the gel falling off. Don't forget he needs to breathe."

"I do know my job."

Six weeks from graduation wouldn't have given him much experience. How many customers had he had?

Nika knelt beside Banjo as Snow slathered the gel on. "Listen to me, Banjo. It is Banjo, isn't it?"

She got something garbled in reply.

"We're stabilizing your face right now." While she waited to be sure he was listening she watched Snow. "Right into the eye sockets. Lots of it there."

Banjo said something else, still garbled, but she figured she had his attention. "The gel will prevent any further damage. Then once the machine is free"—because she was damned if she was going to let a thug like Banjo get in the way of her escape—"we'll set you up in it. It will take a few days to rebuild your face." The eyes would take the longest.

She sat back on her heels, exhausted now that the adrenaline rush had faded, sore all over. All she wanted to do was sleep. Or cry. And she still had to escape from Tamati. "I'm using the machine first," she told Snow. "Set it up for repair." One good thing about the old Netanyus was they did good basic medical repair.

"His eyes. Shouldn't we put him in first?"

"He's a thug. He was about to beat you up. Speaking of." The blood had dried to a sticky red blotch on his face. "You should clean yourself up. Blood around a studio is bad for business."

Not to mention that she didn't want him setting her up with bloody hands.

She stood up to check Snow's supplies. Banjo could sleep rather than wait in the dark. It would be safer. She didn't tell Snow what she was looking for. This fresh out of academy, he was likely to bleat about the need for a customer signature before they gave anyone anesthetic.

His stock was fresh but basic. She guessed he'd spent most of his money on the shop, with little left over for supplies. He did have some nerveseal—she used it on her hands—and a midrange anesthetic that most people would never have considered, but it was a good one for its price.

She used that on Banjo.

"Um, you really should get a waiver before you do that." Snow rubbed his now-clean hands together to get rid of the last dampness.

Nika hardly heard him. She looked at the range of chemicals and looked back at Snow. No newbie would gather this collection of chemicals together. Plus, he'd done a good job on his own aging.

"Let me guess. Your family are modders."

He pursed his lips and looked over at the machine. "We should do your repairs before he comes around." His gaze turned to Banjo and skittered away.

She knew evasion when she heard it. She also knew it was long past time to be fixed.

"I want to be conscious the whole way through," she said, and watched as he set the machine.

4

JOSUNE ARRIOLA

Carlos wanted to break the *Hassim* apart and sell each piece.

"Too dangerous," Roystan said. "As soon as anyone hears about it they'll be after us. Better to get rid of it before anyone knows we had it. Plus, people will pay more for this ship whole than they will for its parts. Who knows what secrets are stored inside it somewhere?"

He disappeared onto the bridge after that—presumably to find a buyer—while the rest of them congregated in the crew room to try to read the memory.

Pol had collected jewelry and other valuables from the *Hassim*'s crew quarters. She doled it out now, keeping the most striking for herself. A long, crimson nen-silk jacket—an exotic purchase that had taken a month of Reba's profit—and a bracelet of Josune's, made from rock Josune had collected from the world the *Hassim* crew had named Sassia.

Josune had machined the rocks so thin they were translucent except for the red veins that showed through. She'd ground up more of the rock to extract the unknown red veins. The red had turned out to be a metal composite, malleable at body temperature, hard and strong when allowed to cool to the regular eighteen degrees Celsius of a spaceship.

At body temperature, the mineral leached red dye that didn't come off. Josune had learned that the hard way. Her wrist had stayed red until she'd gone into the machine to change her appearance before securing passage on Roystan's ship.

Josune shook her head when Pol got around to her.

The *Hassim* crew had marked Sassia as a potential source of income. The red mineral, three plant species that might be medicinal, and another one that might be a potential drug. All this information would be available in the memory of the *Hassim*, which contained a record of everything that happened on a ship. Everything. From the simplest temperature change, to the camera feeds, to every message sent or received, and to every null-space jump. It was write once, store forever, and practically indestructible. And extremely hard to hack if you didn't have the right access codes.

Josune didn't expect the crew on *The Road* to access the memory any time soon.

She didn't care where the *Hassim* had been, which was what *The Road* crew wanted. She had her own records on the reader behind her eyelid; had backups of that stored off-site. But if they could hack Feyodor's access codes, Josune could find how the company men had got on board the *Hassim*. She would see who had died first. Might find out which company they were by the questions they asked. If they had asked any.

And she wanted Feyodor's research.

Roystan joined them two hours later. There were lines of exhaustion around his mouth and his eyes. "Jacques, can you reschedule the next delivery? I've sold the ship."

That was faster than Josune expected.

"Roystan, I told you not to do any deals without us," Pol said. "You're too soft."

Roystan sounded meek. "It was a good deal."

"What about her cargo?"

"Everything that's left, all in the one deal. Ten million."

It was a good price. "Who did you sell it to?" Josune asked.

"Brown Combine."

The Brown family had sponsored expeditions of their own to find Goberling's lode. Had Roystan known that? If so, he knew more than he was saying about the big companies. Not only that, Brown was almost ethical, the company least likely to shoot them all and take *The Road* as a prize.

Least likely, but it didn't mean they wouldn't. As far as Josune knew, *The Road* was unarmed. It wouldn't stay that way, and Josune knew where to get the weapons from. And which weapons she wanted.

"I hope you told them the memory was gone."

"I did. Not sure they believed me, but they'll take it anyway. The meet-up is in ten hours." Roystan ran his fingers through his hair. "We've never run behind on a cargo drop before."

"I'll reschedule," Jacques said. "We have a three-day window, Roystan."

"I know, but—" He stared at the plate Jacques put in front of him.

Josune wasn't sure if it was a mealtime or just a snack. She'd lost track of the time. She discreetly tested a fold of her skin. She'd need time in a machine soon to get rid of the excess weight. Life revolved around food on *The Road*.

"Some of these places go close to the line on supplies. Delays can be problematic. I don't want us to—" Roystan breathed out hard, looked away from the plate. "Is there anything to drink, Jacques? I'd kill for a coffee."

"Coming right up."

Jacques had never said how long he'd worked on *The Road*. Jacques's mission, or passion, seemed to be feeding Roystan. He'd wait on him hand and foot if Roystan would let him. Cargo took second place, but no one seemed to mind.

Roystan cupped his hands around the hot mug and sat back. He looked cold. "How's the decoding going?"

Josune indicated the memory on the table. With its nobbled ends, it looked like a giant femur stripped of meat. The nodes Carlos had attached to it were the color of muscle. "Not good."

"What's taking so long, Carlos?" Pol demanded.

"If you think you can do it faster, you do it."

Ship memory was designed to be indestructible. Even Pol's meddling shouldn't wipe it. Josune didn't believe anything was indestructible. Maybe she should offer to swap her certain knowledge for the memory stick, where she could work on it in her own time. "You might not find anything."

"This is the *Hassim*," Qiang said. "There'll be something."

"And when we find it"—Pol held up her wrist, and the bracelet, to the light—"we'll go exploring. We have a memory full of information that will help us find all the worlds the *Hassim* found."

Roystan finished his coffee quickly. "We've a cargo to deliver. People are waiting on us. Relying on us. Let's not forget that. We're contracted, and a ship that doesn't deliver on time doesn't get any more contracts."

"Contracts." Pol touched the bracelet. "Who cares when we have the *Hassim*'s records?"

"I do. And given we're about to break our perfect delivery record, let's be ready to unhook the cargo as soon as we arrive." Roystan took a top-up of coffee from Jacques with absentminded thanks as he watched Carlos work.

"We're rendezvousing with Brown Combine in ten hours. We have a delivery after that. How do we lock this away so Brown doesn't get it?" He addressed his question to everyone, but he looked to the engineers for answers.

Even a trustworthy company could only be trusted so far. Especially when the *Hassim* memory was involved.

"Strongbox." Josune had a lot of experience locking things away. What could she set up with what they had on the ship? "Start with IDs." Iris recognition and voice. They could do that easily enough. "A minimum number to unlock." So one person couldn't sneak in and steal it from the others. "Three should be enough." She'd like to use all of them in the ID, but if Brown came in fighting, they might not all live.

She didn't mention that to Roystan.

"Later, once we have the time, I'll build extra security into the ship itself. Something only the captain can override." It was poetic, really. "Like the authentications on ship memory." Funny to realize they were planning on using similar security to that they were trying to hack. "It will take time to do properly, and I need you, Roystan, to code in something you'll remember for the override."

Pol said, "What if something happens to Roystan? How do we get the code?"

If only it were that easy. "Captain Feyodor didn't give her codes to her crew." Josune realized too late what she'd said, but no one seemed to notice.

In fact, Roystan said, "What captain would?" Then he made a sound that might have been an *Oh* and smacked his palm against his forehead. "Give it to me." He snatched up the memory and set off at a fast clip for the bridge.

They all followed.

Roystan slid under the panels. "Tools, please."

Josune handed over her repair kit.

Carlos shifted from foot to foot. "I don't know what you're doing, but I'd rather I was doing it."

"You won't know what to do." Roystan opened the memory slot.

Carlos looked to Josune. "Tell me he's not pulling out *our* memory."

She couldn't lie to him.

Roystan slid out from under the panel and handed Josune the ship's memory. "Don't lose that." He slid back under with the *Hassim*'s memory.

"It's not going to work automatically if you put it into our backup slot," Josune told Roystan. "It's coded to the captain. It won't record. It won't display."

"These old ships have a writeable secondary memory. Back then you couldn't rely on the backup. Sometimes it failed. So they wrote to a secondary memory on the ship itself."

"Never heard of a memory that failed," Carlos said.

Josune hadn't either, but she had heard of secondary memory. Every Goberlingophile had. Goberling's first ship—he'd traded it in after he'd sold his first batch of transurides—had it. The memory had contained the first two months of Goberling's trip. After that, it had stopped recording because the memory had been full.

"I can't believe this ship is old enough to have secondary memory." Goberling's ship had been fifth-hand when he'd bought it, and almost ready for scrap. "What does it prove, anyway?"

Roystan's voice was muffled. "The write to the second memory drops a level of security, because it has to write."

"You're telling me it's going to read a fully encoded master memory and write it to memory here on ship?"

"Not just write it," Roystan said. "It bypasses ship security to do so."

"You're deoxygenated," Carlos said. "Spacing out. No old equipment will bypass modern security."

Josune agreed with him.

Roystan poked his head up and over the panel. "Secondary memory used to be for emergencies. To find out what happened in those last moments before a ship was destroyed."

"Never heard of that."

Neither had Josune.

"They had to be able to override it. You'll find you can still do so on modern memory, although most people don't know that."

"Tell us what's happening," Pol demanded. "In plain words. We're not technical like them. And when do we get the *Hassim* memory back?"

"Simple words someone like you can understand, Pol," Carlos said. "Might be—"

Roystan frowned at him.

"He's got old technology on this ship." Josune didn't care what Carlos said, but they were all tired and ready to snap. "Roystan thinks that by swapping the *Hassim*'s memory with *The Road*'s memory, *The Road* will read the memory, and we might be able to hack the read, rather than the memory itself."

"He'd better hurry up and do it," Carlos said. "I don't like not having our own ship's memory in place."

Neither did Josune.

"That's the trouble with this ship," Pol said. "It's cobbled together. So much of it is old."

"Might come in useful now." Roystan smiled as data started scrolling across the screen. "Look at that."

Except the data was only being recorded in the secondary backup memory, and if it was anything like the secondary memory on Goberling's original ship, they'd only get two months' worth. The *Hassim*'s memory stick contained years of data. They'd lose most of it. Josune scrambled for the panel. She still had *The Road*'s memory in her hands. She had to connect it back in. "Carlos, grab me a T5 cable."

She kept one eye on the panel, and prayed. Roystan was crazy. He could lose it all. Was he trying to? It felt like hours before Carlos put the cable into her hand.

Josune snapped the cable into *The Road*'s memory and plugged into a nearby console. She didn't breathe until she was sure data was being rerouted back through *The Road*'s memory.

"Now what?" she asked, when the data had finished copying and they were back in the crew room. "We can read the data, but we still have to decode it. We need Feyodor's personal code for that." If Josune didn't have that, how in the galaxy was Roystan going to get it?

Roystan took the time to drink half a coffee before he looked at what had been transferred to their own ship.

"Well," Pol demanded.

"I'm thinking, Pol. Trying to think like Taki Feyodor."

Did Josune imagine he looked at her?

"She was a sentimental woman. A dreamer."

Dreamer, yes. "Sentimental? Never." Not the woman Josune had known.

Roystan's look was more direct this time. Almost challenging. "You think not?"

"No." Her return look was as challenging as his. He might have told Taki Feyodor she was a formidable foe, but Josune had worked for the woman for more than ten years.

He tilted his head. Looked at her. The hazel in his eyes caught the light of the system statuses on the screens around him and reflected back green with the gray.

They might have been the only two in the crew room.

Jacques cleared his throat. Loudly.

Roystan looked around, then turned back to smile at Josune. "I can do this. Watch." He cupped his hands together. Blew on them. Cleared his throat, took a deep breath.

Josune didn't know why she was breathing fast.

Roystan took another breath. Nodded to himself, rubbed his palms together. "I am—" His voice faded. He took one more deep breath and started off more naturally. "I am the ruler of the galaxy. With my ship, and my determination, no one can stop me."

Josune knew the rest. She whispered it with him.

"I am off to find my fortune. I go places no human has gone before. When I return, I will be rich, rich, rich."

The poem young Goberling had stenciled on the outside of his ship before he'd left to go exploring. It wasn't common knowledge.

Even less common was the wording. Biographer Sandi Tann had transcribed the original words as *I am off to seek my fortune.* Anyone who knew to use *find* instead of *seek* was a serious Goberlingophile.

"He was young." Roystan wrinkled his nose. "Egotistical."

He'd had a reason to be. And it hadn't unlocked the memory.

Josune poured herself a coffee. Her hand shook. "Sentiment isn't cutting it. It's still locked." In fact, it was waiting. "It wants biometric ID." Finger or iris print.

"It won't need it now." Roystan leaned across to thumb off the request on the screen.

Something clicked. Data started scrolling. Words, images, statistics.

It couldn't be that easy.

Roystan looked up and caught Josune staring at him. His smile was half a grimace.

It really couldn't, shouldn't, be that easy. Josune was missing something important.

"It's open," Pol announced, and Josune and Roystan turned to see what the *Hassim*'s records showed.

The explorer Goberling had worked a small, one-man ship somewhere out on the edges of the known galaxy. There were hundreds like him, hunting for exotics—drugs, spices, dyes, and minerals—from the planets that no one had thought to catalog yet, let alone consider for habitation.

His first three trips had been failures. On his fourth he'd come back with chunks of pure transurides kilometers wide.

Transurides were metals—eight stable elements, atomic numbers 122 to 129—never found, or made artificially, on Earth, because they required cosmic forces to create them. They were discovered when humans ventured into areas that had been subjected to immense gravitational stresses unknown on Earth. Despite their high atomic weight, the number of protons and neutrons made them unusually stable—the long-expected island of stability that scientists had predicted for so long in the higher metals.

Although there were eight metals in the series, most people thought of only one element when they talked about transurides. Element 126. Dellarine. Wonder metal that was used for everything from high-end communications—the bionics in Josune's eye were only possible because of dellarine—to body modding. Modders loved it because dellarine had an affinity with the human body that made extreme mods possible.

Goberling's return with an unimaginable prize in the precious metal had sparked a mining rush of immense proportions. Unfortunately, all anyone knew was the rough direction Goberling had gone. They tried everything. Placing tracers on his ship, straight-out following him. But he'd hidden his trail well.

He had made three further trips, bringing back a fortune in heavy metals every time. Then he'd disappeared. That had been more than eighty years ago. People had been searching for the lode ever since.

Captain Taki Feyodor, on the *Hassim*, had been one of those searchers.

Exploration was an expensive business. The *Hassim* regularly ran out of money. When that happened, Feyodor dug into her data banks to find what she could sell. Information about mineral deposits she'd run across in her hunt but had been too single-minded to follow up, potential new spices and drugs from worlds no one knew existed. Exactly the sort of thing, in fact, that Goberling had been looking for when he'd stumbled across his find.

Her journey log was in the *Hassim*'s memory, along with everything else that had happened on ship.

That log was the prize the crew of *The Road* wanted.

Josune didn't care about that. She'd been to those places. She could get to those worlds long before *The Road* did. No, she was interested in the big prize. The one set of information Feyodor's crew hadn't had access to. Feyodor's research into Goberling himself.

Everyone on the *Hassim* had been obsessed with Goberling. That was why they were on the ship in the first place.

She thought she'd known every obsessed hunter of Goberling's lode.

But she hadn't known Roystan, who'd been able to crack Feyodor's codes in less than a day. Anyone else would have taken weeks, if they could crack it at all. Even someone like Josune, who knew Feyodor better than most. What was she missing?

The crew started at the last record. Dates, location, ship statistics.

"Ship was full of fuel." Roystan watched the records roll up.

"We can't use her fuel, remember," Pol said. "She adds synth to it."

Synth was forbidden inside the legal zone. It could wipe out a station if it exploded. Which it did when the temperature rose above 190 Kelvin. But it tripled fuel capacity.

"She was fully fueled, fully provisioned. With empty cargo holds."

Setting out on a long trip.

"We've established that, too. Tell us something new."

Roystan glanced at the scrolling lines. "She came from Pisces III."

Josune leaned over to look. She had, and she'd been there five days. Furthermore, the *Hassim* had only paid two days' berthing fees. The bill for the excess was there in front of them.

Fighting off company people, at a guess.

Based on the smell of the bodies—she tried not to gag at the memory of her friends, her crewmates—those they'd executed in the crew room had been dead a few days. Assume the company people had boarded at Pisces III, overpowered some of the crew, and the rest had spent three days fighting them off.

Then Captain Feyodor had . . . what?

Jumped to where Josune was waiting with Roystan, who knew a lot more about Taki Feyodor than he should have.

"Go back to what happened before the company people arrived. I want to see the attack." Josune thought she'd kept her voice normal. She ignored the sharp look Roystan sent her way.

"Later. I want to know where she's been." Pol stopped on a longer record and switched it to voice. They came in halfway through a low whistle, followed by a moment's silence.

For Captain Feyodor, the longer the silence, the more impressive the feat. Josune held her breath—the longest time she'd ever had to wait—until, finally, she heard a low, admiring "All this time. You cheeky sod." She laughed aloud, then set up a shipwide message. Her voice came through the speaker in an excited boom.

"Today, we set out on our last journey. I have the final clue I need to discover where Goberling found his transurides. Let's get it. We're on our way to be rich, rich, rich."

Josune hadn't seen Feyodor that animated in all the years she'd been on ship.

The silence in *The Road*'s crew room was absolute.

"Do you think she really did?" Guardian asked eventually. "Find it, I mean?"

Roystan rubbed his eyes. "She said she'd found a clue."

She'd been coming to see Roystan. Her instructions to Josune had been explicit. "Get onto Roystan's ship and don't lose sight of him."

But then, with a ship named *The Road to the Goberlings*, he had to be after the lost lode himself.

Roystan ate the breakfast Jacques put in front of him, while the others went back through Feyodor's records. Important records were protected with iris and voice scans. Josune could have cleared the security for them. She didn't offer.

"We'll use the proceeds from the sale of the *Hassim* to buy supplies," Pol said. "Then we'll go. Find what she found."

Roystan finished his breakfast. "I don't recall making you captain, Pol." He got up to get himself more coffee. "Don't forget, we've deliveries to make. We have a contract."

"Deliveries," Pol said. "When we've Goberling's information at our fingertips."

"People spend their lives hunting for that. To date, no one has found it. We go with the job we have. We finish it. We hunt for lost worlds and rare metals in our spare time."

While the people who'd hunted the *Hassim* hunted them.

If Roystan had ever hunted for Goberling's lode—and Josune was sure he had—he'd become cynical and disillusioned. Still, he must have found something, once upon a time, for why else would Feyodor have been after him?

That was what Josune had to find out. Before he kicked her off ship.

"We have the whole of the *Hassim*'s records here," Pol said. "Everywhere she went. Every *world* she went to. We don't need this stupid cargo run."

"We deliver our cargo first, Pol. It's my commitment and my run. We don't drop it simply because we might have a better deal. Cargo runs are hard to get, and once lost, they are lost forever." With that, Roystan took himself and his coffee off to the bridge.

Josune followed him. She waited until they were out of earshot of the others.

"Roystan."

He turned, almost defensive. "We're not walking out on our cargo run, Josune."

She hadn't come to ask him to do that. "Brown Combine will be here in six hours. Please tell me this ship is armed." They had blasters, but she meant cannons or other defensive weapons that could be used against another ship.

"This far inside the legal zone?"

She took that as a no. "I need to go back to the *Hassim*. Get some of their weapons."

"We have shielding. The best money can buy."

Captain Feyodor had been a believer in premium shielding, too. "It's the only thing that stops a havoc bomb," she'd told Josune, many times.

They kept havoc bombs on the *Hassim*, each one stored in its own shielded box, but Josune had never been particularly comfortable having them on board. Sure, they were keyed—and shielded—but if the bomb got loose it would drill its way down to the engine before it set off its mini nuclear explosion.

"Shielding won't stop a determined attack."

Roystan sipped his coffee while he studied her. "Do you know how to install a cannon?"

"Yes." Simple, unvarnished truth.

Roystan sighed. "Why am I not surprised." He flicked on a link. "If you can drag yourself away from plans of exploration and lost metals, Carlos, I've a job for you."

Josune did one more thing before she went over to the *Hassim*. "Let's put this thing into storage." She was not leaving the *Hassim*'s memory out where Brown Combine could take it if they wanted to. "I'll patch it into ship security after I've put the cannon in." In case Brown came early. "But I'll do the first part now, set it so you need three people to open the safe." She made them all line up and put their voice and iris patterns against the strongbox. "Let's go, Carlos."

Carlos followed her onto the shuttle. "You really are paranoid."

"You haven't seen obsessed explorers in action."

On the *Hassim* she went straight to the cannon she wanted. She didn't even pretend to check the others.

"That one." The smaller plasma cannon—two of them couldn't carry the larger one. That took four people, and a large hydraulic lifter, which they didn't have.

Carlos checked the model, then the secondhand prices. He whistled. "Do you know how much we could get for this?"

The trouble with Carlos was that he thought like a shareholder on a small ship, not like someone who was sitting on a potential fortune. Josune knew how much the cannon cost, for she'd been with Captain Feyodor when she had bought it.

"Better to be alive to spend the big fortune when you get it than to make a small amount of extra credits short term." Although to Carlos, it probably wasn't a small amount of credits. "Get me a small hydraulic lift to put this on." They must have used the trolleys to move goods earlier; she shouldn't have to tell him where to find one.

Josune unbolted the cannon in silence. After Carlos helped roll it onto the lift, she turned for the plasma.

Predictably, Carlos balked when he saw how much the plasma could be sold for. "Let's take the cannon, a small amount of plasma, and sell the rest."

"Plasma is hard to get this far into the legal zone, and costs three times what it's worth farther out. We're taking it all. A one-shot cannon is useless. Besides, we're selling the ship in hours, so we'll get nothing extra for it if we don't take it now."

Carlos put the calculator away again. "You know what scares me? Is just how good you are at this."

"I came from the rim," Josune reminded him. "One more item and we're done here."

She collected three of the small fusion bombs that could wreak such havoc. They were deceptively small, given the damage they could do. Each shielded box fit into the palm of her hand.

"What are they?"

"Bombs." Josune didn't expand any more. Carlos wouldn't want them on Roystan's ship. Roystan wouldn't want them either. What he didn't know wouldn't hurt him.

Provided they were locked away and only Josune could set them off.

Back on board *The Road*, Pol was still arguing with Roystan.

"She started just after you left," Guardian said. "Until Roystan told her to shut up and go away. So she went off to her cabin and moaned about it with Qiang. Now they've gone down to talk to Roystan again. I think if he had a brig he'd lock them in it."

Greed made monsters out of everyone. Right now, Pol was Roystan's problem. Josune had other priorities, like making the ship safe. Although, if she got time, she might turn one of the spare cabins into a cell. Just in case.

But then, she didn't like Pol, and she did like Roystan. What did their argument matter to her? She'd be off the ship at the next port.

She was still going to make a temporary lockup, though.

Guardian and Carlos came with her.

"Pol doesn't know when to shut up," Carlos said.

Josune decided to install the cannon up near the ionizer they used to clean up nearby space debris. Not close enough that if one was hit the other would be taken out, but close enough that one person could fire the cannon, and then clean up the debris with the ionizer afterward.

Carlos paced as he watched Josune prepare an airtight compartment for the cannon. "Not sure I like weapons on ship. One more hole that can fail in an emergency."

His pacing was starting to get to her. "Why don't you go and talk some sense into Pol."

"Maybe I will." Carlos turned abruptly on his heel. He stopped halfway down the passage. Turned back.

"Stay away until I'm done, Carlos."

"But what if you—"

"You can check it then. You're getting in my way."

Carlos hesitated.

"Carlos, have I ever done anything to endanger the ship?"

"You've only been here six weeks."

"She's more paranoid about breaches than you, Carlos," Guardian said. "Remember Atalante."

Josune remembered Atalante. It still made her shudder thinking about it.

It was the station where the crew of *The Road* spent all that free time Pol wanted to reduce. An old structure, back when they'd shipped the central station in one piece, then added shuttle bays by bolting on conical spurs.

Unfortunately, the arrival and departure of ships placed stresses on the join where the spurs met the station. So much so that on occasion the joins failed catastrophically. Breach doors inside the station closed instantly, leaving anyone in the shuttle bay exposed to the vacuum of space.

As soon as Josune realized Roystan had a permanent berth there, she'd built a second wall between the shuttle bay and the station—inside the spur—and cobbled together an airlock out of spare parts she'd found on *The Road*. That left a no-man's-land of three meters between airlock and station, but anyone inside the spur when it sheared off would have time to make it safely back to the ship.

Carlos scowled, but he disappeared in the direction of the crew room.

"I don't envy him," Guardian said. "Pol is being a pain. Even if she is right."

Josune didn't argue, but she didn't agree with him, either. Wasn't the captain's word law?

Guardian watched her fit the outer casing for the cannon. "We haven't had cannons on ship before. We work in the legal zone."

"You haven't had to defend a find like the *Hassim* before, Guardian." It was disorienting to think of her old home as treasure, rather than as a means to find it.

Guardian watched for a while, then wandered off.

Outer casing in and airtight, Josune was ready to do the same on the outer hull. She set the markers she would use to locate the exact position when she was outside, and went to find Carlos. It was standard safety procedure to tell someone when you were going outside, and to ensure that they watched for any issues.

She was halfway to the crew room when she heard shouting. Carlos yelling at Pol? Or maybe Pol yelling at Carlos.

An odor of burned metal and plastic wafted down the passage. Josune sniffed. Someone was using a blaster. She ran.

Straight into a firefight.

Carlos was struggling to his feet. Pol had a blaster at Roystan's head. Jacques stood nearby, hands in the air, eyes tracking the blaster.

"We're taking the memory."

Roystan looked over to the safe where the memory was stored. "You know where it is, Pol. You know what you did to lock it."

Look into the iris recognition camera and say the passphrase, which they had all adapted from Feyodor's. Each of them had chosen their own phrase.

But it took three people, and only Pol and Qiang held weapons.

Pol gestured with her free hand. "Qiang. Do yours."

No one moved as Qiang stepped up. "I am off to find my fortune."

"Now, hold your weapon on Roystan here."

Josune had her sparker. She could fire on them. Especially while Pol was distracted with her own identification. She moved her hands so the sparker was easy to grab.

"No one can stop me."

"And there you have it," Roystan said, when they were done. "Stalemate, Pol." There was almost a smile and a—very slight—nod of appreciation Josune's way.

Pol smiled too and looked past Josune. "Guardian."

And Guardian stepped up to say, "I will be rich, rich, rich." His voice was husky.

"Guardian." Jacques's voice broke.

"Sorry." It was barely audible. He didn't meet anyone's eyes.

"Now take it out," Pol said.

Qiang, not Guardian, retrieved the memory stick.

Stalemate. There was nowhere for Pol and the others to go, and if Pol didn't realize that yet, she would soon. They needed a ship, and the only ship they had was *The Road*.

Josune measured the odds. Carlos—looking dazed. Roystan with a blaster to his head. Jacques staring at Guardian as if it were the end of the world. He'd be no help.

Could she rely on Roystan's reflexes? Others in the crew would have said no, but after seeing him in action on the *Hassim*, Josune thought they might be wrong.

She didn't give herself time to think. She pulled the sparker out from under her jacket and fired at Qiang.

Qiang yelped and dropped the memory stick.

Pol swung around to Josune.

Roystan knocked Pol over.

She was right. He could look after himself.

Josune swung around to cover Qiang. Carlos had gone for the

memory stick. He and Qiang were fighting—boots and nails. Both were bleeding. Guardian didn't have a weapon, and even if he did, he would be less likely to fire at her. At anyone.

Pol and Roystan scrambled for Pol's blaster.

"Jacques," Josune said. "Get more weapons."

Jacques blinked at her as if she'd spoken in a foreign language. "Do we have more blasters?"

Roystan kicked the blaster away from Pol.

Jacques finally ran across to pick up the blaster. "Nobody move."

Qiang charged Jacques, grabbed his hand, the one holding the blaster, and aimed at his feet. She fired.

"Aargh." Jacques let go of the blaster and clutched his foot. The burned boot dangled half off.

Josune fired the sparker. Qiang jumped back. "Why the hell did you let her on the ship with a sparker?" she demanded of Roystan.

While she'd been distracted by Qiang, Guardian had sidled over to the memory stick and picked it up. Carlos tripped Guardian. The memory stick skittered across the floor. Carlos scrambled in an ungainly crawl toward it. Pol flung herself away from Roystan and beat Carlos to it. She grabbed it up and raced for the door.

Everyone else stopped, a momentarily frozen tableau, and then Guardian and Qiang raced after Pol.

Josune ran, too. The other way. She knew where they'd go. The shuttles. Their only thought would be to get away. There was a hatch in the engine room that would cut off half the distance. Quicker, and safer.

She heard Roystan shout something after her, but she didn't wait to hear it. He followed her.

"Josune." But by then she was through the hatch and dropping into the shuttle bay.

Pol and the others thundered into the bay. Stopped.

Roystan dropped down behind her.

Pol raised the blaster and fired. Roystan went down.

Josune fired back. Guardian went down. Injured only.

She'd liked Guardian.

"Lifeboat," Pol said to the others. "Quicker to launch."

"Let them go," Roystan said, from the floor. "We can't keep them here."

He was right, but that didn't mean they should get away with it. "Sell them to a cattle ship then." But her momentary pause had given Qiang time to drag Guardian out.

Pol hadn't waited.

"No cattle ships," Roystan said.

"They stole the memory stick." She started toward the lifeboat.

"Let them go." Roystan grabbed her leg and tripped her up. The sparker arced across the metal floor, up the walls, and into the roof. "And turn that thing off before you short everything on ship."

Josune switched off the sparker.

She heard the blaring klaxon that signaled the opening of the lifeboat hatch. The breach doors slid shut. She couldn't get to them now, not without a suit. They were too late to do anything.

"Why should they get the *Hassim*'s memory?" It was hers, by right, if it was anyone's. Not that she needed most of it. She had her own records, but the one set of information Captain Feyodor never shared was information about Goberling. And there was the information about the attack.

"Nothing's worth dying for," Roystan said.

No. Especially not when Josune remembered one important thing. They didn't need the *Hassim*'s memory. They had a copy of it on *The Road to the Goberlings*'s memory.

5

JOSUNE ARRIOLA

The calibrator was cracked.

"Probably the sparker," Carlos said. "You should have known better than to bring a weapon like that on board."

Sad to admit, he was most likely right. Fixing that took priority over installing the cannon, because if they had the calibrator they could at least nullspace if they needed to.

A ship controlled the direction of its movement through space by firing thrusters to create a force to move against. The pilot applied the thrust, but the direction and force of the thrust was controlled by the calibrator. Outside nullspace, a good pilot could control the direction of the ship by small, manual corrections. But you couldn't do that when nullspacing, for even a tiny mistake was magnified over such vast distances. Not only that, the force at which you entered nullspace made a difference to where you came out. If you entered at twice the speed you planned to, you traveled twice the distance.

So it was important to have absolute control—via the calibrator—and to be spot on with direction and force when you entered nullspace.

"You'll get one jump out of it," Josune told Roystan. "After which you'll need to buy a new one."

Roystan was pale under his dressing. "But we get one jump?"

"Yes. The shorter the safer."

Roystan nodded. "We'll wait till Brown Combine collects the

Hassim, and then we'll go to Lesser Sirius and get ourselves patched up. Meantime, I need a coffee."

Josune watched him walk out. "What part of *short trip* doesn't he understand? Lesser Sirius is halfway across the galaxy."

"We always go to Lesser Sirius when we need medical attention," Carlos said.

The CEO from Brown Combine arrived with his aide, the captain, and a cargo master. Plus three accompanying ships, which Josune knew would be armed. They were an hour early.

Josune and Carlos went down to the shuttle bay with Roystan to meet them. Josune came along, because, as Roystan said, "You're the only one who can fight. But if you use that sparker again I might kill you myself."

Josune ignored that. She wasn't going to meet their visitors visibly armed, but she wanted a weapon close enough to use if she had to.

Jerome Brown raised an eyebrow at Roystan's bandages. "I'd heard the *Hassim* could protect itself. I'm surprised you tried it, let alone managed to defeat them. Especially so far inside the legal zone."

Roystan shook his head. "The *Hassim* nullspaced in front of us. A company had attempted to take it over. The two parties had mostly wiped each other out."

If the company trying to take the *Hassim* had been Brown Combine, then this was where they all died, and there wasn't a thing Josune could do about it.

"And your injuries came from fighting off the remaining staff of the company? Or the remaining crew of the *Hassim*?"

"Neither actually. A little internal disagreement. Which is why we only have the ship to sell, and not the memory."

Brown's eyebrows rose almost to his hairline. Josune would bet he didn't show that much expression often. It was unexpected, but a clever thing to do, for now that he knew they didn't have the memory they were suddenly much safer.

"We're also down a few crew, unfortunately."

Except Roystan had just undone all his good work. Couldn't he have left it at no memory?

Brown's captain gave a faint, derisive smile as she clasped her hands behind her back and followed her boss and Roystan. The aide didn't hide his sneer.

"Which crew are you down? I could have them detained for you."

Roystan laughed. "Much as I don't like them right now, I don't plan on setting the companies on them. I'm sure you can work out who they are yourself."

"Naturally." Brown frowned at them all impartially. "I want to go aboard the *Hassim*."

"Of course you do. But let's settle the payment first. That way, the minute you step on the ship she's yours."

That was standard. Once the buyers were on the ship they could kill whoever was with them and take off with the prize. But Josune hadn't expected Roystan to bargain with such experience. He ran cargo and had done so for as far back as her research went. He kept surprising her.

Roystan gestured toward the crew room. "We can discuss it over coffee?"

Coffee was served with cinnamon buns and tiny wafer biscuits, with Jacques and his bandaged foot, hovering.

Brown glanced at the second injury, but he didn't comment. Not on the injury, anyway. He savored the bun with visible enjoyment. "Last time I ate such delightful buns was fifteen months ago, on New France. A little café in the Brest arrondissement."

Jacques stiffened, and for a moment Josune thought he'd go back into the galley.

"It was attached to the most feted restaurant on New France.

You had to book three months in advance to dine there. I always ate there when I was on New France."

"Not sure I'd like to wait that long for a meal," Roystan said.

"Oh, it was worth it." Brown picked up a napkin Jacques had provided.

Josune was sure they were the only ship in the galaxy that had cloth napkins served with every meal. And with snacks.

"The chef went crazy one night. Attacked the restaurant with a meat cleaver. Totally destroyed it."

"Imagine that," Roystan said. "At least we don't have to worry about restaurant dining. We eat too well on *The Road*."

"So, Jacques. It is Jacques, isn't it?" Brown wiped the sticky filling off his fingers with fastidious care. "I have a job for you. Cooking for me. Ten times whatever Roystan is paying you."

Josune saw the look that passed between Roystan and Jacques and the slight shake of Jacques's head.

Roystan's pat to his arm was reassuring, and unobtrusive. "Aren't you afraid he'll take a cleaver to your kitchen?"

"I'll assign security guards."

Jacques turned his back on them and limped into the galley.

"I don't know what game you're playing, Brown." Roystan still looked the gentle, relaxed man Josune knew, but the unfamiliar timbre in his voice made the hair on the back of her neck stand up. "Hassle my chef again and I'll suggest he cook up a batch of arsenide buns for you."

Josune couldn't stop her hand from moving to her inside pocket. Did Roystan have a death wish? People had been killed for less.

Brown's cargo master and the captain both shifted stance. Their hands moved to where Josune was sure they had concealed weapons, too. The aide wasn't a fighting man, but his eyes took in everything, with an avarice that kept Josune on edge. The *Hassim* crew were familiar with being a prize.

Brown frowned at Roystan, but Josune thought he wasn't

frowning at the threat. It was as if the words had triggered a memory, and he gazed at Roystan as if, by looking at him, he'd remember the rest of it.

He shook his head and finally seemed to notice the tense staff around him. "Let's keep this civilized. Rest easy. You too," he said to Josune, and he held his hands out in front of him. "I'll overlook your comment, Roystan. Your reputation precedes you. I'm sure nothing will happen."

"Thank you." Roystan's tone was dry, with none of the gratitude of a man reprieved. In fact, it almost dripped with the arsenide he'd promised a moment ago. "I'm glad we're in agreement." Josune shivered at the tone. She'd never thought of him as a hard man before, but that voice, with its steady calmness, was more frightening than Brown's implied threats of earlier. His confidence was intimidating.

Where had that come from? Why did Roystan hide it? Why hadn't he used that tone on Pol?

"Now, if you've finished threatening my crew and trying to poach them, perhaps we can talk about what you're here for. The *Hassim*."

Executive Brown looked at Roystan, at his bandaged arm, and toward Jacques, now in the galley. She relaxed only when he nodded acquiescence. "What's left on the ship for me to buy?"

"The memory is gone. We took some supplies and personal valuables, but the rest of the ship is intact and in good working order."

"We took cannons." Josune didn't try to match Roystan's tone, but the threat was clear enough. "Ammunition." A direct warning to Brown and his captain. They were armed. They would fight.

They didn't need to know how many cannons they'd taken. Or that the cannon wasn't working yet.

"She was fitted out for a long trip," Roystan said. "Full of supplies. Holds empty, fuel full."

"And the company that attacked them?"

"No idea, although they came from Pisces III."

The purchase went through quickly after that, and then Roystan and Carlos took the Brown people over to the *Hassim*.

Josune wanted to go over with them. She didn't trust Brown, or his watchful aide. Or his smiling captain. Or his silent cargo master. Who ever heard of a cargo master who didn't talk?

She helped herself to the last cinnamon bun, savored it. "Did you really take a meat cleaver to the restaurant, Jacques?"

"It was my restaurant. I could do what I liked with it. That cleaver." Jacques smiled in fond reminiscence. "Big mother. Like an ax. And the edge. I could chop anything with it."

"How many people did you kill?" An axman running berserk in a full restaurant—and it must have been full if you had to book three months in advance—would have done a lot of damage.

Jacques picked up the empty plate. "You're the only one around here who kills people, Josune. *I* pick my times. Like before opening hours."

"Would you ever want to open another restaurant?"

"I have enough challenges here." Jacques collected the rest of the empty coffee cups. "Roystan has a weak stomach. Lots of things set it off. If I weren't around he'd starve."

6

NIKA RIK TERRI

Despite demanding not to be put out, Nika slept through most of her healing. Her body had been awake fifty hours.

Midafternoon, she woke to Snow unclipping the apparatus.

"I didn't put you to sleep," he said, when he saw she was awake.

Eleven days before Tamati came out of his own machine. Or was that ten?

What if she couldn't escape him?

Reaction set in as she tried to stand. She almost fell off the table.

Snow grabbed her arm. "Easy." He sounded worried. "I didn't put anything in there. You shouldn't be unstable."

His after-work manner needed improvement.

She checked her hands and her legs. They were clean and professionally done. As good as she would have done herself. She'd have liked to change her appearance, but not here, not now.

Nika looked over to where Banjo, now cleaned up and his face a flat mask of stabilizing gel, was still out. Snow hadn't tried to move him, which was smart. Just covered him with a blanket. By the looks of it, he'd lost most of his nose to the acid. His mouth was an open O from the breathing ring.

"We'd better get him onto the table."

"I need to clean it down first."

"Of course." She moved aside and pulled on the coveralls she'd bought at the vending machine. She should have bought two pairs. For some of Alejandro's friends she'd put their clothes through the cleaner. A pity Snow hadn't thought to do that for hers.

She yawned as she watched him work. "Did you design a new face for him?"

He indicated the machine. She looked critically at his design. He'd pulled a basic stock face from the archives. One of the models they used at the training schools.

Snow came over to stand behind her, wiping his hands. "I didn't want to waste any talent giving him a custom face."

Which was more than Banjo deserved, but she said, "If he comes after you, how will you recognize him from the hundreds of others with the same face?"

"I hadn't thought of that." He looked around the shop. "I suppose he will. Come after us, I mean."

He'd got it.

"Thugs like Banjo don't like to lose. People might think they can fight back. He'd end up losing everyone along this street. So not only does he lose face"—literally and figuratively—"but you've hit his credit as well. Next time he comes back he'll bring a few friends. They'll trash your shop." If Snow was in it at the time, he'd be lucky to get out of it alive. They wouldn't kill him, not directly, but they'd beat him badly enough that he could die from the injuries. She pushed down the memory of Detective Sanray. Unfortunately, she knew lots of people like Banjo.

Although after Tamati, Banjo was almost tame. He would only beat her. Alejandro had done that, too, at the end. A machine fixed most things—except the memory. Tamati was another matter altogether. He would kill her.

Snow chewed his bottom lip. "I sank all my credits into this shop."

Better to get out alive and broke than dead from making a stand. "You've heard of starting again."

"I can't start again. I don't have—" He broke off, and looked away from her.

Maybe she shouldn't have interfered. "Then don't. Stay and take whatever he dishes out. Me, I'm going off-world." She looked back at Banjo. "Just give him a distinguishable face before I go. If he comes after me, I want to know what he looks like."

Snow opened his mouth to argue.

"Please, just do it. It's been a long day and I'm fast losing patience."

He closed his mouth again, looked at Banjo himself, then said meekly, "Do you want to do it?"

The about-face was suspicious, but she wanted to be gone. "Sure."

Snow tapped some codes into his computer. "Go ahead."

But she didn't design immediately. Instead, she wandered around the shelves, checking what raw ingredients he had.

There wasn't much, given that half his mutrient supply and all his naolic acid had been thrown away. Arrat crystals, five different sodium salts, four aluminum salts, all the basic metals but nothing higher. The seventeen basic plasmas, plus Nu-preon, which was an interesting choice for a beginner.

After that, she looked at the machine. The Netanyu 3501 had six inlet tubes, plus life support.

Had Snow chosen the student template because he didn't want to waste time designing a face for Banjo? Or because he was limited in materials to make a face with? She looked over at him.

His smile was almost condescending.

It was a test, and he expected her to fail.

"How old are you?" He was a cocky young thing, that was for sure.

"What's that got to do with this?"

Everything. She wasn't going to be bested by a kid. She was an artist. One of the best. Even a thug like Banjo was raw material.

There was another place you could get raw materials. From the body you were resculpting. Unfortunately for Banjo, it meant he'd lose a lot of muscle tone—which no doubt he found invaluable in his current job—but that was probably all to the good. "Help me put him on the table."

"So you're going to use my design."

"Of course not. I want to weigh him."

"What?" But he came over to help lift him onto the machine table. Unfortunately, Banjo was a big man. The two of them couldn't lift him.

"What do you use to lift your heavier vats?"

"A hand-lift, but you can't—"

She could, and did. The hand-lift was twelve hundred by six hundred millimeters. It went down flat, which Nika was pleased about. It would have been hard to lift him even a short height. She placed the lift so Banjo's shoulders and stomach would be supported at least, then rolled him onto it. Face down, to make it easier to roll him off on his back.

"I'll hold his legs while you raise him and move him over to the table."

The shop bell chimed as they were in the middle of raising him. They both froze, midlift.

"Be with you in a moment," Nika said. Snow looked as if he'd lost all capacity to speak. "We just need to get this man settled."

"Here, let me help you with that." Their new customer was a rangy male with a deep voice and the burned-ozone smell that Nika always associated with spacers. He came over and helped roll Banjo onto the table. Up close she could see a long burn mark down his neck, disappearing under the collar of his ship jacket. His hand was bandaged. All the way down his arm, at a guess. His clothes hung on him.

"He is a mess," the spacer said.

He didn't ask the questions a normal civilian might, like what was the person doing on the floor in the first place? Why wasn't he on a stretcher? Shouldn't he be in a hospital?

Nika looked at the spacer closely while Snow settled Banjo as best as he could.

His hair was a natural salt-and-pepper gray, and cropped short. His clothes were from a vending machine, faded, as if they'd been through the wash cycle more times than they were designed to. His eyes were gray, flecked with hazel, and his nose had a slight hook that most people would have had removed by now. This was a man who only came to a modder when he needed medical work.

"Free trader?" she guessed. Doing something illegal, otherwise he would have taken his burn to a medical center.

He grinned, showing slightly crooked teeth.

She'd have liked to fix his burn for him, but how much longer would Banjo remain under the anesthetic?

"Sorry, but our machine's otherwise occupied at the moment. If you're short on time you're best to try one of the other shops."

"I'll wait."

Snow made a strangled sound, which might have been him biting down hard on whatever he'd been going to say. Nika hoped so, anyway.

He'd be waiting a long time.

Nika checked Banjo's weight. "Snow, do you want to check this gentleman's neck for him while I set Banjo up?"

Snow nodded and moved over to sterilize his hands. "Why don't you sit down?" His voice was shaking. So were his hands.

"This place has changed." The stranger looked around. "Where's Tilda?"

"Tilda died." Snow's hands steadied as he carefully peeled away the collar from the burn. "I'll need to take your shirt off." His voice was still up and down, but from the way he calmed when he was doing mod work, Nika would bet he'd been around modders all his life. Good ones. She probably knew them.

"Tilda's dead?" A look of panic crossed the spacer's face, just for a moment, so that Nika thought she had imagined it. "I thought she'd live forever."

She lost track of the conversation as she gave herself up to designing Banjo's new face. Given the lack of raw materials, Banjo would have to provide a lot of his own. Waste not, want not, but he was going to be a lot more svelte coming out than he had been going in.

Distinctive face, not noticeably ugly or noticeably attractive. Not a threatening face either, because people like Banjo and Tamati relied on their looks to scare people. A little weakness in the hands and forearms, to make it harder for him to assault people.

A quick analysis of Banjo's body told her he'd been infected with Azovirus. They'd had an epidemic twenty years earlier. It only affected prepubescents, so Banjo wasn't as old as he looked. Azovirus thickened the muscles, made them bulky and sore. Banjo'd had mods. She could see that in the cell changes, but none of the mods had removed the Azovirus itself.

Why were so many modders so ineffective?

She coded to remove all traces of the virus from the cells.

Maybe a special, too, for they were modders, after all, and their job was to make people look good. Sparkling chocolate eyes, to go with his voice. Besides, it was penance in a way, given that she'd thrown acid in his face.

She worked fast, conscious of the limited supplies and the limited timeframe. Banjo's anesthetic would wear off soon.

When she came back to the present, Snow was still dressing the other man's burns. Without his shirt she could see that the burns stretched across his back and down his left side, his ribs stark and prominent against his pale skin.

"You really should get that burn fixed properly," she said. "You'll be waiting a long time if you wait for this machine."

"So your partner here was saying."

Snow bit down on his bottom lip but didn't deny the association.

Nika started setting the controls on the Netanyu.

"I want to see your design," Snow said. "Excuse me," he said to the spacer.

Nika came over to finish dressing the burns while Snow checked out her design. If she were in her studio, she'd have given the stranger something to eat. He looked half starved. "How much can you afford?" she asked.

"Depends."

"I've heard there's a place on the Low Road that might do this sort of thing, no questions asked. But it's pricier than we would be." Alejandro's friends had started going there after she'd kicked Alejandro out.

"Your partner recommended the local hospital."

"Yes, well. He's still coming to terms with the reality of a shop on the docklands. Hospitals have to report damage like this."

"This is not bad." Snow studied the specs. "It's quite clever, actually."

"Of course it is. Now will you come over here and finish this so I can set up the machine."

"It's my machine. *I'll* set it up."

She let him do it. Snow needed to feel he had some control.

Banjo's finger twitched.

"Just do it fast. The anesthetic is about to wear off." Then, because it sounded bad, she lied to the stranger, "He'll be in pain."

Snow clipped everything together with the expertise of someone who'd done it a lot of times before. Maybe she was wrong about how young he was.

He closed the machine cover and flooded the chamber with anesthetic gas just as Banjo started to lift his hand.

The hand flopped back.

Snow looked as drained as Nika felt.

Nika finished dressing the spacer's burns. "Get this looked at. Go to Wazlecki's on the Low Road. Or one of the other shops along the docks here, but get it done. It will turn septic if you don't."

Spaceships were not sterile environments. They carried the bugs of a thousand worlds. Space itself mutated them, and human flesh—particularly damaged flesh—was the ideal breeding ground for all kinds of pathogens.

"Thank you." The spacer stood up. "It feels better already. I can actually move."

That was the nerveseal. "It won't last."

He pulled on his shirt. "I hope that next time I need medical aid you will be available."

He smiled at them both, then left.

The door chime as he exited set Nika's nerves dangling.

"He didn't say *if*," Snow observed eventually. "He said *next time*."

"I expect it's inevitable in his job." Nika turned away. "You should lock the door."

It took him three tries before he set the code properly. "What do we do now?"

He sounded young again. As soon as she was alone with a computer, Nika was going to find out more about Bertram Snowshoe.

"I'm going to ship off-world. I'd recommend you do the same thing." She looked over at the machine, slowly filling with suspension fluid. "The Netanyu has an automatic shutoff. It will disengage when it's ready. Banjo will come around then. If I were you I'd be gone long before that."

Snow chewed at his bottom lip. He looked around the shop. "I *can't* go. I sank everything I had into this shop."

Whereas she, at least, had a successful practice behind her, and while it hurt to walk away from the equipment that had taken her years to acquire, she could afford to start again.

Most people came out of training into an apprenticeship. They didn't buy a shop.

"What about your family? Couldn't they tide you over?"

"I'm not running to him."

Him. Singular. Father? Brother? And why wouldn't he go? Simple pride? Or family disagreement? It didn't matter. In a way, Nika was responsible for what had happened. Sure, Snow would be in a hospital now—or availing himself of his own equipment—but he wouldn't be on the run if Nika hadn't thrown acid in Banjo's face.

She sighed. "You'd better come with me."

7

NIKA RIK TERRI

It had taken Nika twelve months to realize that Alejandro's jealousy, manipulation, and instant rages were classic controlling behaviors. By then she'd lost most of her friends, and she knew that she'd have to escape his clutches by herself.

After her unsuccessful attempt to charge Alejandro with assault, she'd started working on her escape plan. Alejandro wouldn't stop. Ever. Not unless he lost interest in her. Those plans had taken a temporary respite when Alejandro's boss had made a deal with her. It was the day after Alejandro had paid Banjo to beat up Detective Sanray. The first day in the long six weeks while Nika worked, desperately, to keep the man alive.

From the cultured voice and the recognizable SaStudio body mod, she'd thought he was a customer at first.

Sanray was stable for the moment. She closed the door and led her new client down to the office. She'd designed her office to match the Lower Sierras too, but this was based around the colors of the Ramdassan Sea. Aquamarine waters and lilac algae.

"So, Mr.—" She waited.

"Executive Leonard Wickmore."

"Executive. What can I do for you?"

"Please, call me Leonard." He smiled, showing beautiful white teeth. Samson Sa, of SaStudio, was meticulous about teeth.

"Alejandro's CEO." He smiled, disarmingly.

Nika had been wary.

"I like some of the work you've been doing with Alejandro's business associates."

If, by business associates, he meant the wounds she'd been healing, he could like as much as he wanted. "I'm a modder, not a doctor. I don't plan on continuing the medical treatments."

He continued as if she hadn't spoken. "We could help each other. You help my team when they need it. Sometimes we don't want to draw attention to ourselves."

Alejandro had always been vague about his job. He worked for Eaglehawk, one of the Big Twenty-Seven companies, and was proud of it. He'd told her his work was top secret. Nika had never pried. She should have found out a lot earlier. Why would any company have so many injuries they didn't want to take to a hospital?

She waited.

"In return, I'll send Alejandro off-world. He's due a promotion. I'll keep him away from Lesser Sirius while you work for me."

She didn't plan on working for anyone except herself, but it got rid of her immediate problem. And the machines dealt with medical problems. "It's a deal. But if he comes back, the deal is off."

That had been six months before Tamati, and Nika already knew she'd exchanged one death penalty for another.

She had lost four of her new "clients." Two who'd been so badly injured even her Songyan couldn't heal them before their injuries shut down their life functions. The other two had come out of the machine clean and fresh—and one markedly improved—only to find Wickmore, and a heavy, waiting for them.

"You were given one job, Chandra," Wickmore had told the first, his voice as reasonable and gentle as Alejandro's could be.

"I'll fix it."

Wickmore raised his right hand. It contained a small rod. "We get it right the first time."

Blue lighting arced out one end and caught Chandra in a crazy dance. The lights went out, except on the Songyan, where the surge protector clicked in, leaving Chandra to finish his dance in the dim light of the machine LEDs.

"Get rid of the body," Wickmore had ordered his heavy.

It was the first time Nika had seen a sparker. Now she knew firsthand what damage they could do. Especially a sustained blast.

Wickmore had paid for her rewiring, but she'd known since then she had to disappear. Despite the studio. Despite the Songyans. Despite her career. Otherwise one day it would be her dancing at the end of the sparker.

So she had investigated what one needed to do to disappear so completely that no one—not a violent ex-partner, or an executive in one of the Big Twenty-Seven companies—would find her.

She had exit plans, because who knew what Alejandro might do when he was in a rage, or Wickmore might do as calculated punishment. How to escape from the shop if one of them attacked her. How to lock him inside while she got away. How to get away even with the resources of a Big Twenty-Seven company after her. The secret was to be so inconspicuous they wouldn't notice her. Going to a lawyer and changing her name was noticeable. Having a fling down at the docks was not.

The day after Chandra died she had gone down to the docks, found herself a drunk spacer due to ship out the next morning, and convinced him to marry her. As part of the marriage contract she had added her name to his. Legally, she was Nika Rik Terri James.

The minute James shipped out Nika had taken herself and her new identity off to the banks, where she'd opened accounts in the name Nika James.

Next day, after a flurry of I-can't-believe-we-were-both-drunk-enough-to-do-this messages from James on-ship, they'd canceled the contract.

But she hadn't changed her name back.

Nika booked passage for Nika Rik Terri on a liner going to Atalante. It was leaving the following morning and would take four weeks to get there. She booked a bunk for Snow on a tramp going to the Pleiades. It left at the same time as the liner, although from a different dock. Then she booked passage for Snow and Nika James on the first ship doing a business run between this world and the nearest station hub.

She used the time while they waited for the ship to depart to have some business clothes made up for them. They'd blend in better on the ship that way.

"Do you want to design your outfit?" she asked Snow, for that was polite. A modder didn't design another modder's look for them. You made it yours, right down to the clothes.

"Thank you." Snow picked his outfit with care.

"That's an old-style collar for a suit like that," the tailor said. "It will stand out as noticeably different."

Everyone was an expert in their own field. Even tailors.

"That style suits me better," Snow said.

The tailor looked to Nika. She was paying.

Should she remind him that the point of this was to blend in? Then Nika shrugged. What would they notice? An out-of-fashion suit. They certainly wouldn't notice the face that went with it. Except perhaps as someone they didn't want to know.

"It's his choice."

The fashionable color for business suits this year was maroon. Legs were tight, jackets broad. Snow's outfit, with its old-fashioned collar, was dark gray. It looked good on him. He would be a fine modder when he'd had more experience.

Nika stuck to maroon and slicked back her hair in the severe style most businesspeople were wearing this season.

Even with Snow's outré color scheme and his old-fashioned

collar, they fitted in with the other businesspeople streaming onto the shuttle, but Nika didn't relax until the shuttle was in space. So far, so good, but they were a long way from safe.

Snow picked at the prepackaged meal that had dropped onto the food tray in front of him. "I might have been able to save my business if I'd stayed."

He was too young to have a business. "Most people don't buy a studio straight out of school. They do an apprenticeship first."

"I had that sorted."

Nika raised a brow but didn't argue. Snow's life was his own. She turned her attention to her own meal. She had no idea what they were eating. It was green with crunchy purple noodles, and it tasted metallic. She studied her drink. A clear, carbonated beverage. It looked like water with bubbles. Tasted like water with bubbles.

"You wouldn't be able to afford new stock. You'd have spent it all fixing yourself. If you could program the machine after Banjo got through with your hands."

Snow shuddered. "Will he come after us?"

"It depends how angry we've made him."

Tamati would come. Banjo? She wasn't sure. He worked the docks. If he was away too long he'd lose his business. He'd be more likely to spend the time ensuring that the other businesses he took protection money from didn't do the same thing Snow had. She had, Nika amended.

"Was your studio insured?" Maybe he could claim for the damages Banjo was sure to inflict.

"They don't insure shops in the docks." Snow scowled at a purple noodle. "Except I didn't know that before I bought it."

Sometimes you bought what you could afford. Sometimes, too, you had to ask yourself why the business was so cheap when mod studios were so expensive.

"Why Lesser Sirius?" It wasn't an obvious choice for someone just out of school. They'd be more likely to choose Cassiopeia or New France.

"Are you kidding? *This* is where all the good stuff is happening. Rik Terri, Karma, SaStudio."

Nika hoped it was coincidence he mentioned her studio first.

Snow leaned close to her. "I had an appointment with Rik Terri. I had to wait five months."

She didn't want to think about the appointments she'd walked out on.

"I was going to get something small done. Whatever I could afford. Maybe my hair."

His beautiful copper hair. "Is it natural? That color, I mean?"

He nodded. "I like this color." He looked momentarily mournful, then brightened. "But it would be worth it, to see what she would do."

"Nothing. She'd do absolutely nothing." Except pay him for a gene read so she could work on the color in her own time.

Now was the time to tell him who she was. Unfortunately, if she wanted to disappear, she couldn't tell anyone. Not even Snow. Even if it made her uncomfortable.

"She'd do something," Snow said confidently.

"Snow, when you can't improve on perfection, you don't. Artists don't destroy a perfect flower."

"An artist can always make things better."

Or ruin things by trying too hard.

"How long have you been a modder?" Snow asked.

It was the only untruth about her new life. She'd had Nika James's papers forged. She waved a hand. "Seven years, give or take." Half the time she'd actually been a modder.

"What school?"

There was only one school for modders if you wanted to be the best. Landers Academy.

She had thought about choosing another school for her forged papers, but there was always a danger someone would want to talk to her about her education. Even with the mismatch of years there was enough she could say about Landers to convince someone she had attended there. The fewer lies she had to remember, the better.

"Landers."

He nodded, as if it was only to be expected. "Me too."

"What's it like now?" It was a safe subject, and she could use the information he provided to know who to talk about and who not.

Snow shrugged. "Still proud of itself as the preeminent gene-mod school."

"Who's in charge now?"

"Dean Marramar."

"Marramar. Goodness. She didn't even have full tenure when I was there." She'd been a tiny dumpling of a woman, with the most exquisite skin. Her specialty, not surprisingly, had been the epidermal layer.

Snow looked at her as if he didn't believe her. "She's been dean for absolutely forever."

Maybe it wasn't such safe talk. Nika shrugged. "You only think that because you're young."

He didn't argue it. She didn't think he'd noticed even.

They spent the rest of the trip talking about safer things, like where a good designer should start their design. Nika liked to start with the bones. Snow preferred to start with a feature the customer liked.

The walls at Hub Station Five were covered with the plum-and-cinnamon Burnley Company logo. The logos were faded; the walls were scratched. Last time Nika had been through here—as a young apprentice fresh out of Landers—everything had been fresh and bright. It had faded a lot in fourteen years.

Or her memory had.

The Hub teemed with people, most of them busy going somewhere else. It smelled of humans. There was nothing you could do about the smell, and Nika had tried. Get enough people together to crowd a space and eventually it started to stink.

She'd get used to it, but she didn't have to like it.

She bought them both coveralls and undershirts from a vending machine. "Put these on."

He did, but not without a last wistful glance at his designer business suit, which he packed carefully into the bag the coveralls had been in.

The labor pool was out in one of the older modules that looked as if it had arrived precompany. The lifts didn't work; they had to take the safety ladders—metal stairs so steep that if you slipped, and weren't hanging on, you'd be at the bottom before you regained your balance.

The module was one big room with desks scattered around. There were no partitions. People lined up at the desks. Desks in the central part of the room had permanent ship signs and logos, and the staff dealt with each person with impartial efficiency. The queues there were long.

Nika hadn't expected so many people looking for work. Nor had she ever seen so many people who'd never been near a modder.

Around the edges were the temporary desks, set up for the ships that required one or two crew. The people on both sides of these desks changed often. Nika watched them for a while and saw that once a ship had attained the crew it required, the employer vacated the desk. A new person took his or her place and the process started over again.

Snow looked around dubiously. "What are we doing here?" He fit in, with bruises from Banjo's pistol-whipping coming up black on his face, the deep cut high on his cheek still unclosed. She should find him a body studio.

"Looking for passage."

"This is a labor pool. People come here looking for jobs."

Nika's escape-from-Alejandro plan had told her it was also the place to find a cargo ship looking to make a bit of profit on the side carrying paying customers.

There was no day or night on a space station. Always open for business, and hundreds of small ships leaving every day. If Tamati tracked Nika this far, he'd have to sift through them all to find which ship she'd left on. He'd also be looking for a lone woman, not two people traveling together.

She stopped at a screen.

General hand. Must be good with Dekker calibrators.

"We should get a job." She'd spent the first two years in her studio calibrating Dekkers. They were temperamental machines. The calibrations went off fast. You had to sit and watch them all the time. It had taught her a lot about how to assess the progress of rebuilds, and about making minute modifications to the mix as you went. She still modded on the fly now, on occasion, to keep her hand in.

"It's not that sort of calibrator. It keeps the ship on course." Snow paused and chewed at his bottom lip for a moment. "Like one of the mineral drips on a genemod machine. You have to be sure it feeds through at a regular rate, or it can muck up your job."

That was what a calibrator was.

The woman sitting beneath the screen was as unimpressed as Snow. "Lady, the calibrator is the most vital part of a ship, not counting air and food. You get the calibrations wrong and you end up halfway across the galaxy from where you need to be. When I say I want an experienced calibrator, I mean it."

Snow dragged Nika away.

She stopped two desks farther on. This one had a long line. The screen above showed:

General hands. Good at hand-to-hand combat.

Doctor. Dietel FastTrack.

Tamati wouldn't expect her to get a job.

Snow said, "I didn't study for six years just to become a doctor."

The trouble with young people was that they were idealistic, rather than practical. "Banjo will be looking for modders, not doctors." So would Tamati, and she was far more scared of Tamati than she was of Banjo.

Snow scowled. "I've been thinking about that. We shouldn't have run."

Snow was right. She and Snow between them could have faced up to Banjo. Over time he would have learned. Unfortunately, Snow on his own wouldn't have been able to, and she had no intention of staying around for Tamati to find her while she assisted Snow.

Or maybe she should have stayed. Tamati would expect her to run. If she stayed right under his nose, maybe he wouldn't find her.

It was too late now. They'd run, and Banjo—with his new face and svelte figure and glorious chocolate eyes—would be out of the machine soon. The first thing he'd do would be trash Snow's shop.

"We'll go as far as we can." If she could work out how to discover which ships would take paying passengers. "After that we'll start up another studio for you." She'd finance it herself. Same level of equipment and materials as he'd had in his old shop, but in a safer location.

He winced. "I spent everything I had setting up the first shop. It will take years to get enough together for the next."

Nika started walking the floor. "How long did it take to save for the first one?" She half expected to find, with his modder's background and his touch of unworldliness, that he'd been gifted the credits.

"I worked through college." He chewed at his bottom lip. "I always planned to have my own shop."

And she'd killed his dream as effectively as Banjo had. Still, he must have saved hard to make his dream in six years.

She stopped at one of the larger desks. There was a line of people signing up. It looked a large enough ship to take passengers.

"Not here," Snow said softly behind her. "Half his crew die every time he goes out. Plus, he takes a lot of them from cattle ships." His mouth curled over the words like he'd tasted something sour.

"Cattle ships?" She had visions of ships carrying freezers full of slaughtered animals and pens of live animals to other worlds.

Snow sighed. "You know, captured free traders. If you attack a ship, what do you do with the people you capture?"

"Kill them?" Free traders killed each other all the time.

"When you can get credits by selling them to mercenary ships, why would you?"

Nika glanced back at the desk. The woman behind the desk wore a business suit and looked around Nika's own age. She looked normal. "Like slaves, you mean?"

"Not slaves. They sign you up and pay you. Although the rate is low."

The woman looked over at them and smiled. Her face was a little too perfect not to have had work done on it.

"Most times they go to merc ships, because even free traders have standards. But some of them don't."

This ship didn't have standards, Nika presumed. She ignored the smiling woman and moved on to the next desk. "What about this one?"

"No."

After the fourth *no* she started to wonder if Snow was being too picky.

"Is there anyone who'll satisfy you? We're not going to spend the rest of our lives with them."

"We want our lives to be longer than the next two weeks," Snow countered.

Nika sighed. Maybe they should check out the company liners. They weren't getting anywhere here. "Let's get something to eat."

They were standing in the coffee line—which was more crowded than the labor exchange—when a deep, almost familiar voice said from behind them, "Hello. I didn't expect to see the two of you here."

It was the spacer from the shop.

Nika checked the side of his neck. "Passable," she conceded. Just. "Is the rest like this?"

"Don't mind her." Color washed into Snow's face, and out again. Red flush didn't suit copper hair. "She can be a little obsessive." He nudged Nika. "It's not polite." The last was low, hissed through gritted teeth.

"He was almost a customer."

The stranger grinned. "You want to see the rest?"

"I wouldn't mind."

Snow led the way to a vacant table. The back of his neck was still red.

The stranger pulled off his vest and shirt. Two women and a man at the next table catcalled.

Nika ignored them. "A basic machine job," she said. "Dietel FastTrack." The Dietels were cheap and left a characteristic pink stain on the skin. Every hospital had them. Modders—even the bad ones—avoided them because of the color they left. This man had gone straight from Snow's studio to a hospital.

If he wasn't worried about reporting his injuries, why had he come to the shop in the first place? A doctor was a tenth the price of a modder. Although he had known Tilda.

"I have no idea what she's talking about," the stranger said to Snow.

Snow looked as if he wasn't sure either, although he must have recognized the brand.

"Big green machine," Nika said. Their color was the most beautiful thing about them. "Dark emerald, almost glowing."

The stranger nodded. "It was at that." He started to pull his shirt back on. "I'm Roystan, by the way."

"Nika. Snow."

She watched the way the new skin pulled against the old as his muscles moved, and put out a hand. "Wait."

He waited, arms in his sleeves, chest bare.

She closed her eyes as she ran her fingers against the new skin, and then over the old. The catcalls from the next table grew louder. She concentrated on the texture. Yes. The new skin had the characteristic plasticity of hu-skin. She opened her eyes. "How much did you pay for this?"

"A thousand credits."

The man at the next table pulled off his own shirt. "You want to check me out next?"

Snow's face and neck were an unbecoming brick red again. He didn't look at her. Or at Roystan.

Nika ignored them. "They ripped you off." Hu-skin was a synthesized organic they used when the machine couldn't repair the human skin. "They fixed it with hu-skin. There's no reason to do that unless your DNA doesn't take." Then she added, for he was looking bemused, "They usually do that when someone has botched your DNA."

Sometimes even hu-skin didn't work in those cases.

Roystan had started to pull on his shirt again. He stopped, shirt ready to go over his head. "What?"

Snow patted a sleeve and said kindly. "She's not saying they botched anything." He glared at Nika from behind Roystan. "She's saying they charged you for services they shouldn't have."

But they had provided the service they'd charged for. "Which hospital?"

"Old Base."

He'd gone to the nearest hospital after he'd left them. Given its proximity to the spaceport, Old Base was always busy. Too busy to provide services one didn't need. Hu-skin took three times longer to take, far longer than replicating one's own skin with mutrient. That was one genemod machine that might have had two more patients. For Old Base, hu-skin would be a last resort.

"If you have problems that need hu-skin, you're better going to a modder," Nika said. "A good one. Doctors can only run the machines. They have no idea how to fix people."

Roystan blinked, then finished pulling on his shirt, studying Nika the whole time.

She couldn't read the stare. She ignored it and slid onto the seat beside Snow.

Roystan settled opposite them, still watching Nika. "What brings you up here?"

Many people came to the Hub, but those who came down to the labor exchange were looking for one thing. Work. Or occasionally, "Passage."

Roystan nodded. "A pity. It was a good shop."

"Studio," Nika corrected.

They talked about gene studios for the rest of the meal. Roystan had been in a few. Nika was surprised he knew the inside of one, except Tilda's.

Roystan's handheld beeped. It was an old-fashioned, external communicator. They'd been all the rage twenty years ago, a nostalgia fad, until people discovered how inconvenient it was to carry your linking device around with you, instead of having the bioware built in.

Based on that, Nika would have believed that Roystan had last been modded twenty years ago and retained the trimmings. But she'd spent lunch talking to him about body shops. He'd been in one more recently than that, had plenty of time to change it.

Roystan looked down at his handheld, then stood up. "This is my slot. Let me know where you end up. I'll keep an eye out for your shop."

"We look forward to having you as a client." It was the literal truth. Problems that required hu-skin were a challenge.

Roystan's crooked smile flashed. "If I hear of anyone reputable offering passage, I'll let you know."

"Excuse me." One of the women from the next table leaned toward them. "Captain Jai, from the *Boldly Go*. I couldn't help overhearing some of your conversation." She ignored the vocal agreement from both her companions. "I have a spare cabin this trip, if you are looking to pay your way, and you're willing to share." She glanced at her noisy companions. "I'll keep my uncouth crew under control, too."

Nika looked at Snow, who shrugged. "I don't know the ship."

"I do," Roystan said. "Captain Jai is said to be fair. The *Boldly Go* does takes passengers to supplement its income."

"Can we talk it over?" Nika asked Jai.

"No problem. Let me know soon. I'm shipping out at 23:00 today." The captain sent across her contact details.

"Thank you. We'll let you know."

8

JOSUNE ARRIOLA

After the extended jump, the cracked calibrator did exactly what Josune expected. It cracked further.

"Not even going to try to fix it," Carlos said. "Pull it out. We'll use some of those credits to buy ourselves a brand-new one."

While Roystan was off hunting new crew members, Carlos went shopping.

"You coming?"

"I'll stay here and dismantle the old one. Roystan's only booked the ship berth till midnight. That way, if we have any issues with the calibrator we can still buy extra parts."

In truth, she wanted to stay on board. Maybe Roystan would forget he'd told her to go. He and Jacques had gone down world and returned with new pink skin, after which Roystan had taken himself off to the Hub to find new crew members.

Once, she had planned to explore on her own if anything ever happened to the *Hassim*. Now, it wasn't as appealing.

Maybe she could hire Roystan and his crew.

Or maybe not, given what he thought of explorers.

Roystan ran a comfortable ship. He was comfortable to be around, even with his governing more by committee than as sole leader. Not like Feyodor, whose decisions were final as soon as she made them. Roystan and his crew—those that were left—were good people.

In the end, she might have to go. But not immediately. Not unless Roystan kicked her off. Which he would do, unless she could convince him that she wasn't another traitor like Pol. That she wasn't a company person.

She spent the afternoon dismantling the calibrator. Not thinking, just doing. And she kept the ship links open. Jacques spent his time in the galley, preparing a welcome meal for the two new crew members they were to get. He was sweet-talking his oven, which was normal, but not something he'd done since the mutiny until now. Guardian's betrayal had hit him hard. They'd been friends.

Carlos came back empty-handed. "Shop refused the credit. I need to talk to Jacques." He stomped off to find him. "I asked them to hold it for us."

Josune set the parts under a stass field and followed.

"Of course I didn't stop the credits," Jacques said. "Why would I? We talked about it before you left."

"Storekeeper still refused credit. I told him I could have bought his store. He laughed at me."

Brown Combine had a reputation. They honored their word. Surely they hadn't stopped the payment. They couldn't have, but Josune was starting to twitch. "Check your credit."

"I checked it before Carlos went." But Jacques called up the accounts anyway. "We have ten million, fifty thousand—" He looked hard at the screen. "It's a mistake."

"How much?" Josune asked.

"Nothing. It's a mistake. I'll sort it out."

No balance. Zero credits. Someone had cleaned them out.

Carlos called Roystan. "Don't hire any crew."

"But I'm just about to sign—"

"Don't, Roystan. Come back to the ship. We've got a big problem."

He cornered him as soon as he stepped onto the ship. Josune, sitting with Jacques and drinking her second cup of coffee, watched through the link with the sound turned down.

Jacques switched through to the speaker near the airlock. "Welcome-home tea is served." A big, booming sound. "Come and eat this flatbread before it goes cold."

Josune's stomach rumbled at the words. They ate a lot of flatbread. She suspected that was more because Roystan liked it than because Jacques liked cooking it.

Roystan held up a thumb to the camera feed in acknowledgment, said something to Carlos, and led the way down the passageway.

"Not sure how we are going to cope without crew." Jacques sounded morose.

"We'll have to manage." Josune wasn't sure that they would, especially if Roystan forced her to go. She'd have to talk him around, although she was tempted, for a moment, to head off to her room.

Roystan and Carlos arrived. "I'd kill for a coffee, Jacques."

"Coming right up. Bad news is always better on a full stomach."

"Or it gives you indigestion. What's this about no funds?"

"I keep telling you," Carlos said. "Brown cleared us out. Jacques. Show him."

Jacques finished serving Roystan before he brought up the figures. "They took everything."

It was the first time Josune had seen the numbers. 10,050,822.16 credits. Someone had withdrawn the whole amount. The withdrawal had cleared five hours earlier.

"I tried to stop it," Jacques said. "The bank refused. Said it was a legitimate transaction and had already gone through."

"It wasn't Brown." Josune had been telling Jacques that for hours. Brown Combine wouldn't know how much was in the bank. Besides, all they would have done was prevent the ten-million-credit payment being cleared in the first place.

Roystan gave her a sharp look. "Is that firsthand knowledge?"

She shook her head.

"And speaking of, didn't I—"

"Check the codes," Josune said, before he could tell her she was off ship in front of everyone. "The only person who can clean out an account like that is someone who has been authorized. That makes it you or Jacques."

"I did not—"

"Hold it, Jacques. She's right." Roystan rubbed his eyes. "Check the account. See who has access other than you or I?" He pushed away his half-eaten slice of flatbread.

Jacques's gaze followed the bread. He drooped.

"Accounts, Jacques."

"There is no one else." He brought up the accounts with a flourish. "If Josune is so certain of it, then she . . . oh."

Three names had appeared on-screen. Hammond Roystan, Jacques Saloman, Pol Bager.

"Pol." If Carlos got any angrier he'd steam.

Roystan rubbed his eyes again. "She is—was—assistant cargo master."

"I am going to kill her," Carlos said.

No one else said anything, until Josune coughed. "The calibrator's cracked." And it was her fault. She buried the guilt. "We can't use it, and we have no credits to buy another."

Roystan tapped codes onto the screen. Pol's name disappeared off the list. "Any more bad news?"

"What about Josune?" Carlos asked. "She's paid crew, and we can't pay her either. It's time we brought her into the profit share."

"Ah, yes. Josune." Roystan looked at Josune.

"Roystan and I need to talk before that happens," Josune said. "I'll stay for the moment. You need all the crew you can get, paid and unpaid." She looked at Roystan, almost a challenge.

"We'll see," Roystan said.

There was an uncomfortable silence while everyone in the room digested that.

Jacques broke it. "Are you two sleeping together?"

How did you jump from being kicked off ship to sleeping together in one deductive leap? Josune shook her head.

"No," Roystan said.

"Because if you are, don't make the fights uncomfortable for the rest of us."

Carlos leaned close to Jacques. "Why do you think that?" He made it quiet, but the only noise that covered it was the air-conditioning.

"Because. Secrets. There's nothing private on this ship, but they have a secret." Jacques scowled at Josune. "That business when he was decoding the memory yesterday. He was showing off for her."

He was? Josune looked at Roystan. Color stained his cheeks.

He sat back. "It's not that. Something happened while we were on the *Hassim*, Jacques. And no, I'm not telling you what it was. Josune is going to leave."

"I won't leave you while we're in this mess," Josune said.

Carlos patted her shoulder.

Josune and Carlos put the calibrator back together using soft filler on the damaged parts.

"You don't have to leave because of what happened on the *Hassim*," Carlos said.

She'd tried not to think about what happened on the *Hassim*, tried not to think about what she was going to do next. But Carlos's words brought back memory in a blinding, heartbreaking rush. Her home. Her friends. Her old life. Destroyed.

She couldn't see for a moment. Fumbled.

"Or because you went crazy with the sparker and half destroyed Roystan's ship."

Half destroyed was a slight exaggeration. The only thing they couldn't repair was the calibrator.

"Roystan will eventually forgive you."

Was that why he thought she was leaving? "Can we not talk about it?"

"Sorry." Carlos patted her shoulder clumsily.

When the calibrator was in one piece again, they stood looking at the damage.

Carlos circled it dubiously.

"It's not going to work." Josune said aloud what they both knew. "It'll break the first time we nullspace." Who knew where they'd end up. Maybe in a galaxy a billion light-years away, with nothing around them except empty space, and no way to get back, even if they knew where to go back to.

They couldn't risk it. "Let me talk to the captain." Roystan would consider the safety of his crew. "I can loan him the credits."

"He doesn't take loans, Josune."

Maybe he could take a passenger, then. Josune could pay, and she had nowhere else to go.

Light steps heralded the arrival of Roystan. "How's it going?"

Carlos said, "If we'd known this was going to happen, we'd have taken the calibrator off the *Hassim*."

Roystan grimaced. "If I'd known this was going to happen I'd have done a lot of things differently." He leaned against the counter. "You all right, Carlos?"

Josune might not have been in the room.

"Jacques is taking it bad," Carlos said. "He and Guardian were friends."

"What about *you*?"

Carlos traced the crack on the calibrator. "I'll get over it. I never liked Pol anyway, and Qiang kept to herself. Guardian?" He shrugged and waved the word away. "Let's say I don't want to meet him again any time soon. Although I admit, I was spending those lovely credits in my head."

"Let's deliver our cargo, Carlos. Then we'll see." Roystan turned to Josune. "I need to talk to you."

She nodded, and made toward the door.

"Josune," Carlos said. "We'll help you work through it. Don't run. It never works."

"Thanks." Her voice was husky.

Roystan led her to the empty cabin next to his own and closed the door. "What does Carlos think you're running from?"

"Whatever it was you alluded to that happened on the *Hassim*. Or my wrecking your ship." She still wasn't sure which.

Josune sat on the lower bunk, then pulled her knees up so her feet were on the bed and her chin was resting on her knees. "You've a good crew." What was left of them.

Even Guardian had been decent. But it hadn't stopped him from being greedy.

"I do," Roystan agreed. "But I'm not putting up with company spies. Especially as you know as well as I do what's sitting in *The Road*'s memory right now. You're a good worker, Josune. I like you. But I don't trust you, and we've lost everything else."

The only thing Josune had left was her dream. Captain Feyodor had been convinced Roystan was the key to that dream.

Josune blinked on the array behind her eye. She held out her hand. "Give me your communicator."

He hesitated handing it over. "The *Hassim*'s memory isn't linked. You can't retrieve it. Or wipe it."

She sorted quickly through her own records. What could she give him to prove she wasn't a threat? Sassia. The red bracelet that Pol had worn. Josune's notes, her pictures of the rock, subsections as she'd cut it. Her own voice describing what she'd discovered. Her arm, with the indelible red stain. She pushed it down to him.

"I don't need the *Hassim*," she said, when he'd finished watching it. "I told you, I'm not company. I'm an explorer. Goberling's lode is what I'm searching for."

"Josune Arriola."

She shouldn't have been surprised he knew the names of the *Hassim*'s crew without having to look them up.

"Yes."

"Why didn't you say? It was your ship. Survivor rights. We could have—"

"Would I be alive now if I had said?"

Roystan rubbed his nose. "Pol." He looked away. Looked back. "I'm sorry."

"So am I, but there is nothing left for me on the *Hassim*." Except the memory of her crewmates' death. "The only reason I'm alive is because Feyodor sent me to find you. Coming out of nullspace right in front of you wasn't accidental."

"I knew that as soon as I saw the recording." Roystan dropped onto the bunk beside her with a sigh. "I can't help you find that world, Josune. Not *won't*. *Can't*."

"But you know why she sought you out."

"Yes." He bounced to his feet again, hitting his head on the top bunk. "And no. I won't tell you that." He rubbed his head. "Ow."

This time it was *won't*, not *can't*.

"I've no ship. Nowhere to stay. I know you took me on under false pretenses, but I'm a good engineer."

She tried to read his body language. She couldn't see much. His legs and stomach as he leaned against the top bunk. He was almost scrawny. How could he continue to eat Jacques's food and stay so thin, while the rest of them stacked on the weight?

"And thanks to us, you're homeless."

She'd have been dead if it weren't for Roystan. "Thanks to a company. But if it lets me stay, then yes, I'm homeless." Then, because it was Roystan, and he would keep her on because of that. "You know why I'm staying. Always remember that."

She heard his sigh above her. Muffled, as if he'd buried his face in his hands, or in the bunk above. "You know what I wish, Josune?

I wish Goberling had stayed home. Accepted the job his company offered him, and stayed around to become an accountant."

"You don't wish that." Roystan knew too much about the *Hassim* to think that. "Besides, Goberling wasn't an accountant. He was a pilot."

He didn't answer.

It was time to change the subject. "Roystan, if I am staying, I'm not going to risk my life with a faulty calibrator. I'll pay you for letting me stay. I'll buy you one."

"We're not a charity, Josune."

"I'm living on borrowed time. I didn't survive a massacre just to die in nullspace."

"Technically—"

"Technically nothing, Roystan. We are getting a new calibrator."

She knew from the silence that he considered refusing. Eventually he sighed. "I'll let you know how much it is." He turned for the door, then hesitated. "You might want to do something about the eye before you go back to Carlos."

"Put that thing into the recycler," Carlos said, before he left to buy the new calibrator.

She would, but not until they'd installed the other one. Things went wrong. They might need to cannibalize some of the parts.

Carlos hesitated before asking Roystan, "You good with this loan? I know you don't like them."

He'd assumed it was a loan. No one had told him otherwise. Or where the "loan" was from.

Roystan gave his crooked smile. "Josune makes a convincing argument that it's better to be alive with a loan than dead without one."

"We'll pay it off, Roystan."

"Just make sure this thing is worth the money you pay for it."

After they'd gone, Josune and Roystan made their way down to the crew room. There wasn't much to do on a ship in dock. Sometimes Josune thought this crew spent too much time together. On the *Hassim* she'd spent a lot of time in her cabin or down in the engineering workshop.

Roystan spent the time running through the revised delivery schedule Jacques had set up.

If Pol'd had her way they wouldn't have had schedules to rearrange. They'd have been off looking for the lost world right now.

Jacques brought out savory cakes for them to nibble on.

Josune took two. "I died and went to heaven."

Roystan's communicator sounded. He flicked the channel open. Carlos.

"You're ready for your money?"

Josune had transferred the credits through to Roystan earlier.

"They say they've sold out."

"Of calibrators? What about the one they had on hold for us?"

No one ran out of calibrators unless they were a one-man shop on the rim. This was the Hub.

"They couldn't hold it. Sold."

"Impossible."

"Of course it's impossible. He offered me five when I was here earlier."

"Any reason for the change?"

"Nothing personal, he says."

Nothing personal meant someone putting pressure on the shop owner not to sell. Did that mean someone didn't like *The Road*? More likely they'd heard about the *Hassim* and wanted to keep the ship there until they arrived. The only people who could put that sort of pressure onto a store owner in the Hub were companies.

"Try somewhere else. Even a secondhand one."

"I've tried them all. Everyone says the same thing."

"Sold out?"

"Nothing personal." Carlos hesitated. "I've seen a couple of company men wearing that black shiny pin. Like they had on the *Hassim*."

"They're holding us here." Josune pushed her cake aside, a cold, heavy lump settling into her stomach. "They know we can't jump. They'll send someone to pick us off." Probably a trained merc team.

Roystan breathed out in a long sigh. "This is why chasing a lost cause is so stupid." He looked at her. "Everyone will be after the memory. After us."

Nothing Roystan's crew could say would save them. No one would believe they didn't have the memory any longer. Especially not a company prepared to pressure a whole station to hold them here.

"Can you put the other calibrator back in?"

She shook her head. That was an emergency last resort, after all other avenues had been exhausted. "We're smarter getting a calibrator from somewhere the company hasn't banned, and modifying it to suit the ship." She'd done that before. She leaned forward to speak into his handheld. "Carlos, see if there are any genemod machines for sale."

"Genemod. How will that work?"

"They use calibrators, and they're made by the same companies that make ship calibrators."

"You crazy engineer. They use totally different fluids."

"It's still just inlet valves and outlet valves and regulating them." She'd pulled one apart once. Once past the shell, they were almost identical. They could rig up a bypass to ensure that whatever fluids had been in the genemod machine wouldn't contaminate the ship fluids. "Of course, we'll have to readjust our measurements." The flows were different.

"Will it work?" Roystan asked quietly.

She nodded. "Ninety percent sure."

"Which is better than sitting waiting for a company to get to us at their leisure. Carlos. Find us a genemod machine." Roystan clicked off and laid the communicator on the table. He stared down at it.

"If we don't get out of here fast, we're cattle ship fodder," Josune said.

Or dead.

"But we're way inside the legal zone," Jacques said.

"Doesn't matter, Jacques. No one cares when this sort of money is involved."

"We'll tell them we don't have the *Hassim* memory anymore."

"They'll attack us on the chance we might have something, even if we don't." Roystan stood up. "I'll be on the bridge."

Josune stood, too. "I'll go prepare the calibrator slot." There was nothing she could do until the new one arrived, but it was an excuse. She wanted to make good and sure that *The Road*'s memory was protected. And that the ship was better armed. The first place she planned to stop was her own cabin, where Reba's sparker was locked in her safe. One could never have too many concealed weapons.

Josune was on the bridge when Carlos called.

Roystan answered. "That was fast." He put the communicator on speaker so Josune could hear.

"It's fast because there is only one for sale, and it's old."

Roystan looked at Josune.

"Not a problem."

"Buy it."

"Well, I would, but we have another problem." Carlos scowled. "We're in the legal zone. The trader won't sell to anyone who isn't certified to use it."

That was the law. Only doctors and modders were certified to purchase genemod machines. Still, wave enough credits in front of anyone and eventually they'd take it.

"Offer him more," Josune said.

"It's junk." Carlos didn't sound hopeful. "An early model. It probably wouldn't be compatible with the ship. I'm not sure it's worth it."

"Offer him—"

"No. Wait," Roystan said. "I know where we can get someone certified to buy it for us. If she hasn't already left."

"A doctor?" On the Hub? Carlos sounded skeptical, and Josune didn't blame him. The hospital was company run. No one would risk a company job to help free traders.

"Not a doctor. A modder."

It took twelve months to get a doctor's certificate. Most of that was learning how to use the machine, how to make minor repairs, and how to analyze the numerous diagnostics a genemod machine provided. It took another five years to become a modder, to become proficient enough to redesign people's bodies. Modders made big credits. They stayed on-world in their expensive studios, and clients came to them.

"You're dreaming, Roystan. You won't find a modder on the Hub."

"She was looking for passage. She might have accepted Captain Jai's offer."

The way their luck was running, she'd be gone.

Roystan snatched up his communicator. "Come back here, Carlos. I'll send the modder and Josune in to buy the machine. No one will recognize Josune as from our ship."

They had to find the modder first.

"Come on," Roystan said to Josune. "Let's go get ourselves a calibrator."

"Wait. We're not going in unarmed." She pulled out Reba's sparker. "Lift your shirt."

"My—"

She lifted it for him and pulled the Velcro strap of the holster around tight. He was so very skinny, ribs prominent over tight skin. Where did all Jacques's food go? "I want your metabolism."

"I can't take your weapon."

"It's Reba's." She touched her jacket. "I've still got mine."

Should she tell him Reba's weapon was more powerful than hers? No. Best not let him worry about the damage he might do.

Roystan tucked the sparker carefully into its holster and pulled his shirt down. She'd never noticed before just how loose the shirt was.

"You do know how to use a sparker?" She should have checked first. "Have you ever fired one before?"

"A long time ago."

Why wasn't she surprised that he had?

Roystan patted his shirt uncomfortably. "A pity we had to register the *Hassim* before we sold it. People know who we are. That makes it easy to find us."

"I don't think the company has a full team here yet," Josune said. Otherwise they'd have stormed *The Road* by now. "At a guess, they had people nearby. Sent them here to keep an eye on us, and to stop us leaving."

"You've two and a half hours before we have to vacate our berth," Jacques reminded them. "We can't pay for an overstay."

Roystan gave his shirt one more pat. "Then let's not waste any more time."

Josune followed him. "Why don't we just find the trader? It will save time."

"And do what?"

Josune didn't answer.

"We should at least try, Josune. If that doesn't work, we'll do it your way."

They were walking into a trap. Josune was sure of it.

9

NIKA RIK TERRI

The *Boldly Go* worked between the Hub and New France. Snow hadn't found anything to complain of with the ship, and Nika was desperate to leave the Hub. Eight days until Tamati came out.

They shared a four-berth cabin with two other travelers. An older woman returning to New France after the birth of her granddaughter, and a miner around Snow's apparent age, who was going home to visit his wife. He couldn't stop talking about it.

Family. Nika's family had lived for the company they worked for. They'd been fair but distant guardians, ensuring that she was fed, healthy, and educated, but they spent most of their time—even when they were home—working.

Captain Jai, one hundred twenty centimeters tall, with bones for a person a meter taller—height was one thing a modder couldn't change easily—wanted them out of the way while she finished loading.

"Stay in your cabin, or find a bar, but be back here no later than 22:45. We ship out at 23:00 and I'm not waiting for missing passengers."

Nika would have preferred to stay in her cabin, but the others—even Snow—opted for the bar. "After all," the miner had said, "we'll be on the ship a week. Why stay on it longer than we need to?"

The four of them adjourned to the bar closest to the ship. Nika watched the clock and drank water while the others talked. The clock didn't seem to move.

The miner was explaining, for the fifth time, the plans he had for his break.

"Going to the zoo. We met at the zoo, in the giant monitor enclosure. That's where we'll go first, and—"

Snow's eyes were glazed, but he nodded. "The giant lizards." He hadn't known what a monitor was the first time.

"Young people," the grandmother said to Nika. "In love. Have you ever been in love?"

She'd thought she had. Attracted to a dangerous man, but had it been love? It certainly wasn't love at the end. Nika shrugged.

"No? I went through two husbands before I fell in love. But I loved my daughter, right from the start."

The lenses on the grandmother's eyes were starting to cloud. She was heading toward cataracts; she'd need them fixed soon. Nika forced herself to bite her tongue. The woman had confided how carefully she'd budgeted for this break. When her eyes got noticeably bad she'd get them fixed. No point worrying her now.

Two men in business suits stepped through the doorway.

The grandmother stopped midsentence and spat on the floor. "Company grunts. Don't often get them slumming up here."

Nika hardly heard her, couldn't tear her eyes away as light reflected off a black pin in one of the collars. They'd found her. Already. How was that possible?

Maybe Nika, in Tamati's body, had been so badly injured she'd set the time wrong and Tamati had come out of the machine early. No. She knew her job. Tamati must have had people working with him.

"Snow." Nika didn't recognize her own voice. "We forgot the mutrient. We need to get it before we go on board." She grabbed Snow's arm.

"But we can't take mutrient on a—"

"Come on," she hissed. "They found us."

"Banjo." A soundless whisper from Snow.

She wasn't going to argue if it made him move. "Make it look natural. Exiting, I mean. Don't run until we're around the next corridor."

"Who?"

She wasn't going to tell him, because he'd automatically look. He looked anyway, for it didn't take a genius to work out who their pursuers would be. She felt Snow's muscles bunch as soon as they were out the door. "Wait. Don't let them see us run."

But her own muscles were twitching. So much so that she put a hand on the wall to stop herself from taking off.

Snow's longer legs had an advantage. "Hurry."

Nika glanced behind just as someone came out of the bar. "Run." By the time her brain caught up with the adrenaline and she realized it was a stranger, it was too late. They were running.

Around the corner.

Full tilt into a woman hurrying the other way.

"Whoa," said the woman, grabbing Nika before she fell.

In front of her, Snow backpedaled. Nika looked up to find herself staring into a weapon. A sparker.

"Sorry." It was their almost-patient, Roystan. He looked a bit sheepish as he shoved the weapon into its holster under his shirt. "Instinct," he told the woman who had caught Nika. "But well met, since we were looking for you."

"We're in a hurry," Nika said, and couldn't stop herself looking back. There was no one there.

"We're in a hurry, too." Roystan glanced the same way Nika had. "Let's walk and talk."

"Sure." They set off briskly down the corridor.

"You pulled a weapon on us," Snow said.

Nika didn't think Roystan was their enemy. But could she trust him? Maybe he had a problem with his new hu-skin.

Snow must have been thinking along the same lines. He glared at Roystan. "I hope you aren't going to demand medical advice."

Nika couldn't stop the words that tripped out. "He *was* almost a patient." Too much adrenaline. She needed to calm down.

"There's a difference between *almost* and *is*. And that difference could be called stalking."

"I know this looks bad." Roystan glanced behind again.

He was as nervous as they were. Nika looked at the woman following Snow. She was tall and rangy, a good match for Roystan. She had spent time under a machine in the past. Nika recognized the silver skin tint. It had been a Rik Terri color two seasons ago. The long, blue-black, loosely braided hair had a metallic sheen that went well with the silver. It wasn't something Nika had put together, but it was a good fit. She'd have to find out who had done the mod.

Unfortunately, the woman also had an atypical droop in the right eyelid that signaled work under it. That mod included some heavy bioware, at a guess. Expensive, company-level bioware. Her clothes were the same quality as the ones Nika had left behind when she'd run.

And she kept one hand close to the opening of her jacket. Nika would bet she had a concealed weapon. She raised her eyes to the girl's collar. No black pin. That didn't mean much. Alejandro hadn't always worn his pin either. But he had one. He'd boasted that they were only given out after they'd been earned.

The woman blinked on her bioware as they turned into another corridor. "Let's speed it up."

Nika needed no further bidding to quicken her pace. She was almost running.

They turned down another corridor. Then another.

"We haven't much time," Roystan said.

Nika nodded. Neither did they. As soon as she could safely drag herself and Snow away from them, they'd go.

"I know you're both running from whatever happened down on Lesser Sirius."

Snow started to protest. "That's not—"

Roystan held up a hand. "You can go with the *Boldly Go*, but I have a better offer. I'll take you with us." His words tumbled out one over the other. "We have a seven-day layover at Atalante in two weeks. From there I'll take you anywhere in the galaxy you want to go that I can get to and back in that time."

"Why?" Nika asked. No one made an offer like that. "What's the catch?"

"We're in a bit of trouble ourselves," Roystan said. "We've a company after us, and a damaged calibrator. The company has put out the word, and no one will sell us a new one. Josune thinks we can use the calibrator off a genemod machine."

Nika had bought plenty of genemod machines in her life. She knew the process. "You need someone certified to buy the machine for you."

Snow sputtered. "No way. We're not getting involved in a company war."

But they already were involved—or Nika was, anyway, for Tamati was company.

"You'll be leaving soon?" The *Boldly Go* wouldn't wait past their allotted slot.

"As soon as the calibrator is on board." Roystan's fervent words were a promise.

"We get the machine afterward," Nika said. You could never have too many mod machines, and Snow needed something to start with. She hoped it wasn't a Dietel.

"We can't give you the calibrator. We can give you the rest."

"Deal," Nika said.

The goods store was at the end of an arm off the corridor. Anyone coming this way would be heading for the store.

Josune stopped Roystan. "You stay out here and watch. They won't recognize us, but they might recognize you."

It looked as if it was the last thing he wanted to do. "I should—"

"Stay here." Josune swept Nika and Snow in before her.

Nika thought Josune might be older than she looked. Ten years, maybe fifteen. She was too confident for her early-twenties body. There was something about the way young people acted—like Snow. This woman didn't act like that.

The trader looked them over, assessing them. Nika could almost see the droop as he looked at their vendor-purchased coveralls, although his eyes did stop at Josune's boots.

"We're here to buy your genemod machine," Josune told the trader.

The trader raised an eyebrow. A single brow. Modded. He wouldn't have been able to raise it that high if it hadn't been. If Nika weren't in such a hurry she'd have asked him who'd done it. But not today. They didn't have the time.

The screen displayed the view of the camera outside the shop, where Roystan was pacing. Who was he watching for? Was Nika getting herself and Snow into more trouble?

Behind her, she heard Josune. "One of our crew was in earlier."

"Ah, yes. Of course. And as I told him, I can't sell the machine to someone who isn't a registered doctor or modder. I'm sure you haven't forgotten that part."

"We have a modder."

Nika turned as Josune indicated her.

The trader looked Nika over, and the way he sniffed told her she didn't look like a modder right now. "I'll need to see your credentials."

"You'll see my credentials if we agree to take the machine. Not before." Often, the old machines were partially dismantled. You got more for the scrap metal. If Roystan wanted a working calibrator he'd need the flanges as well, and they were usually the first parts to be sold off.

The trader tried to stare her down. Nika stared back, unflinching. Behind her, Josune twitched. At least she stayed silent.

"Very well." The trader looked away first and moved to the back corner. "Here she is." He patted a battered box that looked as if it wouldn't hold together. A big plastic box, gray and stained, double her length, and half as wide again. An oversized coffin on casters, with a clear lid. In the early days, modders had to monitor the changes visually.

Nika sighed. A Dekker. She might have known. What else would be collecting dust in the back of a store on the Hub? Dekkers were ugly machines—nothing like her beautiful Songyans—and had the worst calibrators in the galaxy. Her first genemod machine had been a Dekker and because of that, she'd learned how to calibrate manually.

The company had gone broke, but not because of their calibrators.

The machines also had a nasty habit of bringing the client out early. It had happened so often they'd installed panic buttons inside the box. Not that it helped. Most people died of fright trying to get out.

It had happened to Nika once. It had been awful, waking up, knowing her lungs were filled with liquid, trying to convince her brain that she didn't need to breathe air, that the liquid and the machine were supplying the oxygen for her, but though she knew that, instinct made her try to breathe. She'd hit the panic button, but it had taken time for her lungs, and then the machine, to drain.

Nika shuddered at the memory.

She stored her old Dekker in her lab and used it to mix components. It kept her manual calibration skills active.

The only good thing about the machines was the air cushion they moved on. Nika moved around the Dekker doing a quick check. Surprisingly, the tank was full of mutrient. Any sensible trader would have drained the tank and sold the mutrient off separately. Although, by look and smell, it was old. The tank would have to be scoured to remove all the old chemicals. Better yet, replaced.

"Nika." Snow hung back. He kept his voice quiet. "You're making a bad mistake. There's a reason they don't sell these machines to unregistered modders."

Illegal mods were an unpleasant fact of life, and Nika herself had fixed some appalling—and oftentimes painful—modifications. But desperate times called for desperate measures.

"I'll make sure they can't use anything but the calibrator." She believed them about the reason they needed the machine. Hadn't she seen jobs for people with calibrator experience earlier at the labor pool? "Besides, Roystan agreed to give us the machine."

"They held weapons to our head. We can't stop them from doing what they want."

Right now, Nika didn't care. She wanted—they needed—to get away. If this was how they did it, this would do.

"Haven't you ever locked a machine so no one else could use it?" She hadn't always done that herself. Not until Alejandro.

The calibrator flanges were in a box with some spare cables. They were dented, but workable, although the dents made the volume smaller. They'd have to recalculate for that. She nodded at Josune.

"We'll take it," Josune said.

"It'll cost more. I didn't realize that box was part of it."

"Of course you knew," Nika said. "Are you trying to rip us off, sell us a useless unit?"

Josune's fingers twitched.

The trader looked daggers at Nika, and sideways at Josune. "I need confirmation of your registration before I sell it to you. Doctor."

"Modder." She stepped forward. Stopped. Tamati's associates had found her here. If she gave her details, her new ID would be useless. She turned to Snow. "You sign for it."

"Nika."

"Just do it."

"I am not going to sign my reputation away so they can get a calibrator."

"Snow, I can't sign for it."

Snow opened his mouth to argue but turned as Roystan rushed in through the doorway. "We're about to get company."

Nika looked at the screen. The two men from the bar were coming toward the shop.

Company people, and Roystan and Josune were worried about them. Was it coincidence, or did they have a common enemy?

Had Nika made a mistake by joining up with Roystan? Or was it a setup? After all, Josune's mods screamed company. Or could a company be after Roystan and Josune? It made sense, because Tamati wouldn't be out of the machine yet.

She pushed down the familiar tattoo of fear that started beating at her every time she saw Eaglehawk. Breathe. This was not Tamati. Nor Alejandro. One step at a time. They had the machine. They had to get it back to the ship without dying along the way.

"Snow."

Something in her voice finally made him touch his fingers to the salespoint, then let it read his iris pattern.

The reading confirmed his identity and his status as a modder.

"Satisfied," Josune demanded, her own hand on the reader almost before Snow's read was done. She kept one eye on the outside screen. Nika watched, too.

The trader glanced at the screen. "I'm not getting involved in company business."

"Just take the damn payment." Josune slammed his hand down on the button to accept the deal. "Roystan, Snow. Help Nika get the machine out of here." She turned to face the door. "And keep out of my line of fire."

Nika unclipped the brakes on the Dekker and flicked the air switch. A technique once learned, never forgotten. The machine rose to knee height. That wonderful air cushion that never failed. She turned the machine swiftly. "Snow, help me push."

Roystan guided it with one hand, his other hand hovering close to his weapon. "Remember," he said, as if he hadn't just rushed in. "They might not be after us." Nika might have believed he meant it, except his chest was rising and falling far too much for someone who thought the company wasn't after them.

The trader backed away. He might not recognize the sparker in Josune's hand, but he understood the threat. He edged out a door at the back of the room.

"Let's see if we can walk past them," Roystan said.

Walking past Alejandro's friends never worked. Nika looked around for weapons. Nothing. Except the genemod machine itself. There were cables in the box with the flanges. Not much she could do with that, but she took one anyway and left it to rest on the top of the box.

The Dekker was heavy, but maneuverable on its air casters, and they only wanted the calibrator, so it didn't matter what else was damaged. Nika turned the machine so the section housing the calibrator faced her.

Josune placed her hand on the machine, hiding the weapon she held in her hand.

"Snow," Nika said, softly, as she and Snow pushed the machine out. "When I say push, I want you to shove the Dekker as hard as you can."

Snow nodded, his face set.

The company men stopped in front of the machine, preventing them from moving forward.

"Excuse us." Roystan attempted to maneuver the machine past the men.

"Captain Roystan. Our boss wants to talk to you."

"Be ready," Nika said. Soft, so only Snow could hear.

Roystan straightened, tall and commanding, no longer the stressed, worried man he had been a few moments ago. He could have been a company executive himself. "Sorry, we're on a tight schedule. Your boss can call me if he wishes to talk."

The company man on the left had perfect teeth. SaStudio. Alejandro's boss might send his injured to Nika's studio for repairs, but he and his minions didn't come to her for their cosmetic work.

Nika gritted her own teeth. So be it. Leonard Wickmore had better never come to her for a mod of his own.

"He wants to talk to you personally," Perfect Teeth said.

"Sorry, can't do," Roystan said. "Got deliveries. Got a schedule."

Perfect Teeth's smile was more of a snarl. He pulled out a weapon. "You will wait."

"Perhaps we don't see things the same way." Roystan still sounded calm and in control.

Being calm was fine in its way, but these people didn't make idle threats.

Perfect Teeth's companion shoved at the Dekker, pushing it back toward Nika and Snow.

Nika was ready for it.

"Now," she hissed at Snow, and shoved the genemod machine hard toward the company man. The Dekker hit him forcefully enough to knock him down.

It also spun the machine around, catching Snow on the return. Nika dragged him out of the way.

Roystan kicked at the second company man, catching him in the arm that held the weapon.

Lightning crackled overhead. Sparkers.

Two sets of lightning.

"Get down." Snow dragged Nika to the floor.

"Go," Josune yelled. "Get that machine to the ship."

And leave their backs unprotected. Not likely. Between the casters, Nika could see a pair of suited legs. She shook Snow off and shoved the Dekker at the legs.

Josune hauled her up. "Go. Get this thing out of here." She ducked, pushed Nika down again. More lightning crackled overhead. "Roystan. Get them out of here."

"Doing my best. Let's secure this first. Or none of us will make it."

He was so right. None of them would make it. Nika wasn't going to turn her back on a company man, especially not this company. She wanted them down and out.

The side of the machine crackled; the metal parts got hot. She shoved the Dekker forward again.

Perfect Teeth was on the floor, his leg twisted at an ugly angle. Broken. Couldn't have happened to a more deserving person. Nika hoped the machine had caused the injury. The man's weapon was three meters from his twitching fingers, but he was moving toward it.

She could see Josune's feet, moving around the machine.

Roystan edged toward the weapon, then jumped back as a blast of lightning struck centimeters from his feet.

Nika stood, careful to keep the Dekker between herself and the man on the ground. Where was the second one?

A shadow merged with hers. She grabbed the cable from the top of the Dekker and spun around, raising her arms as she did so. The company man wasn't expecting the cable. It connected under his chin. He stepped back, chin jerking up.

Nika ducked away from his flailing hands, but not fast enough. The cable was torn from her grasp, tossed aside. His hands closed around her neck.

She froze.

She heard, rather than saw, Josune vault the machine. Her feet kicked the head of the man holding Nika. All three of them went down. The Dekker went in the other direction, propelled by Josune's leap, leaving them exposed. As Nika hit the floor, the other man finally reached his weapon.

Josune gave a sharp flick of her elbow and the company man was out cold.

"Josune," Nika yelled, and pointed toward Perfect Teeth. She was too late.

He turned it toward them. His finger tightened.

Josune threw herself in front of Nika. Was hit with the bolt of lightning. She crumpled.

"Josune!" A cry from Roystan, and a long, long blast of his own sparker.

Perfect Teeth twitched. Spasmed from the charge. Kept spasming.

The man Josune had downed groaned. Nika turned, only to find Snow there in front of him, holding Josune's sparker with shaking hands.

"Don't move. I have no idea why anyone is stupid enough to bring a sparker on a station or a ship, but I'll use it." His voice was high. Almost childish. Nika didn't blame him, but she was proud of him.

Roystan used the butt of a blaster to knock the company man out.

Nika checked Josune for life signs, then forced her shaking hands to still. "She's alive." It was lucky this hadn't been a sustained blast. Sparkers did a lot of damage. Most of it was simply disabling, but a sustained blast was deadly, for it often stopped the heart. The man who'd shot Josune hadn't stood a chance. He was most likely dead, but she hadn't checked. Didn't want to.

Snow pushed Nika aside. "I can do this."

And she couldn't? It didn't matter. She let Snow take over. He pushed his palms down hard onto Josune's chest. Fast, quick, pushes. Again and again.

"What can I do?" Roystan's finger twitched on his sparker as he watched Snow work. Nika hoped he would stay focused.

"Watch them. Make sure they don't move." She was certain neither of them would, but Roystan needed to be occupied.

They loaded Josune onto the top of the Dekker as soon as she was breathing on her own. The corridors to *The Road* were empty. Nika wasn't surprised. No one wanted to get involved in company business.

10

JOSUNE ARRIOLA

Josune came around in the Dekker. For an apparently seamless big box, there were hard parts that stuck into her. Worse were what felt like thousands of wasps stinging her from the inside out. She wanted to scream. Instead, she took a deep, steadying breath and forced the pain to the back of her mind. Meditation had to be good for something. Think of something else.

Like that the wasps weren't really wasps, just prickles on her skin. Sparker burn.

Above her Nika listed supplies.

Josune opened her eyes to narrow slits. Nika was giving instructions to Roystan.

"Mutrient." Roystan made a face. "Where can we get that?"

"A hospital."

If no one at the Hub would sell them a calibrator, they weren't going to get any medical supplies, either.

"It won't be enough to fix her completely," Nika said. "We don't have the right fluids, and the machine is damaged."

"Don't you dare." Josune sat up and almost toppled out of the machine. "I didn't spend all this time getting that blasted machine for the calibrator, and going through this, for you not to use it. And we had better have left the Hub, because it will be swarming with company soon, if it's not already. Those men were there to delay us, to *stop* us from leaving. Don't you dare go back."

"Josune." Roystan grabbed her hands, then dropped them again. "Sorry. How are you?"

"I'm fine." Although she wasn't. She swallowed the stinging pain and the nausea that hovered when she thought about how she was. She could take the pain.

She hoped.

"Fine for the moment," Nika said repressively. "You need to get under a machine. The only thing this one can do—without supplies—is give us a diagnosis. We have nowhere near enough medical supplies for your injuries. And yes, we have left the station. You've been out for an hour."

Snow moved Roystan aside and helped Josune off the genemod box. "How do you feel? I want to know where you hurt."

Everything hurt.

He guided her to a stretcher ready nearby. "Roystan. Shouldn't you be on the bridge, keeping us safe?"

Roystan looked as if he would argue.

Josune would have liked him with her, but Snow was right. She smiled, as brightly as she could manage. "I'm fine, Roystan. We shouldn't delay any longer. Once Snow has finished I want to make sure we get that calibrator slotted in. If it's not in already."

"It's not." She hadn't seen Carlos hovering. "They wouldn't move you off that thing until you'd stabilized. Can I take the calibrator out now?"

They were in engineering. At least someone had been sensible enough to bring the genemod box here.

"The sooner the better."

"Good." Carlos started pulling parts off the machine and tossing them to the floor. "I'm glad you're all right, Josune." He sounded gruff. "But—"

"Stop. Not like that." Nika grabbed Carlos's arm. "You'll destroy the machine. Show it some respect, even if it is only a Dekker. Here, let me."

"It's damaged. No use to anyone."

"It might not be to you, but you don't understand these things. Let me do it."

Snow turned to shoo Roystan out the door. "You're in the way here. Josune will be fine. She's going back to sleep."

Josune didn't go back to sleep. Instead, she watched Nika and Carlos bicker over the calibrator while Snow checked her over thoroughly, paying special attention to her burns. She hurt more than she admitted. Did anyone go insane from sparker burns? She would use the sparker with more care in future.

Nika pulled the hoses apart with the sure fingers of someone who'd done this many times before. The modder certainly knew her machines. She assured them that although some of the diagnostic tools had been damaged by the sparker, the calibrator was all right. Josune wasn't convinced.

Carlos paced, fingers twitching. "We're in a hurry. Let me do it."

Snow sprayed nerveseal onto Josune's burns. The sudden cessation of pain was bliss.

He wiped his hands. "I can't do more until we get you into a machine. The nerveseal will last around three hours. You'll be fine until then. After that it will hurt again. That prickling sensation you're feeling shouldn't come back, though."

Prickling! That was an understatement.

"Thank you." She didn't want to think about how much the rest of her would hurt later, but he was right. She felt good now. The nerveseal had eased any stiffness she'd had before, as well as the pain.

Josune drifted off. She woke to a buzz on the internal link and Carlos's irritated voice. "We're in a hurry, you know."

"How's Josune?" Roystan asked from the bridge.

"Same as she was ninety seconds ago," Nika said. "Which is the last time you asked."

"I'm fine, Roystan." Although Josune wasn't sure she was. "Just have those jets ready to fire when we need them."

Through the speaker she heard a sigh of relief Roystan probably didn't know he'd made.

Josune turned to where Nika was asking Carlos, "What liquids are you putting through the calibrator?"

"Hydrogen, oxygen, and CarraFuel," Josune said, because Roystan was still online and the easiest way to make him think everything was all right was to behave normally.

What was normal for her? On the *Hassim* she'd be the one in Carlos's position.

Nika touched a finger to her jaw. "CarraFuel." From the way she held her head to one side she was listening. Linking in.

Josune should link them in to the ship screens. Having access to only an aural link must limit what Nika could do.

"Won't go with mutrient," Nika said, eventually. "We'll need to flush the calibrator, and get new hoses."

"Mutrient doesn't go with anything." Snow sounded mournful. Josune glanced at him. He looked mournful, too.

"Mutrient is fine. They build bodies out of that. It's what you put with it."

"I use naolic acid all the time. It's a staple for any modder."

Josune struggled to pull herself together. Nobody had mentioned naolic acid, had they? Had she blanked out and missed part of the conversation?

Carlos came over to the stretcher. Snow glanced at him, then at Josune, and went over to join Nika. Carlos watched him go.

"Josune." He made it quiet. "I'm not trusting our ship to someone who doesn't have engineering experience."

Josune looked over to where Nika was saying, "If Landers didn't teach you how to store mutrient, they've slipped a lot since I was there."

"They said it was a stable compound."

"In the jar. Not when you start mixing it with acids. Are you sure you didn't miss that lecture?"

"I've been lugging jars of mutrient since I was eight years old."

"I bet you never used naolic acid with it, though."

"No-o."

"She looks competent," Josune said.

"She's a modder. Airy-fairy artist type who'll try to give you gills and a tail."

"I heard that." Nika sniffed at the hose she was holding, then wrinkled her nose. She looked over at them. "You've insulted us both. Gills were fashionable ten years ago. Tails fifteen. We"—she put a hand to her heart—"make trends. We don't follow them. And sometimes we just make people look better. And I'd really like to work on your nose, Carlos. I could do it before we put the calibrator into your ship."

Carlos put his fingers up to cover his nose. "Just hurry on pulling that thing apart, so we can put it back together again. Besides, you don't have the materials."

"I can make do. I could do your nose in fifteen minutes. Josune will take hours."

They didn't have fifteen minutes to spare. Josune wanted to jump. She wanted to jump now.

Nika said to Josune, "We need to store the old mutrient and flush the calibrator. What have you got to clean it with?"

"Water?"

Nika shook her head.

"Steam?"

Another shake.

They eventually settled on a slightly acidic compound Nika and Snow mixed up from pure alcohol and a mineral salt. Nika was fussy about the result.

"A pH of 5.6," Nika told Snow. "That will clean out the mutrient. Then we'll wash it with a neutral bath."

"Of what?"

"Water, set to a pH of 7 with the addition of either a harmless acid or base."

"But isn't that—"

"It's to clean it. To be sure there's no mutrient left. Now, I want you to wash those rings." Nika pointed to the ones that clipped the hoses on. "In the same acid, and then water." She looked at Josune and Carlos. "What sort of hoses are you using?"

"Standard geomembrane." The third pipe was coming out of the molder now, the ship end flaring twice as wide as the calibrator end. At least the pipes didn't need to be cured for this. Otherwise they'd be hours.

Nika nodded. "Do you have the calculations to account for the reduced flow?"

"Yes," Carlos said.

"I want to see them."

"We *are* engineers. We know our job."

Josune was starting to develop a healthy respect for modders. Or this one, at least. Nika James knew what she was doing.

"I still want to see them." Nika looked at Snow. "I want you to calculate them, too."

"I'm not sure—"

"Second year. Fluids and flow." Nika thought about it. "They probably had some junior professor teach you. They don't think it's important. Would have said something like 'trust the machine.'"

"They said that a lot."

Nika grunted.

"This time it's trust the engineer," Carlos said. "Can we cut the lesson and get on with the doing?"

"The kid's got to learn."

"He's not a kid, either."

"And I'm going to check his figures." Nika looked over at Carlos. "If I didn't calculate it myself, it hasn't been calculated." Then she turned back to Snow. "Measure the diameter of each outflow and inflow. Get the volume in each of the tanks. The volumes in the Dekker tanks are one cubic meter, 0.8 cubic meters, and 0.6, respectively. They're dented, so you'll have to measure it manually."

The flow was tiny compared to the regular flow of fuel through the jets. Still, it wasn't so much about quantity as quality, but it would need a fine hand on the controls to get the mix right.

The calibrator was in good hands. Provided Carlos didn't murder Nika before she finished setting it up.

"I'm going up to the bridge," Josune told Carlos. "I'll check the controls."

Roystan jumped up as soon as Josune stepped onto the bridge. He took her hands in his, then dropped them. "Sorry, that probably hurt. How are you?"

She would have preferred him to keep holding her hands. "Fine. I can't feel a thing." She wished Jacques hadn't said that about him showing off to her, because now she was thinking . . . no. She wasn't thinking.

He smiled. "I'm glad." Then he scratched his head. "Not glad that you can't feel anything. Just glad you're all right."

That, she wasn't sure about.

Jacques, in the co-pilot's chair, said, "You look terrible. But I'm glad you're all right, too."

"Thank you." The burns were coming out in a red branching pattern over her arms. And probably the rest of her body if she looked, including her face. Josune tried to smile. Her skin was tight.

Jacques looked odd sitting in front of the calibration controls. Normally, Guardian sat in that seat, with Qiang as Guardian's backup.

"Any sign of company?"

Roystan gestured at the screen, which had been split into six different displays, each one displaying the status and position of an amber dot. "The ships we can't identify. I'd guess at least one is a company ship coming our way." He pointed to the screen top left. "Probably that one."

Josune watched the figures change underneath it. "They're taking their time."

They wouldn't have traveled that slowly for the *Hassim*.

"They don't think we're a threat. Easy game. And running without a calibrator. Either that or they want to get some distance away from the Hub. We are in the legal zone, after all."

Whoever it was, it wasn't Burnley Company; the Hub belonged to Burnley and they would have simply marched in and arrested them. There wouldn't have been any messing around denying goods or fighting in the corridors. Nor was it a company that Burnley was on good terms with, for they would have handed them over. There were two of those. Nor Brown, who would have attacked at the *Hassim*.

That left twenty-three of the Big Twenty-Seven companies. Who else could invoke that sort of blanket refusal from traders?

"They'll be here in four hours," Roystan said. "Can we be gone by then?"

"Yes." Definitely, from what she'd seen. "Nika certainly knows what she's doing."

Roystan didn't look surprised. "She's a good modder."

She was halfway to being a good engineer as well, if the way she worked on the calibrator was anything to go by. "Have you seen any of her work? Or is it all theory?"

"I haven't seen a finished mod, no. But she knows what she is talking about. I'd trust her to do the job."

Josune nodded.

"But can't Carlos rebuild the calibrator? I didn't mean them to do all the work."

"Tell that to Nika James. She's a control freak."

Roystan grinned. "I could imagine that. But we should at least feed them."

Jacques said, "I can't feed them while I'm stuck here helping you."

Roystan pulled himself to his feet. "Well then, Jacques, let's go and do something about that. I'd like to check in with Carlos, too. It should be good here for the moment. Watch those ships for me, Josune. I won't be long." He hesitated. "Can you? Will you be all right?"

"I'm fine." Provided the nerveseal kept the pain away.

Josune sank into Roystan's vacated seat with a sigh. She couldn't feel anything, and they were short crewed. She hoped Nika and Snow would help while they were on board.

She focused on the ships. They should get the calibrator in soon, provided Carlos didn't upset Nika too much and she stripped it back again to do a nose job on him. Josune rubbed her own nose reflexively. Maybe it was lucky for all of them they hadn't received supplies with the machine.

One of the ships she was watching nullspaced. It reappeared a few moments later four light-seconds closer. At least she assumed it was the same ship. It was the same type of ship, with the same heat signature, and no identification.

Josune opened the ship link. "Roystan. We need you back on bridge. The company ship will arrive earlier than we thought." She switched to engineering. "Carlos, how are we going? We need that calibrator in yesterday." *Yesterday* wasn't a word she'd used six weeks ago, not to mean *quickly*. It was something she'd picked up on this ship.

"Not too bad, actually," Carlos said. "Ten, fifteen minutes."

It would be enough. The company ship would get close, but not close enough to board.

There was a clatter of feet on metal. Roystan dropped into the pilot seat as Josune stood up. "What's happening?"

Josune tapped the screen to show the ship that had jumped. "It just nullspaced. It's here now and will reach us in another hour. I'll go help Carlos. The calibrator should be ready, but you'd better be prepared for things to go wrong. It will work, in theory, but no guarantees."

"I'm prepared. Just give me something I can use." Roystan called Jacques. "Leave what you're doing and get back up on the bridge."

Josune left at a run. She stopped at the plasma cannon she'd installed earlier and set it to power up, then continued on to engineering. "How's the calibrator?"

Nika and Carlos ignored her. Both were absorbed in tightening the inlets to the tanks. Snow stood to one side, looking as if he didn't know what to do next.

"How's it going?" Josune asked him.

He shrugged. "They sound like they know what they're talking about."

Carlos turned on the flow. Gently at first.

Josune called Roystan. "Looks like it's all together down here. You might experience some fluctuations soon."

"Happening right now." It sounded as if Roystan's teeth were gritted. "Glad we're not nullspacing this very minute. The gauge is all over the place."

Nika looked around. "Where's the controller?"

"On the bridge," Josune said. "I'm going up now." She didn't ask Carlos if he was all right down here. He'd have to be.

"Come on, Snow," Nika said, and followed Josune at a run.

Roystan was sweating when they arrived.

"The company ship nullspaced again." He was trying to help Jacques keep the calibrator steady and watch the screen while he set the jets up for a controlled burn. "They'll be here in twenty minutes."

Roystan's burn set the calibrator swinging wildly. Jacques over-compensated. The company ship would think they were crazy, gyrating in space like this, wasting fuel.

The run had depleted the last of Josune's energy. All she could do was watch. "They'll be certain we're without a calibrator, at any rate." Which was good, provided they could control the calibrator now that it was working.

"Let me," Nika said.

"I might not be good at this," Jacques said, "but I have to be better than a modder."

"From where I'm standing, even Snow would be better. And he hasn't had much calibrator experience."

The ship lurched again. "Let her try," Josune said. "Modders know their calibrators." She hoped Jacques didn't see Snow's pursed lips or the slight shake of his head. Nika knew what she was doing—Josune would bet on it—and Roystan was one lucky bastard to have picked up the only modder in the galaxy who knew her way around the machines.

The company ship gave a long burst of its own rockets, heading straight toward *The Road*.

"Give her the chair," Roystan told Jacques. "Because how much experience have you had on a calibrator anyway?"

"I don't like trusting my life to a stranger." But Jacques moved out of the seat.

Nika slipped in under him.

Roystan turned to Nika. "A calibrator on ship feeds the fuel to the jets. They fire a controlled amount of fuel for a controlled amount of time. If the burn's off, even a thousandth of a degree, when we jump through nullspace we'll be light-years away from where we want to be."

"No pressure, of course," Josune said.

"No pressure," Nika agreed. She didn't look the least bit stressed, and her hands moved surely over the board.

"It's like a genemod machine," she told Snow. "Getting the feed exact is important. Otherwise a perfect modding job turns into something less than perfect."

"Nowadays," Snow said, "a calibrator calculates to the exact cubic milliliter. You let it do what it needs to do."

"Snow, that's the difference between a *modder*, and a modder." She made the first sound reverent, the second blasé, and accompanied it with a shrug.

Over Snow's muttered "It's just buckets of plasma," Roystan said, "You know, I wouldn't mind less talk about the technique and more doing. I'm about to fire the jets."

"Gently first," Nika said. "I need to get the feel of it."

Roystan fired.

Nika trimmed the feeds, eased the flows.

The ship stabilized.

"Fifteen minutes," Roystan said.

Josune moved up beside Roystan. "You okay?"

"I am now." His fingers moved over the pilot console in an uncanny imitation of Nika's at the calibrator.

Josune put a hand on his shoulder. "You chose well, Roystan."

Roystan glanced up at her.

She smiled at him.

"Josune." Carlos's tense voice came through the communicator. "I need you. Now, as in yesterday."

"Coming." Josune left at a run but slowed as soon as she was off the bridge. If she ran she'd fall flat on her face. The nerveseal might be hiding the pain, but her body was telling her it had taken on damage. She stopped on the way to flick the safeties off on the cannon.

Carlos was holding the calibrator in place, muscles straining, sweat pouring off his face. "Bastard thing started to move. Too much juice going through this end. It's too light. Grab me some straps, will you?"

A regular ship calibrator was built in.

Josune clipped supporting bands to the wall, then around the calibrator.

"Thanks," Carlos said, when it was stable.

Snow arrived in the doorway. "I can't do anything on the bridge, but I can handle weapons. I saw a plasma cannon as we went up. Do you want me to man it?"

Josune could have hugged him. "Snow, you are a lifesaver. It's all yours."

Carlos looked doubtful. "Let's hope he really does know how to use it."

Josune ignored him and led Snow down to the cannon.

"Will you be all right here?"

"I'm good." Snow looked grim but determined. "I thought I was past all this. That's all."

"I'll send you the coordinates."

Carlos's voice crackled through the speakers. "Josune, you'd best get back to the bridge. They're totally out of control up there."

It had been under control when she'd left.

"It's in better hands than mine, Carlos."

"So why are we still headed straight for the company ship?"

"I'll check." All she wanted to do was drop, but she made her way back to the bridge, more slowly than she wanted to. "What's wrong?"

Roystan's grin was wide and glorious. "Nothing's wrong. It's as smooth as a regular run."

Josune checked the coordinates. Carlos was right. He was still heading toward the other ship. "For goodness' sake, Roystan. Use the reverse rockets."

"This way they don't suspect anything," Roystan said, and he and Nika grinned at each other. "They think we're helpless. They're probably kitting up for a landing party."

"But you can't—"

"We were waiting for you. But now you're back, let's do it. Ready?"

"Plasma pulse from company ship." Snow's voice.

Roystan seemed to crackle. "Right. Don't fire back. Don't let them know we have a weapon. We might need it later—"

"But—"

Jacques started praying aloud.

"Ready," Nika said.

Josune watched, one eye on the flow of plasma coming toward them, the other on the calibrator. Nika kept the balance exact.

The plasma was almost on them when Roystan touched the console delicately. "Jumping now."

They jerked into the momentary disorientation of nullspace, then came out the other side.

Roystan flicked stats with one hand as he used his other arm to put a gentle hand on Jacques's shoulder. "We're through, Jacques. Safe, secure, and"—he looked at the charts—"right where we planned to be. On the way to our next delivery." He smiled over his shoulder at Nika. "Well done. That was impressive." He looked at the link screens. "How are you, Snow?"

"As well as anyone can be watching plasma come at me without doing anything."

Josune hid a smile, and saw Roystan's mouth turn down in a similar quirk. She hadn't met many modders before. Maybe she should have. But now the adrenaline was gone, she was starting to get a headache. "I'll go see how Carlos is doing." Before she dropped. She couldn't keep going for long.

11

NIKA RIK TERRI

Done, and they wouldn't need the calibrator until they fired the jets again. Which, according to Roystan, was after they left the space station on the edge of the asteroid belt they were heading toward. Nika stretched and took time out to look around.

She'd been on ship bridges before. Not many, admittedly, but when a renowned modder was aboard, it was almost obligatory for a captain to invite his—or her—esteemed guest onto the bridge.

This one was small, cramped, and shabby.

Roystan, sitting back now, one eye on his instruments, saw her looking. He patted the console with affection.

"She's a beautiful ship. Runs like an angel." Then he made a face as he guessed what she was thinking. "Seriously, she does. Even with a faulty calibrator."

Nika wasn't sure what an angel was but didn't ask. Why did no one ever decorate the bridge when so much time was spent on them? She would have added color and warmth to the walls, made it more welcoming.

Snow arrived back on the bridge. Jacques went down to his galley, calling on Carlos to check the cargo, leaving Nika, Snow, and Roystan alone.

Roystan checked the screens, then smiled at Nika. "I haven't thanked you properly. None of us could have done it."

"Tell that to Snow here, who thinks that calibrations are a technical job."

"They are," Snow said. "The design's the thing."

Roystan laughed. "There's a lot to be said for technique, Snow." He stood up. "But we've been remiss. Working you so hard as soon as you came on ship. You haven't tried Jacques's cooking yet. Or been properly introduced." He locked the screens. "Come on, you're in for a treat. I hope you're hungry."

Nika nudged the calibrator straight and turned both inputs down. She'd have to clean the left jet. But they were on course and wouldn't need the jets for a while, so she silently followed Roystan.

She was more tired than hungry. It had been a long day and now that she had stopped all she wanted to do was sleep. From the whiteness around Snow's mouth and eyes, he probably wanted to do the same. Would it be rude if she asked where their cabin was?

The appetizing smell of hot coffee and freshly baked bread wafted across to them as they entered the crew room. Snow brightened. So did she. She was hungrier than she realized.

The crew room was circular, with three doorways, and a central round table. An unusual design. Something to consider for Nika's next studio, something she could use if she needed a fast exit. Screens lined the walls.

Jacques dumped a plate piled with steaming buns into the middle of the table and poured coffee for them. "Eat while it's hot." He patted Nika on the shoulder, awkwardly. "Not a bad job, for a modder."

Nika snorted and took a bun. It was chewy, hot, and melt-in-your-mouth delicious. She nodded appreciatively. "For a calibrator controller, you're a far superior cook."

From the looks of him, Jacques was almost certainly too fond of his own food. She didn't blame him if this was the standard he produced, but her first job for him would be a basic rejuvenation to get rid of most of the fat, and to fix any problems his unhealthy lifestyle had introduced.

His nose, at least, was a snub. The only one on the ship so far whose nose didn't need work. Excepting Josune, but she'd had work done.

Carlos entered through one of the other doors. "Cargo's fine. The fastenings in the large cargo hold moved but didn't break."

Nika took time to study him, as well. His body was covered with arcane symbols, inked, not part of a mod. Religion, or visual effect? She couldn't tell. The image was marred by a thick pink line down his left arm. He'd spent time in a Dietel.

Carlos's shoulders were narrow, his neck long. At a guess, he'd once been a she. If Nika had done the mod, she'd have given him broader shoulders and a more prominent Adam's apple, to take away the slight delicacy. He didn't look female, but the tells were there.

Josune followed Carlos. She looked ready to drop. The nerveseal was wearing off.

"Let me check you before you sit down." Nika stood. "Outside." Most people didn't want an audience.

"Here will do." Her voice was hoarse. "I need food."

Nika checked her over quickly. Snow had done a good job. She was pleased.

"Nicely done, Snow. You could get a job as a doctor any time."

"I didn't study six years to become a doctor."

She thought it might be a sore point with him. "It's useful to know how to fix a body." She got a mug of warm water and gave it to Josune.

"I'd prefer coffee."

Roystan got up to get her one.

"No problem," Nika said, soothingly. "As soon as you finish your water. We need to keep your fluids up." She watched Josune drink. She couldn't do anything about the burns except ensure they didn't turn septic before they got her to a genemod machine, and keep up the fluids in the interim.

More worrying was the slight tic in her right eye.

When Leonard Wickmore had used the sparker at Nika's shop, he'd fried all the electronics that hadn't been protected. That little piece of electronics in Josune's eye connected directly to her brain.

"Who did your last mod work?"

Snow sighed.

Roystan laughed. "Nika takes a serious interest in her work. She can probably tell you where you had it done."

"I can tell you what type of machine was used. I can't necessarily say who did it. Not unless you went to one of the big names."

"Nika Rik Terri?" Snow asked.

Nika couldn't stop her wince.

Josune looked at her.

Nika covered it. "Josune didn't go to one of the masters. I'd recognize their work."

"I went to Mattise on New Earth."

Nika might check them out. They'd done a competent job. "I'm more concerned about the bioware. Did they do that as well?"

Josune shook her head.

"You had that before?"

Josune hesitated. Roystan moved restlessly but didn't intervene. "Yes."

"The shop you went to. Either they'd had no experience with bioware or they can't integrate other people's designs into their own." Nika studied Josune's face. "It's a nice job, but—" Right now that was working in Josune's favor, for had it been fully integrated, the sparker jolt would have fried the electricals, possibly destroyed the eye.

The eye looked to be fine.

"It is hard to integrate bioware," Snow said. "That's why they have shops specializing in tech. They never do a good modding, but they don't have to. That's not their specialty."

"A good modder should be a generalist as well as a specialist, Snow. There's no excuse for shoddy workmanship."

"They're two different fields."

Roystan's handheld pinged. He picked it up. "When you open your new shop, Nika, I'm coming to you for all my work." He flicked the channel open.

"Does the bioware still work?" Nika asked Josune.

"I haven't tried it."

Jacques and Carlos looked puzzled. Roystan—on the communicator—looked as if he wanted to shut her up. That meant they hadn't known about the implant. What a waste of cutting-edge electronic equipment.

"Do you want to continue this conversation outside?"

Josune looked around the table. Shrugged. Shook her head.

"I need to see that it's not damaged. Turn it on." Nika would have preferred to wait until they were close to a genemod machine, or forbid Josune to use it, but who could stop someone from blinking, even by accident. Especially as her eye was already noticeably twitching. "It might have shorted. Can you still see out of that eye?" She wasn't going to mention the potential for the sparker to short out brain synapses. There was no way Nika could pick that up without equipment.

Roystan clicked off. "Can you see, Josune?"

"I think so. But my vision has been different ever since it was put in." Josune blinked five times. The color under her eyelid changed as light and images passed through.

"Can you access anything?"

"I don't . . . I haven't tried." Josune looked at Roystan. "I've never tried to use it here."

Jacques crossed his arms. "You've had that spy thing in your eye all this time and you didn't tell us."

"Nonsense, Jacques," Roystan said. "I knew about it. Josune, you've linked to my handheld before. Try that."

Carlos crossed his arms, too. "No one would have that technology and not use it."

They'd moved together, in an unconscious solidarity.

"I want to know how she got it, and why," Jacques said. "She said she came from a rim ship."

"With company-quality electronics like that?" Carlos looked around at them.

Roystan said calmly, "I know where Josune's from. I know where she got the credits for the technology. I know why she has it. She's welcome aboard my ship."

"She lied to us. You lied to us."

"Roystan did not lie to you," Josune said. "I told him after I arrived on board. You know him better than that, so don't even think of it."

Carlos and Jacques looked at each other.

Nika ignored them. "Can you contact Roystan's handheld?"

The light under Josune's eyelid brightened momentarily.

Roystan's communicator beeped. He glanced at it, then nodded at Josune. He glanced at Carlos and Jacques but didn't say anything.

"Answer it." Nika held her breath until Josune answered Roystan, with no visible effects. "Headache?"

"A little. I've got face ache, and I'm starting to hurt, but that's not the bioware."

No, it wasn't, but something about the way the lid drooped had changed. Nika didn't trust the change. "Don't use it until we can get you into a genemod machine. You're lucky few people can integrate bioware properly. Otherwise your brain would be fried right now. And you wouldn't have an eye."

Snow said apologetically to Josune, "Nika doesn't have a good bedside manner." Like Nika, pretending there wasn't any tension in the room.

Nika turned to Roystan. "Do you have any more nerveseal?"

Back in her studio she had a four-liter container of it, and she'd only ever used it for Alejandro's scummy friends. In that same studio, she had two beautiful Songyans. Josune would have been in and out of one by now.

Tamati would still be in the other, almost halfway through a total body remodel. Nika rubbed her arms, cold suddenly.

"A little."

"Josune will drop shortly. Once she starts to feel the burns."

Roystan nodded and stood up. "And that's soon, from what you're saying. Come on, Josune. I'll escort you to your cabin."

"I'm fine."

"She's not fine," Snow said. "She's in shock."

And he said Nika had a bad bedside manner.

"Captain's orders," Roystan told Josune, and indicated the door.

He stopped on the way out. "Almost forgot. That call, Jacques. That was Bellatrix Station. We have to take the secondary landing bay. The main one's in use."

Jacques scowled after him. "Now he tells us. We'll have to use the small crane, and the small carts. Everything's set up for the big one. The loads have to be rearranged."

He stomped out.

"He should have told us about Josune," Carlos said. "We don't need any more lies on this ship, not right now."

"Don't you trust Josune?"

"I do, but that's company-level bioware, and we've a company after us."

"Would Roystan let Josune stay on the ship if he thought the two were related?" Nika didn't think he would, but she could see he cared for her. Would he be thinking clearly?

"I suppose not." Carlos stared broodingly at the table. He sighed, and straightened. "We're lucky we have a calibrator. Even if it isn't a proper one. We have to curve around the station. You can bet our flight path isn't set for that."

Snow collected Roystan's and Josune's empty plates. "You don't need a calibrator for that. You need an experienced pilot."

"A calibrator's still going to make it easier."

Nika yawned. "So if a good pilot can do it, why do you need a calibrator at all, then?" She wanted a bed.

"Nullspace." Carlos drew a circle on the table with his finger. "Start here." He placed his finger in the center of the circle. "Go a little way, like around a space station." He moved his finger but didn't lift it off the table. "Nothing. You can correct with the jets, and like Snow said, a good pilot can do that. Nullspace now." He moved his finger to the edge of the circle. "Out by a fraction of a degree." He moved another finger thirty degrees around the perimeter. "When you get where you're going, you find you are a long way away from where you want to be."

That was the last Nika heard. She fell asleep.

12

JOSUNE ARRIOLA

The nerveseal was wearing off, the pain starting to seep into Josune's bones, scratching at her nerves so that she wanted to scream.

"How bad is it?"

She jumped. Roystan's question in his deep voice buzzed through her body. She'd forgotten he was there.

Roystan reached out to steady her. "Careful."

"I'm fine." Her voice was scratchy. Had the inside of her throat been burned as well? Neither of the modders had mentioned it. "Thank you for using the calibrator to save us all, rather than just to save me."

"Can't say I liked it. Especially since you saved us beforehand. And you saved the calibrator." He stopped at Josune's door and waited for her to enter. Followed her in.

Josune sat on the bed, glad to do so. She rested her head on her knees.

Roystan knelt at her feet. "Let me get your boots."

Josune lay back. She was too sore to argue, even though she planned to only rest a short while. "How long before we reach Bellatrix Station?" Bellatrix was next on their delivery route.

"Six hours." Roystan hesitated over the boot he'd pulled off.

"You don't know if it's six hours?" But then, six hours was what it would take to get to the world if the jump had been optimal. Most jumps weren't. Not unless they had high-level, fine-tuned, computer-controlled jets and a processor that could react in a fraction of a millisecond. Which the company ship must have had, for it had taken only two jumps to reach *The Road*.

He shook his head. "It's definitely six hours. Spot on. As accurate as I could have done with brand-new equipment. She's good, this modder of ours."

More than good, given Nika's handling of the calibrator.

"So what's the problem, then?"

"We need to get you to a doctor. We can get to Atalante in two days if we skip the deliveries and go direct."

Josune sat up fast. The pain made her dizzy. "After all that fuss about delivering our goods, don't use me as an excuse not to do so."

Roystan steadied her. "Maybe you should lie down again."

"Don't give me that, either." The effort to stay upright was exhausting, but she wasn't going to lie back and accept it. "Don't make me something special because you feel guilty."

"I'm not."

"When I came around you were talking with Nika about getting medicine for me, when you should have let Carlos get at the calibrator. You'll get your crew killed."

"I'll get my crew killed either way. Josune, please. Two minutes to listen."

She kept her mouth shut, but only because she couldn't talk through the pain that assaulted her after the sudden movement. She was almost grateful for Roystan's hands, gentle against her burns. That centered her and dulled the other pains.

"Thank you." Roystan sounded as if he'd run a marathon. "I've been thinking. If we deliver that load we're walking into a trap."

She looked up at him. He was serious.

"The company knows who we are. They know our route. They know where we're going." He scrubbed at his eyes, tiredly. "Us finding the *Hassim* won't be a secret forever. Everywhere we go, people will be waiting for us. Just in case we did find something. Not just that company."

They *had* found something, and anyone who attacked them would get that something. Josune wasn't going to let just anyone get the *Hassim* data. She'd destroy it first.

The *Hassim* had built its reputation as a fighting ship. Deepak and Reba had both been trained in warfare. They'd trained the others. The ship itself had been heavily armed. People thought twice before attacking it. Not like *The Road*, which had a nonfighting crew, one cannon, and three havoc bombs.

"We need more weapons," Josune said.

Roystan laughed. "It's not always the solution, Josune." His face showed naked exhaustion. "We can't keep running. I'll sublease the run. It's too dangerous to continue."

"To whom? You'll never get your run back."

"Captain Kahurangi will be good for it. We go way back. And she will be happy to have the work. She runs close to the breadline sometimes. Once we drop off our modders, we'll get new identities. Start again. A long way from here."

Josune leaned into the warmth of his chest. It was unexpectedly comfortable. "We'll work something out. You'll keep your run." Since he wanted it so much. "You'll keep your ship. You'll keep your crew."

She could feel his smile, rather than see it. "Aren't I supposed to be encouraging you, not the other way around?"

"Even captains need support." If Feyodor had got it, it hadn't been from Josune. "You know, until I came on board I never realized just how autocratic the *Hassim* was."

Roystan chuckled, deep in his chest. "Taki Feyodor was a born dictator."

She wanted to ask how well he'd known the other captain but didn't want to spoil the moment. There was time enough for that later.

Provided they survived.

Roystan sighed, and gently eased her back down onto the bed.

"Get some rest, Josune, since both our modders are convinced that's what you need."

The pain he'd been holding away by his touch came back in waves. "Airy-fairy artist types, Carlos would say." Josune tried not to sound breathless. "What would they know?"

"For modders they make damn fine doctors."

"I won't tell them you said that. I believe it's an insult."

Snow was a surprise. He'd known how to use the cannon. He'd been in battles before. He'd dealt with battle-injured people. Josune might talk to him later, see if he had any strategies for staying alive.

Roystan knelt at her feet again. "Let me get your other boot."

"I wonder what Nika is running from."

Roystan grunted, which told her he knew, but he wasn't telling.

There was also the way Nika had been so uncomfortable when Snow had mentioned the modder Nika Rik Terri, whom even Josune had heard of. What had that been about? If she hadn't been so sure Snow would know Rik Terri, she would have considered they might be one and the same, especially with the same first name.

Roystan sat back on his heels, a boot in each hand. "I never noticed before how expensive your clothes were." He waved a boot. Soft, exquisite, sap-green. "We must be poor rustic cousins compared to what you're used to."

"Hardly." It was good to close her eyes. "Most of the time we were in the middle of nowhere, chasing up whatever crazy lead we had. There was us, the ship, and nothing else. Except when someone decided to attack us." She tried to smile at the memory and found she couldn't. "We spent a lot of time linked in, planning what we'd buy when we got back." Some of it had been equipment, but there'd been clothes, and shoes, and mods—including bioware.

Beside the bed, Roystan was silent. She opened her eyes.

He was watching her, boots neatly on the floor beside him.

"Why do you do it, Josune? The *Hassim* had everything Goberling wanted. How many worlds did you find? Six? Eight?"

"Fourteen."

"Fourteen! All Goberling ever wanted was to find one. And you're chasing after a dream that . . . I don't know." He rubbed his face. She heard the scratch of his stubble. They'd all been up a long time. "You, Feyodor. You had everything you could possibly need."

"But we had a dream," Josune said. "It's out there, Roystan. Somewhere. I will find it." Except it didn't seem so important, here on Roystan's comfortable ship. What sort of dream was it when it could be so easily forsaken?

Roystan groaned. "What sort of dream is that to waste your life on?"

She changed the subject. "Later, when all this settles down, I want to go over the last days of what happened on the *Hassim*. I want to know more about the people who destroyed my friends." No one killed her friends and lived to get away with it.

He expelled a long sigh. "That's fair. I'll give you access here, in your cabin." A smile twisted up the corner of his mouth. "It's one way to keep you in bed, I suppose."

Josune crossed her arms, then uncrossed them again, because it hurt. "I'm injured. Not an invalid."

"You still need a genemod machine." He hesitated, curious now. "How did you manage on the *Hassim*? When you got injured, I mean."

"We had a safe port. In the Between, halfway out to the rim."

The legal zone was—supposedly—policed. The rim was uncharted space. Few people—except a foolhardy few like Feyodor and her crew—ventured out past the rim where there was no safety net if anything went wrong. The space between the legal zone and the rim, informally known as the Between, was the most dangerous. "One of the Big Twenty-Seven had a mining venture out there. It wasn't making any profit, so they abandoned it."

There was more to it than that, she knew, but Declan, the leader of the settlement, had never told her the story.

"Just up and pulled out, leaving everyone there. The survivors banded together, started a protection business. You pay their premiums." Hefty premiums. "They guarantee your safety." The annual fee the *Hassim* had paid would have fed the whole community. "They have a private army. A hospital. Even a flourishing artists' colony."

"Artists' colony?"

"They turn out some amazing stuff." She'd kept aside some of the red mineral she'd picked up on Sassia for one of the artists. That had gone to Brown now, along with everything else on the *Hassim*.

"This agreement you had with them? Was it an annual fee, or pay-as-you-go?"

How would a cargo runner from the legal zone know how these agreements worked? "Annual."

"So if the *Hassim* turned up there and asked for sanctuary, and maybe repairs, they'd get it, at no cost?"

"*The Road* isn't the *Hassim*," Josune said.

"What if someone from the *Hassim* turned up. Without their ship."

She couldn't read his face. "What are you getting at, Roystan?" Was he dumping her?

Roystan tapped some codes into his communicator as he stood up. "I've given you access to the *Hassim* feed. If you can't sleep, stay here and look at it."

"Read-only, I hope. Have you stored a copy of this off-site?"

He tapped something else into the communicator and confirmed, "Read-only."

"Roystan!" He was too trusting.

"And yes, I have an off-site copy." A line creased his forehead as he looked down at her injuries. "Once I've sublet the run and gotten you some emergency repairs, we'll see if your safe site will give you sanctuary as part of the *Hassim* contract."

What if she didn't want to go? Would he kick her off his ship? "And then?"

"That depends on you, doesn't it?" He tapped his handheld. "Everything here is rightfully yours."

Far too trusting. "Did you even check to be sure I was who I said I was?"

"Credit me with some brains." He brought up an image. A teenage girl, surrounded by electronic equipment and spare parts, staring at the camera, as if whoever was taking the image was wasting her time.

Back then Josune's head had been shaved. Impatient teenager that she had been, she'd hated wasting time doing her hair.

"Josune Arriola, aged thirteen. The day she won the Inter-Worlds engineering championship."

"She looks nothing like me."

"She has the same direct way of looking straight at you." Roystan looked down at the image and smiled. "I think she's rather cute."

Josune threw her pillow at him.

He escaped out the door.

It was a good thing, she thought, as she settled down to scroll through the data Roystan had left her—on the screen in her room, not through her eye, for she was mindful of Nika's warning—that the mascot she'd carried with her everywhere as a youngster was out of that particular picture. A battered old spaceship. She'd had it since she was five years old. The *Determination*. The ship Goberling had owned when he'd found his lode of transurides.

13

NIKA RIK TERRI

Nika had a vague recollection of Roystan talking to her, trying to wake her up. She stayed asleep. She was safe here on this ship in the middle of space where neither Tamati or Alejandro could get to her.

She woke, stiff and sore, at the table where she'd fallen asleep.

Snow sat watching her, his back to the wall, eyes half closed, head drooping. He looked lost in his too-old body. Defenseless and defeated. Carlos sat next to him, half napping as well.

Roystan sat at the table, talking to Jacques through the ship link. "All of it," he told him. "Everything that's there."

Jacques stood in front of a crane. Nika vaguely remembered seeing the crane as they ran through the cargo area coming on board.

"You're giving away our only source of income."

"We're cattle bait if we stay on our route. Or dead."

He was right. You didn't outwit a company by going where they expected you to go. Which was why Nika was on this ship and not on a passenger liner.

"We've no money," Jacques said. "And no way of getting any more if we don't have work."

"We'll get some, somehow. Load it all, Jacques. That's an order."

Roystan sighed as he clicked off the communicator. "I'll miss this route. I was happy here."

"How long have you been doing it?" Nika asked.

"Forty—" He stopped, made his voice lighter. "I knew everyone's children. Their grandchildren."

If Nika had to guess, she'd have put his age at around thirty. A good modder could take years off someone's age, but there came a time when, no matter how good the machine was or how good the modder was, age showed. You were only as good as your raw materials, and once the cells started to break down you couldn't stop the thinning of the hair, the buildup of fat on the stomach and loss of fat under the skin. Or more obviously, the loss of color in the iris, and slight changes in balance. Roystan hadn't reached that stage yet.

If he'd grown up on the ship, that forty might literally be forty years. Along with some mod work to make himself look younger. "Who did your mod?" It was as skillfully done as Snow's.

Carlos opened one eye. "We always go to Lesser Sirius."

Roystan hadn't come to Nika, and he certainly hadn't gone to SaStudio, for he wouldn't have walked out with crooked teeth.

"Tilda. The woman who owned the shop before you did."

"It was *my* shop," Snow said.

Nika would have to train him not to call it a *shop*. That was halfway down the ladder to being a doctor, something Snow didn't want to be.

Roystan bowed his head in apology. "Sorry. Your shop."

Train them both.

He looked at Nika. "You worked for him?"

"What do you think?"

Roystan shook his head.

Snow took a deep breath. "You've been disqualified from practicing, haven't you? Deregistered. You've lost your accreditation." He blurted it out, as if he couldn't hold the words back any longer. "You wouldn't use your ID when we bought the Dekker. You know you would have been refused. I should have guessed when you were all black and white. Color is big in modding, and you haven't any."

She would have laughed if she didn't think that would make it worse. No one banned Nika Rik Terri. "Color is last season, Snow. As modders we make trends, not follow them. And no. I haven't been disqualified. I didn't use my name because I don't want anyone to find me." She couldn't tell him she was Nika Rik Terri, but if she was honest about running, he might understand she had secrets and forgive her for that deception. Maybe.

"Another one on the run," Carlos said. "You'll fit right in here." Did he mean himself?

"Everyone has secrets," Roystan said.

But Snow, now started, couldn't seem to stop. "You didn't go to Landers, either."

"I went to Landers." Long enough ago now that it wasn't important anymore. Not the way it was to a kid fresh out of college.

"Marramar has been dean forever. You would have known that."

"Maybe it was more than seven years ago."

"How long?"

Fifteen. "Marramar was teaching the epidermis. Nassaf was dean." *He'd* been there forever. "Farinor was teaching biological sex." He—or she, for he/she changed on a whim—had the worst ideas for modding Nika had ever come across.

"I heard about Farinor." At least she'd momentarily diverted him. "They said you couldn't tell what sex he or she would come in on the day."

"But he didn't change much else," Nika said. "You could always recognize him as Farinor. Different-colored hair, but same nose, same lips, same hands."

Same feet, too, for she'd worked the machine for him in class on occasion. No way would she have ever let a student mod her body.

She thought about the other lecturers. "There was Chatty, of course." Igor Chatsworth, genetics expert. He'd taken Nika on as his own special student.

Snow brightened. "Professor Chatsworth was retired, but he came in and gave us a guest lecture every year. You must have been at Landers when Nika Rik Terri was there."

Now was the time to tell him who she was. But a secret wasn't a secret when you told the world.

"I was."

"What was she like?"

Nika thought about her younger self. A know-it-all, sure she had all the answers. Already knowing she'd own her own studio. Already with big plans, and enough talent that her professors let her get away with it.

"Arrogant. Obsessed." Lonely.

"Sounds like all modders I know," Carlos muttered.

Roystan's lips twitched.

"But you must have thought she was good. You named yourself after her."

Now he was assuming too much. "Never change yourself to imitate someone else, Snow. That's a bad way to begin. Nika was a common name back then. One year at Landers there were four of us with the name."

Roystan stood up. "It's time I showed you two where your cabins are. Given that we set you to work as soon as you stepped on ship."

The bedrooms were on the top level.

The lift opened onto a landing, with passageways leading off in four directions, making a cross. Heavy breach doors stood open at the start of every passage.

Someone—a long time ago—had painted the walls a deep crimson. They were faded now, scuffed, and marked after long years of use. Still, it warmed Nika to see some personality in the otherwise featureless ship. The walls she'd seen to date had been a practical, drab olive—also faded.

The passages all looked the same. "How do you tell which passage is yours?"

Roystan grinned. "They're not marked, if that's what you're asking."

It was.

He pointed to the leftmost passage. "I'm down there." To the one past it. "Jacques and Carlos are down there." To the passage the other side of Roystan's. "Josune is here, to the right of the stairs. She's a quiet neighbor. I'll put you alongside her."

"Thank you," Nika said.

Roystan indicated the small terminal beside the lift. "There's a public node here." He stopped beside it. "While we're here, I'll link you in to the ship. That will allow you to use the screens. As well as the screens, it will give you access to general systems and allow you to contact us anywhere on ship."

"Thank you." It had been tiresome earlier, checking facts aurally. There was only so much information you could hear before you forgot it.

Roystan keyed an override into the node. "Link in."

Nika touched a finger to the node in her jaw and heard the familiar *pling* that signified she was in. "Iris, voice, palm recognition, and code," Roystan said.

Her own node would provide the iris, voice, and palm details.

Snow had a jaw node, too. Given his worry about credits, or lack of, Nika half expected him to have his in his tooth. Although tooth links were cheap and could turn off or on when you ate the wrong food. So far, Snow had demonstrated a good sense of when to cut costs and when not.

"Confirmed, both of you." Roystan led the way down the passage to the first room. "The door only recognizes a code. It's currently four zeroes. Key in the number to open the door. Do you want to reset the code?"

Nika had nothing worth stealing. "I'm fine with your code."

The cabin contained two bunks, a built-in desk at one end with drawers underneath, and a cupboard over the top of the desk. Spacers traveled light, obviously.

At the other end of the cabin was a door. Roystan indicated that way. "Toilet, shower. Water cycle is two minutes."

These walls were the same faded crimson. Nika mentally redesigned it. Light colors. Maybe a restful aqua, with a scene on the wall behind the bunks. A pastoral scene on the top bunk, something water-based for the bottom.

She followed them to the room across from hers, which Roystan had chosen for Snow. "Keypad locks are old technology." She'd investigated it when putting her own locks in against Alejandro. Biometrics had been around hundreds of years now. Keypads were a fad, like handheld communicators and palm recognition systems.

She'd implemented one as an extra layer of security against Alejandro. Had Roystan implemented his for the same reason?

"This ship is old. You'll find a lot of old technology on her. It works, and why change something that works?"

The ship was an antique. Or built by someone who didn't trust electronic locks. Nika could understand that.

"I'll leave you to get settled." Roystan hesitated at the door. "I seem to have landed you in a worse mess than before. I'm sorry, but we'll work something out."

He knew what they were running from. Or thought he did, anyway. Banjo. But the crew of *The Road to the Goberlings* were running, too.

"What are you running from?" She had to know how bad it was.

"We found a ship everyone thinks can lead them to a big find. It nullspaced in front of us. We went over to check it out."

"Salvage?" Snow asked.

"Yes."

Nika had no idea what they were talking about.

"There'd been a fight." Roystan's expression changed. Sorrow. Or regret? "The company—the one that's chasing us—tried to take over the ship, but the crew had killed most of them."

"You shouldn't take on a company," Snow said. "Not for salvage. No ship's worth it. Not unless it's something like the *Hassim*."

"It *was* the *Hassim*," Roystan said.

Snow opened his mouth to speak. Closed it again.

"There's nothing left from the *Hassim*, Snow. We sold it, and then some of our crew stole the proceeds and ran. Unfortunately, the company doesn't know that."

He turned to go. "We'll do what we can to keep you safe, but the safety of my crew is important to me."

In silence, they watched him leave.

Snow dropped onto the bunk. "On the *Boost* we had six to a cabin the same size as this. Except Gramps and me, where they turned the other four bunks into cupboards. We used to keep the drugs there. People always tried to break in."

The more Nika heard about Snow's old home, the less she was impressed with it.

"Then I went to Landers, and even the cheap scholarship rooms only had two beds to a room. Beds, mind you. Not even bunks. We each had a desk, and a cupboard to store clothes. Everyone complained about the lack of room. It was four times the size of this."

He looked up at Nika. "I complained too, because everyone else did."

Why Snow felt compelled to confess to her, Nika had no idea. "You must have had better quarters at the docks." The two-story apartment above her studio on Salamander Street had been large. The studio itself had been made up of the small studio, the main studio, a consulting room where she walked customers through her designs, two large storerooms, and three smaller ones. True, she had turned half her apartment into a lab—she'd built the exchanger there, and countless other mods—but there was still plenty of room.

"It was just a shop," Snow said. "I slept on the storeroom floor. I didn't have anywhere to stay." He chewed at his bottom lip. "Banjo must have wrecked it by now."

"Probably." There was no point denying the truth.

Snow nodded. They sat in silence for a moment.

"This ship is not safe," Snow said. "If a company's after you, there's no escape. We shouldn't have run from Banjo."

Nika sat on the other end of the bed. "You didn't have any choice, Snow. I dragged you along." She didn't regret running, but Snow had never been up against the likes of Alejandro, Wickmore, or Tamati.

Tamati's body would still be rebuilding. The first of her clients would have arrived and found the doors locked. Would they do anything about it? If they went to the police, what would the police do? They'd think Alejandro was back.

"You saved me from getting beaten up." Snow drooped. "But I don't have anything now. No shop, no machine."

She was going to have to get him back into a body more befitting his age. These sudden mood changes didn't go with the thirty-five-year-old casing. "Studio, Snow. Studio. Shops are for those cheap places along the docks."

"I wasn't cheap."

"First lesson in modding, Snow. You want to be a respected modder, behave like you're one." The docks might be a good place to learn the trade, but it was a career killer all the same. "You should have apprenticed yourself to one of the big names."

"You have to pick a good modder. Someone you admire." Snow paused. "I sent a request to Nika Rik Terri. She didn't answer."

Of course she hadn't. "She gets"—had got—"a hundred requests every term for people asking to do an apprenticeship. She doesn't take apprentices. Pick sensible targets, Snow. SaStudio takes on an apprentice every year." Sa's version of immaculate teeth was spreading across the galaxy.

"She was the only one."

Talking about modding didn't solve their immediate problem. Should they run again, or stay on *The Road*? How much trouble was the ship in?

"What's this *Hassim* they keep talking about?"

Snow turned his incredulous gaze to her. "You don't know what the *Hassim* is?"

"I wouldn't have asked if I knew."

"You have heard of Goberling, though?"

"Some old explorer who found a big source of transurides." Roystan had named his ship after him. Was that a coincidence?

Snow sighed. "That's like saying a Songyan is just a genemod machine. He didn't just find transurides, Nika. He found the biggest haul of it ever. In the whole history of the galaxy no one has found a source like it."

"What's that got to do with the *Hassim*?" Goberling was long dead. She'd learned about him as a child, in history. And later, in modding, which benefited from the use of the transurides Goberling had brought back. The current glow to her own skin came from dellarine, which was a transuride. And it was an essential part of the exchanger.

Gino Giwari, the modder Nika's first boss had been so enamored with, had used them with abandon. Back then everyone had believed Goberling's find was the start to a cheaper supply.

Snow sighed again. "Goberling disappeared without telling anyone where his lode was. The *Hassim* was searching for it."

"And?"

"The *Hassim* has a record of everywhere it's been. Unexplored worlds. That information is a treasure trove on its own."

"But they haven't found the transurides." Everyone would have heard if they had.

"Not Goberling's lode, no. But they found new worlds. Unexplored worlds worth billions of credits on their own. You sell the location of these worlds to a company, and live comfortably for the rest of your life. If you've a good lawyer, you can negotiate a percentage of profits from the world, as well."

Company lawyers, Nika had found, could bypass any legal contract.

"Taki Feyodor was a company lawyer before she went exploring. There are smaller companies that have gotten rich just from managing what the *Hassim* sold previously. The *Hassim* hasn't sold anything for years. They haven't needed to."

Nika didn't get the logic jump between Goberling and the *Hassim* not needing to sell anything, but Snow apparently thought it obvious.

"Maybe they don't have anything to sell." Even Nika knew how hard and expensive it was to find new worlds. How many worlds could one ship find in a lifetime?

Her own world, Lesser Sirius, had started out as a company world. The company had gone broke. The residents—Nika included—had bought shares in it.

"There's at least one world." Snow stood up to pace. "Everyone knows about it. Well, maybe not you, but everyone else does. You should get out more. Feyodor was negotiating with XGRC."

XGRC had gone broke two years earlier. Which was why the Big Twenty-Eight was now the Big Twenty-Seven.

"Rumor is Eaglehawk sent them broke, then bought the bankrupt company."

Nika couldn't stop her shiver at the name. She well believed they could send another of the Big Twenty-Seven companies broke. Eaglehawk played dirty.

"They tried to get Feyodor to honor the deal, but she refused.

The contract hadn't been signed." Snow's eyes took on a faraway look. "Just that one world would make you rich."

"What if the world turns out to be a waste of money?"

"A company will pay for it, regardless. But she was asking a lot for this one.

"So they think Roystan's got the location of this world from the *Hassim*. But he hasn't."

"He might be lying."

He might be, but even if he wasn't, it wouldn't matter when you were up against Eaglehawk. They'd tie up any loose ends. Especially if the crew of *The Road* had witnessed what they'd done on the *Hassim*.

They were still safer on the ship. Roystan had said he would take them where they wanted to go. Nika thought he'd honor that.

"When this is over, Snow, I'll buy you a studio. With whatever brand of mod machine you want in it."

"*You* don't have to patronize me."

"I wasn't trying to."

"I'll make my own way."

"Snow, you were right. You didn't have to run. *I* did. I'll replace what I helped you to lose."

Snow flung himself back onto his bunk. "Banjo would have trashed my shop no matter what. Probably destroyed the Netanyu. We both know that. I was going to lose everything."

Nika leaned back. "Where would you like your new studio?"

He stared at the bottom of the bunk above him. "Salamander Street. Right next door to Nika Rik Terri's."

Nika had news for him. Nika Rik Terri didn't practice on Salamander Street anymore.

Why not? He was a good modder. "Sure."

Snow raised himself on an elbow. "Do you know how much the rent is on Salamander Street?"

She didn't. She'd owned her studio, and owning shares to Lesser

Sirius gave her benefits noncitizens didn't have. Like not having to pay rates. On a new world, she'd have to worry about things like that. And decide what to do with the studio on Salamander Street. Rent it out, she supposed.

"We're not going back to Lesser Sirius."

"No." He flopped back onto the bunk. "I suppose we're not. Let me see. I want a Songyan, of course."

Songyans had to be custom-made. It took experience to know what you wanted. "Maybe you should start off with a later-model Netanyu."

"They're no good. You have to buy too many add-ons. You're better off buying a 3501, like I had."

Nika smiled. "My first-ever machine was a Dekker. Older even than the one on the ship here. Awful machine, and not just the calibrator." She shivered, remembering the time she'd come awake early.

Snow raised himself up again. "I'd never heard of them before yesterday."

Yesterday. Tamati had another seven days in the machine.

The tiny cabin felt oppressive, suddenly. Nika stood up. "Let's go back to the crew room."

14

JOSUNE ARRIOLA

Josune fast-forwarded the memory to the *Hassim*'s last hours, set it to play, and promptly fell asleep.

A lancing pain around her eye woke her. Her stretched-tight skin throbbed, her head ached, her eye burned. She couldn't think.

She struggled to sit up and slowly became aware of an unfamiliar voice on the screen, and Feyodor's voice answering. It was the *Hassim* playback, still going. Feyodor was talking to the company man Pol had killed.

She should go back and listen earlier, to see how they had got onto the ship, and what had happened then, but right now, she didn't care.

The company man's voice was cultured and pleasant. Provided you didn't listen to the words.

"We will track your crew down and kill them, one by one. Including the one who's missing. So why not give up this farce and call for them to surrender."

He wouldn't keep his word. Josune clenched her fists.

A red haze of pain engulfed her. She barely heard the next words.

"As if you would keep your word." Feyodor's voice was cultured too, evidence of her own background as a company lawyer. She put the accent on different syllables, though, and pronounced her *i*'s and *e*'s differently. "If they surrender, you will shoot them. I know that. They know that."

The company man laughed. "Today I am feeling generous. Just tell me the whereabouts of Goberling's lode."

"If I knew that, would I still be here?"

"But you're closer than you have ever been."

Feyodor didn't deny it. "And I'm wondering how a company man like you knows that."

So did Josune.

She switched cameras to see who else was in the room. Her eyes blurred, then cleared. Jervois and Dani were dead. Dani had a knife in her back. Thrown, at a guess. Ricaro and Chen were silent, arms above their heads. She looked at the two men holding weapons against them, then looked at the weapon the boss held at Feyodor's throat. Plasma guns. One hit would melt a person—and half the bridge—into a heap of slag.

Feyodor should have called their bluff. They wouldn't use guns like that near the backup memory. Then she looked at Jervois's melted face. Wrong. They would use them.

It took skill to use a plasma gun. What sort of skill did it take to use one and only take out the person you used it on, rather than the whole area?

She checked the other cameras. Watched as two company men fought it out with Sammy. He was good, but these two were professionals.

Watching him fight, hand to her mouth, helpless, Josune understood what her crewmates must have known. These people were specialists. Her presence would have made no difference. The crew of the *Hassim* was outclassed. Roystan's team should have been dead, would have been if she hadn't fired first, hadn't known the ship, hadn't had her bioware.

Josune felt a surge of grim satisfaction. These were the two she'd shot when Roystan's boarding team had first gone across. Roystan was lucky he'd arrived so late. Lucky she'd known the codes.

One of the men punched Sammy. His head rolled back, his neck at an impossible angle. Almost certainly dead.

They dragged Sammy down to the rec room, where nine of her

crewmates were already tied up. Peng wasn't moving, would have been flat on her back except she was wedged tightly between two other crew.

The person with Feyodor, presumably the boss, called then. "Time to make an example. You've a full ten down there."

It wasn't a question. He knew where his people were. "Kill them."

"Do that and none of us will cooperate," she heard from Feyodor.

"But you weren't cooperating anyway, Captain. This lets you know just how serious we are."

The two men in the rec room took out blasters.

Josune closed her eyes as they executed her friends.

"It's always so boring, shooting them while they're tied up," the one who'd killed Sammy said. "A good fight is so much more fun."

She wanted to kill them all over again.

The other man grunted. "Dead is dead. It's just a job. I like mine easy. Besides, there's ten more to kill. You'll get your fun."

Josune wished she had a weak stomach, like Roystan. She wanted to purge the sight—the memory—of what she had seen. She bookmarked the feed and turned the link off. She couldn't watch any more, and her headache was burning a hole in her brain.

They nullspaced when she was halfway to the crew room. A smooth jump, with no firing of the rockets after. She guessed Nika was at the calibrator, and Roystan the pilot. Indeed, by the time she'd made her way down to the crew room—it was hard work, and she had to stop often for her panting to subside—Roystan and Nika were coming down from the bridge.

"Josune," Roystan said. "Should you be up?"

"Couldn't sleep." Which was the truth.

Nika came over. "Let's look at you." She touched a hand to Josune's skin, pressed gently. "Does it hurt?"

"What do you think?" Of course it hurt.

Nika nodded. "That's good. Second-degree burns. You've still got the nerve endings."

Right now, she rather wished she hadn't.

Nika looked at her face and frowned. "It means that when we put you in the machine, you won't be in there for weeks having a complete skin repair." She looked at the dendritic pattern on Josune's arms. "Nice design, though. I wonder if I could use it."

"Nika." Roystan sounded like Snow. Or maybe it had been Snow, for he was standing in the doorway behind them.

The two women exchanged sudden, companionable grins.

"Ideas are everywhere," Nika said.

"But not in someone else's misfortune."

"If you can't drag beauty out of pain, what can you get out of it?"

"Don't judge most modders by Nika," Snow said. "She's odd, by anyone's standards."

Odd, maybe, but as Roystan himself had said, a damned good modder. Snow should have heard of her. And, from her reaction when Snow had mentioned Nika Rik Terri, he probably had.

Carlos came in. "You look awful. Should you be out of bed?"

"No," Roystan said.

"I couldn't sleep." If they sent her back to bed she'd scream. Or tear her eye out, which was burning a hole in its socket.

"She probably smelled the food cooking," Nika said. "I did." And everyone, blessedly, shut up about whether she should be up and made room for her at the table.

In this new order of seating—Pol, Qiang, and Guardian gone, and Nika and Snow here—she found herself sitting beside Roystan. He was comfortable, and quiet, and his deep voice rumbled against her sensitive skin when he laughed once, but she missed being able to look into his eyes.

He glanced at her occasionally, and was ready with a hand every time she moved, but he didn't say anything.

Most of the talk was about the cargo exchange. "We can't afford the docking fees," Jacques said. "Nor can Kahurangi, unless she's making a lot more credits than she used to. We should do a space-to-space transfer."

Roystan didn't look at Josune. She knew it was deliberate. "We've got hurt crew here, Jacques."

"But we—" Jacques buried his face in his hands. Josune watched as he struggled to compose himself. He finally looked up. "Sorry, Josune."

Josune reached across and touched a hand to his. "It's your job."

Jacques flinched. He turned Josune's hand over. "Does it hurt?"

Right now, the thing that hurt most was her head, for she was working up to a headache to beat all headaches. She shrugged. Even that hurt.

Jacques let Josune's hand go and stood up. "I suppose we should be grateful you forced us to Atalante instead. Despite my slaving down there in cargo for hours before anyone remembered to mention that." His voice was harsher than it normally was. "Atalante should let us run a tab, at least."

Roystan flushed. "Sorry, Jacques. But I had to be sure Kahurangi could do the job first."

Jacques moved to the galley and patted the stove top. "At least I can rely on you. You've never let me down. Roystan, you'd better put us straight onto that cargo door. You know as well as I do how awkward our lock is when it's on an angle."

"Have I ever docked badly before?"

"Last time. Remember?"

"In his defense, he did have the use of only one arm at the time," Carlos said.

Jacques brought a coffee over and placed it in front of Josune.

She looked at him, surprised. Jacques only ever waited on Roystan.

"You look like shit. You probably couldn't get up to get a coffee if you tried."

"Thanks." The smell of the coffee made her headache worse, but she smiled anyway, and hoped Jacques put any weirdness in her expression down to her sparker burns.

She closed her eyes and sat back, listening to the banter, which had a forced edge to it. Maybe she should go back to bed. Before her headache got so bad she couldn't move.

She didn't notice Nika talking to her, or feel the hand on her arm. Not until Roystan leaned over. "Josune?"

Nika batted his helping arm away. "Josune, I want to talk to you about a way that might ease the burns." She pulled Josune up and away from the table.

Roystan started to follow. Nika glared at him. "You stay here. Haven't you heard of client confidentiality?"

He sat down again. "Sorry, Josune."

Snow slid out in his stead.

"*I* know more about burns than you do," he pointed out.

"True," Nika agreed, and let him follow them out.

Josune didn't care. Her head was going to fall off, or implode, she was sure of it. She was glad of Snow's supporting presence behind her.

Nika stopped in the next passage. "But I know a lot more about bioware than you do, Snow." Her voice was brisk and professional. "Can you make it to your room, Josune?"

Could she? Josune wasn't sure.

Nika nodded, as if she'd expected nothing less.

"You keep watch," she said to Snow, and pushed Josune against the wall. "Let me see your eye."

"It's fine." It was red-hot, raw pain.

Nika's touch was inexorable. "This is going to hurt. If you scream, Roystan will come running. Is that what you want?"

She couldn't even hear now. Or not much. She wanted to die.

"Cover her mouth, Snow."

"What?"

"She'll start screaming in a minute." Nika stripped off her own top and shoved part of it into Josune's mouth. "Bite on that."

Josune bit down gratefully.

"What are you going to do?" Snow's voice rose.

Nika pushed back Josune's right eyelid. "Did you use the bioware?"

"No. I don't know." It came out unintelligible through the gag. She shook her head. If she had, she hadn't meant to.

"It's frying your brain. This is going to be messy. I need to cut the connection. Snow, do you have any tools on you?"

Josune felt the movement that was Snow shaking his head. A tiny movement, but that caused a wash of agony that blinded her. She wanted to die. Anything would be better than this. She bit down harder.

"Damn. Get Roystan. He'll find something."

"Wait." She had to take the gag out to say it so they could understand. "Tool belt." Nika was halfway to an engineer. She might be able to use some of the fine electronic tools there.

"Thank you." Nika seized on it gratefully. The rattle as she sorted through it sent knife bolts through Josune's head. She pulled out the snippers Josune used for delicate work, and some tweezers.

"You can't use that on her eye. Stop." Even Snow's words were agony. "What are you doing?"

"If she wants a functioning brain I can." Nika shoved the shirt back into Josune's mouth, prized the eyelid open again, and cut, in one quick movement.

The pressure in Josune's head stopped. She cried with relief. Tears mixed with blood. Her legs gave way and Nika guided her down to the floor.

"You've cut her eye."

"You can fix a slashed eyelid with a genemod machine. You can't fix brain damage." Nika took her now damp and bloodied shirt back from Josune and put it on. "See if you can stop the bleeding."

Snow was almost crying too as he crouched in front of Josune and tended her eye. "You are a butcher. I'm so sorry, Josune. I didn't know what she was going to do. She's stark raving insane."

"Snow." Josune tried to calm him down. "She had to do it. I was crazy with pain."

But Snow didn't hear her. Not until Nika said, over the top of them, "Snow. Never go to pieces in front of your client. They need to be able to trust you, and if you fall apart like that, they won't."

"I'd rather fall apart than do that to them. Even if I did look trustworthy while I was doing it."

"Snow." And the modder finally listened. "Nika *helped* me. She's right in what she did." Josune knew she was, given the agony that had been spiking into her head.

"I don't know why you're defending her."

"It was a white-hot soldering iron in my skull. It needed to come out." Now she was one big pain all over, but her head was blessedly painless. Comparatively.

Nika found the nearest first-aid kit and pulled it open. "Roystan doesn't stint on the basics." She sounded approving. "Here." She handed over a wad of gauze, which Snow carefully applied to the eyelid.

The blood dripping down Josune's face was sticky.

"Getting thicker. Good."

Nika handed over plaster. Snow applied that, too.

Josune wondered if he knew he was deliberately keeping his body between her and Nika. To protect her?

She looked past him, to Nika. "Thank you."

Nika nodded and looked at her critically. "Lucky you'll be in a machine soon. If we let that heal by itself you'll end up with a scar, and an eye you can't close."

Snow scrubbed at his own hands, where the blood was. "She has no tact either."

15

NIKA RIK TERRI

Nika washed as much blood off her shirt as she could and wrung it out. She wasn't much on hand washing. It dripped and was clammy on her back, but the only other clothing she had was the business suit she'd used to travel up to the Hub—which she knew would be a bad choice to wear.

Once she was as clean as she could be, she made her way across to Josune's cabin. "Can I come in?"

"Of course." Josune lay limply on the bed, still in her blood-spattered clothes.

Snow wasn't there. Was he up with Roystan? What would he be saying?

Nika sat on the edge of the bed and used the back of her hand to test the skin around Josune's eye.

"They have a hospital on Atalante." She'd checked. "Unfortunately, the only machines on station are Dietel FastTracks. We've booked one. While Carlos and the others are unloading, Snow and I will take you down."

If Snow was talking to her. Later, they'd find a better machine and do a proper mod.

"I thought Snow might be here, protecting you from me."

Josune managed a smile. It must have hurt. "I appreciate what you did, even if he doesn't. He doesn't know who you are, does he?"

Nika stiffened. Josune obviously knew.

"It's not hard to guess. You get uncomfortable every time he mentions a certain name."

She'd have to remember that, and modify her behavior. "Where are your shirts?"

Josune pointed to the cupboard. Nika took that as permission to open it. Josune's cupboard was tidy, and mostly bare. There were no personal trinkets. Just two changes of clothes. She traveled almost as lightly as Nika and Snow.

Nika brought a clean shirt over. "Do you want to shower first?"

Josune shook her head.

Nika helped her sit up and deftly pulled the bloodied shirt off over Josune's head. She slipped the other one on. There was nothing she could do to make it painless, so she made it fast.

"You're not so bad yourself," Josune said. "At doctoring, I mean. Most modders don't know how to heal."

You had to know your tools, and the human body was the most basic, and most important, tool in a modder's toolkit. If you didn't know what could break it, how could you presume to change it? You had to be able to undo what you had done. Nika had seen irresponsible mods, dangerous mods, mods that had been supposedly irreversible.

"A good modder should be able to heal, even if it's not their primary function."

Simply being able to fix things didn't mean you couldn't improve on them, however.

"You'll come out of the machine a patchy pink. We should make it a feature, so you don't look like you've come out of a Dietel."

"Pink." Josune looked down at her burned skin. "I suppose." Doubtfully.

"Think about it," Nika said. "We'll get rid of the pink when we get to a real machine, although we can still use the pattern. I'll draw you a design." She'd talk the doctor into letting her take over the machine. Maybe she could hire it for the mod, so she could control it, rather than the doctor.

"We won't have time. The quicker I'm in and out, the better."

"There's time to decide. Roystan said it will take two days to get there. You should get plenty of rest in the meantime. Your body's in shock."

Nika would come up with the design regardless of whether Josune used it or not. There was always room, even in basic repairs, for some style.

Josune touched her hand to Nika's. "Thank you again. Do you ever think about anything except modding?"

Nika shrugged. "Not really." It was all she had. "It's what I live for."

"I understand obsessions." Josune closed her good eye. "I've lived one all my life." Nika thought she was asleep until she whispered, "What do you have left when you start to doubt your obsession?"

"Loneliness." An obsession ate your life, except you didn't know that until you didn't have it anymore, and you were left with nothing.

Josune opened her good eye again. "All I ever wanted was to find Goberling's lode."

There was far too much Goberling on this ship, in Nika's opinion.

"But Roystan's right. All Goberling ever wanted to do was find new worlds. *He* would have been happy with half, a quarter, of what we found."

She wasn't talking about what *The Road* had found. At least, Nika didn't think so.

"What would I do when we found it, anyway? Retire?"

"You'd probably keep exploring."

"Maybe I could sign on as Roystan's crew. Settle down and work a cargo run."

It wasn't hard to see where that came from. It was clear Roystan liked Josune. It was nice to see that Josune reciprocated some of the feelings.

"Get fat on Jacques's food."

"If you do, make sure you drop in to a good modder regularly."

Josune laughed, then sobered. "I can't stay." Her expression was a mixture of despair and determination. "I can't shut out the noise, Nika. My crewmates. Until I fix that . . . I can't drag Roystan into that."

Josune didn't need time alone in her room right now. She needed sanity, and people around her. She could sleep surrounded by her friends.

Nika stood up and collected Josune's pillow. "Let's go back to the crew room. Get you some coffee."

"I'd rather stay in bed." But Josune followed her out.

Snow wasn't in the crew room. Nika thought about going back to his cabin and talking to him, but the others swamped Josune then.

"What happened to your eye?"

Maybe later, when Josune was settled.

"The bioware was giving me a headache, so Nika cut it out for me." Which was the literal truth, but Nika was glad Snow wasn't there to embellish the story.

Movement caught her eye. Snow, hesitating in the doorway. This might be awkward.

But it wasn't. Snow entered, hunched in on himself, not looking at anyone directly—except at Josune, and that was the quick look of a professional for his client.

They made room for him next to Nika. He hesitated before he sat down. One day she would find out why he lacked the confidence to stand tall. He was good at what he did. He knew he was good. So why did he hunch in on himself all the time?

Nika chose the safest conversation a modder could think of. "I'm doing a design for Josune. Do you want to try one, too?"

She saw the interest quicken in his eyes and approved. A good modder should always be interested in the chance to design.

"Remember these things. She wants to be in and out fast. She wants to be repaired, and we're using a Dietel, so she'll come out pink."

Snow curled his nose at the mention of the machine. Did he realize he had done so? "My Netanyu would do a better job."

At least he was talking to her. Nika settled down to her own design, keeping an eye on Josune while she did so. The engineer looked exhausted but no longer looked as if she wanted to die. She even smiled once at something Jacques said, and asked in reply, "How long will it take to unload?"

"Four hours if Roystan can sweet-talk them into extending us credit for a landing berth. Eight, maybe ten, if we have to do it ship-to-ship, with another hour out while Roystan takes you down. And we still need credits for your shuttle landing."

Four hours. It wasn't much. "If we have the funds, can we stay longer?" Nika asked. They didn't know what supplies the doctor had on hand.

"Roystan doesn't like loans," Carlos said.

"It's not a loan." Although Roystan was the sort of person who'd take out a loan for one of his crew. Even if it lost him his ship. She'd talk to him in private later.

Josune started to say something. Roystan hushed her by putting a hand over hers, but he nodded at her.

That was a conversation Nika wasn't party to. She turned to Snow. "Let's see your design."

"I want to see yours first."

She handed it over. He passed his own back, then looked at hers in silence.

His design was good, but basic, with an eight-hour window for the whole thing, and clever coloration to blend in the pink.

She'd kept hers down to six, blending in the pink similar to the way Snow had, but adding a layer of darker dendritic branching as a feature, much like the burns themselves. She would have liked to make the skin glow as well, but that took more transurides than she had. She'd changed the hair—Josune's old metallic blue-black wouldn't work with the new look—and it now tapered from short on the right side to long on the other. The long side, she'd made a deep black. That was easy and fast. The shorter side retained the black underneath but had an overlay of pink to blend with the skin and dendrites, and a top layer of electric blue.

"This isn't bad," Snow said. "Although I'm not sure about the hair. You said color was out."

"It's last season. Josune doesn't need to be cutting-edge. We do." She looked over at the other woman. "I'll cut your hair before we go. We can fix it properly after you come out."

Snow pushed the design back. "It won't work." Was that a challenge she heard in his voice? "You need transurides to start the reaction on the skin."

You never needed more than a trace of transurides. It was far too expensive to use more.

"As to that." Nika reached into her pocket and pulled out the sliver she'd taken from Josune's eye. "It's damaged," she told Josune. "Do you mind me using it?" It wasn't just a transuride, it was pure dellarine. The best of the best.

Snow let his head drop to the table. She heard the *thunk* as it hit. "You're a cannibal. Certifiably crazy." He lifted his head. Grudgingly, he said, "But it might work."

"Cannibal?" Roystan looked at the sliver in Nika's hand.

She didn't know if he recognized it.

"She reuses parts of people."

"Snow. Your body is the best source of material for a re-mod. It doesn't reject its own." You could push through changes the body would otherwise reject when you used the body's own DNA. Not that the transurides were a natural part of Josune's body—of anyone's—but a body didn't reject transurides either.

Snow said, "Give me nice fresh mutrient any day. At least I know what I'm putting in then."

Atalante Station was a good match for *The Road*. Way beyond its prime, stitched together seemingly with random pieces of metal. It looked like an egg with spines all over it.

"It used to be one of the central places people went to get supplies, crew, passage," Roystan said.

A former-day version of the Hub.

"But as the legal zone moved out, so did the hubs." He smiled fondly as it came closer on-screen. "Now it's limping along with a tenth of the people. But it's got plenty of room, and the docking fees are cheap."

"Is that why you came here?" Nika asked. They were seated around the table in the crew room again. They practically lived there.

Roystan brought up the image of Atalante again. "It's our second home."

What would it be like traveling permanently through space, with long stays at a space station as the only break?

"Won't the company know we're here?" Josune asked.

"I'm hoping they'll think we're still on our route, doing deliveries. They'll come, of course, but we should still have enough time to fix you, sublease our load, and get out of here."

"And then what?" Jacques asked. "Where do we go then, Roystan?"

"We drop Nika and Snow where they want to go." He looked at Josune. "Then we find this safe station of yours, work something out."

Josune gripped the edge of the table. She didn't look at Roystan.

"We've no credits," Jacques said.

"We'll be fine, Jacques." Roystan looked at Jacques, but his eyes moved toward Nika and Snow. "We'll think of something."

He had plans, but not for their ears. Nika didn't mind. She was looking forward to having the sun on her back and being able to walk down the street again, instead of being locked in a tin box. In fact, she was looking forward to the station, for there'd be more room than there was on a ship.

Terrible medical facilities, though. She'd looked up the hospital when she'd booked the machine. Four Dietels and two of them out of commission. She wasn't surprised. They were as old as Snow's Netanyu. Nika hadn't thought Dietels lasted that long.

Roystan was known here. "You know your bay," the controller said, when Roystan booked a slot.

"It'll have to be on credit. Our funds are tied up for the moment."

"You're good for it, Roystan."

It was a good thing the controller couldn't see Jacques's face right now.

"Thanks," Roystan said easily, and asked Nika to join him on the bridge. "Despite what Carlos says about not needing a calibrator when you're not nullspacing, it's always good to have one. And you have a light touch."

Nika was glad for time alone with Roystan. She wanted to talk to him about his mods. She was starting to think someone had done genetic work on him in the past, and they'd botched it. He was half starved, so his body wasn't metabolizing food well. He had a weak stomach, which meant his body was rejecting what was put into it. She wanted to know what he'd had done.

"Have you ever had medical treatment or mods done here on station?"

"Carlos did once, when he sliced his arm." His eyes danced, a smile that didn't reach his mouth. "He has pink down his arm, but Carlos doesn't seem to mind. Look, Jack's all right, if that's what you're worried about."

"Jack?"

"Sethu Jackson. The doctor. Everyone calls him Doctor Jack. I've known him for years. He's a decent man."

"But you've never been modded by him."

"No."

So there wasn't any point talking to Doctor Jack about any mods he'd done on Roystan.

"Who have you been modded by?"

Roystan looked away, into the screens, and nodded at the image in front of them. "We're getting close to the station. We'll need to maneuver soon. Is the calibrator ready?"

It could have been the timing. More likely a deliberate attempt to change the conversation.

Closer in, the egg shape looked patchy. Parts of it were well lit, others in darkness. At intervals around the ovoid, jutting out from the central core, flexible arms reached into space.

"What are the arms for?"

"The technical term is *spurs*. Each spur is a docking bay."

Now that he'd pointed it out, she could see three of those arms bright with activity. A ship rose and moved away as she watched.

It cleared the station and nullspaced within minutes.

"They don't make stations like this anymore," Roystan said. "Even with maintenance, the spurs shear off. It doesn't happen often, but enough that the insurance companies wouldn't insure them now."

She wished he hadn't told her that. Especially since she could see a broken spur in front of them. It was patched with white metal, brighter than the metal surrounding it. They didn't make space stations out of metal anymore, did they? Wasn't it some baked-earth ceramic-mineral alloy? Or was it fiberglass, like the genemod machines?

Roystan smiled reminiscently. "Josune was with us on the last layover. She took one look, then went shopping. Next thing, the maintenance people roll up with supplies. She added a new wall and installed an extra airlock inside our spur. Plus emergency lighting, heating, and air. She says if anything goes wrong at the spur now, at least we'll stay alive."

That didn't make Nika feel any safer.

"Although if you get caught between the breach door and the airlock, you're toast."

"Toast?"

"Finished. Dead."

Nika didn't know where Roystan had grown up, but his vocabulary contained some strange words.

Roystan fired the jets. A gentle nudge. One of the spurs came closer. A landing pad glowed with the number thirteen.

"The ship at spur twelve is the *Promise*. Kahurangi's ship. She's on time; that will make the changeover easier." Roystan's fingers moved over the controls. "Thirteen is ours. Let's keep Jacques happy. Ready?"

"Ready." Nika held the calibrator steady. They coasted into their landing slot.

"You are good at this."

"Lots of practice. You're not bad yourself."

"Thank you." Nika looked at the screen, where the mobile passageway was extending out to meet them. Red warning lights blinked an outline.

Down in the cargo bay Jacques was talking to the auto-controller on the other end. "Come on, you piece of integrated circuitry. Nice and steady and don't make an angle into the passage. We want a straight doorway to unload to."

It seemed like Jacques always talked to his machines, although he saved his best flattery for the kitchen items.

Roystan stood up and stretched. She heard his bones creak. From the sound of that, he was older than he looked. Another thing she'd have to add to her list to watch for.

"Do you need me to come with you to the hospital?"

He'd helped already, by convincing the doctor to let them use their own design. "It's organized." She had the directions keyed into her communicator. Four passages down, two floors up.

"Thanks. I'll finalize the sublease, then, while you look after her."

Josune, Nika was sure, would say she could look after herself.

Roystan said, "If you have any problems, call me."

16

They left for the hospital as soon as they had clearance to enter the station.

Four passages and two floors wasn't much, but Nika glanced at Josune and seriously thought about hiring a station cart.

Josune might have read her thoughts. "I can walk if it's not too far."

Define *too far* when your body was covered in second-degree burns and you only had the use of one eye.

"It's not far," Snow said.

"Let's go." Josune didn't say anything until they were in the lift, when she pressed a hand to the gauze over her eye. The skin on her arm pulled tight. "I'll be happy to get this fixed. It's hurting today."

Nika looked at the skin on Josune's arm. She'd be glad to get the burns fixed, too. The skin was starting to harden and scab in places. "So will I."

Doctor Jack waited for them. The hospital was a single room with wall-to-wall cupboards and two emerald boxes, one on each side of the room. The Dietels. Visitors' chairs were placed discreetly beside each machine. In the center of the room, a desk took pride of place. Opposite the desk, a wall screen ran a news feed.

"I have to tell you I don't like other people using my machines," he said. "Even if they are certified modders. If it hadn't been Roystan who asked for this, I wouldn't let you do it. I want to see your certification, and your blueprint, before I let you try any of your experiments."

Nika looked at Snow. He sighed and put his palm to the reader.

Doctor Jack checked his credentials. "You're too young to insist on your own plans."

Nika sent the plan across. "It's copyright, of course." She passed the hospital robe over to Josune. "You get ready while we sort this out."

Josune nodded. She'd been in a machine before. She knew the process.

The doctor looked at Josune rather than at the plan. "She needs medical help, not modding."

"Of course she does." The sooner the better. "But she doesn't want telltale pink skin, and that's a Dietel sitting over there. You know as well as I do that's what will happen."

"It's not all about beauty, lady. Sometimes it's about saving people's lives." But after he studied the plan he moved over to the built-in cupboards in the wall under the screen. "This is what we have."

Mostly, the supplies were what she'd expected, although there were dendrian salts, which she hadn't. The container was old, and the print had faded, but the salts didn't go off. She could use them. "Is that all you have?" It wasn't much for a full station. He'd have a second store cupboard somewhere.

"What were you expecting? Fancy supplies like one of those modder shops?"

She straightened up and turned to look at him. "I was expecting more mutrient."

"We've spare plasma. Acid. Arrat crystals. If the machine wants more, I'll get you some."

"We need it now. What type of acid?"

"KT18." Which was the one in the cupboard. "And this, of course." He held up a glass jar of sulfuric acid. Modders used it to clean off the metal that collected around the modding plate after prolonged mutrient use.

"Very funny." Nika did a quick calculation. "We'll need another liter of mutrient, and the same of KT18."

Doctor Jack scanned the blueprint again. He looked over at Josune. "Are you good with this?"

Josune nodded tiredly. "Whatever Nika wants."

Snow frowned, but he didn't argue. Nika was glad.

The machine was clean. Nika wiped it out, anyway.

She turned to Josune, who'd placed her folded clothes neatly onto a chair. "Let's get you started."

Josune climbed in. Nika set her up quickly. She stood aside while Snow checked her setup.

"All right," he said, eventually. "Your work is sound."

Nika hid a smile. Snow would misinterpret that. Josune wasn't as polite, but there was affection in her smile.

Nika closed the lid and set the cycle going.

Then they waited. At her own studio Nika had plenty to do. New designs to create. Add-ons to build. Clients to follow up. Here, there was nothing to do except talk to the doctor or watch the vids.

The doctor fell asleep at the desk, and from the suddenness with which he did so, Nika suspected he did it often. She felt like doing the same. Instead, she watched the telltales on the machine.

Snow settled on the floor, back to the wall, and watched the news on the wall screen. "It's a pity we can't change the channel."

Five hours of news wouldn't hurt them. Meantime, could Nika convince the doctor to sell them extra mutrient and acid? Roystan would buy a spaceship calibrator as soon as he could, and when that happened they'd have a working genemod machine. They'd need supplies.

The news droned on in the background. Some starlet sponsored by one company was having an affair with the CEO of a rival company. Nika hid a snort. News never changed. People never changed. But the starlet had interesting purple mods in her hair that flickered as she spoke tearfully to the camera.

Nika watched and waited for a tear to fall. It never did. Mods? Or clever management on the girl's behalf, for crying in public was a problem. Eyes filling with tears gave the desired result. But crying? That made your eyes and nose red, streaked your makeup, and did all sorts of other things no one in the public eye wanted.

She turned her attention back to Josune. The build was going well. Blood flow on the eyelid was gradually moving down. The skin was knitting without any problems.

Snow made a strangled sound. Nika looked over at him. He was staring at the news feed.

She looked at the screen. A smiling, open-faced reporter said, ". . . wait to find out. Until then, this is Banjo Yoxall, signing off from Lesser Sirius."

The voice was familiar, and so was the face. Familiar in the way Nika always remembered the faces of clients she had worked on. This man had been one of her clients.

"Banjo," Snow whispered.

Nika looked at the screen again, which was now showing the results of a two-man shuttle race. "Are you sure, Snow?" But she didn't forget a body she'd modded, and yes, now prompted, she recognized him.

"A reporter," Snow said. "How—"

Nika could see how. Banjo's voice had always been his strongest point, and there had been good bones beneath that heavy exterior. Take the bulk away and he'd turned out rather presentable. If she said so herself, it had been a nice job.

Something beeped, making her jump. She swung around to the Dietel, but it was fine.

The doctor woke with a mutter, and nearly fell off his chair. He swiped the screen in front of him as he did so. A message alert.

The news on-screen changed to a woman wearing the distinctive collar of the Justice Department. The Justice Department was a combined initiative of all companies. Companies paid them a percentage to maintain law inside the legal zone.

"Citizen watch," the justice said. "We are hunting a criminal who might be seeking medical attention."

"We used to get these on the *Boost*," Snow whispered. "Gramps used to ignore them."

A picture flashed up on-screen. Grainy, enlarged, but instantly recognizable.

Josune.

"Wanted for destruction of property and actions endangering life on a space station. Believed to have burns to much of her body. The burns will be characteristic of sparker damage."

For one frozen moment Nika couldn't move.

She stared at the telltales on the machine. If she pulled Josune out now she'd destroy her eye. And leave her skin vulnerable to infection.

On-screen the relentless voice of the justice continued. "The unidentified woman is believed to be traveling on the cargo ship *The Road to the Goberlings*. The crew of *The Road to the Goberlings* are considered dangerous. Captain Hammond Roystan is armed. He is wanted for actions endangering life on a space station, along with damages to said station." The images of the crew, including Snow, flashed up on the screen.

"Me." Snow looked as if he couldn't decide if he should be outraged or worried. "I'm not crew."

He'd signed for the Dekker.

"Roystan," Doctor Jack said, making Nika jump again. "He wouldn't hurt anyone. Much less damage a station." He switched off the screen. "What are you going to do?"

Nika looked back at the genemod machine. "Wait." And stop this doctor from calling the Justice Department.

He grunted. "Some people would run."

She wanted to. She looked at the machine again. "We're not leaving Josune behind, and you can't make a genemod machine run any faster."

"That's the truth, lady."

Nika looked at Snow. "It's your image that's being splashed around. Go. You should be safe on *The Road*."

Snow hunched in on himself. "What good would that do? They can still find us there. I can't go anywhere else. Banjo—" He glanced at the blank screen and took a deep breath. "Running won't help. Besides, *they* attacked us. Why are we the wanted ones?" The plaintive note on the last sentence made him sound young again.

"Because we're not company." That was how it worked. Nika tried not to be bitter. Once, she'd been a citizen of Lesser Sirius and thought she was protected. She'd learned otherwise.

"Roystan's well known on this station," the doctor said. "Most people will ignore the message."

"But you can't. You're a doctor." Part of the legal requirements of a doctor's certificate was to assist the Justice Department in their inquiries. And to report any suspicious injuries. It was the reason Nika had suggested, back when she had first met him, that Roystan go to a cosmetician rather than a hospital.

"This is my off-duty time. I don't normally come into the hospital till 08:00, excepting for emergencies. Won't be listening to messages for half an hour after that."

"Thank you," Nika said, fervently. They'd be gone before then.

Doctor Jack settled back in his chair. "I'm not the one you have to worry about. Calli will be fine, too."

Calli Mattins was the station manager. She'd called earlier to check why Roystan was arriving out of schedule. From what Nika had overheard of the call, she'd sounded concerned. Roystan had told her it was because Josune needed medical care.

"She has a soft spot for Roystan. Always has. Aubrey would be a problem, except he'll be playing sho by now."

"Sho?"

"Cards."

"Who's Aubrey?"

"The night manager. You should be safe."

"Thank you. I'd better let Roystan know." Nika touched her jaw to open a link. "Roystan. Can you talk?"

There was a lot of background machinery noise. That was the problem with those old handheld communicators. You didn't get that background noise with an internal communicator. Then, from the sounds of it, he dropped his communicator.

"Sorry. A little busy here," he said when he'd picked it up.

Why did he insist on such an anachronistic tool? With an internal communicator, he could have both hands free right now. She'd be able to hear him without him having to raise his voice.

"The Justice Department has put out an alert to medical staff and station managers."

"Josune?"

"In the tank for another three hours."

Three hours, nine minutes, and forty seconds precisely.

"Tell me about the alert."

"It identified Josune. That she was burned. It identified you, your ship, and your crew, including Snow. Asks people who see any of you to get in touch with the Justice Department."

"The Justice Department?"

"We damaged the Hub when we escaped," Nika reminded him. She glanced at the doctor to see what he thought of that. He was staring at his hands.

"How long have we got?"

"No idea."

She could hear the rasp of something. Roystan scratching his head, or rubbing his face. "Aubrey will be playing sho by now. He shouldn't be a problem. What about Jack? He has to report it."

"Doctor Jack doesn't start work till eight." She smiled at the momentary silence on the other end of the line. "Josune will be out of the machine before he acts on the message."

"Thank goodness for that," Roystan said fervently. "Meantime, I'll keep an ear out to be sure no one else has reported us." A soft sigh. "I am so tired of running. Look after Josune for me. I'll get Kahurangi on her way, and then scout around, see what's happening." He clicked off.

There were worse things than running, Nika decided. Waiting to run was one of them.

"You ever had to bring a patient out of a machine early?" she asked Snow.

"No. I hope you're not thinking about it."

"Of course not." A good modder wouldn't. But it might be prudent to work out what they could do, and when, if they had to. Nika didn't want to stand around waiting. She'd rather have something to do, even if it was contemplating nightmare what-if scenarios.

"*If* we had to take her out early, what can we do?"

"Why are you asking the question if you're not planning on doing it?"

Snow and Doctor Jack were both looking at her, and frowning.

"Because I'm twitchy, and I need something to occupy me."

And because it might be a matter of life or death for Josune. For all of them.

She knew what she'd sacrifice. It wouldn't be the eye. She wanted that whole and working, and she'd bet Josune would, too. Right now, the way she had set up the machine, the eye would be the last thing finished.

She checked through her program to see what she could change. The hair was done. The dermis was mending nicely, although the machine hadn't started on the epidermis. The eye—halfway through. If she switched the processes around, so that the machine concentrated on the eye first, the lower layers of the skin next, and the epidermis last, she'd add half an hour to the final build. An unfinished epidermis was not life-threatening, it only looked bad. Josune would shed dead skin for a week. Was it better to simply let the process go through as fast as it could?

Snow put a hand over the screen. "Nika. You don't change a program halfway through."

"I know." Although she had, when she found something wasn't working. "But, Snow, let's pretend for a moment that we have to. What would you do?"

"But you—"

"A theoretical exercise. We have enemy coming. They'll be here before she's out of the machine."

"They won't be. You heard the doctor. No one will know. Not until we're gone."

"Theoretically."

Snow chewed at his bottom lip. "The skin enhancements," he said, finally. "To cover the pink. That could go."

"Good." Some modders Nika knew would be more horrified at leaving the pink, but you couldn't prevent it with a Dietel; all you could do was enhance it, make it look like it was supposed to be there.

"Her eye. We'll never be able to fix that in time. She'll have to wear a patch until we get her to another machine."

Not if Nika could prevent it. "The eye is important to Josune."

"But her skin."

"You ever heard of sunburn, Snow?"

"Of course I have. Planet-bound people get it. It's common on worlds where the sun emits high ultraviolet radiation and newly landed visitors forget to cover up."

They didn't go to a modder to get it fixed, they went to a doctor. But Nika had one client who participated in extreme outdoor sports. His skin burned regularly. He had a standing appointment with her when he came back after a session.

"Not that common on a space station," Doctor Jack said, unhelpfully.

The hospital door opened. Nika's hands clenched over a weapon she didn't have. She should have borrowed one from Roystan. She glanced over her shoulder and relaxed. The man who'd entered was breathing heavily and perspiring slightly. He'd had work done. His look was a poor copy of a CEO Nika had modded twelve months ago.

Snow took an awed breath. "That's a Nika Rik Terri design."

"A copy," Nika corrected. It wasn't even a good copy, for the skin around the hairline was mottled and silvering. Not a bad effect itself, but certainly not part of the design. The nails were silvering, too.

"Has Roystan brought anyone in to be treated?" the newcomer demanded.

"Roystan?" Doctor Jack ran his fingers through his hair. "Aubrey, you know he's not due back for a ten-day."

Nika moved quietly over to the controls of the Dietel.

They had to get Josune out of the machine as fast as they could. And warn Roystan.

Her fingers flew, rescheduling the build, reassigning the priorities.

She was glad Snow watched Aubrey, not her. He would have tried to stop her from making the changes.

"He's here," Aubrey said. "He's in my jail right now. He had an injured crewwoman with him. One of the crew will be bringing her here."

He spotted Nika and Snow then. Did a double take as he recognized Snow. "That's him. You're under arrest." He put a hand to his chin to tap his link on.

"Calm down, Aubrey," Doctor Jack said.

Nika pulled everything but the essentials out of the design. The eye, completion of the dermis layer of the skin, and the basal layer of the epidermis. The burns would heal themselves from there. They'd be mildly painful for a day or three, and the dead skin would flake and look terrible, but it wouldn't kill Josune.

She pushed affirmation of the changes through and watched as the machine concentrated mutrient and other trace elements around the eye. Thank goodness for that tiny piece of dellarine, to speed up the process.

"That man is a wanted criminal."

Snow hunched in on himself again. Nika sighed, and said more to distract Snow than anything else, "What happened to your game of sho?"

"So you know about that, do you?"

"Everybody knows," Doctor Jack said.

"Well I tell you, Lady Criminal. If you were counting on that, it's your bad luck that Executive Mattins banned sho."

"Knowing Calli she probably threatened to sack you for slacking off during business hours," Doctor Jack said.

Aubrey swung around so fast Nika thought it might have been true.

"Doctor, why haven't you reported these two to me?"

"What?"

"Don't you read your messages?"

"It's the middle of the night."

Nika glanced down. Josune's mod was going nicely. Pulling her out early would be tricky, but provided the first part of the mod was completed—and if they needed to—they could pull her out without finishing the last part of the build.

She increased the timer by half an hour. The new finish time was displayed on the screen, counting down. If anyone looked at the time, they'd think they couldn't move Josune before that.

In reality, Nika could pull Josune out any time in the hour beforehand.

It would give them an hour. They might need it.

The doctor took his time scrolling through the messages. He eventually found and replayed the one from the Justice Department. "It says watch out for Roystan, and a woman with burns. This woman"—he gestured toward Josune—"had her eye gouged out."

Gouged was a little strong, but Nika appreciated what he was doing.

"Oh." Aubrey looked toward the Dietel. "Maybe I'm—" His gaze moved on to Snow. "You wouldn't recognize a criminal if he robbed you. Look at that man. Look at his face."

The doctor looked at the image on-screen, at Snow. He shrugged. "You didn't really arrest Roystan, did you?"

"Of course I did. And I let the Justice Department know." He looked at Nika. "Don't think you'll get away with this. I'm not stupid."

"So you keep telling us." Could they keep him talking long enough to get Snow away? She looked around for a weapon.

Snow moved to stand in front of the supply cupboard.

Right now, Nika would have liked a handy container of naolic acid to threaten Aubrey with. Not that Aubrey would have recognized it as a threat.

"Roystan's part of the station," Doctor Jack said. "He's been coming here forty years. Longer than you've been alive, Aubrey."

There was nothing loose that Nika could use to hit Aubrey with.

"It's irrelevant. When the Justice Department calls, I answer."

"He does a lot for us. He lends us his engineer when he's here. He brings supplies. This won't be popular."

"I'm not here to be popular, I'm here to do my job."

"It's a pity you chose tonight as the night to do it."

Nika moved Snow away from the supply cupboard.

"Nika, you can't—"

Much as she'd love to, she wouldn't. It wouldn't help Roystan's chances, or their own. But she did want to be armed. She rummaged through the cupboard.

"These two," Aubrey said. "They're under arrest."

"What have I done?" Nika waved a hand at the screen. "I'm not on the wanted list."

"Aiding and abetting a criminal."

"That's not for you to decide. I'm not going anywhere. I paid for time with this machine. If I don't get the time I paid for, I'll sue."

Nika's clients were mostly high-end, powerful executives and entertainers who used the threat of legal action as one of the base tools of trade. Anyone who did that to her didn't get return appointments.

Aubrey laughed, but she heard the faint doubt.

"You think I'm joking. Why don't you call your boss and ask her? Will she be happy about breaking a contract?" Every minute they stayed out of jail was an extra minute for Josune to recover.

If she could work it so she stayed with Josune, Snow could help break Roystan out of his cell. Nika turned back to the supply cupboard for the small glass container of sulfuric acid Jack had placed there. They were on a station. And no matter how dangerous a criminal was, space doors had to open. There was always a manual override for when the lock was damaged. And sulfuric acid would certainly damage a lock, if you put it into the right place.

"I have every right to arrest *him*," Aubrey said. "You can stay here. Under guard."

"I'll be here until she's out of the machine." Nika handed Snow the tiny bottle. "Don't forget your fixative. You know you're due to take it in an hour." Aubrey, eyes on the bottle, didn't see the horror on Snow's face. The machine countdown was two hours and five minutes.

"What is it?" Aubrey demanded, taking the bottle.

She gambled he didn't know his acids well. "Something he needs to take every day. Otherwise his skin goes patchy."

"Patchy." Aubrey rubbed discreetly at his own hairline, and she worried for a moment he might keep the bottle.

"Brown blotches. A skin mold. Kills the mold."

He handed Snow the bottle as if it would bite him.

"Remember," Nika told Snow. "Put it on the joints. Opening and closing orifices."

Was the hint too obscure for Snow to understand? At least he recognized what was in the bottle. Doctor Jack turned away, covering his mouth with a hand.

"Get someone else to put it on for you, if you prefer."

Aubrey stepped away from them. "That's disgusting."

"An hour," Nika said.

Snow looked at the bottle in his hand. "An hour."

The security team arrived. Four guards. One of the guards had a cut on his lip, another a mark high on his cheekbone that was going to turn into a bruise. And probably a black eye.

"The whole damn team," Doctor Jack said. "What'd you wake them all up for, Aubrey?"

"These people are dangerous. They destroyed half a station."

Half a station? That was an exaggeration.

"As dangerous as Roystan," the doctor said. "Did it take all four of you to arrest him, too?"

"Don't be stupid, Jack," the lead security said. "Roystan came quiet as a lamb. I was embarrassed arresting him. I'm going to have to apologize when we let him go."

They wouldn't let him go. These people might think it all a misunderstanding, but Nika knew better. Snow looked at Nika.

"We'll get you out. Don't forget that, will you?" She pointed to the acid. "An hour from now."

He slipped the bottle into his pocket and allowed two of the guards to lead him away.

Aubrey looked at the remaining two security people. "Lexie, Kane. Bring the woman when she comes out of the machine." He turned to the door. "I've got forms to fill in."

Nika had hoped they'd leave her there on her own. Now she had to work out how to disable these two—and the doctor—long enough to help Josune escape.

One hour and fifteen minutes before Josune was due to come out of the genemod machine—according to the timer—Doctor Jack lumbered to his feet. "I'm for a coffee. Anyone else want one?"

Nika watched the telltales on the machine.

How much had Doctor Jack noticed? The timing couldn't be coincidental. Fifteen minutes before Josune could come out of the tank. Fifteen minutes before she had to do something about the two guards.

What could she do? There was nothing in the supply cupboard she could use. Not without harming them, and despite what Snow imagined, she didn't plan on harming onlookers.

Unless she absolutely had to.

One unarmed woman. Against two armed guards. She went through the cupboard again. Found the spray bottle Doctor Jack used to wipe out the machine with. Tipped most of the antiseptic out and filled the rest of the bottle with water. Straight antiseptic would damage the eye, but watered down, it would merely sting, and maybe give her enough time to get out the door with Josune.

She put the spray bottle on the bench above the machine.

Ten minutes.

A message chimed. The female guard, Lexie, pushed it onto a wall screen. It was the station manager, Calli Mattins.

"What the hell is going on?"

"Justice Department identified some wanteds," Lexie said.

"Did you seriously arrest Roystan?"

"He's comfortable."

"Why didn't you just keep an eye on him?"

"The orders were to restrain him."

"What about his crew?"

"They're with him. Resisting arrest. Jacques was demented. Clocked Kane a beauty. He's taking time in the tank when he goes off duty."

Mattins scowled.

"We've arrested the redhead as well."

"The injured woman?"

"She's coming out in one hour and seven minutes."

Seven minutes, provided they didn't stop Nika, and if the time was going as slowly as it had for the last eight minutes, the next seven would be the longest seven minutes of Nika's life.

"Aubrey's called the Justice Department," the other guard— Kane—said. "They'll be here in an hour."

Some news at last. They had less than an hour to escape.

"An hour," Mattins said. "So who's demanding landing slots? *Immediately.* To take the dangerous criminals off our hands."

It wouldn't be the Justice Department, who came when they said they would.

It had to be the company after Roystan. Eaglehawk? The Justice Department was, once again, aiding a company.

"You leave me no time to do anything except hand over an old friend to the law. I wish Aubrey had spoken to me first." Mattins clicked off with a savage thrust of her hand.

Five minutes.

"Suits," Kane muttered. "She thinks she's above work rules because she's station manager. She's going up against the Justice Department. What about us? What happens to our jobs?"

Nika didn't feel so bad about what she planned to do.

"Nothing," Lexie said. "Except that we get Aubrey as boss instead of Calli."

"He's not likely to lose his job for insubordination," Kane said.

His companion scowled. "If Aubrey weren't such a sanctimonious prig this could have been sorted. We could have warned Roystan quietly and let him move on."

Maybe Nika wouldn't be so hard on the female guard, although she'd be tougher to subdue.

"What's with you all?" Kane demanded. "Why would you warn him?"

"Roystan's a good man. I've known him since I was a kid."

"You station-bred people need to get out more, learn what it's really like to work for a company. It's not all like this, you know."

"I know," Lexie said.

Two minutes.

Lexie looked to be around ten years older than Roystan, yet she said she'd known him as a kid. Either Roystan's modder Tilda was a genius, or the years didn't add up. Nika had never heard of Tilda, and if she was that good, why did she have a studio down on the docks?

"You said you knew Roystan when you were young," she said to Lexie, before the waiting got too much for her and she did something stupid, like pull Josune out early.

"We all did. We'd wait for his ship, just to get a glimpse of him. To us, he's a hero. The new people here don't understand." She slid her eyes in the direction of Kane without moving her head. "You saw our station as you came in?"

Nika nodded.

"You can see where we've lost spurs. Roystan was here when the first spur broke loose. It didn't shear off at the join as it was supposed to. Part of the station tore away as it went. Lots of people died. We were losing air faster than we could shut down breach doors. Roystan was incredible. None of us would be here without him." She shrugged. "You had to be there. You had to see it."

Roystan hadn't told Nika about that when he'd told her about the spurs. Maybe it was a good thing. She'd never have believed she'd feel safer in Roystan's old ship than she would on a station. But she did right now.

It was time.

Nika gently touched the override and set the closedown. All she could do was wait.

"They've fixed it all now," Lexie said, and Nika had to force herself to remember what they'd been talking about. "Roystan helped there, too. The spurs break off at the stress points, where they're supposed to. We've had two break since then."

The box drained slowly.

Lexie didn't notice. Her expression was raw. "Lost good people both times, but not too many. Not like that first time."

The Dietel beeped.

Nika opened the cover.

"You're not supposed to open them before their time," Lexie protested. "I'll call the doctor."

"It's fine. I know what I'm doing."

Josune opened her eyes. Blinked three times, moved her hand.

Nika picked up the spray bottle with the diluted antiseptic. "You coming out?" she said to Josune.

Josune surged up and out of the tank.

Nika sprayed the liquid into both guards' eyes.

"Hey! What?" They scrabbled wildly, trying to clear their eyes.

"Don't move," she ordered. "You'll make it worse." Which was a lie. "I'll call Doctor Jack."

Josune pulled on the robe Nika handed her, snatched up her clothes, and hunted through them. She pulled the sparker from an inside pocket. "Let's go."

Nika wished she'd known about the sparker. She could have used it.

She pressed the exit button.

Out into the corridor, where the station manager—a company man with her—was raising a hand to the entry button.

"Calli. Thank goodness," Nika said. "Call Doctor Jack. Those two people in there. They need medical help. Their eyes."

Kane started yelling, "I can't see."

Calli called the doctor.

"Excuse us." Nika stood between Josune and the company man. Josune didn't look the same anymore. Some of the mods had started to take—the patterning on her skin, the warm, pink tones.

The pin on his collar was all she saw. And the movement of his hand as he raised his blaster.

Something crackled past her ear.

Josune's sparker.

The company man jerked. The blaster shot arced.

Josune pulled Nika and Calli down.

The shot passed overhead.

Josune's sparker crackled again. This time she'd aimed for the arm holding the blaster, and followed up with a kick that sent the blaster halfway down the corridor. Josune followed that up with an elbow to the company man's head. He dropped and lay still.

"What's going on here?" the station manager demanded as she picked herself up.

Nika crawled across to get the blaster. She trained it on the company man, in case he moved.

"What's going on?" Calli demanded again.

"I lied to your security guards," Nika told her. "I said what I sprayed in their eyes was dangerous. It isn't, although it stings. Tell the doctor it's diluted antiseptic."

"I wish someone would tell me what's going on."

Josune snatched up Kane's weapon. Checked it. "You ever used a stunner like this before? No?" She swapped it for Nika's blaster and showed her how to fire it. "It won't kill anyone, but it should stop them."

They took off running.

"Wait," the station manager called after them. "You're going the wrong way."

Nika wouldn't have stopped. Josune did, looking back at her.

"Lockup's Sector C. Level 5."

"Thanks." But they kept running, and turned down two corridors before Josune stopped. "Do we trust her?"

"Probably. They seem mostly pro-Roystan. That was Calli Mattins. The station manager." Nika tried to inspect Josune's skin. "How do you feel?"

"Deaf and blind," Josune said.

Nika inspected her eye.

Josune pushed her away. "I can't connect to the station. I feel helpless. Patch in and find which sector we're in, and what level we're on."

"But you can see out of your right eye?"

"I can, and I feel unbelievably good, and pain free. I'll thank you for it later, but right now we need to know where Sector C is, and how to get there."

Nika activated the link in her jaw. "Station directory," she said, as the screen in front of them illuminated. "Tell us which sector we are in."

"Current location is Sector E, Level 17."

"How do we get to Sector C, level 5? The fastest way possible?"

"Follow the blue arrows." The floor in front of them illuminated with discreet blue arrows.

The fastest way wasn't through the public halls. "We should have specified a route you had access to," Josune said, as they backtracked from a locked door. "Still, no one will expect us to come this way."

As they ran, Nika told Josune what had happened. "Justice Department put a call out. For you, for Roystan, for Snow, and for the crew. They've all been arrested. I pulled you out of the tank early or you'd have been arrested as well." She hesitated. "I didn't finish the job. Your skin will flake for the next few days. It's not pretty, but it's not dangerous."

"You did what had to be done. Now let's rescue Roystan and the others and get out of here."

"I gave Snow some acid to use on the door seals, but I don't think he understood."

Josune grunted as they came to another restricted area and had to retrace their steps again. "That sort of understanding takes years to develop. He hasn't been with you long."

No, he hadn't, and if Snow had his way, he wouldn't be around after they stopped running. Nika would miss him.

"If the floor plan is right, this is Sector C5." Josune slowed. "Ask the station to switch off its guide. Someone might see the arrows as we get closer. We can see which direction to go from here."

Nika did as asked. "The company will expect us."

"So we shoot first. I wish I had my eye." Josune looked at Nika. "I don't, but it would be useful right now, and I have to rely on you for all communication. It's frustrating."

"Think of it as a feature, rather than a disability. They can't see you in the system."

"Genius. They won't, will they?"

There was more than one way to see on station. "What about the station cameras? Won't they pick us up?"

Josune waved a dismissive hand. The skin on the back of it was flaking, starting to peel. Nika didn't think Josune had noticed. "I don't look the same as I did before. No one will expect me to change my appearance." She grinned, and skin flaked off around her mouth. "Unless they are looking for you now, we should be good. They'll be relying on IDs. Do you think the company is at the prison yet?"

Nika thought Calli would give them time. So would Doctor

Jack, once he ensured she truly hadn't injured the guards. "I don't think so. Did you kill the company man?"

"I certainly hope so."

Nika wasn't sure killing someone would help their cause.

Josune grinned. Her lips were chapped, and the grin made them bleed. Some of the moisture from her lips had been redirected to other parts of her skin. It was the worst, most unfinished job Nika had ever done. "Let's assume we're not walking into a trap. If Mattins is helping us, we'll only have station staff to deal with. How many guards?"

"Two." If Doctor Jack had implied correctly. "Two at the hospital, two at the lockup. But they're station staff, and we don't want to kill them. They were trying hard not to kill Roystan."

Josune nodded. "If we can avoid it." She looked at the stunner Nika had forgotten she was carrying. "Can I take that? We need to take them out long enough to escape, and I don't want to kill anyone."

Nika handed it over with alacrity.

"Thanks." Josune tucked the weapon into her robe to hide it, then stepped out into the passage.

A noisy crowd had gathered outside the lockup. Two guards were trying to quiet the mob. One of them—the woman—held a weapon. "Under orders from the Justice Department. I can't do anything." It looked as if she had been saying it a while now.

"What's Roystan ever done to you? He's one of us. Give him a chance to disappear." The speaker was an older, fine-featured man whose skin looked as if it had never seen sun.

"Let him go. We know Roystan. If he did anything to those company men, they'll have deserved it." The mob surged forward and the two guards pressed back against the door to the cells.

"Keep back or I'll be forced to shoot," the second guard said.

"You wouldn't want to be responsible for deaths, Niall. Our orders come from the Justice Department."

"It's not the Justice Department out there," yelled a woman with equally fine skin. "Roystan's been set up. We won't stand by and let them take him away."

The mob pressed closer to the guards. "Open the doors."

The first guard raised her weapon higher. "Keep back or I'll shoot."

The alarms on the door behind them sounded. A long slow beep. Both guards glanced back.

Niall chuckled. "That Roystan. He's escaping. Open the door."

The guard raised her weapon and tightened her finger on the trigger.

Josune stunned her.

"Apologies for that," she said into the silence that followed. "She's only stunned, but she was going to fire." She looked at the other guard. "Drop your weapon."

The crowd parted before her, backing away.

"Drop your weapon," Josune said again.

The guard did. He moved away with the others. "It takes two of us with the door code, and you've dropped Pad here. You won't get in."

"Maybe not," Josune agreed. "Nika?"

Nika picked up the weapon.

Not that anyone was looking at the weapons. They stared at Josune and backed away, until they were stopped by the wall.

The woman next to Niall dropped to her knees to check the guard. "Stunned," she told the crowd. "She's fine."

"Lot of good that's going to do her if she catches a pox," a voice in the crowd said.

Pox? Nika glanced at Josune and grimaced. With her shedding skin and the distinctive pattern showing beneath the flakiness, who was to say what she had wasn't viral. She did look bad.

So too did the blood-rimmed lips.

Two residents broke from the back and ran.

Moments later, a siren blared, and a message was broadcast throughout the station. "Warning, contamination alert. Please stay in your area and remain there until the station has been cleansed."

The door behind the guards opened a sliver. Manually forced.

Niall lent his weight from his side while everyone else kept an eye on Josune. The fear was palpable.

Roystan came out first. He looked around, and his gaze passed over Josune and stopped at Nika. "Josune?"

Nika pointed to Josune.

"Josune? Are you sure?"

Nika nodded.

"But she doesn't look like—"

"It is me, Roystan," Josune said.

"You look . . . terrible. Your face. Are you . . . all right?"

Roystan certainly knew how to make a newly modded person feel bad.

"I'm fine. Itchy, but fine." Josune pointed to Pad's blaster on the floor beside her. "Get that so we can get going."

He took the weapon and looked at the downed guard. "Pad?"

"She's fine. Stunned."

"Thanks." He looked around at the crowd.

"They're here to rescue you," Nika said.

"Thank you." Roystan bowed at them, then turned to his fellow escapees. "Let's get out of here before we get these people into any trouble."

Jacques glared at Nika. "That's not Josune. You've left her in that machine. Unprotected."

"This is me, Jacques," Josune said. She turned to Carlos, who was looking equally dubious. "When the *Hassim* arrived I was curing the fly gear."

They didn't have time to stand around and talk while they debated if Josune was Josune or not. "Can we discuss this on the way?" Nika asked.

"What did you do to her?" Snow demanded.

"Got her out early." Snow's timing stank. "We'll talk about it when we're back on ship."

"Out, all of you," Josune said, aiming the order at Roystan.

He nodded. "Come on." He led the way.

"Move," Nika said. "Before they lock the station down for contamination."

"But she's not—"

"Later."

Roystan backed inside the door again, hands up, blaster facing up. Carlos and Jacques backed with him. Two company men followed them in. Blasters aimed. They both wore black pins.

Eaglehawk's thugs. They'd shoot straight and fast, and wouldn't miss.

Nika risked going close. She raised her voice to a screech and pointed at Josune. "Didn't you hear the contamination alert. Look at her. Keep away. Let us out of here."

The two men glanced over, then backed away without realizing they had done so. Nothing scared people in space more than an unchecked, unknown virus. It was enough. Josune took one out with her sparker, while Nika and Roystan took out the other.

Both company men still managed to fire, taking down the woman who'd checked the guard earlier and two others.

Nika hoped they would be all right. Doctor Jack was going to be busy.

Niall snatched up one of the blasters. "Get going," he told Roystan. "Or you'll never get away."

"Sorry about—"

"Go," Niall, Josune, and Nika said at the same time.

Roystan didn't linger.

"Go," Josune said to the others.

Carlos threw another dubious glance at Josune. Was he going to start arguing again?

"She's fine," Snow said, oppressively. "It's just a botched mod." And with a glare at Nika he grabbed Carlos with one hand, Jacques with the other, and ran.

He was an intriguing mix of young and sensible. You just couldn't tell when he'd be young, and when he'd be sensible.

"Thanks for your help," Josune said to Niall. "Appreciate it. Nika, go."

Nika paused. "Talk to Doctor Jack later," she said softly to Niall. "Tell him to read the machine. He'll tell you it's not—" She didn't need to state the obvious. "You'll be fine," she said, and raced out after the others.

17

JOSUNE ARRIOLA

Two corridors. Three. Roystan was ahead of her. At the next passage he paused, slowed.

He was going to wait for them. Josune waved him on. "Get ready to take off," she said, although she didn't think he heard her.

She waved him on again. "Call Snow," she ordered Nika. "Tell him Roystan has to keep moving. He needs to be ready to take off."

"I don't know Snow's ID."

It surprised Josune enough that she stumbled. A plasma bolt sailed over her head. That was worse than using a sparker on station. She swung around and fired the sparker in an arc. The resulting bang was deafening. The corridor went dark, and there was a strong smell of scorched plastic and hot metal.

The emergency lights came on.

"Run," Josune ordered Nika. "As fast as you can. Don't look back. Don't stop. Don't wait for me. If Roystan is stupid enough to wait, knock him out and drag him with you."

"And you?"

"I'll be right on your heels." But she'd glimpsed two company men before the lights went out. There would be more. How could she stop them?

They made it onto Spur Thirteen.

Roystan waited inside the huge breach door that separated the thirteenth arm from the central station. They had barely cleared the door before he thumped the emergency switch. The door slammed shut.

Any door into space could open if the electronics said it could, so there was always a manual override lock to prevent any accidental doors opening to deep space. The lock prevented the breach door from being opened. Roystan turned to the manual controls and broke the seal. He grunted as he turned the lock.

Josune moved over to help him. It was stiff, hadn't been serviced in years. She would have to fix that next time they were here. If they were welcome after today's fight. She was doubly glad, suddenly, of the extra airlock she'd installed. But that was why she had installed it, wasn't it? Because one day that breach door was going to break.

"Why aren't you on the ship? Ready to take off."

Roystan sagged against the door as the lock clicked into place. "No point." He wiped his forehead.

She was sweating as much as he was.

He pulled out his handheld, tapped, and brought up the image of near space on a nearby screen. Two ships hovered, each fifty-one kilometers from the station on opposite sides of *The Road*. Both were stationary.

Fifty kilometers was the minimum distance one could go without incurring landing fees.

These two ships didn't plan to land.

Roystan brought one of the ships into close visual. He overlaid infrared. Three hot spots jumped into focus. "Plasma cannons, primed, and ready to fire."

They surely were. Josune calculated the distances, as she was sure Roystan had already done. "They'll know as soon as we start our engines."

The Road would take time to come up to speed. They wouldn't be able to avoid either ship.

"We're safer staying on station," Roystan said. "Those two are already mobile. As soon as we take off, they'll shoot us."

They wouldn't kill them straightaway—at least not all of them—but they'd damage the ship so it couldn't fly, and once they'd done that, the crew of *The Road* would be at the company's mercy. Once the company got whatever it wanted from *The Road*—the *Hassim*'s memory or the knowledge Feyodor had been seeking—or found they didn't have it, they'd kill the crew. The same way they had slaughtered the crew on the *Hassim*.

They were dead if they stayed. They were dead if they left.

Thumping started on the other side of the breach door, near the manual lock. Then came the distinctive whine of a cutter. Their pursuers were pulling off panels, trying to reach the override.

Roystan fused the override lock on the airlock she'd installed. Josune smiled grimly. No one was going to bypass that. It gave them a second level of protection the company men wouldn't expect. They didn't know it was there.

Could they use it?

"How far out before we can nullspace?" she asked Roystan.

"A thousand kilometers."

They'd never do it. Not with two ships sitting fifty-one kilometers out. They had to get past those ships before their enemy realized *The Road* had moved. As soon as Roystan fired his rockets they'd know he was ready to move, and as soon as he moved away from the docking station they'd attack.

Fifty-one kilometers wasn't far.

What if the initial boost of speed didn't come from *The Road*?

What if Roystan didn't fire his rockets until after he passed the company ships?

What if he didn't move away from the docking station until after he'd passed them either?

The spur was weak, easy to break. Put some decent rockets between it and the station, and it would blast out a hundred kilometers before anyone realized what had happened. *The Road* could then fire its own rockets and split away, leaving the spur as protection between them and the company ships.

It would give them time. Not much, but it might be enough, and Roystan was an experienced pilot.

The airlock—her airlock—would give her time to blow the spur and get back onto the ship before *The Road* split.

Josune reached for her tools, then remembered she didn't have them.

"Lend me your handheld." When you didn't have a comms-link of your own, having someone who carried around a portable device was useful.

He handed it over.

"Carlos." Carlos was hovering at *The Road*'s entrance. "Bring me a toolkit. The one at the airlock there." Otherwise Carlos would run and get her own. He knew how particular she was about her tools. "And hurry."

"You think you can hit nullspace in under a minute?" she asked Roystan.

"Yes." No hesitation. "But they'll fry us long before that."

Josune smiled. She loved his confidence. And his realism. "Can you detach from the Hub in that same minute?"

He looked back to *The Road*. "There's an emergency detach. It takes twenty seconds. I could have Jacques or Carlos ready."

"Good." She looked at the spur and did a quick calculation. "How many rockets have we got?"

"Twenty." Roystan knew his cargo better than Jacques did.

Josune called Jacques. "Jacques, bring me ten rockets." She'd have preferred to use them all, to get more speed, but the company would be through the breach door long before she could set up all twenty.

She snatched the kit from Carlos and pulled out the Insta-Hold, the glue designed for emergency repairs. It set instantly and held everything.

She used Insta-Hold around the breach door.

"Like that's really going to stop them," Carlos said. "They've got a cutter."

"Sometimes an extra minute is all you need." She thought she'd get five.

"Carlos, take Snow and help Jacques with the rockets. We need them yesterday." She turned to Roystan and Nika. The modder had been silent throughout.

"I'm going to blow the spur off the station," Josune said. "They'll be watching your jets to see when you take off. The explosion will propel the spur away from the station. It will make *The Road* hard to control." She grimaced. "That can't be helped. Those ships out there will lose a minute while they try to work out what's happened. As soon as the spur is between you and the ships, you fire the jets and Jacques and I will push the emergency release. It won't give us much time, but it should be enough."

Roystan looked at Snow and Carlos, running out with the rockets. She saw the struggle on his face as he looked at her, and thought he was going to argue, but didn't. Instead, he clapped her on the shoulder.

"I like the way you think, Josune." His face was gray and shiny with a sweat that didn't go with the words. He nodded to Nika. "Let's get ready for the bumpiest ride of our life. I hope you haven't lost any of those calibrator skills. That gauge is going to swing."

Josune was glad he didn't argue. Roystan was the best pilot they had. If anyone could get them through this, he could. Each to the best of their abilities.

Roystan didn't go far. He came back with a space suit. "Suit up, Josune."

Josune opened her mouth to argue.

"No time to be stupid. Anything could go wrong. Let's cover all bases."

The suit would make things that much clumsier, but she put it on.

"Don't forget to show Jacques how to detach." The worst thing would be to do all this and then find they couldn't detach the spur before nullspacing. They couldn't nullspace with the spur attached to *The Road*. The flexible corridor would whip all over the place, turning their ship into a tumbling, out-of-control nightmare. The stresses from the whiplash would pull the ship apart.

"Will do," she said, but she hardly heard him. There were so many other things to do.

"Snow, can you work the cannon?"

"Sure. Turn it on now?" Snow asked. "The heat signature."

"Good thought. Wait until we start moving." If the company ships had any weapons detection system at all—and it would—they'd recognize the cannon as soon as it came on. They'd react to that.

A minute wasn't enough to warm a cannon properly, but it would make them pause. Maybe long enough to nullspace without needing to fire the thing.

She didn't watch them go. Rockets next.

Roystan's voice came through on the communicator. "Nika and I are on the bridge. Ready when you are."

"I'll let you know the moment I'm inside."

She set the rockets with speed. This was practical engineering. Velocities, force, mass, trajectories. She'd used rockets before. Never to tear two pieces of metal apart, but the physics was sound.

The insistent whine of the cutter added a high-pitched urgency to her work. She kept an ear out for it, for when it stopped it meant they had broken through into the controls. Then she'd only have the precious minutes afforded by the Insta-Hold to trigger the rockets.

The breach door was a buffer between the spur and the station. If the spur broke away, the door would close. Josune's airlock would seal the air in the passageway up to the ship. If the door was forced open before the spur broke away, she'd kill everyone in that part of the station.

Which would have been fine if it had just been company men, but it wasn't.

The cutter stopped. Seven rockets set and she was out of time.

It would have to be enough.

Josune ducked inside her airlock and closed it. "Triggering the rockets in . . ." She watched the lights on the door. "Three. Two. One."

The force from the blast knocked her off her feet. She bounced against the airlock she'd just closed.

She struggled to her feet against the pressure of the acceleration, and ran for *The Road*. It was like trying to run uphill against a strong gale.

The whine of the plasma cannon warming up was comforting in her ears. Snow was fast, or cocky, or both. She smiled grimly.

The company wouldn't be expecting plasma. It would make them pause.

"Hurry up," Jacques called.

She made it, although she wasn't sure she would.

"You took your time."

"You try running against an acceleration like that. In a suit." She could hardly get the words out. But she was glad to be inside. "Ready to disconnect from the spur," she told Roystan, through the link, as Jacques closed the airlock.

Did he even understand what she'd said?

"Jets ready."

"Do your thing, Jacques."

Jacques pulled the emergency bar down.

Nothing happened.

Jacques stared at the handle.

"Jets ready," Roystan said again.

If Roystan didn't fire his jets in the next minute they'd lose their window to escape.

"The disengage is sticking," Josune said. "Fire anyway, Roystan. I'll clear it while you're accelerating." She couldn't clear it from here, but Roystan didn't have to know that. She'd have to go outside the airlock to do it. "It'll be rocky for a minute."

The spur was bucking under the combined forces of the rockets, each component reacting to its own forces and stresses. If she didn't get out there and clear it, the oscillations would tear the ship apart before they could nullspace.

"But how—"

The distinctive crackle of a plasma burn hit the side of the ship. Lights went out. Emergency lighting came on.

"Fire those damn jets."

Josune pulled the handle up. "I'll have to go out to reset it," she told Jacques. "As soon as I give the word, you pull that handle. Understand?"

He nodded.

She recycled the airlock and was glad of the battery backup, for they had no power to this part of the ship.

The oscillations were making her giddy. She swallowed the reflux and kept her mouth shut so she wouldn't lose the contents of her stomach.

Through the speaker helmet she heard Roystan, talking to his ship. "Come on, girl, you can do this."

At least, she thought he was talking to the ship.

The twisting spur knocked her off her feet. She rolled partway down the passageway before she righted herself, and finally thought to turn on the magnets in her boots to stop flying any farther.

Too much precious time lost.

"What's keeping you?" Jacques demanded.

She inched back to the airlock, one hard-won meter at a time.

"Josune."

She almost didn't recognize it as Jacques's voice.

"It's rocky out here."

She heard the distinctive splat of fire from a plasma cannon hitting the ship. She imagined she could smell the nose-searing plasma burn, even though she knew she couldn't.

"Josune!"

"Got it." The latch had hooked. She hammered it up, clumsy in the suit, but she had enough grip on the wrench to apply the pressure required. A pity she didn't have her own suit. The tools were built in on that.

The latch sprang free.

Tearing part of the outer metal of the airlock away with it.

Josune reached for the emergency foam in the suit to plug the hole. It was instinct, because the last thing she needed to do was add in any way to what was keeping the spur attached to the ship. "Jacques. Pull the release. Now."

If she opened the airlock she'd kill Jacques, who wasn't wearing a suit, and Snow and Carlos, for they were in the same section of the ship. No one had time to suit up.

She might as well already have been in the deep of space. She was so cold. But she'd calmed now, an icy calm that matched the imaginary ice creeping into her fingers and toes.

She opened a channel to Roystan, trying not to think about what she was about to do. "Start the nullspace sequence. Jacques will disconnect in a moment."

"I have never been so glad to." Roystan sounded as if his teeth were gritted.

Josune smiled. "You're the best pilot I know." She cut him off when she heard the nullspace alarm. "Jacques. Come on. Push that release down. Now. Otherwise everyone will die."

Snow and Carlos whooped in her other ear.

"Got him," Carlos crowed.

Roystan was a good pilot. He'd keep the others alive.

Silence from inside.

"Jacques," Josune said. "The airlock's damaged. I can't get back in. Everyone will die if you don't pull that lever down."

More silence.

Josune silently counted down with the nullspace alert. Twelve. Eleven. Ten.

In the short time she had left of her own life, what could she do to help the others stay alive?

"Jacques. Put on a suit. Don't open the airlock until everyone is in suits. Tell Carlos the outer airlock door is gone. He'll know what to do. Just press that damn lever down."

18

NIKA RIK TERRI

A splat vibrated through Nika's body. An electrical pulse, but it sounded like someone slinging mud against the side of the ship. Was that even possible in space?

Ship metal screamed and an acrid odor filled the bridge.

Light blossomed on the screen in front of them.

Snow, breathless. "We hit one. I can't tell the damage."

"Start the nullspace sequence. Jacques will disconnect in a moment," Josune said over the link.

"Thank God," Roystan muttered, and reached for the nullspacer controls. "I have never been so glad to enter nullspace. Ready, Nika?"

"Wait." It was Jacques, so panicked Nika didn't recognize his voice for a moment. "Josune lied. She's still outside."

Roystan's hands hovered over the nullspacer.

"Roystan," Josune said through the link. "If you don't jump, you'll kill everyone on the ship. I'm in the spur. I'm safe."

The countdown behind them continued. "Eight. Seven."

Another splat against the side of the ship. The other side this time. More metal screamed. The pulse went through their bodies again. What sort of damage did a pulse like that do to human cells?

"That was close to me." Josune sounded calm. "They're strafing, and they'll hit the spur next. That *will* kill me. Don't hang around and get everyone else killed as well."

"Three. Two."

"You're cutting it close."

"Jacques. Do not. I repeat, do not push that lever." Roystan shoved the controls down.

Nika kept the calibrator right on the line.

Nullspace rippled, with the usual mind-numbing colors that your brain couldn't get around. But this time they tumbled end over end, until even the calibrator became a crazy kaleidoscope of colors. Nika focused on the line. Narrowed her gaze until there was nothing but the line. Until finally she couldn't even do that.

19

JOSUNE ARRIOLA

Josune was flung around the spur. End over end over end.

Roystan had nullspaced. Thank God for that, but Jacques hadn't disengaged the spur. Roystan had no control over the ship. Nika wouldn't be able to calibrate. Who knew where they'd come out? Who knew what they'd hit when they did come out?

She hit the wall of the Hub again. The twelfth time. Not that she was counting, but her suit was.

"Tear in the left sleeve," the suit told her.

In the psychedelia of nullspace she didn't even understand what it had said, but her subconscious did. She increased the magnet strength in her boots and latched on to the nearest metallic surface. She'd repaired the suit before she realized she'd done it.

They exited nullspace. From her position of relative safety against the wall, she could see that the spur was hanging on only by the lock Jacques hadn't released. He should have. It would shear off soon, and the resulting loss of force would send *The Road* far, far out of reach. A body in space was tiny. Impossible to find.

No time to think.

She fired her jets.

And prayed to any gods who might be listening as she moved with speed toward *The Road*.

The spur broke away.

The ship accelerated.

Josune increased her jets to full power.

She wouldn't catch it.

20

NIKA RIK TERRI

They came out of nullspace.

A grinding sound could be heard over the whole ship. Then the ship ride smoothed.

"No." A cry from Roystan. His fingers flew over the boards. There was a flash of orange, followed by a reverse thrust so hard it pushed Nika back into her seat. Another orange flash.

She kept the calibrator steady, not even sure if he wanted that or not.

Reverse. Forward. Reverse. Forward. Each one pushing her back into the chair. Then releasing the pressure so she was almost floating. Less and less each time, until she could feel the pattern of the thrusts.

Roystan was piloting by feel—and maybe instinct—for there was no way he could have calculated what he did. Or waited for the ship to calculate it for him.

Eventually the ship stopped. As stationary as a ship this size ever could be in space when it wasn't tethered to a larger object.

Roystan stood up. Grabbed a bag out of a locker on the side of the console. Threw up into it.

Nika put a hand to her own mouth, stifling the gag reflex and her body's memory of the gyrations it had just been through.

He handed her another bag, one-handed.

She took it, but the urge had subsided.

Roystan wiped his face. "Sorry." His eyes were bruised black holes in a skeletal face. He zipped his own bag.

She tried not to look at it.

Roystan opened the communications channel. "How is everyone?"

Snow's voice was shaky. "Carlos is banged up a little. Concussion, but otherwise fine."

"And you?" Nika asked.

"Me?"

"Yes, Snow. You. Clinical assessment." Otherwise he would gloss over any problems. She needed to know he was all right.

"I'm not a doctor." But he gave an honest assessment. "Bruised. My left elbow is swollen. Twisted, and the bone chipped. Emotionally shaken, but I should be fine."

He might not be a doctor, but he sounded like one. A good one.

Roystan sighed. "The young. They bounce back from everything." He turned back to the link. "Jacques?"

There was no answer.

"Jacques."

Roystan pressed a series of buttons, and there was another orange flash.

"Markers," he told her, although she hadn't asked. "Not that it's going to help. We've a million square kilometers of space to search. It's as close as I can estimate to where we parted ways with the spur, but the spur is nowhere in sight. A human body is tiny, compared." His voice broke on the last word.

Roystan would find her. Nika was sure of that. Whether she'd be alive when they did was an entirely different question.

Roystan choked off a sound that might have been a sob. He made for the door. Nika followed, trying not to think. Josune had been the closest thing to a friend she'd had in a long time.

21

JOSUNE ARRIOLA

The Road accelerated away.

Josune would never catch it. She looked back toward the spur, so far behind her now she couldn't see it.

She was here, alone in space, with—she checked the suit stats—fourteen and a half hours of air left, and a ratty suit communicator with a range of only 3.6 kilometers.

Being out in space had never bothered her before.

Now it was just her and black, empty, lonely nothing. Except for the stars, which were bright points of light wherever she looked. But oh so far away.

She was in an open-air coffin.

And she had fourteen and a half hours to contemplate her future. Or lack of.

Her shipmates had gone, long before her. The *Hassim*, the ship she had called home for more than ten years, was gone. *The Road* was gone. Roystan was gone.

She was alone.

Josune switched on the suit emergency beacon.

Nothing happened.

She looked down at the arm of her suit. The distress beacon was smashed.

She closed her eyes momentarily, took time to savor the fact that she could. At least if she was to die she'd do it with two functioning eyes. So the old-fashioned way. Through the link then.

Where the signal would travel all of 3.6 kilometers.

Roystan would come back for her. There was comfort in knowing he would. But he would be too late. He had a million square kilometers of space to search. How likely was he to get within three kilometers of her? And if by some miracle he did, she had to know he was there, for she couldn't keep up a manual send for the full fourteen and a half hours.

She cut the suit jets. No point in wasting what little fuel she had.

The suit continued on, following the trajectory her initial burn had set. It was as good as any other path. She imagined she could still see the yellow burn of *The Road*'s jets as they cooled. Which was impossible, of course.

But she could.

The ship was coming back.

She stared at it for long, wasteful seconds. Impossible. And yet not.

It wasn't coming back on the same path. No one was that good a pilot, but it was close, spatially speaking. Nika and Roystan, between them, made a perfect team. Josune kicked her jets on.

She'd only get one chance at this.

Her distress beacon might not be working, but the homing guide was. She set it to the ship, coming up faster than she wanted it, and let the automatics do the rest. They would take her home.

She hit the ship hard.

Her chin went down onto the suit communicator. She heard something crunch, loud in her ears, thought she'd broken her jaw. Realized after a second she'd broken her communicator.

She blacked out.

22

NIKA RIK TERRI

They found Jacques curled up on the floor. Bleeding, but not badly. Bruised, but not broken. The cacophony of alarms around him was deafening.

He rolled away when Roystan and Nika knelt beside him. "She said she couldn't get back in."

Nika could hardly hear him above the noise. She checked him over, trying to make it as professional as Snow might, although her hands were shaking.

Jacques covered his eyes with his arm. "She told me not to open the door."

Roystan stood up and turned off three of the alarms. He looked around, his eyes scanning the docking area, a hand to his mouth. For a moment Nika thought he was going to throw up again.

There was a groan from behind. She turned. Snow, with an arm around Carlos. Shuffling, weaving. Neither of them steady. Snow held his left arm awkwardly, but otherwise his analysis of his own wounds seemed to have been accurate. Nika expelled a breath she hadn't realized she was holding. Snow was fine.

Roystan circled the area. Looking. Not touching. He didn't say anything. Nika thought he might have struggled if he had tried to speak.

"She said it would kill us all," Jacques whispered as Carlos and Snow reached them.

Roystan bent to inspect the airlock. He opened the cupboard marked *Emergency Repair Kit*.

It was empty.

Carlos staggered. "Gave it to Josune. Remember?" His voice was slurred.

Roystan nodded and walked silently down the passageway. They stared after him. No one spoke.

When he came back, he had a repair kit in his hands and his voice was normal. "There's foam on the door. She repaired it."

Nika looked closely at the airlock door.

There was foam. Two tiny hardened tendrils, where it had forced itself through the door and hardened.

Carlos went whiter than he already was. Nika hadn't thought that possible. "If the foam came through this far—" He didn't finish, but Roystan nodded, grimly, at what he didn't say.

"I'll get a suit."

"No." Snow and Roystan said it at the same time.

"You're concussed," Snow added.

"There's a massive hole out there. Someone has to fix it."

"I'll do it." Roystan looked at Jacques. Then at Snow and Nika. "I'll need help."

Nika nodded.

"I'll do it," Snow said. "Nika's probably never been out in a space suit before."

Which she hadn't. "What can I do while you're doing that?"

Roystan looked at Jacques.

Nika nodded. She watched Roystan and Snow suit up before turning to Carlos first. "Let's get you to bed."

"I need to check the rest of the ship."

"Can't it wait?"

"We were hit twice." Carlos wove his way across the width of the passageway. "Josune would check it."

Josune would have, too.

"Jacques," Nika said quietly. "He's too heavy for me on my own."

Jacques dragged himself up and moved to Carlos's right side. She moved to his left.

"I can check the ship for you, if you tell me what to look for."

"I need to check—"

"Even I can check oxygen and temperature from a control panel. You're not going to let a mere modder beat you at that, are you?"

"I know what you're doing." Carlos staggered to the left, into Nika. "I can see."

"Well then, you can see that I'm doing what needs to be done. The sooner we have you sitting down, the better. You can use machines to do the initial testing, surely."

"Of course I can."

"Then tell me or Jacques where to go to look at any problems."

"I'd rather have Snow. At least he'd recognize the problem."

"You don't have Snow. You have us."

With Carlos ensconced in the crew room, Jacques made for the galley.

"Let him go," Carlos said, putting a hand out to Nika when she went to stop him. "He's stressed."

"So tell me what you want me to do."

"Give me time." Carlos tried four times to pull up screens.

Nika bit down on the knuckles of her right hand, so she wouldn't tell him to hurry. The ship could be falling apart while he was fumbling around. Probably was. Something was tap-tap-tapping over her head and Carlos hadn't noticed it. Neither had Jacques.

"Temperature in the cargo bay is down," Carlos said. "I need you to look at that. Take some oxygen."

"Oxygen?"

He looked at her. "You really don't know?"

If she'd known, she wouldn't have asked, would she?

Carlos saw her face and stood up. He went to the nearest cupboard marked *Emergency* and took out an oxygen bottle and a face mask. "Technically you should suit up. But I bet you don't know how to suit up, do you?"

She shook her head.

Carlos sighed. Long and dramatic. "Save us all." He held up the mask. Put it over his face. Flicked a button on the cylinder. He switched it off and took the mask away. "If you can't breathe, put this over your face. Then get out of wherever you are."

"Understood."

"And if you find you're freezing cold, get the hell out of there as well."

She took the oxygen and the mask. "Shouldn't we be fixing the things we know are broken first? Like whatever's causing that tapping." It sounded like a sail flapping in the wind.

"What tapping?"

"That tapping." But the tapping had stopped. "It was there a minute ago."

"You're imagining things."

The tapping started again. *Tap. Tap-tap. Tap-tap-tap.*

Tap-tap-tap-tap. Pause. *Tap-tap-tap-tap-tap.*

"Counting," Carlos whispered.

Jacques came out of the galley to listen.

"How do we contact Roystan?" Nika asked. No one else was moving.

"His handheld," Jacques said.

"No," Carlos said. "Ship suit. He gave the handheld to Josune." He brought the link up on the screen, the view from one of the suits. "Roystan. You out there?"

Roystan grunted. It was Snow who answered. "He's busy right now. What do you want? He'll hear you."

"Where are you?"

"Airlock." Roystan sounded as if he was gritting his teeth. "Hold. There. Perfect."

"Both of you?"

The suit view stopped on a sheet of what looked like plastic, or maybe metal. "Why do you ask?"

The sheet floated up, and away. Someone, probably Roystan, snagged it.

Carlos was silent a moment.

Snow swam into Roystan's view. Gestured. Roystan nodded. "More to the left," he said, and lifted a screwdriver attached to his arm. "Why did you ask, Carlos?"

Carlos waited until he'd finished fastening the bolt. "There's a noise—" He hesitated.

"Sounds like someone's up there," Nika said, because Carlos was never going to get to the point. "They're tapping. Counting."

Roystan screwed in another bolt. "Up where?"

"Above us. Above the crew room." But it couldn't be, could it, for the crew room was in the center of the ship. "They're inside." They had to be.

"Not necessarily." Roystan screwed in another bolt with maddening slowness. "Seal the edges," he told Snow.

Nika almost didn't recognize his voice. She saw, through the display coming from the helmet camera, that his hand was shaking as he screwed the next two bolts in.

"I'll check it as soon as I can."

One last bolt. Roystan watched Snow seal the patch.

"Where should we start, Carlos?" Nika wanted a weapon. A blaster, or even Josune's sparker. No matter what damage the sparker did.

"The overhead compartment?" Carlos suggested. "There's a cabling duct up there. You have to crawl, but if it's big enough to fit—"

Roystan said, "Some of the cables lead outside. If anyone knew that, they could use it to get your attention." He held out an arm to Snow. "Latch on to me." And Snow had only just latched on before Roystan fired his rockets.

His voice still didn't sound like him.

Tap. Pause. *Tap-tap.*

Roystan and Snow sped around the ship so quickly Nika's stomach flopped just watching.

Roystan fired the brakes before he even came up on the final curve. Before he could see.

Before they could see through the camera on his suit.

A space-suited figure. Twisted awkwardly out of place. One leg free in space, the other trapped in what looked to be a hole in the side of the ship.

Roystan came to a stop in front of the figure.

Josune.

They didn't see much from Roystan's suit camera. Didn't hear anything either. Roystan wasn't talking. He and Josune had a silent conversation. Josune pointed down. Roystan's suit camera bobbed up and down in a nod.

"What's going on?" Carlos demanded.

No one answered him.

Nika wiped away tears she hadn't known she was spilling. "Do you have another camera out there?" She sent a prayer of thanks to any god who was listening. Things like this didn't happen. Not in real life.

"No."

Roystan indicated to Snow, who nodded. It was impossible to see what he was thinking inside his suit.

Roystan's suit moved close to Josune's. The drill came out. Or was it a blade? He cut carefully around the metal of the ship. Josune pulled her leg away, bringing the cut-away metal with her.

Snow used sealant around the metal on her suit leg.

Roystan raised the other arm of his suit and sprayed out something into the side of the ship. It foamed up and hardened instantly, filling the hole he'd made.

"Where will they come in?" Nika asked.

"The airlock," Carlos said. "Roystan finished that repair first. Get down there. I'll keep watch."

Jacques hadn't waited. Nika arrived as the door started to open.

Roystan and Snow shed their suits, then turned to help Josune out of hers. Afterward, Roystan hesitated, as if he'd forgotten what he had to say.

Josune put a hand to his shoulder, briefly. "Thanks."

Why didn't they just hug each other and be done with the awkwardness?

Josune limped over to Jacques. She did hug him. "I'm sorry I put you through that, Jacques."

He hugged her back. Hard.

Nika, standing behind Jacques, saw the agony Josune bit down. Cracked ribs, at a guess. And a mildly sprained ankle, for she could still walk on it.

Jacques pushed her away. "I've got flatbread in the oven." He looked at Roystan, who looked in worse shape than Josune. "Bring her down to the crew room."

Roystan nodded.

Jacques left.

Nika looked around. They were in the cargo bay. There'd be a medical kit here. There was. She moved over to check the supplies.

"Bandages," she told Snow. "Painkillers. Nerveseal." She pulled it out. "You'll need to renew your medical supplies," she told Roystan. To Josune, she said, "Let me see your ribs."

Josune started to lift her tunic, then stopped. "I can't do this right now."

Nika turned back to the medical cupboard for the scissors she'd seen.

Josune winced as she cut it away. "My favorite top," she told Roystan, who hadn't said a word.

"We'll get you another one." He bit at his bottom lip, but it seemed to have broken the silence. "What happened out there?"

Josune's ribs were red. Whatever she'd hit, she'd hit it hard. She'd be bruised tomorrow. Nika ran careful fingers over them. "Sorry about the pain, but I have to know if you have any broken ribs."

She couldn't feel any bones jutting out. "We'll put you under the Dekker to be sure, but I think they're only cracked." She looked at Snow. "What about her ankle?"

"Sprained. But Nika, the Dekker doesn't calibrate. And we don't have supplies."

"We can still diagnose." She'd repaired the broken diagnostics on the way to Atalante. She sprayed nerveseal onto Josune's chest.

Josune hissed with pleasure. "That feels so good."

Or didn't feel, in this case. Nika, having recently been on the receiving end of nerveseal herself, could imagine the relief it would be.

Snow bandaged Josune's ankle silently. Roystan checked his own suit and Snow's, and refilled the oxygen tanks.

"Try to breathe properly," Nika told Josune. "Real breaths, not shallow ones. Even if it hurts."

She checked the medical cupboard again and found some anti-inflammatory pills, which she handed to Josune. "Take two of these when the pain gets too much. No more than two every three hours."

Josune nodded. She looked at the last suit. Her own. "Put that one in engineering. I'll see if I can fix it."

Roystan put the two good suits into a locker. He took the damaged one out with him, and came back sans the suit, but with a front-buttoning shirt over his arm. "Arms down and a little back, if you can. One at a time."

Josune stretched her arms out with a sigh. "You know exactly what I need, Roystan."

Roystan carefully pulled the sleeves up over her arms. The shirt was long and loose. Not Josune's size. Roystan's.

Josune hobbled out of the cargo hold, favoring her sprained ankle. "The lock didn't disengage properly." She finally answered Roystan's question.

Roystan gently caught her elbow. "Lean on me when you put your foot down."

Nika smiled at the two of them. Serious, focused, each deliberately not concentrating on the other.

"I had to go back into the spur to release it."

"You should have left it."

"The oscillations would have torn us apart."

Roystan nodded.

"I cleared it, but the oscillations had already damaged the airlock. I couldn't get back in." She stepped down harder than she'd meant to. Grunted. Cut it off. "You should have made Jacques disengage."

"Humans can't nullspace outside a ship." Roystan managed to smile, at last. "Or some sort of container."

Like the spur of a station.

"Well, I appreciated that you didn't disengage. But the damn thing broke away anyway. All I could see was *The Road* disappearing into deep space."

"It must have been bad."

Josune patted his arm. "For a few minutes, it was. But you came back." She looked from Nika to Roystan. "That was the most beautiful piece of piloting I ever saw."

"Nika calibrates with a steady hand. I probably shouldn't admit this, but maybe better than a machine, even. She anticipates."

Which machines could never do. They could only respond, and anticipation was responding to a different set of stimuli.

"I hit pretty hard," Josune said. "I couldn't move, and my suit was damaged. Otherwise I would have waited at the airlock. I knew someone would be out to look at it."

"What about linking in?"

"Suit link was broken. I lost your handheld at the spur. And my eye link was gone." She shivered. "That bit was horrible, actually. To be so close and unable to do anything. Until I remembered the cables to the antennae, and I knew you would hear it in the crew room."

They gathered in the crew room. Jacques served them a thin grain porridge, or it might have been soup. It was delicious. Roystan had his own version, which looked like slimy gruel. The smell of it turned Nika's stomach.

Roystan ate it with enthusiasm.

Carlos saw her looking. "That's Roystan's special porridge. It's awful."

Jacques deposited a plate of bread and two bowls of dipping sauce onto the table.

Carlos took a piece of bread in each hand and dipped one in each bowl. "This is good," he told Nika and Snow. "Try it."

"Not you." Jacques reached out to rap Roystan on the knuckles as he reached across for a piece. "You know your stomach won't take it."

Nika took a piece of bread. "We have the Dekker here. After we've checked Josune, why don't I check you as well, Roystan? Maybe we can work out what to do about your weak stomach."

"Don't waste it on me, Nika. When you're settled in your new place, I'll come and visit and you can go over me with as much detail as you like. Until then, I'll wait."

Nika chewed thoughtfully. Roystan was hiding something.

23

NIKA RIK TERRI

The diagnostics on the Dekker proved what Nika knew already. Josune had three cracked ribs and massive bruising. Her ankle was sprained, but not broken. She was still shedding skin, but the Dekker confirmed it was mostly dead topical layer, and that the skin underneath was good.

The pink and red patterning was barely visible yet beneath the flaking skin. The final look would be amazing, nothing like someone who'd come out of a Dietel. She neatened Josune's hair with the scissors from the first-aid kit. The layering suited her. Maybe Nika should have stayed with color for her own new-season look.

"There's not much we can do for you until we get you to a machine with a calibrator."

After that, Josune insisted on checking the ship.

Roystan sighed. "Why don't Snow and I inspect the lower deck and work up. Josune, take Nika as a helper. You can start at the top and work down. We'll go prow to bow, starboard side. The top and bottom decks are most likely to be damaged."

He'd very neatly gotten out of his own diagnosis, Nika noticed.

"Roystan's digestion is a worry," she said now, as she waited for Josune to—carefully—buckle on her tool belt. "How long has it been like that?"

Most of Josune's attention was on her belt. "I don't know. I haven't been crew long. To be honest, I thought it was Jacques justifying his existence in the galley, rather than in the cargo hold. Pol did most of the cargo work." Josune stopped to look up at the overhead compartment. "That's why she had access to the accounts." She frowned, looked around, then called Roystan.

She used an old handheld Roystan had dug out from Nika-didn't-know-where. Roystan had found one for himself, too.

"Are you using the welder or the foam?"

"A problem?"

"Not sure. Looks like we got hit by a plasma bolt."

Nika would have said two or three.

"We'll bring it up for you."

"Thanks." She clicked off.

"So how long had you been with the crew?" Nika asked. This was the sort of ship where "not long" was probably two years. Surely Josune would have noticed something about Roystan's eating habits in that time.

"Six weeks."

That short. "You're very comfortable with a captain you've only known six weeks."

Josune smiled. "Comfortable." It was soft, affectionate. "That's what he is. But not just comfortable, Nika. He's competent. He does what needs to be done, things other people only think about, might even balk at."

"Such as?"

Josune smiled again. "He's practical. He's full of surprises. He hoards obscure information that nobody thinks about."

Her non-answer was an answer itself. Roystan's choice to ignore Banjo when they'd first met at Snow's studio showed how practical he could be.

"Jacques feeds him well."

"We're not complaining."

Yet while everyone else on ship showed the effects of all that food, Roystan himself looked malnourished. And he'd been treated with hu-skin for blaster burns, when there were cheaper and more effective methods.

Skin that didn't take. A stomach that didn't digest well, especially after stress.

Nika didn't like the conclusions she was drawing.

A botched mod.

Sometime in the past, Roystan had gone into a modder's studio and come out damaged.

24

JOSUNE ARRIOLA

The plasma cannon hadn't been damaged, which was a tribute to Roystan and Snow's foresight in not turning it on until the last minute, for it was the first thing an enemy aimed for. Unfortunately, that was the only thing that was okay.

"The area surrounding the cannon is so brittle that if we fire it the housing will shatter," Josune reported to Roystan. "It will be the last shot we make with it."

"Told you we didn't need another hole in the ship," Carlos muttered.

"Put a patch over the area," Roystan said.

Josune agreed, although she would have liked more than a one-shot working cannon. What other weapons did they have?

Three havoc bombs.

A two-shot cannon was better than one, and if she put a bomb on the outside of the cannon she could send it on its way fast, using the handheld. No one would know it was coming.

Provided they didn't fire the cannon before she sent the bomb on its way.

With Carlos's help, she made up a quick, airtight panel from what they had in the workshop. They'd need a second one for the outside.

Roystan and Snow put it up, and she was glad of that. But she insisted on inspecting the outside damage herself. She had to, unless she asked Roystan to set the bomb.

He'd say no.

"You can't," Roystan said. "You've cracked ribs, a sprained ankle, and you've just got your eye back."

"Plus, you've some sort of flaking disease," Carlos said. "You're a walking hospital case."

"Her healing was incomplete," Snow said repressively, with a side glare at Nika. "She was brought out early. Something no registered modder would do to a client."

"I'm fine." Josune's ribs hurt, but she didn't plan to sit around and wait to be attacked.

Roystan looked at Nika.

The modder was watching Josune. *Please let her understand she needed to do this.*

Nika nodded. "She's not fine. As you say, she has cracked ribs and a sprained ankle. Both of which happened *after* the mod. The mod, that part's fine."

"Botched mods," Snow muttered. "She takes risks. Stupid risks. They both do."

"Josune's mod is *not* botched." Nika sounded exasperated. "Her skin will clear up in a week. Sooner if I could get her into a machine. Can't you see the pattern coming out? Does it look botched? It's the outer skin shedding. Don't tell me you don't recognize it as dead skin, because I will not believe you."

She turned to Roystan. "There are calculated risks and there are foolish ones. Josune knows her body's limits."

Thank goodness for Nika, who understood.

"If you're worried about her flaking skin, don't be. Snow still has things to learn."

Josune bit her lip at Snow's outraged expression, determined not to laugh. She turned away, only to have Roystan corner her.

He pitched his voice low. "Josune. You wouldn't send a crew member out in your state."

She had to set the havoc bomb. Otherwise they had almost no

weapons. "If I don't go out again, I'll lose my nerve." She hated misleading him. She just hoped her words weren't prophetic.

Even Roystan couldn't argue against that.

A plasma cannon did a lot of damage. Luckily for *The Road*, this particular hit had melted the metal onto the ship frame, rather than sheared it off. Luckily also, they had good shielding. Otherwise they'd be looking at a massive hole right now.

Unluckily for them, that made it harder to repair. She had planned on removing the damaged panel, replacing the wires underneath it, and welding the new one back over the old.

"It's a mess, Carlos," Josune told the other engineer, through the link.

"I didn't need to hear that."

Snow swam past her with a grace that said he'd spent time in freefall before. She felt his boots click on to the outer hull. Good. He knew what he was doing.

"The panels won't work." Better to spray the whole thing with foam and take the ship in for repair. Foam didn't last long in the brittle cold of space. It was emergency use only. "You ever done a foam repair?" she asked Snow.

"No," Carlos said through the link. "Please tell me we can fix it, Josune."

"You won't fix this without a shipyard and a workshop."

"How bad is it?" Roystan asked.

"It's slag. The panels have melded to the frame. You're not going anywhere, except heading in for repairs."

She could imagine Roystan's anguish from the silence. "I'll get Snow to start spraying while I patch what electronics I can." She surveyed the molten mess. "I'm not sure what we can rescue."

Snow was competent in a suit, but not confident around repairs.

She should have brought Nika, who might not have worn a suit before but certainly knew her engineering.

"What sort of training do you get repairing genemod machines, Snow?" She'd brought out two cameras to replace the ones they'd lost. She moved back to the nearest working camera to get a connection.

"Training?" Snow looked up, his helmet a blank mask.

"Fixing them. Modifying them. Nika has had some experience."

He went back to spraying foam. "That's because she does things a legal modder wouldn't."

Did he remember that Nika was listening to this conversation?

Josune taped the camera down carefully. If she knocked against the slag, the metal would break off.

"They teach you to call a technician," Nika said, through the link.

"As we should. We're modders, not engineers."

Josune heard Nika's sigh. "Snow. There are good and bad technicians, just as there are good and bad modders. What do you do if you get a bad one?"

"Technician? Or modder?"

"Both."

Snow sprayed foam with an intensity that said he didn't like the question. Josune pointed out where the foam was thin. It was better to use too much foam than too little. Although it was a long time since she'd been on a ship where you had to count the cost of supplies.

"A technician," Snow said, eventually. "You find another one next time you're on station."

"And the modder?"

"You sue them."

Nika's voice was soft, not meant for over the channel. "Did you sue your modder?"

There was no answer, but she could only have been talking to Roystan. It was an interesting question to ask. As if she assumed automatically that Roystan would have needed to sue his modder at one time.

"I'd be tempted to do it the other way around," Nika said. "But you need to know how to fix things, Snow. How else will you know what the end mod will be?"

"You do a design."

"You tell me a design will come out the same on your Netanyu as it will on a Songyan."

"Well, no. But it will be mostly the same."

"So you don't need a Songyan, then. You can stick with the Netanyu."

"But a Songyan gives you more control."

"You said it didn't make any difference."

"It has more outlets. It's more precise. With a Songyan, you control flows down to fractions of a milliliter."

"You said it was all in the design."

Josune had a private bet with herself. By the time these two left *The Road*, Snow would be Nika's apprentice. He was in everything but name now.

"Nika, sometimes your work is only as good as your tools."

"Exactly," Nika said. "Jacques might not have the best knives in the galaxy, but I bet he knows how to keep them sharp."

"My knives *are* the best in the galaxy."

Snow threw up his hands, knocking the canister. He had to swim after it to collect it. "What do Jacques's knives have to do with it?"

"They're tools, Snow. You are only as good as the tools you have. You need to keep them honed. Not rely on someone else to do it. I bet Jacques doesn't wait for someone else to sharpen his knives for him."

"Of course not. They'd be blunt."

Snow's shrug was evident in the slight lift of his suit. His voice was a mutter. "I'd still get a technician to service my machine. *Especially* if I had a Songyan. If you service one of their machines yourself it goes out of warranty."

He sprayed more foam. Nothing came out of the canister. Empty.

Josune's first camera was ready. She pulled out the havoc bomb. "You ever use one of these, Snow?"

He shook his head. But he recognized it, she could see that from the way he stilled.

She clipped it to the front of the cannon and set the mechanism to target and release at an order from her handheld.

"You're insane. That's . . . Why?"

"Insurance. Don't fire the cannon unless I say so. And make sure no one else does either." She opened her link to Carlos. "Let's test this camera, and then I'll bring the panel back in. It's useless. We need more foam."

"Sure. Camera panning now. Full control in engineering."

She hoped he wasn't too concussed to check properly. "What about you, Roystan? Do you have full control from the bridge?"

"Fine control here." Then Roystan stopped, panned back, and zoomed in. A speck grew larger.

"There's a ship out there."

Carlos laughed. "Here? At the ass end of nowhere?" A pause. "You didn't jump us into a shipping lane, did you, Roystan?"

"No. I jumped to the Outer Pamirs. They have a cargo delivery twice a year." A pause. "The next one's due in two months, and we are where we're meant to be."

Josune couldn't see a ship yet, but she saw the dark space it made against the stars.

"They're not answering any messages," Roystan said.

If they were close enough for *The Road* to see, they were close enough to answer messages.

"Salvage?" Carlos asked, but not in an enthusiastic way. "I mean. If they're not answering."

Roystan's cheery "We're all allergic to salvage at the moment" cut through the awkwardness. "And how likely are we to come across two ships to salvage in the same week?"

The *Hassim* hadn't been a coincidence.

"Especially inside legal space."

Legal space or not, this was an isolated sector, and if anything happened to them, there was no one around to witness it. Josune shivered. "Let's get that foam, Snow. I want inside as fast as I can."

The view through the suit camera changed as Roystan switched away, onto another speck, and zoomed in.

Josune really wanted the bioware she'd had before.

"Another ship," Roystan said.

Carlos said, "If you're seeing ships out here, Roystan, you're seeing things."

But it was a ship. They'd run from two ships at Atalante. Now there were two, in a place no one expected to see ships. There were coincidences, and there was cause and effect.

Half the *Hassim*'s crew kept a watch for attacks. Josune should have known better.

Roystan said, intense, quiet, "Josune, Snow. Come back inside."

Snow started back. Josune hesitated. "I should fix the second camera."

"Inside. Now."

"Can we finish—"

"No."

In her other ear Carlos swore, violently for him. "The bastard nullspaced. Right in front of us. They're an hour away now."

Josune had never heard him swear before.

"The second ship nullspaced, too," Roystan said. "It's closer than the first. Josune."

Josune gathered her tools. "Coming." Had Carlos jumped with a plasma-damaged ship before? "We didn't finish sealing out here,

Carlos. If we jump, nullspace might breach it. We need to seal off the area."

The breach was above crew quarters, which was a plus, because there were two compartments.

"That will take out cabins one to eight," Carlos said. Roystan's, Nika's, Snow's, and Josune's cabins. "We can't keep nullspacing, Josune. We haven't the fuel."

Josune didn't plan on sticking around while two ships came close enough to fire another plasma cannon. Especially two ships that were capable of nullspacing but weren't talking.

"We have no choice, Carlos. Those of you in cabins one to eight, go and rescue anything you can't lose. Nika, you collect Snow's."

"Shall do. What do you want, Snow?"

"My gray suit."

"You too, Roystan." Josune caught up to Snow, slowed him while she clipped her line to his suit, then fired her suit jets in a fast sweep to get back to the airlock, and reversed just as hard. The welder, heavier than the rest, kept going, bashing into the wall beside the airlock.

"We heard that right through the ship. Don't damage what ship we have left."

"Sorry, Carlos." And she was, for even though *The Road* was battered, Roystan loved every centimeter of her. "Coming in the airlock now." She pushed Snow in, with the panels and welder close behind.

She watched the feed on the screens through her suit camera as she waited for the air to cycle through. Both ships had fired long jets. They were, as Carlos said, less than an hour away.

25

NIKA RIK TERRI

"I'll jump as soon as they're in," Roystan told Nika, when she came back with Snow's gray suit. "Keep the calibrator steady on my word."

Roystan pulled up star charts and picked coordinates seemingly at random. He was sweating, the only outward sign of stress. His hair had a tiny curl when it was damp, something Nika would be careful to retain when she worked on him. Josune probably liked it.

Nika was past sweating. Being afraid was part of her life now. Ever since Alejandro had lost his temper that first time, and she realized how much trouble she was in. Or, to be honest, not the first time. The second time. The first time she'd believed him when he'd apologized, and said he'd never do it again.

Alejandro wasn't here. Nor was Tamati Woden. That meant she was still better off than she might have been.

Josune called as soon as she was inside. "We're both in."

Roystan checked the cameras near the airlock. "They really are," he told Nika, as if he hadn't quite believed it. He set the null-space countdown.

Jacques called him. "It's probably a bad time to remind you, but nullspacing takes a lot of fuel, and we have no credits to buy more."

"One jump, Jacques. If they find us again, we'll be sure they're chasing us."

Josune and Snow came onto the bridge as Roystan jumped. Carlos and Jacques not far behind them. There was solidarity in numbers, safety even.

They nullspaced.

Roystan scrubbed at his face as he checked the readings on the star chart. "Right where we planned to be, anyway." He relaxed. "Must be time for some spicy flatbread, Jacques."

"What spices do you use, Jacques?" Nika asked. Roystan had a weak stomach, so the spices must contain trace elements his body required, given he liked it so much.

"My own secret recipe, of course."

"Of course." It was a wonder he'd shared that much. Nika thought back to the first time she'd eaten the bread. "It had Rendo spice in it."

Jacques turned away huffily. "That's part of the secret recipe."

The ship rocked, knocking most of them down, then spun fast enough for the extra gravity to momentarily pin them where they'd fallen. Five alarms went off.

Snow was the only one who stayed upright. "We've been hit."

Roystan pulled up the star chart again. His fingers flew, so they were almost a blur. "I want that calibrator on true. Now."

Nika dragged herself up and into her seat. She nudged the calibrator with a sure hand. "On track."

They nullspaced again. Or tried to. Everything slowed and went psychedelic, then snapped back into real space. The star charts looked the same.

Roystan's hair curled with dampness, and when he ran a hand through it, sweat sprayed off. "Let's not do that again."

"They hit the nullspacer," Josune said. "They knew where it was. We can't run. Not without nullspace."

"It's always the first thing you do," Snow said morbidly. "Disable the enemy and move in for the kill. If you can't nullspace, you can't hide."

"They hit us this side of the jump," Roystan said. "Deliberately fired on us. They knew who we were, and where we came out. What are the chances of that?"

Remote.

"They're tracking us."

26

JOSUNE ARRIOLA

Tracking them? How was that possible? Josune had already destroyed Feyodor's marker, and the enemy hadn't made it on board to plant another one yet. Not as far as Josune knew.

Roystan rubbed his eyes. He looked tired, and his eyes were starting to redden. "Let's worry later about how they got here. Let's find them first. We need to know what we're up against, so we can escape." He linked his screen to the cameras Josune had recently installed, and brought up a full 360 view. Visible spectrum, infrared, ultraviolet, radio waves. "Nothing. Not a ship, a rock, not even the trace of one."

"Maybe we hit an asteroid as we came through," Carlos suggested.

Roystan shook his head.

Snow shook his head, too, in a silent imitation. "There'll be a ship."

Roystan stood. "I'll suit up. I want to check the external casing of the nullspace drive."

"You need an engineer," Josune said. "Carlos can't do it."

"And you can?"

Snow grabbed Roystan's sleeve, pulling him back. "Whoever goes out there will be murdered. I've seen these attacks before. This is a typical cattle ship attack. Hit the nullspacer, wait for someone to go out and fix it. Then pounce. They'll kill everyone you send out. Until you eventually surrender, because that's all you can do."

"You're right, Snow." Roystan rubbed his chin. "It *is* characteristic of a cattle ship—although I'll bet it's a company ship this time."

Snow looked surprised, as if he didn't expect Roystan to agree with him.

"When do we stop running?" Carlos demanded.

"We don't," Roystan said. "Not with the ghost of Goberling behind us. Not with news of the *Hassim* salvage shadowing us. We keep running until either we're dead or we reinvent ourselves."

Josune turned to look at him. That sounded like experience.

"Let's find the ship before we decide what to do next. Snow, where would it hide?"

"These body modders know a lot about things they couldn't be expected to know," Jacques said. "Like nullspace drives and ships hiding."

"I know nothing about nullspace drives," Snow said. "I do know covert attacks."

Where would a body modder learn about covert attacks?

"You're free traders. I'm sure you know about them, too."

"We're in the legal zone." Roystan scanned the screens again. "We don't get attacked."

"What are covert attacks?" Nika asked.

"See. She doesn't know about them," Jacques said. "Why do you?"

"Snow spent half his life on a mercenary ship; I didn't. Someone please tell me what is going on."

"Which ship?" Jacques demanded.

"The *Boost*."

Even Roystan winced.

"The captain of the *Boost* is too miserly to employ modders."

"They employed doctors," Nika said. "And Snow's a registered body modder."

Roystan didn't speak, but he frowned—first at Jacques, then at Carlos.

"Sorry," Jacques said gruffly to Roystan. "Nerves."

On the *Hassim* everyone had their own rituals while waiting to be attacked. Feyodor paced. Josune and Reba checked the weapons. Deepak did deep breathing exercises. Here on *The Road*, there were no weapons to speak of, and no one except Josune—and maybe Roystan—had ever waited for an attack before.

The trick was to relax, however you could, to save your adrenaline for the fight. Josune thought she knew what might work with Jacques. "Roystan's probably hungry," she said.

Snow's mouth dropped open. "We're about to be attacked, and you want food. Josune—" It was tragic, as if he'd thought better of her.

But it relieved the tension that had nowhere else to go. "Spicy flatbread coming up," Jacques said.

"Since we're going into battle," Carlos said, "you should cook something we like as well. Like cinnamon cakes."

"You wish," Jacques said.

He hadn't refused outright. Josune put out a hand to stop him on his way to the galley. "Nothing you can't leave. If you have to fight, Roystan won't want the galley burning down."

Josune moved over to Roystan, who was scanning the boards again.

"Thank you," he said quietly, so only she could hear.

"You've good crew." Equally quietly.

He stopped at something Josune couldn't see. "Take a look at this."

Josune brought it up on her own boards. Maybe. "Anomaly? Or shielding, do you think?"

They spent the next five minutes triangulating the anomaly and making sure there were no further ones. Roystan rubbed his arms, as if he was cold. "Let's flush these beasts out. Snow, you say if we send someone out to fix the nullspacer they'll target them. If they do that, then we'll know they're enemy, and we can take them out. Josune, how much damage can the nullspacer take before it breaches the ship?"

Josune checked figures. "We could contain the breach. For safety, we should block off the whole upper floor. The jets are around the circumference. They should be fine."

"We've still got the crew room, here? And Jacques's galley."

"Yes."

"You can't send someone out there," Snow said. "They'll be killed."

Roystan grinned. "We don't have to send anyone out, Snow. We just have to make them think we have. We've a damaged suit. You and Nika can wire something up for us that's vaguely human in shape, and the right temperature. They won't look hard."

"He's as crazy as you are," Snow told Nika.

"But it's going to work, Snow."

27

NIKA RIK TERRI

It took half an hour to wire up a pseudo-body. Nika and Snow worked on that, while Josune worked on a remote controller for the damaged suit. The ship didn't attack again.

"Probably waiting for the second ship," Roystan said. "Assuming these are the ships from Atalante. They think they have us. They won't hurry."

They'd fight this ship, and maybe win. Or maybe not, but it was better odds than fighting two of them together. After that? They'd sneak off into the vastness of space that was this sector and try to lose themselves for a while.

Tamati would be out of the machine in another three days. Or was that two. She was losing track of time.

Josune frowned down at the pseudo-body. "Carlos. Do you think you could control this suit?"

"Of course."

People did what they had to do, even if they were injured. Carlos was still seeing double, but he'd manage.

"I can," Snow said.

"We need you on the cannon, Snow. Roystan to triangulate the ship, with Nika on the calibrator if we need it, and Jacques to assist Roystan."

"And you?"

"I have to send that bomb before you fire the cannon."

Roystan looked up from the boards. "Bomb?"

"A havoc bomb," Snow said. "She put it on the front of the cannon."

"Havoc." Roystan was noticeably paler than he had been. "I hope that's the only one we have."

Josune didn't answer.

"Don't I have any say in what comes onto my ship?"

Josune put her arm across his shoulders, halfway to a hug. "I'm in charge of weapons." She turned away, so that only Nika saw the sweat the movement had cost her.

They were running low on nerveseal.

"Since when?" Roystan asked.

"Since Pol."

"How many?"

"Three."

"All on the cannon?"

"Just the one."

"I don't know if that's good or bad. Where are the other two? No, don't tell me, I don't want to know."

"Down in engineering."

"He said he didn't want to know," Snow said.

Josune smiled. "He does, Snow. And no matter what he says, he'll direct the other two bombs, not me. But," she told Roystan, "I'm not altogether crazy. I pulled the filaments out of the two in engineering. They need to be assembled before we can use them. That will take time."

"Thank gods for something." Roystan was shaking as he turned back to the boards. "I don't like havoc bombs, Josune. Let's take them off any future shopping list."

"They never were on the shopping list," Jacques said. "Where did they come from, Josune?"

"The *Hassim*," Roystan said. "Where else?"

"We didn't pick up any bombs from the *Hassim*."

"Josune and I went over later," Carlos said. "Got the cannon. Remember?"

"Cargo master should know what's on the ship."

"It wasn't cargo," Josune said. "Can we use it, now? Please."

"Only if we need to," Roystan said.

Nika silently put the final touches to their warm, wired body—which was nothing more than a stick with four branches, and a circle of wire for the head. She'd ask Josune later what was so bad about havoc bombs.

No one spoke as they maneuvered the suit out to the airlock, and Josune set it free. She tested the controls, nodded to herself, and gave them to Carlos. "You can work the suit. And Carlos, don't damage Roystan's ship."

"I would never do that." He took the controller and concentrated hard, tongue between his teeth with the effort.

"What now?" Nika asked, as Snow left them to make his way down to the cannon.

"Now we wait," Roystan said.

They watched as Carlos clumsily maneuvered the suit around to the nullspacer. Behind it all, Nika heard a faint clicking sound. Eventually, she realized it was Roystan's teeth. He was shivering, trying to hide it. She moved over, touched him.

He was freezing.

"As soon as we get somewhere safe, you're going into a mod machine."

Roystan leaned across the boards. "Firing. Coming from—"

"Got it." Josune tapped something onto her handheld.

"Hold till they hit. We don't want them accidentally triggering the bomb close to us." Roystan gripped the edge of the panel. "Brace yourselves."

The jolt was minor. The camera on the damaged suit went down.

"That's just mean," Carlos said. "Cold-blooded killing."

"Bomb away," Josune said.

They waited. Tense. Nothing happened.

"Maybe it was a dud," Nika said, just before a sudden mini-sun lit up outside.

"Not a dud. A havoc bomb." Roystan didn't even try to stop his shivering. This time Nika thought it was reaction, not cold. "Let's see what damage we've done. Nika, calibrator."

He fired the engines, a long thrust. His hands were steady on the controls, despite his shivering.

One moment Nika was watching Roystan's empty screen, with half an eye on the calibrator; the next it was filled with spinning debris.

"Snow, have you got the ionizer?"

"On it," Snow said, and the path in front of them miraculously cleared.

The debris came closer.

Roystan glanced at Nika. "Can you control the calibrator? I need to move two degrees positive."

She nodded.

Their new position put them into space with less debris. Slower debris, too. They gradually outran it.

"I want a sweep of the whole area," Roystan said. "I don't want anyone going out there and getting accidentally hit by a piece we missed. Pulverize everything close. The ionizer will work for that."

"I'll help Snow," Josune said.

It wasn't long after that Nika heard Josune say, "You all right?" through the link.

Snow muttered a reply, which might have been, "Fine."

Roystan looked at Carlos. "Check for survivors. Nika can help."

Carlos moved to the board next to Nika and started to scan.

"What do I look for?" Nika asked.

"Heat traces," Carlos said.

Which was no help. "What does a heat trace look like?"

"Really?"

"Really."

"Color," Roystan said. "Red or yellow, mostly." He fired the jets, a gentle movement.

Something large hurtled by, close.

Behind it, Nika caught a glimpse of yellow.

Carlos's eyes crossed. "Maybe I should go to bed. Seeing everything double made that look huge."

It had been huge.

"There," Nika said. "Something warm."

Carlos zoomed in. A body, dead, from the way the neck twisted. The yellow fading as the body cooled. Rotating lazily in free space, the body rolled to face them.

Carlos gasped, cutting off a gurgle that might have been a choke. "Qiang."

The ship had imploded from the inside. It had a massive hole through the middle, but parts of the hull remained undamaged. Nika counted twenty-one yellow blips before the last heat trace faded to nothing. It didn't seem possible that one bomb could do so much damage. There were no survivors. There were bodies.

Qiang was the only one not wearing a business suit.

Roystan was white around the mouth, the red blotch of his healed skin a stark, pink patch against the alabaster of the rest of his neck and down into the collar as far as Nika could see. She thought for a moment that he would clap his hand over his face and reach for a zipped bag, but he didn't.

"I don't care that she's dead." But Jacques's voice broke.

The only time Nika had heard him mention his former crewmates, he'd sounded ready to kill them himself.

Roystan got himself a coffee, and almost gagged at the taste. "It looks like Qiang and Pol sold out to the company."

They hadn't found Pol's body. Or Guardian's.

"Part of the ship looks intact." Roystan hesitated. "Josune, how are your ribs?"

"Fine."

It was a lie, but Nika thought Josune was sore enough to take care with her own body.

Roystan hesitated, then said, "Take Jacques and Snow. See if you can find their nullspacer, and if we can salvage it. I'll send the bodies sunward."

The nearest sun was a light-year away.

Snow leaned close to Nika. "No one wants to carry dead bodies. You send them into the nearest sun."

She must have looked bewildered, for Snow sighed. "There's no room on a spaceship for dead weight."

Dead being the operative word, obviously.

"It keeps space tidy. Gets rid of unwelcome objects floating around in space, waiting to hit an unsuspecting ship."

"You really don't know anything," Carlos said.

Nika raised her hands in defense. "Airy-fairy modder, remember."

Jacques thrust a bowl under Roystan's nose. "Eat. You know how useless you'll be if you don't keep up your energy."

Roystan pushed it away.

"You've a crew, remember. They're your responsibility."

For a moment Nika thought Jacques would spoon-feed him. Maybe Roystan thought so too, for he took the bowl and raised it to his lips. His hands were shaking. With nerves? Or fatigue?

Maybe his body produced too much adrenaline.

Carlos said, "Remember that time they discovered those bodies circulating New France? Hundreds of them. Must have been a whole ship destroyed. They sent them sunward and the planet gravity caught them."

Nika shuddered.

Roystan put down the bowl abruptly. "Let's get suited up and get this grisly business over with."

"What if the second ship arrives before we're done?" Josune asked.

They all knew there would be a second ship.

"They won't jump close to their own ship. We'll have time to get away, and if we can get their nullspacer, it might be faster than repairing our own, which has been hit twice now."

"Grisly as it sounds," Josune said, "we should keep Qiang's body. For her ID. She does, after all, owe you ten million credits. Well, Pol does, but I can't see Qiang leaving all the credits with Pol. If we can get someone to hack it, we might be able to get some of it back for you."

Fingerprint and iris identification were basic work to Nika. If she had a machine like the Songyan, she could probably do it.

Roystan clamped his teeth together, as if the food he hadn't yet eaten wanted to come up again. He nodded. When he finally spoke, it was to say, "Do what you can with the nullspacer while we clean up the bodies."

Josune nodded.

Alone on the bridge with Carlos, Nika watched the screens and spent the time planning Roystan's new stomach.

There were three reasons someone had such a poor gag reflex.

Reason one. The stomach rejected foreign matter. That was easy to fix. Find out the cause of the rejection and fix it. This often had an added advantage that the person enjoyed exotic food more.

Reason two. The body had trained itself to gag based on an event or events that had happened in the past. That was harder to fix. You had to know what the memory was and change the association. Changing memories was bordering on illegal, and had to be done delicately so that you didn't change anything else at the same time. She didn't know Roystan well enough to fix a bad earlier association.

Although she might have been able to do it with the exchanger. Back when she'd first built it, not after she'd used dellarine in it.

Neither of those was likely to be the problem. No. Nika was becoming increasingly convinced it was botched DNA.

Change on a molecular scale had to be done carefully, and properly. It took a gifted modder to do it.

Nika's first job, before she'd bought herself the Dekker and branched out on her own, had been with Hannah Tan. Because Hannah was the leading expert on DNA changes, many botched-DNA jobs came her way. Young modders, straight out of Landers, convinced they could do anything. Not-so-young modders, who should have known better. Nika had learned to recognize the symptoms. Roystan was exhibiting many of them. The only reason she wasn't certain it was a botched mod was that he didn't exhibit the most common symptom—rapid aging.

Josune's voice broke into her assessment. "Promising piece of debris at five hundred points to the center. I'll check it out."

Through the link, Roystan instructed Snow and Jacques. "Work with Josune. Follow her orders. I'll finish the bodies. Snow. Jacques. Keep your links open, to both Josune and me. I need to know everything that goes on out here."

Nika heard the assent. She shivered. She wouldn't like to be out in space on her own, hunting up dead bodies. Especially not when they were expecting an enemy ship any moment.

Roystan arrived back before the others did. He dropped wearily into the captain's chair. Nika studied him carefully, one eye on the calibrator. Sometimes food intolerances showed up around the eyes. Like the black ring that indicated signs of a liver problem, maybe leaky gut syndrome.

"What?" Roystan asked, at Nika's scrutiny.

"Just thinking about mods." His eyes didn't have any black rings.

"And you're looking at me?" He looked wary.

"She's an *artist*," Carlos said. "No doubt she wants to change your body to suit her artistic ideal. Next thing you know you'll be three meters tall with green hair and a fish tail."

"A true artist doesn't take away the essence of the person. Their aim is to enhance what's already there, not to disguise it." Nika turned back to Roystan. "Who did your last mod?"

"Do you ever think of anything other than modding?"

Her whole life had revolved around her work. And Alejandro. She shook her head.

"Why am I not surprised. Tilda, of course."

Tilda, the previous owner of Snow's studio. "And she botched your mod?"

"Botched?" Josune asked. "How?"

Nika had forgotten the link was open, everyone on the same public channel. You didn't talk to a patient about their mods publicly. She shouldn't even have done it with Carlos there. Sometimes her obsession took over, and she wasn't safe in her studio right now and free to discuss it.

But Roystan didn't seem to mind. "I went to Tilda all the time. She never botched a job."

Nika would believe that when she got Roystan under a machine.

"I know what you're thinking. She wasn't in your class, but she was a good modder."

Snow's disembodied voice came through the link. "Tilda apprenticed to Hannah Tan, you know. I found some old letters on the shop link. They parted on bad terms."

Nika bit her tongue to stop herself from saying she'd also apprenticed to Hannah Tan, and was glad she hadn't spoken when Snow added, "Nika Rik Terri apprenticed to Hannah Tan, too. She was the first apprentice Hannah took on in twenty years."

Nika said, "Hannah hated apprentices. Thought they were worthless." It had taken a lot of work, hanging around Hannah's studio, talking mods every time she got the chance, before Hannah finally gave in and even let her inside.

"Tilda stole money from her," Snow said. "That's also why Hannah never acknowledged her as an apprentice, and why Tilda came to Lesser Sirius rather than Pisces III."

"Pisces III?" Josune sounded suddenly breathless.

Should they pull her in?

"Hannah's studio was on Pisces III," Nika said. "Back then it was the hub of all things modding." All the big modders of the golden age had come from there. Giwari, Stephenson, Jens, Patel, McLannard, diGiovambattista. Nika herself had come to Lesser Sirius to get away from the influence of all those masters. She'd found the modders on Pisces III steeped in tradition, set in their ways, always looking to the past, not the future. Lesser Sirius was the modding hub now. In a hundred years, Lesser Sirius would go the same way as Pisces III.

"I found court papers," Snow said. "Justice Department. Tilda nearly went broke paying the fines."

If Tilda had studied with Hannah Tan, then she'd know how to fix a botched genemod, for that had been Hannah's bread and butter. No wonder Roystan had gone to her.

"Hannah Tan refused to have another apprentice, until along came Nika Rik Terri."

Who'd been an arrogant little piece, and refused to take no for an answer. She wanted to learn from the best modders around.

Josune cut in. "We've just picked up some salvage."

Nika was almost glad for the interruption.

"You are not going to like it, Roystan."

Snow and Jacques dragged a net between them when the salvage party arrived back. The contents looked like junk.

As soon as they were all in, Roystan set *The Road* on a new course. "We're lucky the other ship hasn't arrived yet, but it will. Start thinking. We need to know what we brought on board that they could be tracking."

They all adjourned to the crew room.

"Bodies headed sunward?" Josune asked.

Roystan nodded. "Except Qiang." He looked momentarily green. "I've stashed her in the outermost cargo hold. Did you get the nullspacer from the ship?"

"Most of it. We can fix the rest."

"Good."

Jacques helped Snow lift the net onto the table. "Look what we found." He pressed the release. Strands dropped away. "Snow says they're weapons."

They didn't look like weapons. Nika picked up one of the smaller pieces. "How do they work?"

"That one's a Mark 27 Skol hand weapon," Snow said. "Military grade. It can burn half your body off if you're within twenty-seven meters."

Nika dropped the weapon hurriedly.

"Twenty-seven to eighty meters," Snow said. "We might be able to save you, but you'll spend weeks in the regen machine."

"Outside eighty meters?"

"No range."

Nika touched it cautiously with the tip of her middle finger. "So if you see someone with one of these you run like mad and hope you're out of range before they fire."

Snow had a great repertoire of withering looks. Nika would have to cultivate some of them.

"Hmm." Roystan picked carefully through the weapons. "Military grade, you say."

Snow nodded.

Roystan tapped the table thoughtfully. "Salvage is salvage. But I've never sold weapons before. I wouldn't know how to."

"Qiang would have known," Jacques said.

Roystan gave him a sharp glance. "None of us are Qiang, are we? Does anyone know how to get rid of them without getting ripped off?"

Alejandro's boss would have known.

Roystan sighed. "We'll work something out."

Nika picked carefully through the weapons. They didn't look dangerous. In fact, only two of them looked like traditional weapons.

"Don't," Snow said. "You don't know what you're doing."

Nika knew how to handle an iron bar. Or a hefty plasma jar. But the first time she'd held a real weapon had been on Atalante Station. She held her hands away in surrender.

Roystan grinned sympathetically. "You're the expert on this," he told Snow.

"They're all old." Snow picked through the bundle. "This one"—he pointed to one that looked like something Nika might have used for jimmying the lid off a can of mutrient, back when they came in cans rather than screw-top jars—"can slice a man in half at the waist as neat as you please. Cauterize the wound, too."

Roystan looked gray around the mouth. "Let's change the subject."

"To this?" Josune brought out something else. At first glance Nika thought it was a giant femur, for it was roughly the same shape. Then she looked closer and saw it was a ceramic-metal alloy, that peculiar gray-purple of alloys designed to withstand extreme temperatures. It was still crackling as it warmed up now that it was no longer in the near absolute zero of space.

The word on the side was *Hassim*.

Roystan rubbed his eyes. "I suppose destroying it isn't an option."

"No." Josune put another one beside it. This one had *Pierre* down the side. "You know what it means, Roystan. They didn't need us at all. They had the *Hassim* memory. But they came back for us."

Roystan moved his hands away from his face. He looked at her.

"They came back. They're looking for the same thing Captain Feyodor was."

"Something on the *Hassim*'s or the *Pierre*'s memory will tell us why," Jacques said.

Josune opened her mouth to speak, then closed it.

Roystan rubbed his eyes again. "Let's put these back into the safe. You might reprogram it, Josune. Add Nika and Snow, and have any four of us open it."

"This conversation isn't finished." But Josune picked up the ships' memories and took them out.

28

NIKA RIK TERRI

After that, things slowed down.

As Roystan pointed out, you couldn't go anywhere in space fast. Not when you couldn't nullspace. Josune and Carlos worked on the nullspacer. They'd taken the one from *The Road*, and the one from the *Pierre*, and were trying to patch something workable out of both of them.

Jacques and Roystan searched the supplies they'd brought over from the *Hassim* to see if they could discover how the company was tracking them.

Since Nika and Snow had no idea what they were looking for—Jacques didn't either, Nika was fairly sure—Josune set them to curing the nullspace parts as they came out of the molds. Nika was glad to do something. Anything.

They had one curing machine and a dozen gears on the table in front of them.

Carlos hovered, watching the curing while he worked at his own tasks. "Do it properly. I don't want something breaking because it wasn't cured properly."

Neither did Nika. "They teach us how to cure at Landers, Carlos." Or they had when she'd been there. "Two hours a week for a whole term."

"Two hours a week."

"They don't do that anymore," Snow said. "They expect the molding machine to cure it for you." He glanced at Nika. "Of course, most modders don't make their own equipment. They buy add-ons."

He was winding them up. Nika didn't mind. His curing technique was far superior to hers. She'd bet that on the *Boost*, the medical team had repaired a lot of their own equipment. Now all she had to do was to convince him that making your own add-ons, rather than purchasing them, was a step up, not down.

Roystan came by engineering when they'd finished searching the cargo. "Nothing. And no ships, either. Maybe we've lost them."

An alarm sounded.

Roystan opened a link. "A ship just arrived."

Nika's heart raced. Reaction, even though a ship couldn't possibly get to them for hours. After all, they'd waited hours for the *Pierre*.

"Normally, I'd hail them, say hello," Roystan said. "But we don't want anyone to know we're here. Let's wait for them to hail us."

Nika calculated the vectors. The ship was turning to intercept *The Road*. She hoped she was wrong, but Roystan confirmed it.

"Right in our way," Roystan said, as the path of the other ship stabilized. "We'll meet them head-on in three hours. They haven't called us."

"It's a standard safety measure," Snow told Nika. "Even before you can see a ship, you know by the transmissions that another ship is in the area."

Roystan stood. "Let's change our own path, Nika."

Josune followed them.

"How can you see them, if they can't see you?" Nika asked.

"This ship belonged to smugglers when I bought it. It has some of the best long-range surveillance equipment money could buy back then. Old now, but still effective." Roystan turned to Josune. "How long before the nullspacer is ready?"

"Nineteen hours."

Nika had seen the number of parts left to cure. They needed all of that nineteen hours.

"Can we do anything in the next two that will allow us to null-space, even if we break things coming out the other side?"

"No."

"I was afraid of that." Roystan settled into the pilot's seat. "One degree," he said to Nika. "That way, if they're only watching us, they'll think we're still coming."

"Shouldn't we head the other way?" It would take them longer to catch up.

"If they know we've seen them, they'll nullspace in. This way, they'll think we're making a minor course adjustment. Ready?"

"Ready." She wished he sounded more hopeful.

The adjustment was so gentle she didn't feel it.

They watched the boards in silence.

Three minutes later, the other ship adjusted its course, too.

Roystan sat back in the pilot's seat. "They're too far away to respond that fast to a visual, even if they noticed a one-degree change. Which means they know where we are." He bounced to his feet. "If we don't find that marker, we'll never escape from them."

He opened a link. "Jacques, I need you to watch the ship while we go through everything we've brought on board. Everything." He looked at Josune. "Do you need to help Carlos?"

"Snow's with him."

Josune rubbed at her flaking skin. "If you didn't find it earlier . . . The food maybe?"

"Jacques has already checked that."

"The only things I brought on were the havoc bombs and the cannon. And some plasma. They wouldn't have markers. I know them inside out. I don't think they could be tracked. Feyodor was—"

The color drained from her face. "The black pins." She turned and ran. Roystan and Nika followed.

Snow and Carlos looked up as they burst into engineering.

"Don't come back here until you've found what's tracking us," Carlos said.

Josune yanked open a drawer and pulled out some pins.

Nika put out a hand to take one. A black, polished metal bird of prey. Her hand shook. No matter how far you ran, they always got you in the end. "Eaglehawk."

"Eaglehawk?" Josune's voice was sharp. "Are you sure?"

"Absolutely." She'd been sure back when they'd purchased the Dekker. She just hadn't known for certain whether they were after *The Road* or her.

Nika held the pin up to the light. Alejandro had never let her touch his. The metal had an oily sheen, typical of a substance that contained trace amounts of transurides.

"I never knew it contained a marker." So that was how Leonard Wickmore always turned up at strategic—and inconvenient—moments. He didn't trust his people. Not even his elite thugs. How many of them knew the pins were trackable?

"Eaglehawk. Now I know the company." Josune closed her fist around the pins she held, her face grim. "They can start counting their days."

"The people who wear these pins beat up or assassinate other people. How long do you think you'll last?" How had Josune and Roystan collected so many?

"I'm still going to destroy them."

"Where did you get these?" Nika asked, to stop herself from saying any more about how stupid that was.

"The *Hassim*."

The *Hassim* had been destroyed. "So they've been following you since then. They never give up, you know."

Josune took the pin out of her hand. "Neither do I."

Josune sent the pins off in a drone—in the same direction the ship was currently traveling—then took over from Carlos. Nika went back to the bridge, where she and Roystan carefully turned the ship 62.7 degrees from its current course. After that they retired to the crew room, where Jacques was cooking honest-to-goodness Reta-potato chips from Reta. There was no mistaking the spicy smell of them.

Carlos hovered. "Even my saliva's got saliva. How long?"

"Less if you sat at the table and waited."

Carlos gave a long, overly dramatic sigh and came over to sit beside Nika.

Roystan took Carlos's place in the galley entry. "How's it going, Jacques?" Jacques didn't order him away.

"So-so," Jacques replied.

Checking on his crew to see that they were okay. He'd take time for a quiet chat with Carlos later, if he hadn't already done so.

"How long have you been with Roystan?" Nika asked Carlos.

"Twenty years."

Carlos wasn't much older than she was. "You must have been quite young."

"I was on the run."

Jacques said something soft to Roystan, who said something equally soft back, then moved to the table so Jacques could bring out an enormous bowl of retchips.

Carlos dived on them. "I haven't thought about that in years, you know. I was apprenticed to an old prospector out in the Pleiades. He was a weird man. Believed in rituals for everything. He had this ancient pen-and-ink set that he used to burn symbols onto flesh." Carlos glanced at his inked arms. "There was literally no uncovered skin on him. I think that's why he took on apprentices." Carlos shrugged. "And why he decided to sell me off. He needed a new body to ink. Wouldn't sign the qualification papers unless I signed on to a merc ship. He got more by selling a geologist's contract and I knew that I wouldn't get qualified if I didn't sign."

Geologist. She'd thought he was an engineer.

"So I signed. Then I took my bag and tried to lose myself between the two ships. There's been a bounty on my head ever since, for breaking contract. Roystan found me trying to break into his cargo. He was taking Earth chocolate to one of the Colcannon worlds."

Roystan smiled reminiscently. "He was skinny, half starved. He threatened to brain me with my own chocolate, although to be honest he'd crammed so much in his mouth it was hard to understand the threat at all. And he stank. He hadn't bathed for months. We cut his clothes off him in the end, left them in a bin near the vending machine where we bought him new coveralls."

"We?" Nika asked. If Carlos had been there twenty years, maybe Pol or one of the others had, as well.

Carlos winced.

"Barr and me," Roystan said, and the conversation shut down.

A warning sounded. Then another. Nika was almost glad for the interruption.

"Two more ships," Roystan said. "Busy little sector of space, all of a sudden." Another signal. "The original ship has jumped closer." He shook his head. "The pins are still too close. Any ship intercepting the pins will see us on visual. We should have destroyed them."

He brought up the paths of the three ships on-screen. A red line, a green line, a yellow line. Then he added a blue line for the path of *The Road*, and a paler blue for the marker. All five lines converged. He called up engineering. "Are you seeing this, Josune?"

"Unfortunately. And they're close enough to see us without the marker."

Roystan rubbed his eyes. "Which do we think is the weakest ship?"

"The first one," Nika guessed.

"Agreed," Josune said. "After all, it waited until the other two ships arrived before it jumped in."

"Let's move away from the two new ships," Roystan said. "Head toward the original ship. Nika, I need you on the calibrator."

She went with him to the bridge, where he fired the rockets gently to change their course, making away from the other two ships, more on an angle to the first.

In less than five minutes, all three ships had adjusted their own courses to meet up at Roystan's ship again.

Roystan sighed, and linked into engineering. "All of you drop what you're doing and come up to the crew room. We're out of time."

29

JOSUNE ARRIOLA

"We've two and a half hours before the first ship reaches us," Roystan said, when they were all assembled in the crew room. "Josune, Carlos, you say we won't have a nullspacer ready before then?"

"Nowhere near then," Carlos said.

Josune nodded agreement.

"We can't take on three ships," Roystan said. "I propose we make a bargain to get us out of here."

Josune shook her head. "They might agree, but they'll double-cross you."

"Credit me with some brains. We still have a bargaining tool."

If he meant the *Hassim*'s memory, that wouldn't work. "The *Pierre* had the memory, remember." These ships had come back for Roystan, for the same information Feyodor had wanted from him. He'd better not offer them that. It was the only thing keeping them from being blasted out of the sky.

"That company isn't the only one who'll pay for the memory," Roystan said.

"No one will take the memory and leave us alive."

"Jerome Brown might."

"Jerome Brown might kill us, too. We're vulnerable, and he'll know it." But Roystan's idea was a good one. Brown, so far, had been fair in his dealings. He might agree to the bargain to get his hands on the *Hassim* memory.

"I trust him," Roystan said. "His grandfather was a good man, and had a lot of influence on young Jerome. Jed practically brought him up."

His grandfather. Josune kept forgetting that Roystan—no matter how much he claimed to hate exploring—was a Goberlingophile, too. Jed Brown had been a friend of Goberling's. They'd grown up together. Of course Roystan would know of him. Would know that Jed's influence was one of the reasons Jerome hunted Goberling's lode himself.

Brown was almost as obsessed as the crew of the *Hassim* had been, although he was more discreet about it. Feyodor had sold him information once. She'd wanted fast credits, and it was quicker than setting up an auction to sell the information.

"Maybe," Josune agreed. "But he'll need to do it in the next two hours. Otherwise he'll get caught in the fighting."

"I'll set it up," Roystan said.

He was forgetting one thing. Josune caught his arm as he turned to go. "Qiang came back."

"I know that."

Nika looked at them, as if trying to work out what she wasn't saying. Josune wasn't sure Roystan had worked it out either.

"They must have cracked the *Hassim* code." They would have the best hackers in the universe working on it, although it was fast, even for them. "They learned something on that feed. They learned what Feyodor knew. They learned why she wanted to talk to you."

Roystan nodded.

"Brown will learn that, too."

"I know, Josune. But at least we'll be alive."

Roystan left to contact Brown. Josune considered their options. They had two havoc bombs, but she'd pulled the filaments out. Did she have time to set them up? Was it worth it, given that the enemy ships would be expecting havocs now? Might even be able to send them back.

Better to concentrate on checking over the *Pierre*'s weapons.

"I want something that makes me feel safe," Nika said.

So did Josune, although her safety was in knowing she had a crew who could fight and the weapons to back it up.

"We have the out-of-date mutrient, but I'd give anything for some naolic acid, right now."

Snow shuddered. "No way."

Given Snow's reaction, it sounded dangerous. Something they could use?

"What does it do?"

Nika didn't answer immediately. She stared into space, then said, "Naolic acid isn't the only—"

Snow stepped back. "No."

Josune said, "If it helps us, Snow."

"You're not going to like this."

"Mutrient and acid. Burns the skin," Nika said. "Spray it on them as they come through. They'll be so busy trying to get it off, we can stun them while they're doing it."

"You're right," Josune said to Snow. "I don't like it."

"If they get hold of us, they'll do worse," Nika said. "Believe me."

A link opened. Two images, Roystan and Jerome Brown. Sound came with it. They stopped to listen and watch.

If Roystan had planned to make his call public, why hadn't he called from the crew room instead of going down to his cabin?

Maybe he didn't want Brown to know it was public.

"Atypical droop on the left eye," Nika murmured. "He's got bio-ware. Unusual they put it in the left eye. Most people put it in the right."

Josune's had been in the right. She touched her own eye, then closed her left eye to reassure herself she could see just as well with the other one. "Did I ever say thank you for saving my eye before you fixed the rest of me?"

"It's the logical way to do it when you can't do a full mod. Fix the worst damage first."

On-screen, Roystan said to Brown, "Last time we dealt, there was one thing we couldn't supply you with. That's back in our possession now. We're wondering if you're interested."

Brown's eyes narrowed. "I might be."

His left eyelid glowed momentarily. Checking up on them?

"Subvocal transmission of commands to his link," Nika said. "He didn't buy that from his modder. That's a specialist tech firm there."

"We have that item back." Roystan ran his hands through his hair. Josune thought he might be worried, but it didn't show on the screen. "But we'll only have it for the next two hours."

Brown's eyes narrowed farther.

They had closer to two and a half hours, but there was sense in making it earlier, to avoid the company ships.

"We'll sell it to you. Provided you collect it within the hour."

"The price?"

"Take us with you."

Brown twitched. The first reaction they'd gotten out of him. "Take you where?"

"To a central hub. Somewhere we can re-equip."

"And your ship?"

"It's a write-off."

"So I can wait until the ship dies, and come in and take it."

"It won't be here in two hours."

"I . . . see." And Josune saw that he did. "Captain Roystan. You are asking me to rescue you and your crew. Put my own ship in danger."

"Yes, Executive, I am. But the prize is worth it. The backup memory from the *Hassim*. I will give you coordinates that will bring your ship in close to us. If you get here within the hour, you should be safe."

It was the first time he'd mentioned the memory by name. Josune thought that was deliberate.

Brown shook his head, and almost smiled. "I admire your effrontery, Roystan."

"Thank you."

Brown's eyelid glowed again, in silent communication they weren't party to. "What are your coordinates?"

"Do we have a deal?"

More silent communication. "How many of you?"

"Six."

"We have a deal, but I can't do an hour. It will be ninety-five minutes."

That was cutting it closer than Josune liked. Closer than Roystan liked too, by the way he blew out his breath. But he pushed the coordinates through without saying anything. "We'll expect you in ninety-five minutes, then."

"Ninety-five minutes," Brown agreed, and closed the link.

Roystan called the crew room. "You all heard that."

"Every single word," Carlos said.

Ninety-five minutes of sitting around, waiting to be collected. Hoping nothing would go wrong. On the *Hassim* Josune would be checking the cannons, checking the blasters, doing what she could to protect her ship.

Here? She was doing nothing.

She stood abruptly. "I'm going to look over the *Pierre*'s weapons." She looked at Nika. "Do you want to try out that mutrient mix of yours?" Every extra weapon they had to hand was a bonus.

"You really should tell Snow who you are," Josune said, as they walked down to the storeroom together. "He'll never forgive you when he does find out."

"I know. But I need to disappear."

"What are you running from?"

Nika looked around the storeroom. "Can you unlock that?"

The dangerous-goods cupboard. Josune silently unlocked it. She didn't press for more detail. Nika would tell her if she wanted to. Otherwise, it wasn't Josune's business.

She piled the weapons from the *Pierre* onto a trolley, while Nika picked out the container of phosphoric acid that Josune and Carlos used to clean the rust and grease off the ship panels.

"This should do."

Josune helped her lift it onto the trolley, along with the out-of-date mutrient from the Dekker.

"It's simple, really," Nika said, long after Josune had thought she wouldn't. "And rather stupid. My ex, Alejandro. He was—"

Josune saw the way she flinched. Didn't ask what.

Nika looked around the store. "I need salts, and something that works like Arrat crystals."

Salts were easy. "I don't know what Arrat crystals are."

"They're a softener."

The only softening Josune understood was softening water. Water from different worlds, different stations, came in varying degrees of hardness. Water that was too hard left scale in the pipes. "Lime? Citric acid?"

"Either of those." Nika took both.

They walked back in silence to the engineering workshop, detouring on the way to the crew room, where Nika begged a steak from Jacques. And a knife.

The steak was easy, but getting a knife was like asking Jacques to part with his firstborn.

"I'll take an image of the knife if you like," Josune offered. "Make sure it's returned in the same condition."

"It's not the look of it that's important. It's the feel of it."

She didn't point out that they might not be alive in three hours for him to use it.

In the workshop Nika measured out careful samples of mutrient and phosphoric acid.

"Alejandro was everything I wanted. Someone who cared about how he looked. Someone who—" She stared at the ingredients she'd laid out. "I don't know what that makes me. Because I care what I look like."

Josune laid the weapons on a workbench. Started at the Mark 27 Skol. The fuel gauge on the Skol was almost empty. She put it on the reject pile and picked up the next one. "You're a modder. It's your job."

Nika diced meat without seeming to see it. Josune watched to make sure she didn't cut herself. "I can't imagine you putting up with—"

"I can't imagine me doing that either. By the time I realized what he was like, it was too late. By the time I knew how bad . . . I was in too deep."

"You killed him?" That was what Josune would have done, but for all Nika's toughness, she wasn't a killer.

"I wanted to. You can't imagine how badly I wanted to sometimes, but no." She tipped mutrient onto the first cube of meat. Then tipped phosphoric acid on top of it. The liquids combined, sizzled a little.

"I set up an escape plan. New identity. Credits stored away. I was ready, just couldn't take that final step." Nika tipped mutrient onto the next piece of meat. Then a larger amount of phosphoric acid. This one sizzled louder.

Was this a weapon Josune had the stomach to use?

More mutrient. More acid. A lot more sizzle. Nika scraped away the liquid. Half the meat was gone. She nodded. "Just a little more phosphoric acid."

First, she mixed up a salt and lime solution, although Josune wondered how much attention she was paying to it, for she stared at the wall a lot. "I didn't use the escape plan. Not then, because

Alejandro's boss, Leonard Wickmore, offered to send him off-world. Provided I helped them out occasionally."

She turned back to the meat. This time, when she scraped the mix away, the meat was mostly gone.

Josune shuddered. "Why not just the acid? It will burn."

"Mutrient has an affinity for the skin. That's what it's for. It binds with both the skin and the acid, takes it right into the skin, not just onto the surface. If you let it go, it will work its way through your body.

Josune hadn't known mutrient was so dangerous. She put the blaster she'd been checking down onto the okay pile and picked up the next weapon. "What did helping out Wickmore involve?"

"Repairing people who couldn't go to the hospital because someone might ask questions. I don't know why they bothered to hide it. The police couldn't do anything."

That sounded like the bitter voice of experience.

"My patients worked for Eaglehawk. Most wore those pins."

Maybe Josune could use Nika's knowledge in her attempt to avenge her crew.

"The worst of the worst of them was a man called Tamati Woden. He had this scar." Nika shuddered. "It was supposed to be the last thing you saw before you died. Everyone in Wickmore's team was terrified of him." She shuddered again. "He was Alejandro's hero, so I heard a lot about him, long before I met him.

"Anyway, Tamati got injured before he could finish a job. He's an assassin. He came to me because Alejandro had told him I'd made a body exchanger." She looked at Josune, eyes veiled. "It's a device that allows your brain to swap bodies for a short time."

"Impressive." Only Nika could casually say she'd made a device that allowed people to switch bodies.

"It was."

Josune nodded.

"Tamati forced me to swap bodies with him."

"He did a job using your body?"

"While I cured his, yes."

"So now you're wanted for murder?"

"I hadn't thought of it that way, but yes, probably." Nika scooped up the experiment and tossed it into the recycler. Josune wasn't sure she wanted that corrosive combination in *The Road*'s recycler. "I'm running from Tamati. He never leaves witnesses."

"You think he'll chase you down and kill you."

"I know he will."

"I see." Josune was a realist. She thought Nika might be, too. "You know that one day you might have to kill him." Because if Nika thought he would chase her till he caught up, he probably would. "And he can mod his body to change his appearance, so even you won't know what he looks like until he's about to kill you."

"I'll recognize him."

"Nika, anyone can get rid of a scar." She was a body modder, for goodness' sakes. She knew that.

Nika smiled. "He doesn't have the scar anymore."

She was playing with fire. She'd taken away the one advantage she'd had. The scar, which would identify Tamati. "That makes him more—"

"Distinct. I know what he looks like, Josune, and he can't change those looks. Not anymore." She looked around. "Now. Something to neutralize this."

She prepared another meat sample and took it over to the Dekker to measure the pH. Then measured the pH of the solution she'd prepared.

Josune held the beaker for her.

"He doesn't blend in, Josune. He's the best mod I ever did. No one will ever know except me. The body took two years to design.

And an hour to redesign it so he can't hide." Nika put mutrient on the meat, then the phosphoric acid, and finally the salt solution. The sizzling stopped instantly. "That will work. Now, all we have to do is set up a weapon to spray it."

Poor Roystan's ship if they ever did spray it. "Just don't shoot it anywhere near a containing wall." With luck, Brown would come through and they wouldn't need to use these weapons at all, because they'd never catch every bit of acid spilled.

Still, if things got that bad, it wouldn't matter what happened to the ship, would it. Roystan would be devastated.

She linked in. "Have we heard from Brown's ship?"

"Not yet."

"We've got our solution down here. We're about to build containers to put them in. How's everything else?"

"Quiet."

She nodded, and clicked off. "Two containers," she suggested to Nika. "Each with a nozzle. Spray the mutrient first. Then the acid. And a sprinkle can of the salt solution hanging at our side, ready to grab and spray if this stuff gets past the enemy and falls onto the ship."

Add a safety, tuned to the firer's iris, so that only those from *The Road* could fire them.

Nika nodded.

Josune assembled the makings quickly. She'd watched Nika work, already had an idea of what she needed to contain each liquid. The containers were acid-proof. "What will you do if Tamati comes for you?"

"I don't know, Josune. I don't know."

Sometimes, fighting back was the best defense. People like Nika, like Roystan, thought they could run forever. But running was the stupidest thing to do. Ten years on the *Hassim* had taught her that.

Roystan joined them in engineering as they finished the third makeshift weapon. "I'll take the *Pierre*'s memory, in case Brown tries to double-cross us. Josune, you take the *Hassim*'s memory. It's rightfully yours anyway. Don't hand it over until we're safe on station. Grab a bag of essentials. That's all we can take."

He looked around the engineering workshop. "She's been a good little ship. The best I've ever had. I'll miss her."

"We'll get you another."

"Josune." He looked around. Looked back at her.

She was aware of Nika, moving quietly out of the workshop.

Roystan brushed a gentle finger over her cheek. "I'm sorry about everything. I wish—" He looked into her eyes. "I wish things could have been different for us."

Josune stared back into his gaze, not daring to breathe.

"I'd hoped—" She saw the moment he changed his mind, changed what he was going to say. "I'm asking a lot, but if anything happens. Carlos. He's been with me years. I—"

She'd hoped too, but that was stupid, especially in the middle of potential danger. It made her angry. "That's not very optimistic, Roystan." What had he been going to say?

He smiled his crooked smile. "Sometimes you have to think of worst-case scenarios."

Sometimes you did. And sometimes all you could do was concentrate on the words. Otherwise you'd be crushed that the other person hadn't said what you wanted them to say.

"Jacques might stay with Brown and cook for him. He'd be safe there."

Worst-case scenario. "You're very confident of Brown."

"Jed Brown always said Jerome was the best of his offspring."

"You're too soft, Roystan." She looked at the weapons in front of her. A belt for the *Pierre* weapons. Nika's homemade device would fit into a backpack. And Josune's sparker. "We're going armed, regardless."

No matter what Roystan thought.

Brown's ship arrived twenty-seven minutes later.

"That's fast." Roystan chewed his bottom lip. "I suppose it would be rude to ask them to confirm identification."

"It's never rude when lives are at stake," Josune said.

But she hadn't needed to, for Roystan was already saying, politely, to the captain on-screen, "This is a valuable artifact we're bringing on board. You understand we need to be sure you are who you say you are. We require proof."

"Of course," the captain agreed, equally politely. "Captain Miles Darcy, of Brown Combine, ship XD-237-Y." He permitted himself a smile. "Otherwise known as the *Dreadlord*. Pushing the details through to you now."

"Thank you. If you will give us a moment to confirm your credentials."

"Of course."

Roystan ran the checks. "It's definitely the *Dreadlord*." He tapped the table and frowned. "They're too early. I don't like it."

Each ship had its own signature. Theoretically, you linked into the ship registry, plugged in the signature, and the registry confirmed or denied the registration. It also sent back public details of the ship. Make, model, registration number. But there were lots of ways to claim to be a ship you weren't. The easiest was to switch the feed that was returned to the person making the query.

That sort of switch took company-level hacking skills.

Josune checked her blaster.

They were all armed. Nika had three weapons. A stunner, her mutrient, and the triangular class five laser. She'd ducked back to the engineering workshop for wire and glass and spent five minutes working the whole of it into a striking piece of jewelry, which she then fashioned into a pendant.

Now that was a way to wear a weapon. Publicly, and Josune bet no one would notice it for what it was; they'd be too busy admiring it as a work of art.

"Two purposes for everything," Nika had said, when Josune had nodded approvingly. "This one is beauty and function. I hope Snow is right about which way to point the thing."

"Aim it low enough and a good modder can put your body back together anyway," Carlos said. "Isn't that what you say?"

"I'm the best modder around here, Carlos. That's the problem. Who's going to put me back together?"

"Hey," Snow said, but without much force.

Nika ignored him and looked at Josune. "Your sparker is a slim rod. I can make it a hairpin if you like. No one will recognize it then, either."

Josune handed it over. "Just remember, I need to be able to press this button." She pointed to the small depression that was the sparker control.

"I'll angle it so that when you've got your hands stuck above your head, you can press down, and zap, bad guy electrocuted."

They grinned at each other.

Nika finished converting the sparker and knotted it into a coil of Josune's hair at the same time as the two ships connected.

30

NIKA RIK TERRI

Ten days. Or was that eleven? Tamati would be out of the Songyan soon. Nika fingered the laser pendant she wore. A weapon like this might be enough to save her life when Tamati did find her.

In another few hours, that was all she'd have to worry about again. If they lived that long.

That, and helping Snow set up a modding studio. She doubted he'd appreciate her help.

She'd get him another Netanyu. The Songyan wasn't a machine you bought to learn on. You earned the right to use one, learned the basic machines first.

Josune and Roystan would go exploring, with Jacques to feed them and Carlos tagging along. Roystan wouldn't go back to his run, not while Eaglehawk was after him. But before he went any-where, Nika was going to fix his DNA.

If he'd let her near him.

Roystan paced.

"I'll be glad to see Josune looking like herself again," Carlos said.

Some people clung to the past. "She looks better than she ever has."

"She doesn't look like Josune, that's all."

Nika shrugged. It was unlikely that Josune would ever again look like the Josune that Carlos knew. He'd get used to it.

Jacques said, "I might offer to cook Brown a meal."

"Make sure it's something we can all eat," Carlos said. "Not just porridge that Roystan can."

"If I'm cooking it for Brown—"

Roystan cut across Jacques. "If Brown said his ship would be ninety-five minutes, they'll be ninety-five minutes."

Both he and Josune jumped as the linking passage hit the outside of the ship. Their unease was infectious. Nika took out her stunner and made sure her backpack was easily accessible.

"Both ends secure," Captain Darcy said. "*Dreadlord* lock opening."

Roystan pulled the handheld from his pocket and opened a link. He keyed in numbers. "I hope I remember the code. I've forgotten so much."

A startled Jerome Brown came up on-screen. "Where did you get this code?"

"Your grandfather gave it to me. Apologies for using it, but you said the ship would take ninety-five minutes."

"Roystan, I can't get it to you any faster."

"That's what I thought. It appears to be early. I'm wondering who else you mentioned our deal to. Or if your security is not as secure as you think it is. Would you mind checking where your captain is right now?"

"It's not possible. She's coming from the Antares system. About that code—"

The airlock clanged as Jacques and Carlos opened it from their end.

"Jacques. Carlos." The sudden authority in Roystan's voice stopped them. "Don't. It's a trap. Close the lock."

Josune moved before they did. Slammed the door shut. Sealed it.

"What's going on?" Brown demanded. "Roystan, are you accusing me of something?"

Josune jumped to one side.

The airlock glowed red, started to melt.

Nika holstered her stunner and reached for the mutrient mix. She felt more comfortable with mutrient.

Roystan dropped the communicator, grabbed his stunner, and fired as the first suited man came through.

The company man went down under Roystan's stunner, the second under Josune's blaster.

Snow took the third one down.

Silence.

"They'll throw something through to gas us," Roystan said. "Or they'll take off and leave us open to space." The airlock was destroyed. "Time to retreat."

"Roystan?" The voice came from Roystan's communicator on the ground. Roystan scooped it up as he went and turned off the link.

"Split up?" Josune suggested.

Roystan's gaze swept them all. Lingered, Nika thought, on herself, Carlos, and Jacques. "It's safer if we stick together."

They backed away, watching the entry.

No one came through.

Roystan—the last person out—locked the door behind him.

"Bridge?" Josune asked.

"Crew room. We can do everything from there except pilot the ship. The first place they'll head for is the bridge. There are more weapons in the crew room."

Nika looked at him.

"Jacques's knives."

Jacques's knives were in the kitbag on Jacques's back. Including the one Nika had returned.

"Pots. Things to throw."

Jacques's best pots were dangling from the bottom of his kitbag.

Josune locked the doors to the crew room. "Locking down the lifts as well."

Roystan opened a link and set it to display the airlock and the corridors. "Smoke," he said, because the airlock was hidden under a thick, slow-moving cloud.

"Closing down nearby vents," Josune said, and did, but the first acrid tendrils were already starting to drift into the crew room.

They heard the sound of running feet.

"Oxygen." Roystan motioned to Jacques and Carlos.

Carlos made for the cupboards. He handed out oxygen.

Men with gas masks emerged from the smoke. Ten, fifteen.

"Gas masks only," Roystan said. "They think the smoke will be enough to stop us."

"Lucky this is such an old ship," Carlos said, as Josune and Roystan worked the controls. "Modern ships wouldn't have a control center in the crewroom."

Roystan said, "There's no luck about it, Carlos. It's one of the reasons I like this old lady."

"That one is wearing a pin. Aubergine suit." Nika squinted to get a better look. He looked familiar. "The ones with pins are the more dangerous."

"We should cut oxygen to the bridge," Josune said.

Roystan ran his hands through his hair. "That leaves us vulnerable. We'll have to carry oxygen."

"We're carrying it now," Carlos pointed out.

"Well, whatever we do, don't any of us get in the way of a blaster, or there'll be one almighty explosion."

Their enemy reached the bridge.

Roystan slid the door closed behind them. Locked it. "It won't hold them long."

Indeed, it wasn't going to hold them at all, for Aubergine Suit was issuing instructions.

They watched as more people came through the damaged airlock.

Aubergine Suit, on the bridge, shoved aside the man trying to open the door. He took out his weapon and blasted the lock.

The door didn't open but dented enough to allow them to force it.

Carlos watched the feed, then hefted a blaster in one hand and a stunner in the other. "We're stuck. They can destroy these doors and we have no way out. All we can do is take them out as they come in, and hope they use one door at a time."

This was one time when Nika would have preferred fewer than three doors into the crew room. They had to survive here until Brown's ship arrived, even after they defeated these people.

If they defeated them.

"Suits on," Roystan said. "Keep your arms free, and helmets off for the moment, but if your suit starts beeping, let it seal. If they destroy *The Road*, wait until Brown's ship arrives, then turn on your emergency beacon. And let's hide the memory for the moment. Wouldn't do for this lot to get them."

"Good idea." Josune stowed both the *Hassim* and the *Pierre* memory sticks behind separate panels, well apart.

The company men had spread out around the ship. "Find their secondary bridge," Aubergine Suit said. "Wrap this up fast. Brown's ship isn't far away. I want only debris by the time it arrives." He turned to the men working unsuccessfully to override the controls. "There's six of them, and twenty of you. And don't forget, we need them alive. I'm going back to the *Dreadlord*."

"I can take him out before he reaches the airlock," Josune said.

"No," Nika and Roystan said together.

"He's wearing a pin," Nika said. Josune would get slaughtered.

"Those, then." Josune tapped two men in a nearby corridor. "Open that door there." She pointed to it.

Roystan hesitated, and Josune slipped out before he could say no.

They watched on the screen. She fired around the corner. Two men went down. She was back before the bodies stopped moving.

Roystan looked green. "You're very good at this."

"We learned to be, Roystan. To stay alive."

Nika gripped her own makeshift weapon and waited. They would fight soon. She was ready.

At least, she hoped she was.

There were three exits to the crew room. Josune used another exit to surprise two more. She managed to hit one. The other was scarily fast. She only just managed to avoid being shot, and that was because Roystan had ducked out after her.

"That was too close. No games from here."

"They'll corner us eventually. The fewer people out there when we do, the better."

"We don't want fewer of us, though. We need delaying tactics. We have to give Brown time to get here." Roystan put a hand on Josune's arm. "Your people survived three days. We can do this, but we need you alive to show us how."

Josune took out one of the homemade weapons. "This is how they survived, Roystan. Picking them off, one by one. Otherwise, when Brown's ship arrives, they'll pick us off while we load. And probably Brown's crew as well."

Nika watched the screen. There were so many of them. Enough to guard the stairways, enough to search the rooms. Josune was right. Doing nothing was deadly, and it wouldn't take long to be discovered.

If she was going to die here, she would go down fighting.

She held up her mutrient pack. "Let's at least take out the ones on the stairs. Roystan can lock any intervening doors. Josune can keep the ones on this floor occupied, while I do the stairs."

"We don't have time to think about it," Josune told Roystan. "Or we'll lose our opportunity. We can't stay here and wait to be caught."

"You're both certifiable. All of us are." Roystan slammed doors shut all over the ship. "Go. Stairs only, Nika. Don't go down."

Nika ducked through the exit close to the stairs. Two of the enemy turned into the passageway as she did so. Both raised their weapons. A beam of light shot over her shoulder. One of the guards went down. Nika glanced back. Josune. The second guard went down. Snow.

She ran to the stairs, aiming both nozzles, spraying liberally even before she reached the steps. Mutrient and acid splattered on the stairway and surrounding walls. The mixture started to sizzle. Someone screamed. She could hear blaster fire getting closer.

Snow grabbed her arm and pushed her back toward the crew room. "Go."

The door slammed behind them. Josune came in another door at the same time.

"Enough." Roystan had a greenish tinge to his mouth again. "We'll pick off the rest as they try to get into this room."

"It was close," Josune agreed breathlessly. "Thanks, Snow." She looked at the screens. "Did it work?"

Roystan pointed wordlessly to the stairway. Two men were down, both screaming, scrubbing at their faces. He put his two containers to one side. "I think I'll stick to my blaster."

"I am going to look at modders in an entirely different way after this," Carlos said.

"We're not all crazy," Snow said.

"Glad to hear it." Roystan indicated the men converging on the crew room. "Be prepared. I'm sorry it came to this, in the end." He checked the locks on all doors into the crew room.

"Jacques, with me." Jacques moved to his side, a meat cleaver held firmly in one hand, a blaster loosely in the other.

"Josune, you and Nika at door two. Snow, Carlos, door three. Be ready."

They moved into position. "Remember, they want us alive."

They might not be as gentle as they would have been had they given up without a fight, but none of them would go quietly. Neither would Nika. This was Eaglehawk. They gave no mercy.

The man who'd been left in charge was giving orders. "Melt the locks. Take them down." Nika readied her mutrient sprayer.

Roystan's door opened first. His blasts hit the two lead men in the chest. Nika's door opened. She and Josune brought their weapons up, spraying indiscriminately, emptying their backpacks. The men clawed at their faces, howling.

Josune had her blaster out, and her sparker. She put them out of their misery.

Snow dived for the weapons on the floor, then rolled to avoid being blasted by one of the three men left standing. She scattered the weapons and rolled again to avoid another blast.

"Left, Snow, left. Roll left," Nika yelled, because he was about to roll into blaster fire.

Roystan aimed for the man firing at Snow.

Nika smelled burned flesh and heard a grunt of pain from Roystan. She aimed her empty mutrient weapon at one. He backed away. She needed to get to the mutrient mix Roystan had put to one side.

Snow dropped him with the stunner.

Nika pulled out her blaster, fumbled, and dropped it. She bent down to grab it.

Electricity arced beside her. Josune's sparker.

The power went out.

Something heavy thunked over near Roystan. Fist hitting flesh. A grunt.

"Everyone all right?" Roystan asked.

A long orange beam of blaster light flared out, catching Roystan, the force of it turning him before he dropped. The light kept going. On around to Josune, who dived, but not fast enough. Snow dropped seconds later.

Nika was out the door before the beam found her. She ran. To the stairs, and up.

Exposed wire dangled at the top of the stairs.

Nika ducked under it but fell forward as a hand closed around her ankle.

"Nowhere to run. Nowhere to hide. Come quietly now, and I *may* think about letting you live." Her captor wasn't smiling.

Nika dug her heels in, resisting the pull. Above them, the exposed wire sparked.

She had the laser, which she couldn't get to in time, hampered as she was by the space suit.

She did have oxygen, and oxygen and sparks were a bad combination.

There was a breach door between the two of them and the rest of the ship. It would close with the explosion. If the others weren't dead, they might have a chance. She had seconds.

She kicked out.

Her captor let her go. "We don't need you all. Come quietly, or don't come at all."

Nika nodded and stood up. She pulled off her oxygen tank and aimed the nozzle at the spark above them.

She saw the moment it caught, and knew it was futile but snapped the helmet down on her suit. The force of the explosion hit her and blasted them both down the stairs.

The breach doors slammed shut in front of her, closing out the fire. Wrong way. She staggered upright.

The man beside her groaned. The only weapon she had was her helmet. She used it, bringing her head around to meet his in a hard crunch. He went down.

Alarms sounded all over the ship.

Something hit her with a force so bad she almost didn't realize that part of the pain was the prickle of a stunner.

31

NIKA RIK TERRI

Nika regained consciousness to the sound of Jacques shouting.

She opened her eyes.

Jacques crashed against the bars. "I will kill you."

Bars? She squinted. Honest-to-goodness bars. Wall-to-ceiling. They were in a cell.

Nika looked around. It was literally a bare space with nothing in it. The cell bars separated them from the other half of the room. Guards stood on either side of the outside doorway. Two chairs occupied center stage. A stage to view the prisoners.

Aubergine Suit sat in one of the chairs. Nika recognized him, now she saw him in the flesh. Benedict, Wickmore had called him. He'd been one of her clients, and Wickmore had waited all the time he'd been in the tank. After Nika had taken him out, Wickmore had leaned forward, taken a vial out of his pocket, and tossed it in Benedict's face.

Acid. That was where she'd learned that acid could be a weapon.

"You made a mistake, Benedict," Wickmore had said. "Make that your last mistake." He'd stood up. "Don't clean it up," he'd told Nika as he walked out. "Or you'll get the same."

She shivered now, remembering. Wickmore had been charming. Like Alejandro.

The acid burn on Benedict's face was gone. He'd found his way back into favor with Executive Wickmore. He'd also had work done. The squareness to his jaw, almost as telltale as the gleaming teeth. SaStudio.

But it wasn't Benedict that Jacques was screaming at. It was a woman standing to one side. Dark-eyed and tired, with no expression on her face at all.

"Come over here, you coward. See how brave you are when you have to face us."

Nika crawled to her knees. Carlos and Roystan were on the floor behind her. Neither moved. Josune sat propped up against the far wall. Her left side was burned, from the cheek down. Nika's beautiful patterning ravaged. At least the blaster hadn't gotten as high as the eye. She managed to smile as Nika looked at her. It must hurt.

They'd been stripped of their old clothes and were wearing uniform brown coveralls. Strangely, they'd left Nika with her pendant.

Or maybe not so strange. Expensive jewelry—and this looked expensive—was ID-chipped. If they were still inside the legal zone, and Nika could claim ownership to her "jewelry," she could take it to the Justice Department and bring a case of theft against the company. Smaller things than that had tripped up companies before.

Not that Nika had any illusions about being allowed to go free. Not with what had happened so far, but any smart company would play it safe until they'd disposed of the bodies.

Snow had a burn across his shoulder and down his back, but it didn't look too bad. He knelt beside Roystan.

"You're nothing but a thief." Jacques tore at the bars, trying to rip them out. "Let me out of here, Pol, so I can kill you."

Pol. Nika looked at the woman again. She was as tall as Josune, but bulkier. She had a silver tint to her skin, and the curves Nika had made fashionable three seasons ago. So, a body mod, but not too recently. Pol's hair was black, cropped short. A cheap job; a good modder would have silvered the hair to match.

Jacques rattled the bars again. "You sold us out. And now you have the cheek to stand here and gloat."

"I'm not gloating, Jacques." Pol pretended disinterest, but she stood tense.

Nika crawled toward Snow, using the time to catalog her own injuries. Major burns over a third of the lower half of her body, mostly down the left side. They'd turn septic if they weren't treated. She was as bad as Josune.

She stopped at Carlos. He'd taken a full spray. Fifty percent burns. Luckily for him, most were only second-degree. But he was in a bad way. How did a blaster do that sort of damage?

She moved on to Roystan.

Snow looked at her, shook his head.

Unfortunately, she agreed with his prognosis. If Roystan didn't get into a body tank in the next three hours there was nothing she could do for him. She nodded, glad Jacques was otherwise preoccupied, and Carlos was out.

Josune crawled over to join them. They were all in bad shape. Jacques and Snow looked to be the only two capable of standing.

Benedict stood and walked down the line of the cage. Nika waited, tense. His gaze rested on each of them in turn, cold and malevolent.

"You have put me in a very difficult situation, and I am most unhappy about that." He walked the length of the cage again, stopping to look at Jacques. "Unfortunately, I need you alive."

He continued his slow walk. Was that meant to unnerve them? Because if it was, it was working. Nika tried to make herself small.

Benedict fixed his gaze on Snow. "Keeping you alive does not mean keeping you whole. You will wish you were dead soon enough." He turned his gaze back to Jacques. "I don't mind doing this the hard way. You have caused me a lot of trouble."

Nika bet they had. Wickmore didn't give second chances. Benedict was dead if he didn't deliver.

"Captain Feyodor jumped directly to your ship. I want to know why. What did she find that took her to Pisces III and caused her to send a spy to your ship?"

Nika kept her gaze on Benedict, glad Josune looked different now. Pol would have pointed her out if she'd recognized her.

Benedict turned and walked back to stop in front of Nika. "Perhaps you can tell me."

She shook her head.

Jacques rattled the bars one final time. "Feyodor jumped to escape your people, who were killing her. She didn't set a course." He had been listening. "If you haven't worked that out, how do you expect to work anything else out?"

Josune took a deep breath. Nika was glad she kept silent. Did she know she hadn't been recognized? Of course she did. Josune wasn't stupid.

Benedict ignored Jacques and kept watching Nika.

Josune's face was a mask, but her fist clenched. Nika half expected her to go for her sparker there and then. It was crazy, but they'd left her the sparker too. Another expensive piece of jewelry they worried would be ID'd. Nika pressed her lips together to prevent a smile. Two purposes for everything.

Benedict had to have seen Josune's reaction, but he ignored her and kept his gaze on Nika.

"Feyodor found something. Something she didn't tell her crew. Wouldn't you call that strange?"

He was hypnotic. She couldn't look away.

"My people spent three days on the *Hassim*. We hunted down the crew. We tortured them. They died slowly. They knew nothing. We recorded everything. I've been over those records fifty times. That was no random setting she jumped to." His smile hardened. "There was only one thing at that location. Your ship. And Arriola."

Jacques broke the spell. "Tell him, Pol. He's nuts."

"He's telling the truth, Jacques."

Benedict continued as if they hadn't interrupted. "And when the *Hassim* arrives at that location, there you are waiting for us. You board my ship. You kill my men. You take my ship, and you sell it."

Josune gripped the bars. "It never was your ship!" If she gripped any tighter she'd break her fingers.

Please let Josune not say anything that would make Benedict realize who she is.

This time Benedict did look at her. "Salvage law, my dear. There was no one left alive on that ship." His smile was all teeth. "There will be no one left alive on your ship either. But we are not wasteful. As long as you answer my questions, I'm sure we can come to some other arrangement. No one needs to get hurt."

Snow had explained salvage law to Nika. No one left alive to claim ownership of the ship. But Josune hadn't been on the *Hassim*, she'd been on *The Road*. She was dead if Benedict discovered who she was.

His gaze turned back to Nika. "Who, on this ship, has the information Captain Feyodor needed to find Goberling's lode? I want that information. I *will* get it."

"She wasn't there," Pol said. "She's new."

"So why don't you tell me who I do want, Pol?"

Pol raised her chin. Nika could almost read her thoughts. Would lying benefit her?

"I don't want a guess, Pol," Benedict said.

Pol lowered her eyes.

Nika looked at *The Road*'s crew. Jacques angry. Josune tense. Carlos and Roystan unconscious. Snow, sitting by Roystan, worried.

If they told Benedict it was Roystan, would Benedict get him into a machine to save him?

It was the only thing that might.

"If you want to talk to him so desperately," Nika said, "maybe you should get Roystan to a machine. He'll die if you don't, and you won't get any answers at all."

"No." Josune struggled to stand up. "I'm the one you want. Not Roystan. You don't need him." Nika saw the struggle in her face. To protect Roystan, or to have him healed.

Pol looked at Josune contemptuously. "You'd know, of course."

Jacques rammed his shoulder against the bars again. The whole wall shuddered.

"Enough. Maybe she does know, Pol." Benedict pointed at Josune. "What's wrong with you?"

"Me?"

"The flaking skin."

"Burns."

"Botched mod," muttered Snow.

Benedict turned to him. "Snowshoe Bertram, is it?"

Snow sighed. "It's Bertram Snowshoe, actually."

They'd used Snow to buy the Dekker, and his name was around the wrong way on his modding certificate. Benedict must have gotten that particular snippet from the Hub.

"That isn't what it says on your ID."

"It doesn't matter what it says on the ID," Nika said. "What matters is what he's telling you." Benedict would listen to the person he knew as the modder, and get Roystan into a machine. "Tell him, Snow."

Benedict looked Snow up and down. A long, leisurely look. "According to your records, you're a new graduate. If it took that long for you to graduate, maybe we shouldn't be trusting your knowledge."

They didn't have time for this.

"I'm a body modder," Snow said, with as much asperity as Nika herself would have used. "Haven't you heard of people changing their appearance to look older or younger?"

"Most of them do it to look younger," Benedict said, but this time he looked Snow over thoughtfully. "Well, body modder, what can you do to bring Roystan around? I need to talk to him."

"I can't," Snow said.

"Mr. Bertram, come here. Over to the bars."

Snow didn't move.

Benedict brought out his blaster and turned it on Nika. "Come to the bars or I'll shoot your friend."

Snow stood up, hands above his head. He moved slowly to the bars.

"That's better," Benedict said. He pressed the blaster into Snow's neck. "Now, I ask you again—and think carefully about your answer. What can you do to bring Roystan around?"

A bead of sweat dripped down Snow's face and dropped onto the blaster. Nika clasped her fist tightly around the laser pendant. She so badly wanted to turn it on Benedict, but if she did, people would die. Her people.

"Put him into a machine."

Benedict moved the blaster closer. "Are you sure there's nothing else you can do? He doesn't have to live long. Just enough for us to talk."

Something in Snow seemed to snap. They all saw his posture change. He reached up and pushed the blaster away. "Are you questioning my knowledge?"

Nika pulled her pendant free. She wouldn't be able to save him in time.

Benedict didn't fire.

"I am a body modder." Snow pointed to his chest. "I am a *good* modder. I *know* what I'm telling you." He pointed to Roystan. Nika couldn't tell if his finger was shaking from rage, or if he was just shaking. "That man will die if you don't put him into a machine."

Benedict indicated Josune. "Not your work, then?"

"No." Snow turned his back on Benedict and walked back to Roystan.

Pol had a blaster. She raised it.

"Snow." Nika pulled him down fast and rolled on top of him.

The laser dropped from her hand.

Benedict turned, so fast he was a blur. Pol's blaster skittered across the floor. Pol gasped and clutched at her wrist.

"Don't ever presume you can fire on *my* prisoners," Benedict said.

32

JOSUNE ARRIOLA

Roystan was dying.

Josune picked up the laser Nika had dropped while Benedict was facing Pol. Her fingers were numb. She didn't want to think. She slipped the pendant around her neck and dropped it under her coveralls. It was hell on the burned side of her neck, but better than on the floor where Benedict would see it. The nerveseal was wearing off. Her ribs hurt, reminding her that she couldn't do much.

They would pay for what they had done to Roystan. They would pay for the *Hassim*. She had a name. And a face. Benedict was a walking dead man.

As for Pol, it couldn't happen to a more deserving person.

Snow shook, so badly his teeth chattered. Nika shook too, but she remained between Pol and Snow.

"Well, you certainly behave like a modder," Benedict said, as if the interlude with Pol hadn't happened.

Snow sat up. He was still shivering. "Get him into a machine. Otherwise he'll die on you."

Benedict nodded at Pol and returned to his chair. Pol took over the questioning. Her voice wavered slightly.

"What happened to that mad engineer, Josune?"

"Got in the way of a blaster," Jacques said. "As will you when I get out of here." He rattled the bars again.

"Dead?"

Jacques, bless him, didn't look her way. "You should be so lucky. No. She'll be coming for you. You won't even see her coming."

That was for certain.

Josune missed what Pol said next, for Benedict's right eyelid glowed and she turned her attention to him.

There was a pause before he blinked it off. A message.

He looked speculatively at Josune, Nika, and Snow before interrupting Pol midsentence. "We'll continue this conversation later. Let's get Roystan repaired and see what answers he has for us." He turned to one of the guards. "Book a slot. You know which hospital."

"If you want to live," he told Snow, "keep him alive until then. As for the rest of you, I'll give you time to think about what you do know, and how best you can help your captain. Pol, it's time you and I had another chat."

Benedict came back with the station doctor, who brought a stretcher. She didn't bat an eyelid at the burns. Or at the bars, although she did look at the injuries of those assembled behind. She frowned at Josune. "What's wrong with that one? Is she contagious?"

"Botched mod, they say. I'm sure you can confirm that."

The doctor clucked sympathetically. "Can't have that, can we." She turned back to Benedict. "What are you doing with them when you are finished?"

"You mean the ones I don't kill?"

"Yes. They look young and strong and healthy. A cattle ship would take them."

"We are not going onto cattle ships," Snow said.

"You'll get double for them if they go in whole." She beckoned to Jacques and Snow, and pointed to Roystan. "Lift him onto the stretcher for me."

"Not if you're going to sell him off to a cattle ship."

"Snow," Nika said. "He'll die if we don't get him into a machine."

"It's better if he does. At least it will be fast."

Was it better if he died? No. While there was life, there was hope, and Roystan hadn't come this far fighting to give up now.

"He has no hope if he's dead."

Josune pushed past him, tried to lift Roystan's legs, and hissed as her ribs objected. "Just get him on the stretcher."

"You don't—" But Snow helped lift Roystan onto the stretcher.

"I'll do a deal," the doctor said to Benedict. "I'll fix them all and we'll split the sales fifty-fifty."

Once Roystan came out of the machine, Josune would enjoy fighting it out with this doctor.

"And do something about that one." She pointed to Carlos. "He's worth nothing if he's dead. I'll send someone back for him shortly."

"Your expense?"

"I'm sure you wouldn't have it any other way."

Benedict smiled. "You have a deal."

The doctor brought up a form. She thumbprinted and irised it, and nodded to Benedict to do the same. "One for each of them. Make sure they sign it. Without it, it's not legal."

"It'll be legal."

"Pleasure doing business with you." The doctor wheeled Roystan out. Benedict followed.

Josune stretched carefully. Her body was seizing up from her injuries. If they didn't escape soon she might not be able to fight.

If Roystan didn't survive, what was there to fight for anyway?

She'd made him a promise. If Carlos stayed alive long enough for her to keep it. He was collected shortly after. Nika looked relieved to see him go. Josune thought the modder might have agreed with the doctor's assessment of Carlos's chances of survival.

Half an hour later Pol returned.

"Hey. You." Pol looked directly at Josune, keeping far enough away from the bars to avoid the arm Jacques thrust through. "I need to talk to you. Privately."

"Why?" Did Pol know who she was? Had she given herself away?

Jacques fisted his hand and swung. Pol jumped back, though he was nowhere close. "Where's Guardian? Hiding? Too afraid to come out and face us?"

"Guardian." She spat the name out. "Couldn't even finish the job properly."

"Wasn't much of a job he had to finish."

They'd been friends, Jacques and Guardian. Guardian had been the only one, outside of Roystan, who could sweet-talk Jacques into cooking treats he liked. Jacques must have been hurting about the defection ever since, but Josune had never thought about it.

Roystan would have known. He knew his crew.

"He tried to sneak back to *The Road*."

"I'd have killed him if he'd turned up. I still will, when I find him."

"He's dead."

"You killed him. What did he ever do to you?"

It wasn't a smiling matter, but Josune couldn't help herself. Jacques might have been angered by Guardian's betrayal, but he wasn't happy about him being killed. Friendships were funny things.

"I didn't kill him. Qiang did."

Josune didn't believe her.

"Why? Fewer people to share with?"

"He got upset about us taking the money."

Josune spared some pity for Guardian, who had taken the time to be nice to a newbie, and who, at the end, had been decent enough to care that he'd left his former crewmates destitute.

"It was ours as much as yours. Besides, Roystan still had his precious run, while we needed to finance our expedition."

"How sad for you." Josune didn't mean a word of it.

"Because of him sneaking off, Benedict separated us. Doesn't trust us. Guardian got what he deserved."

So had Pol.

"Then you come along and blew up the ship Qiang was on, along with the memory. So here we are."

Josune didn't point out that they hadn't "come" anywhere.

Jacques turned away, disgusted. "And you need Roystan for what? The memory's gone."

Pol's eyes glittered. "It's not about the memory. Benedict was following the *Hassim*. Captain Feyodor discovered something on Pisces III that led to Roystan, or to something on *The Road*."

She lowered her voice and looked directly at Josune. "That's why I need your help. Benedict will kill me once he gets what he wants. I'm no use to him. But together, we can find out what it was. We can all be rich."

Pol certainly didn't lack front, trying to strike a deal in front of people she'd recently robbed.

"Why would I deal? We already have Roystan on our side. What could you give us that he can't?"

"You won't have him after Benedict has finished with him." Pol leaned closer. "We help each other. You look like you can fight. I have information you don't. We can share."

"What information?" Josune glanced back at Jacques. What was he thinking? That she'd sell them out? Nika, at least, would trust her. But Jacques?

Jacques gave a half nod. Almost imperceptible, but it said volumes. She took a deep breath. Roystan's crew had been a team, more than any crew she had known. She'd do anything she could for them.

Even lie to Pol.

Pol's voice dropped lower. Josune had to put her ear to the bars to hear her. Jacques moved closer to hear, too.

"Josune Arriola came from the *Hassim*. She'd been questioning Roystan behind our backs."

Did she really not know who Josune was?

"Do we have a deal?"

"Last deal you made, Pol, ended up with us broke and on the run," Jacques said.

Pol ignored him. "Work with me. I can help you escape." She gripped the bars. "Help me find Josune. Once we have her we can follow Feyodor's trail and work it out ourselves."

Nika's laser was hard against Josune's chest, the sparker in her hair. She took a deep breath and forced herself not to reach for either. Forced herself to continue listening.

"They think I know nothing. But they—" Pol stopped as Benedict entered with two guards.

"That one." Benedict pointed to Snow. Pol might as well not have existed.

One of the guards moved over to the locked door. Beckoned.

Pol slipped out of the room.

Snow looked at Benedict.

"Yes. You. The body modder." Benedict smiled, and the smile held a touch of grimness to it. "Your captain isn't responding well to the tank."

"Snow," Nika said, urgently. "His DNA." She turned to Benedict. "I need to come."

"I only want the body modder." Benedict turned away.

Snow hesitated. "I know how to heal people, Nika. Better than you."

"This is not basic medicine, Snow."

"I know what I'm doing."

Nika looked as if she wanted to shake him. "Call me as soon as you know you're in too deep."

Benedict must have heard them, but he appeared not to notice.

"I know what I'm doing, Nika. I've spent years healing people. I don't need your help." The guard unlocked the door.

Snow followed Benedict out into the passage. He didn't look back.

Carlos returned a few hours later, his body covered in pink repair work but otherwise healthy.

Nika spent the night pacing.

Josune wanted to tell her to settle. When the time came to fight, they didn't need people who'd already expended their strength.

"Snow hasn't come back," Josune pointed out. "Neither has Benedict." He couldn't have missed Pol's little talk, even if he'd ignored it. "Maybe Snow is actually fixing Roystan."

Nika snorted and continued her pacing.

Josune considered her options. She had her sparker and Nika's laser. Benedict had multiple ships, lots of weapons, and crew enough to use them. They'd already proven in a head-to-head fight that Eaglehawk would win. They needed to run. But first, they had to escape. The longer they sat here in this little cell, the harder it would be to do so, because Benedict wasn't feeding them. Did he intend to starve them into submission?

"They could at least give us something to drink," Carlos grumbled.

Which only made Josune thirsty.

They wouldn't leave without Roystan. They had to wait for him to come out of the machine. But the rest of them grew weaker while they waited.

They couldn't afford to wait.

Pol hadn't returned. Because Benedict forbade it? Or because she wasn't alive any longer?

The door opened. It was the doctor, with a suited company representative.

"I'll take the youngest one first," she said, indicating Josune. "The younger they are, the better value. Get her print."

This company representative looked as young as Josune did. He wore an obsidian pin on his lapel. Shiny and new, and from the way he admired it as he passed his reflection, he hadn't had it long.

He grinned. "Come on out now. Aren't you the lucky one. Your burns are about to be healed."

"Just as soon as you sign the form," the doctor said. "I'm not wasting good mutrient if I don't get any value out of it."

If she only had to sign, good. If she had to use iris or thumbprint, they'd discover her identity. They were running out of time. She forced herself to breathe naturally. She was carrying two weapons, but if she used them now she'd get them all killed.

"What am I signing?" she asked, as she allowed herself to be pushed along.

"Just a little something that says you accept responsibility for my saving your life. And it gives you a job at the same time."

Cattle ship. "You know, it's illegal not to warn the signee what they're getting into."

"You don't get the cure if you don't sign. You must be hurting." The doctor glanced sideways. "And starving."

If this doctor was in the way when they finally started fighting, Josune wasn't going to point her weapon away to spare her. Her returning look was cool. "I'll survive," she said. "But I admit I'd like to stop the pain."

"Good. You'll sign, then."

"I'll sign," Josune agreed. "But I want to read it first." She was stalling for time. She needed to get rid of her weapons. She didn't want to leave them unattended on a bench while she went into a modding machine. Except, how?

"It won't make any difference."

"I know that, but I like to read my contracts."

"More fool you. I don't care. Just don't take long about it."

They came into the hospital. A smallish room, crowded with four emerald Dietels, the machines Nika despised so much. Three of them were occupied.

Snow sat by the one nearest the door. He looked haggard. Roystan was in the machine in front of him. Josune could see his outline against the green glass. He was so still.

But then, wasn't everybody once you got them into a genemod machine?

She stopped beside Snow. "How's it going?"

Snow's eyes were rimmed with red. His face was gaunt. He indicated the displays. Everything was red.

He shook his head.

"We turned the alarms off," the doctor said. "The noise annoyed me. You don't get time to chat to your friend. You get time to read the contract."

Josune sat down. "Pull it up."

"What, you can't pull it up on your own?"

"I had a hand link," Josune said. It was easier than explaining. She didn't want to explain, anyway. Not to this doctor who sold bodies for half the profit.

"I didn't think they made them anymore." The doctor looked at her consideringly. "No ship wants someone who can't communicate."

Josune shrugged and waited for the doctor to think it over. The loudest noise was the swish of the inlet valves on the machine on the man farthest from Roystan.

"Josune," Snow said, suddenly, urgently. "I've done everything I can for Roystan."

She looked at him.

"I've stabilized him as much as I can. The machine's keeping him alive, but only just. I can't do any more." His eyes glistened with unshed tears. "It's not going to keep him alive forever."

"Not much longer, I'd say," the doctor said.

Josune could see that Snow agreed with the diagnosis by the way he rubbed his palms together. How did she point out that Nika was a body modder too? Without him closing down on the idea completely?

He said, "I know Nika does some dangerous things. Like when she pulled you out of the machine early."

Maybe she didn't have to.

Snow closed his eyes. "I know she's been deregistered, but she's still a modder."

If Rik Terri—one of the best-known modders around—had been deregistered, it would have been all over the media.

"I know she's crazy. I know she's never done any medical work. And I'm still not sure if she lied or not about going to Landers."

He took a deep breath. "But Roystan's dying, Josune. And sometimes Nika thinks differently than other modders. She might—"

Josune's own eyes were watering. "She might."

"I can't think of anything else to do, and he'll die soon."

"Snow." Josune hugged him. Almost too late she remembered the weapons, and swiftly transferred Nika's laser from her coveralls to his, pulled the sparker out of her hair, and dropped it down there too.

She pressed a palm to his chest, so that he wouldn't touch the weapons. This might have been a bad idea. "I hear you, Snow. I was thinking of what Nika used to say. Two reasons for everything."

"Two reasons?" Snow sounded out the words, as if the syllables didn't make sense. They probably didn't, but at least she'd stopped him drawing attention to the weapons she'd transferred to him.

"I come here to be cured. You needed me here to reassure you that it's all right to call Nika in, no matter what the consequences. Two reasons."

She'd said her private good-byes to Roystan earlier, in that stuffy little cell where she thought they'd all die. She'd hardly dared believe they'd put him into a tank. Snow had been convinced Roystan was dying, and so had Nika. Josune hadn't hoped. Now, Snow was giving Nika a chance, and she knew she shouldn't believe it would make a difference, but it did.

Snow blinked and put his own hand to his chest.

She thought he was going to give them away, but he was only settling the load. "Right. Two reasons." He turned to the doctor. "I need the other modder to look at him."

"Not sure I like having a deregistered modder in my hospital."

Josune hoped the conversation was all that she'd followed.

"You can't do anything. Snow says he can't. Why not let Nika try? Can she do any worse?"

The doctor looked around. "Deregistered. She'll probably waste expensive product. I can't afford that." She waited expectantly.

Josune was used to bargaining, but this was blatant extortion. "How much?"

"Three thousand credits."

When the average wage for a crew hand was three hundred credits a week. If she promised twice as much as she supposedly earned, they would suspect something. Or not believe her. "Eighteen hundred. I've got six weeks' wages in my bank. That's it."

"My cut's ten percent," the company man told the doctor. "For not letting it go any further than this room."

"It's all I have," Josune said. "I can't give you any more." They didn't have time to bargain.

Snow twitched. He glanced at the silent machine.

"If you don't take it," Josune said, "it will be too late." She should have kept her weapons.

She looked around for something else to use. "Maolic acid?" she asked Snow hopefully.

"It's naolic acid."

"Deal." The doctor handed the scanner to Josune for her payment.

Josune paid, praying Benedict hadn't told this doctor he was looking for Josune Arriola.

He hadn't, it seemed, for the doctor only glanced at the receipt, nodded, and looked at the company man. "You get the deregistered one while this lady here signs her other contract."

33

NIKA RIK TERRI

Nika was half dragged, half helped across to the end Dietel. She glanced over to where Josune was installed. The machine would destroy Josune's lovely detail. It had been good work.

She flashed Snow a quick smile before turning to Roystan. She was nearly too late. Why had Snow left it until so late to call her?

Benedict walked silently into the room and settled in a chair. Pol was with him. By the look on Pol's face, it wasn't her choice to be here. The doctor glanced at them, glanced at Nika, then turned back to her work.

It was eerily silent, although every light on Roystan's machine was flashing red. Nika turned up the volume. Sometimes you could hear the problem before you saw it.

"Oh, please," said the doctor, as the hospital filled with the cacophony of alarms.

Nika ignored her. The first thing she did was switch off the rejuv, inflow by inflow, until there was nothing left except life support.

"You can't do that," the doctor protested. "He's liable to die from his injuries."

"Nika," Snow said. "It's what's keeping him alive."

Nika hardly heard them. She was counting under her breath. Six, seven, eight.

The alarm on the first inflow cut out. Then the second, then the third, until at last there was blissful silence again.

She leaned against the side of the Dietel, her legs shaking, and watched Roystan's vital signs. His heartbeat was settling from the erratic pulsing induced by the forced mods. Brain activity was normal for a man in an induced coma. He wasn't going to die immediately. Good.

The rest of him was a mess.

"I don't think you should have done that," Snow said.

The doctor came to stand beside her. "What do you expect him to do? Get better by himself? It'll take months."

It was always an option when nothing else worked, although Nika thought that in this case his body would probably break down first. "Do you have any hu-skin?" Roystan had needed hu-skin to fix his blaster burn.

The doctor laughed. "You're joking, right?"

Nika wished she were. She scanned the monitors. The lack of food and liquid didn't help. She had no balance, and everything had a double image.

"I need food," she said. "Water."

"It's in the drip."

"For me. For Snow too." He looked as if he was ready to drop. "They haven't fed us. They haven't given us anything to drink. We're weak enough to make stupid mistakes." She looked at Benedict.

"Get them something," Benedict ordered one of his company people. "Water. Rations. Nothing fancy."

The machine was set up for heavy burns. Nika had used similar settings on her own Songyan for blaster burns on Alejandro's friends. There was nothing wrong with that. It would have worked on a normal body.

No, the damage was more integral than that.

Old Base had used hu-skin. To Nika, that was another signifier of a DNA problem. She pulled up the DNA read. It took three tries.

Another Dietel sounded completion. It made Nika jump. The

doctor shook her head and she moved over to open it. "I want you to know," she said to Benedict, "if he dies, it's nothing to do with me."

Nika thought she didn't care, either.

"You're the doctor," Pol said. "He's your responsibility. The man's been in a fight. You say you can't fix it. You're lying."

Pol had better hope she never had reason to come to this doctor for mods. Not the way the doctor looked at her. "We've a body modder here, and he can't fix him either."

Neither Pol nor the doctor would come out of it well if Roystan died. They were already laying the blame elsewhere. Snow wouldn't come out any better, but his situation was settled. Cattle ship. Snow would hate that.

"Body modding is not basic medicine," Snow said. "Few modders make good doctors. They don't have the experience."

Snow might be welcome at the hospital—he was saying things the doctor liked to hear—but Benedict was listening, and he didn't need to hear things like that.

"This is not basic medicine," Nika said. "His DNA has been modified."

"Liar," Pol said. "Roystan wouldn't even go to a modder when he broke his nose."

Nika checked. She hadn't been looking for tiny cosmetics like that. Sure enough, there was the hairline crack and the mend that pushed the nose out of true. She should have seen that when she'd first observed his nose on ship.

"It took months to set and he still refused to see a modder about it. There's no way he'd go for anything larger."

He'd gone to Tilda, who'd studied with Hannah Tan, who knew how to fix botched DNA mods.

"If either of you wants to take over, you can," Nika said. She knew neither of them would. She tuned them out and concentrated on the details scrolling up the screen.

"You hear me?" Pol demanded.

Nika hardly noticed.

She recognized DNA changes. She recognized it now, as Roystan's DNA scrolled up.

The changes—always in the same places. Coding that Nika hadn't looked at since she'd left Hannah Tan's studio to start her own.

Pure Giwari. Except for the telomere at the end.

The only problem was, Giwari had been dead eighty years.

Nika clung dizzily to the edge of the Dietel while she tried to think, gulped the water Snow handed her. "Thanks."

Roystan looked to be in his late thirties. Maybe he was older. Even so, he'd have been a child when Giwari got hold of him. Why would anyone change the DNA of a growing child?

The alternative—that one of Giwari's changed subjects had bred—was less likely, but what else could it be? Nika revised her opinion of Giwari. Maybe Hannah had been right. Maybe he had been a genius. Changing one's DNA normally made you sterile. Had Roystan's parents—or grandparents—bred true? Had Giwari had an apprentice? She'd never heard of one.

Or was Roystan older than he looked?

The lack of food didn't help her think. She scrolled back through the DNA, blinking, trying to focus.

The numbers ran together.

"She's stalling." Pol reached for a weapon she didn't have at her hip anymore. "It's an excuse."

Nika tuned her out again.

Roystan's DNA was a Giwari design. No question. The only question was whether it was first-generation or second-generation Giwari. But while it was classic Giwari, the mods on the telomeres at the end weren't. Either Roystan had been modded twice, or that was the change that had allowed the first generation to breed.

Nika touched her finger to her jaw, linked in, and copied the results to her own personal memory. She'd study it in detail later.

Roystan's heart and lungs were both strong, but he was struggling to breathe—the Dietel had to continuously drain his lungs and help the heart keep pumping. He'd be dead without the machine.

His skin was supple, although his bones were brittle and fragile. He had the body of a man in his thirties, and the bones of someone three times that.

A goodly portion of that body was covered in hu-skin. More of it was covered in a synthetic that took half an hour's analysis to identify. Nuagahide. She hadn't been born when they last used nuagahide. Regeneration had improved so much since then. Nowadays they used the person's own skin to repair damage, and if they couldn't, they used hu-skin.

Nika sat back and stared at the screen as she considered the results.

Roystan looked to be around her own age, but the machines didn't lie. Here, in front of her, was the body of a man whose skin had first been repaired before Nika was born.

With a DNA change done by a man dead eighty years.

Hammond Roystan was an old man.

Nika came back to the present to find everyone watching her. The only sound she could hear was the low music piped through the speakers, and the soft hum of the other mod machines working. Roystan's machine missed every third revolution. It needed servicing.

"Discovered a problem you can't fix." There was a hint of smugness about the doctor.

"There's never a problem I can't fix, provided I have the time to do it in." And the tools. But what did she have?

She turned to Snow. "See how I've stabilized the body by turning off any mods?"

He nodded. "But the doctor's right. It will take months for him to recover this way. He won't make it. His kidneys, heart, and lungs will give out beforehand."

They wouldn't be the first to give out. "You forgot his blood. In a couple of hours his blood won't be able to carry any more oxygen. If we can't keep the oxygen to his brain, it won't matter if he does live. He'll be brain-dead."

It wasn't as if the Dietel wasn't trying to force the oxygen through. That was the problem with nuagahide, one of the reasons they'd stopped using it.

"In fifteen minutes we'll have to push more oxygen through to him. Watch him in the meantime. Let me know if anything—anything at all—changes."

Snow nodded.

Now to see what raw materials were available. She looked around the room.

The doctor stood, arms crossed, smiling faintly. Benedict sat in the only chair—presumably the doctor's work chair—elegant and watchful.

He reminded her of Alejandro, back when she had thought she was in love with him.

She looked around further. Supply cupboards would be . . . over there.

"What are you doing?" the doctor demanded, as she made her way across.

"Seeing what you have."

"I didn't say you could use anything."

The supply cupboard was locked. Nika looked at Benedict, rather than the doctor. "I need raw materials."

Benedict glanced over at the Dietel. At the doctor. "Open it."

She opened it, with a backward glance that might have been sullen or might have been scared.

Nika went through the cupboard. They had large vats of mutrient, some basic salts, naolic acid, and some of the more basic acids. Not a lot here she could use on a man whose DNA wouldn't replicate outside his own body.

"Do you have transurides?" Giwari always used transurides in his work.

The doctor laughed. "You're joking, right."

"No. I'm not." If Roystan truly had been modded by Giwari, she'd have to get transurides from somewhere, and the only place she knew of any was the tiny bird of prey on Benedict's lapel. He wouldn't hand that over.

Maybe if she told him about it being a marker? She'd think about that later. She took some mutrient and naolic acid and placed them on the bench behind the Dietel, with as much distance between the two as she could. "Just in case," she told a wide-eyed Snow. "You know what it's for."

He moved as far away from them as he could.

She looked down at Roystan again. If he'd been Banjo she could have used his own muscle tone for some of the work. Would probably still have to do that anyway. How much did he weigh?

"He'll come out of this weak. No energy reserves." And thin. So very thin.

Roystan's blood oxygen levels were becoming dangerously low. "We need to restart the healing process," Nika told Snow. "Let's turn on inflow three—the mutrient. It will force oxygen into his blood, but it will also stress his heart. Start with ten milliliters a minute."

"Me?" Snow said. "Aren't you—"

"If you're going to be my apprentice, Snow, you have to learn. Ease it in."

"I'm not . . . I have a shop, remember." Then Snow turned to the Dietel and carefully set the feed. "Had a shop," he muttered.

"I still don't get why you can't stick him in a box and let the machine do its job," Pol said. "It works for everyone else."

"That is why we are the modders, and you're not." Nika looked at her newly declared apprentice. Had she said that? Out loud. She never took apprentices.

"Run that for five minutes, Snow. I'll get more mutrient."

Fresh mutrient this time, not like the solution she'd left on the bench. They had to keep the food up to his body. If she did it properly she could feed him a little faster than he used his own cells, so at least he wouldn't starve. Or not much, anyway.

"Hey," the doctor said. "That stuff's expensive, and you've already got some out."

"That's for emergencies." They didn't have to know what type of emergencies. "I need fresh mutrient, not something that's getting close to its use-by date." Now, all she had to do was convince Roystan's body to take it. "I need to talk to Jacques," she told Benedict. "A link is fine."

"So I'm your personal aide now, am I?"

"You're the one who has to agree to it."

She thought he only agreed out of curiosity.

"Jacques," Nika said when he'd joined the link. "I need to know every single ingredient you put in that spicy flatbread. Everything. How much of it, and what brand. No secrets this time, Jacques. Not if you want to help Roystan."

She noted every item and brought up the chemical composition for each.

"And the porridge?" Which turned out not to be porridge at all. In fact, it was a mushroom slurry.

"Really?" No wonder it had looked so bad.

"Genuine shiitake mushrooms, from Earth," Jacques confirmed.

And most useful when Roystan was badly run-down. If he was reasonably healthy—healthy for Roystan—then the mushrooms weren't required. It was the spices in the flatbread that worked.

"I don't suppose you have the ingredients here," she said to Benedict. "So he could make some up."

Benedict leaned back in his chair and crossed his arms. "Earth foods. Imported here. Even if I did have, I wouldn't. I'm not covering those costs."

What had made Jacques try the mushrooms—and the spices, for they were also from Earth—in the first place? But Benedict was right, she'd never get them here. Therefore, she had to work out what it was that was helping Roystan's body, and somehow manufacture them.

She watched as Snow added a minute amount of mutrient to the feed, just as she was about to tell him to do it. He learned well.

His movements were slow and heavy.

"Get some sleep after this, Snow. You need it. I'll need you to take over from me later."

Snow nodded, found a space on the floor, and fell asleep almost instantly.

Nika opened a link and worked through the ingredients in the foods Jacques had listed. She began with the porridge. The shiitake mushrooms provided two promising leads. Vitamin D_2 and beta-glucans.

Weak bones were a symptom of a lack of vitamin D, and Roystan certainly had weak bones. She carefully added vitamin D_2 to the mix going into Roystan's body.

Every fifteen minutes she turned on the feed of mutrient on the Dietel and cleansed Roystan's blood for three minutes. The vitamin didn't seem to change anything.

Nika started to build beta-glucan molecules.

The doctor had no equipment for mixing molecules, but one of the Dietels wasn't being used, so she borrowed it.

"What are you doing?" one of the guards said. "Sabotaging it?"

She looked up. Benedict had gone. So had Pol and the doctor. They must have been gone a while, for the second guard had been dozing, coming awake now with a start at his companion's voice.

"Mixing molecules. This hospital doesn't have anything that will let me create them. It's primitive."

Their talking had woken Snow. He yawned hugely and came over to check Roystan's status.

"He's still alive."

Nika wished he hadn't sounded so surprised. "Of course he is. That's what we're here for. To save his life."

"I know, but—" He yawned again and scratched his head. "He shouldn't be."

Nika tapped the second Dietel. "What we're doing here, Snow, is making our own polysaccharides."

He blinked. At least he didn't ask what a polysaccharide was.

"This is the one we're making." She brought up the formula. "I'm taking the results from inlets one to four and outputting them into five. You make sure that what comes out into inlet five is this, and only this."

The guard said, "It's not really an inlet, then, is it. It's an outlet." He sniggered at his own joke.

Nika ignored him. She went back to figuring out what the spices were. Jacques had called them chili peppers. Nika had never heard of them, but she dug through the historical records until she found something. Capsaicin, 8-methyl-N-vanillyl-6-nonenamide, which turned out to be a major irritant for mammals.

Why would Roystan's body react well to that? If it did.

"Done," Snow said, as the secondary Dietel beeped. "What do we do with it?"

"Now we see what the impact of giving this to Roystan is." Nika disconnected the whole inlet tube and took it across to Roystan's machine. "Disconnect inlet five for me, please."

He did it swiftly. "We had Dietels in our first year at Landers. We all had to use them. Except Nika Rik Terri, who refused to. She was allowed to use the second year's Netanyu instead."

Nika connected the inlet lines she was holding. "I'm sure she didn't refuse to use them. Just refused to use them on herself."

She'd refused to be pink.

"You said you went to school with her. You must have known what she was like."

"Unfortunately, yes." Around third year, Nika decided she needed to learn all the modding machines. She couldn't use something if she didn't know how it worked, so she'd sneaked back on the weekends to run herself through the Dietel, observe the results, and then run herself through another machine to hide those results. By then, Chatty had given her a key to the labs.

"That was a long time ago, Snow." Nika eased the gauge up on inlet five, half a milliliter at a time.

She stopped at six.

At first it didn't seem to be doing anything. Until Nika went to do the next blood cleanse and found that Roystan didn't need it.

An hour later they both agreed. Roystan's body was taking oxygen again.

"But it doesn't change anything," Nika said. "As you pointed out earlier, his heart, lungs, and kidneys will fail if we can't do it fast enough."

It took four hours to mix up a compound from the base components. She added the capsaicin to outlet three. "Let's see how this goes." She slowly moved the inlet feed up, delicately and carefully.

They waited.

"His temperature's rising," Snow said. "We should turn it off."

"No. Wait." By all accounts that was what capsaicin did. If that was so, then something would happen as the body got hotter. Rather like running a fever.

They watched as his temperature crept up. 37.5. 37.6. 37.7. 37.8. 37.9.

"How far?" Snow whispered.

Roystan's temperature jumped to 40.2.

"Turn it off." He reached over to turn off the feed.

Nika reached out to stop him. "No. Wait. Everything's stabilized. Look."

"At 40.2 degrees?"

"Turn on the mutrient feed, Snow." It came out as a whisper.

"He's running a fever."

She turned on the feed herself. The alerts on the screen went green.

"That's impossible. He's 40.2 degrees."

At least the temperature had stopped going up. Nika leaned back against the wall, suddenly aware of how exhausted she was.

She watched the screen, the tiny green dots spreading through Roystan's body. Slowly, ever so slowly. Watched the other vitals. Heart, lungs, liver, kidney. Calculated the time the machine told her they had before the organs deteriorated too much to use.

They didn't have enough time.

"Nika."

Snow was experienced with death. He'd recognize what he was seeing.

"I know," Nika said. "We have to speed up the process, or he'll still die."

34

NIKA RIK TERRI

Gino Giwari had used transurides in everything. Especially della-rine. He believed the body would accept that metal even when it rejected everything else. When Nika had worked at Hannah Tan's she'd learned to use dellarine to quickly rip apart a bad gene mod and stitch it back together. Other transurides worked, too, but not as well.

If Nika could get hold of some, she was sure she could hasten the healing. Enough to do something about the organs that were failing.

She only needed a trace amount.

Which was fine, because trace amounts were all you ever got. Until Goberling had found his lode, transurides were found in small quantities in the soil on some worlds.

She'd have to take Benedict's pin. It wouldn't have dellarine, but the transurides it did contain might be enough.

Nika looked at the mutrient. At the naolic acid. There was only one way.

Snow looked uneasily in the same direction.

But first, she'd ask again.

Benedict arrived well rested and smelling of coffee. Her stomach gurgled at the scent of it. They'd need proper food soon.

"They spent all night making things in another machine," the guard who'd stayed awake said. "They seemed happy with what they had. Until about an hour ago."

"What happened an hour ago?"

"Not sure. She said"—he nodded at Nika—"they have to speed up the process or he'll die."

"Get the doctor here," Benedict told the guard. He turned to Nika. "How long before he's ready to talk?"

"We need transurides."

Benedict sat down and crossed his ankle over his knee. "Even if I had some, I wouldn't waste them on you. Or him."

The doctor arrived, out of breath. "What's happened?"

"You tell me," Benedict said.

She checked Roystan's monitor. "He's still alive?" There might have been some respect there. She turned to Snow. "Nice job."

Did she realize he was dying?

"It wasn't me," Snow said.

"It was teamwork," Nika said.

"Teamwork. Hah. When you spent the night asleep, leaving him to do all the work."

Benedict leaned forward. "Why do you say that?"

"Look at her. Skin glowing with life, refreshed. She's had eight hours of healthy sleep."

Snow looked at Nika. "You do look fresh. Don't you need sleep?"

"Of course I do." She'd crash soon. "That's the sign of a good mod, Snow." And the dellarine that added the translucency.

Dellarine.

She clutched his arm. "Snow. I've got del . . . It's part of my mod." She dragged him over to the Dietel they'd been using. "We can get it from me."

"Hey," the doctor said. "You can't use that machine."

Nika's fingers flew over the panel, programming it. "Watch me, see what I do. You might need to do it one day."

"You're too fast."

Next time, then. "Collect every single molecule in inlet five. We'll need everything we can."

"Don't touch that machine."

"Keep that woman away from the machine. Away from me." If either of them understood what she was doing, would they let Snow keep the metal? No. She hoped they didn't understand. "I'm not giving this stuff up for anyone except Roystan. Understand that?

"And Snow. Don't touch the controls on Roystan's machine. No matter how bad you think he is. Ready?"

She stripped and was in the tank before Snow had time to object. The last thing she saw before the machine took her under was Snow bumping the doctor out of the way. She hoped she'd come out of this alive.

Nika came out of the tank feeling better than she'd gone in. The Dietel had done some basic healing. The burn on her side was gone.

Pink skin. No! She shouldn't have been in such a hurry. She should have thought first.

"Satisfied," the doctor said to Benedict. "She planned this all along."

"You look terrible," Snow told her. He had a graze along his cheek and the makings of a black eye.

Nika grimaced. "You ever tell anyone I came out of a Dietel, Snow, and you're dead." She pulled on her coveralls as she moved over to Roystan's tank. "Where's our supply?"

He handed over the precious container from inlet five.

She checked the solution. It had the characteristic oiliness of suspended transurides. It wasn't oily, it was the way the particles trapped and captured the light.

"Roystan?"

"Still at 40.2 degrees. Body repairs up 0.5 percent to 7.3. Deterioration of vital organs increasing." He bit his lip. "We're too late, Nika."

"You're never done until you're done, Snow." She connected the dellarine to input six on Roystan's machine. "Now, watch carefully. This stuff is expensive and you can't afford to get it wrong."

She turned down the capsaicin feed. And the mutrient. "First, we stabilize his temperature, because this metal only spreads through the body at a temperature of 37 degrees."

They waited as the temperature went down. While they did, Nika reprogrammed the Dietel. Old, familiar programs that she hadn't used in years. Coding she'd learned from her time with Hannah Tan, back when fixing bad DNA mods had been part of her job, and transurides had been a necessary part of the process to tear the DNA apart, rather than now, when she used it mostly to add mods. Like the glow to her skin, now gone.

"I thought it was bad when you used Banjo's body for modding Banjo," Snow said. "Now you're using the contents of someone else's body."

If Snow thought this was bad, wait until they really got started. Nika knew that only Roystan's body could be used to repair his damaged organs.

"Is that really dellarine?" Benedict asked, making them jump.

Nika had forgotten anyone else was there. She looked around. The doctor had gone. "What's it to you?"

"And it gave your skin that glow?"

"If you wanted cutting-edge mods you should have come to my studio. Instead, you went to SaStudio and got perfect teeth and a square jaw."

Benedict stiffened. "How do you know where I got my mods done?"

"Samson Sa," Nika said to Snow. "He's obsessed with teeth." He'd probably had bad teeth as a child. "And he loves a square jaw. What you see there is classic SaStudio. It's like a signature."

Snow looked at Benedict. Benedict looked at Nika. Both were a little openmouthed.

"What you're aiming for, Snow, are mods so unique no one knows who did them. And every season you come up with a different look. Go ahead, have a closer look. I'll watch the temperature."

Snow shrugged apologetically and declined to go closer. "She does it to everyone," he told Benedict. "She did it to Roystan when she met him."

"Thirty-seven," Nika said, as Roystan's temperature dropped to that. It kept dropping. She hand-fed the capsaicin flow until it settled at the required temperature. "Let's get this stuff in, Snow. Very, very gently, now."

She kept the temperature steady as Snow carefully fed the dellarine in.

"Good. Good. We're done." She waited half an hour to be sure it had dispersed. "Now, I'm taking his temperature back up again." She'd never heard of transurides working at that temperature before, but Giwari's mod seemed to require it.

At 40.2 degrees, they added mutrient again. This time the alarms stayed silent. One by one, the telltales went green.

"Look, it's taking," Snow said, as the dellarine kicked in, sped the process, the effect doubling, then doubling again. "He's getting better. You're a genius."

Nika hated to dampen the sense of wonder. "No, Snow. That's just the start. Now we get to work. We've repairs to do, and I can tell you now that we'll have to use his own body to do it. There's nothing in this studio, or out of it, that will work on him. Let's get to it."

35

NIKA RIK TERRI

Roystan came out of his tank six days after Tamati came out of his—if Nika had calculated Tamati's times properly.

"Hello, old man," she said.

Roystan blinked at her.

"Don't mind her." Snow helped Roystan sit up. "She has a terrible bedside manner. You're just lucky she knows what she's doing."

That wasn't what he'd said to her the second day, when he'd asked her if she knew there were ways to use a genemod machine without stripping the customer's muscle to do so.

"You look old right now," Snow continued. "But that's because you've lost so much weight." He threw an accusing look at Nika. "Once you get some muscle tone back you'll be fine."

The guard assigned to watch them opened a link. "Prisoner's awake, Mr. Benedict."

Roystan looked down at his hands, skeletal on the machine bed. Despite what Snow claimed, he didn't look old, just pared down, and intense. With a healthy glow.

"How long have I been out?" His movements were shaky as he obediently ate the garfungi Nika gave him. Benedict had been surprisingly obliging there.

"Seven days."

"Seven!" He looked at his hands again, at the machine he was sitting up in. There were no other patients today. He, Snow, Nika, and the guard were the only inhabitants of the hospital. The doctor had taken the day off. Even Pol had stopped dropping by for updates. "Did I . . . did you?"

"Yes. We did." He had to know how dangerous it had been. Euphoria was starting to set in, overlaying the exhaustion. A mod like that. Snow didn't realize what they'd done. And to do it under the masterpiece that had come before.

Roystan looked around. "Where are we?"

"No idea." They'd been too busy to find out. "We were captured. Eaglehawk's in charge. A man named Benedict. And Pol's here. They want to interrogate you."

Roystan pushed his plate away. "My crew?"

Nika pushed it back. "Eat everything in front of you, even if you don't want to." She guided his hand back to the spoon. "So far, no one's dead, or on a cattle ship, because no one knows what you told your crew." She hoped Roystan understood her subliminal message.

They'd all been interrogated. Nika had been grateful for the doctor's insistence that Roystan would die if they took Snow or her away for the same treatment.

"What was Gino Giwari like?"

Roystan stopped, spoon to his mouth, while he considered. "Confident. Very sure in what he could do." He smiled. "You remind me of him. Obsessed."

She wasn't sure it was a compliment. "Eat your protein."

"Gino Giwari has been dead eighty years," Snow said.

When Roystan regained his weight, he'd look much as he'd looked before. A man in his late thirties, except for the salt-and-pepper hair. He'd look as if he'd never been near a genemod machine. Not even to fix his nose. Her old boss had been right. Giwari had been more than a technician.

"Tell me, when did your hair start to go gray?"

"I . . . that might have been part of it, actually."

Naturally graying hair was a trend that came and went. It was used to show maturity, to show that the person who went gray at the temples was less concerned about themselves than they were about managing their business. It was popular with high-end executives, and had last been fashionable ten years ago. The style was difficult to maintain, because the silver tended to proliferate on its own. If Roystan had retained the same percentage of gray over that many years, Giwari had been very, very good. Nika tried to hide how impressed she was. "And your nose?" Noses grew over time.

He rubbed it reflexively. "I'm not sure."

Benedict arrived, the doctor not far behind.

Nika nearly asked that they move Roystan somewhere more comfortable, but who knew what they would do to him, so she made sure he was sitting up properly, crooked a finger at Snow, and moved over to the doctor's station to get some hot, sweet tea for Roystan.

"Shouldn't we stay close to protect him?" Snow asked quietly as he joined her there.

She shook her head. It was better if Benedict forgot all about them for the moment. Otherwise he'd lock them back up with the others.

"Where are my crew?"

"They're safe," Benedict said. "And they'll stay safe while you cooperate with us."

"No thanks to him," Snow muttered quietly. It had taken a lot of talking to ensure that the others were all right.

"Will they still be safe once I tell you what you want to know?" Roystan looked around the hospital. "I want to see them. All of them." And he lay back and closed his eyes.

Snow rolled his eyes. "We told them so," he said quietly. Benedict couldn't have heard, but he glanced their way.

"It's time you took your patient back, Doctor. These two modders have taken enough of your resources."

"Be sure I'll be billing Eaglehawk for it."

Sometimes the doctor didn't know when to shut up.

"He's weak," Nika said. "Don't push him too hard or he'll collapse." If that gave Roystan ideas, then good. "Feed him garfungi."

Benedict waved two guards in to take them away.

"And don't put him in a machine without one of us there."

"Oh my god," Benedict said, and she knew she was meant to hear the parting remark. "I pity anyone having to work with her."

36

JOSUNE ARRIOLA

Day lighting. Night lighting. Day lighting. Night lighting.

Josune lost count after day four.

Each morning, when the day lights came on, Josune worked through a set of exercises. Lethargy could destroy escape plans as easily as anything else.

Benedict hadn't killed them. Nor had he sold them off to a cattle ship, as the doctor must be pressing for. She took that as good news. Roystan must still be alive. Otherwise they'd be on their way to the nearest war by now, ready to give their life in service. Nika and Snow too, neither of whom they'd seen for days.

That they hadn't meant Benedict was keeping Roystan's crew to pressure him when he was well enough to talk.

Twice Benedict took each of them away to ask them what Feyodor had wanted Roystan for. The second time, Jacques came back in berserker mode. It had taken an hour to calm him. Carlos curled up on the floor and refused to talk to anyone for at least a day after his sessions.

Josune's sessions had been unpleasant. She'd told the truth—as much as Benedict had asked, anyway. She knew Roystan was hiding something. No, she didn't know what. Yes, it was Roystan that Feyodor was after. Josune didn't see any point lying about it, not after Nika had told Benedict that.

It had been a clever move, had kept them all alive and together days after they should have been. She hoped she'd get to tell Nika that face to face.

Pol visited twice.

"I can't help you if you won't help me," Josune told her, the second time. "I need out of here. I need a weapon, I need somewhere to go." She needed to take everyone with her, too, but she didn't add that stipulation, for Pol would find a way to prevent it.

Nika and Snow returned not long after Pol's second visit.

Nika looked terrible.

"What happened to you?" Josune asked, while Carlos and Jacques crowded around sympathetically.

"Nothing a week's worth of sleep won't cure." Nika checked Josune's arm, the one that hadn't been damaged by the blaster fire and subsequently repaired by the doctor in preparation for sale to a cattle ship. "A pity. That would have turned out well."

Josune glanced down. "One side still looks good." She'd forgotten all about the mod. "How's Roystan?"

Nika said something that might have been, "Fine," but it was overlaid with a huge yawn that rendered what she said unintelligible.

"You look really bad," Carlos said. "Are you sure?"

"The Dietel didn't help." Nika grimaced and yawned at the same time.

Snow said, "I wasn't walking around with a load of priceless transurides inside me to make me look healthy. She's fine, Carlos. This is just her as she really is. Unmodded."

"Unmodded?" Would Nika even remember what her unmodded self had looked like?

"Half modded. And by a Dietel, no less." Nika shuddered. "It can't get much worse. At least unmodded you have an excuse."

"How is Roystan, Nika?" *Get to the important bits.*

"He's alive," Snow said. "Although he shouldn't be."

"Roystan will be fine, Josune. He's weak. Keep him warm. He'll need Jacques cooking for him. Lots of porridge and flatbread."

"He'll get that," Jacques promised.

Josune hadn't dared hope. They'd been gone seven days. The longest seven days of her life.

"They're interrogating him right now."

"He's tough." She hoped he was, anyway. He'd just come out of a machine. He should be healthy and fit. Even if it had taken seven days to get him that way. She looked at Nika's face. He wasn't. She could tell.

"He'll look bad when you see him, Josune. It was . . . tricky."

Snow said, "You didn't have to tell him he looked old, though."

"I didn't say he looked old. You told him that. When he recovers, he's going to look exactly like he does now, with more flesh, less skin and bone." Nika slid down the wall at her back and rested there, eyes closed. "Gino Giwari was an absolute genius." Her voice filled with reverence. "I was so wrong about him."

Snow sighed. "I don't know what got you talking about Giwari, Nika, but he's mostly discredited nowadays. People don't use his techniques anymore." He said to Josune, "She asked Roystan what Giwari was like. He's been dead eighty years. Nika should know that."

"Who's Giwari?"

Nika opened her eyes. "When Tilda died, Snow, did her family, or whoever owned the studio, clean it out?"

"What's that got to do with—" He stopped at her frown. "Her grandson sold the whole thing sight unseen. Why?"

"Because I'll bet she's got transurides there. To treat Roystan."

"Transurides. In my shop?" Snow brightened, then deflated. "I didn't even know what they looked like before . . . before—"

"Studio," Nika corrected.

Jacques laughed. "So you threw the transurides out."

That would be a costly mistake.

"I haven't thrown anything out. I didn't have time. Except some mutrient that was past use-by date. Some old salts. And some—" Snow stopped. "I probably did throw them out."

"What about the safe?" Nika asked.

"I couldn't get the safe open."

"Relax, then. They're in the safe. No one would leave transurides out. Not even me."

"You kept yours in your body." Almost an accusation. "That was a very expensive look."

"Do you know where I learned that technique, Snow? Gino Giwari." Nika's face glowed with wonder. "To think I thought he was just a technician. I was so wrong."

"What happened up there?" Josune asked. What had changed?

Nika smiled and closed her eyes. "We met a ghost, Josune. We saw a miracle."

"She needs sleep," Snow said.

"No miracle?"

Snow chewed his bottom lip. Nika seemed to have taken his advice. If she wasn't asleep, she wasn't taking part in the conversation any longer.

She was still smiling.

"There's no ghost. No Giwari."

He didn't say no miracle. "How is Roystan? Really?"

"He's alive, but he's weak."

Which was as frustrating as Nika's earlier report.

"He nearly died, Josune. She . . . she was amazing." Snow glanced at Nika. "He shouldn't be alive." He slid down the bars and settled on the floor.

"Is he conscious? Can he walk?"

"I don't know."

"You don't know if he's conscious?"

"I don't know if he can walk. He looks so awful now. She used all his muscle to—"

"To what?"

"Well, to fix him. She does that all the time. She needs to learn other techniques." Snow scrubbed at his face with his hands. "When they pushed us out they were asking him questions."

She couldn't do anything about that. What she could do was work on their escape plan. "How many people did you see who worked for Benedict?"

By careful questioning she worked out that Benedict had at least four staff and he was expecting his boss soon. That had been a conversation through the link the previous night. Josune touched her hand to her stomach. No weapon.

"Snow. Do you still have Nika's pendant? My hairpin?"

Snow stifled a yawn. "I gave Nika her pendant. I thought it better than naolic acid and mutrient." He handed the hairpin to Josune and closed his eyes. Josune coiled her hair and slipped the sparker into place. Armed again. It felt better.

After Snow fell asleep, Josune settled down to plan. She had her sparker. Nika had her laser. Now they had to wait until Roystan was with them, and only a small number of enemy nearby.

She was dozing when Benedict arrived in the outer doorway of the prison, sans Roystan but accompanied by two men in suits and two guards. One of the suits was the most beautiful man Josune had ever seen. The other was older, with more muscle, and clearly the boss. He wore a black nen-silk suit that Josune couldn't guess the price of. Obsidian pins gleamed in their lapels.

Josune stood up.

That woke Snow and Nika. They stood as well, Snow knuckling sleep out of his eyes.

Nika glanced at the visitors and froze completely. If her base look hadn't been white, she would have paled.

Benedict and the boss looked at the handsome man.

He ignored Nika and looked Josune up and down. His eyes rested on the patterning on her arm, then looked up into her eyes.

He shook his head. After that he looked at the men, dismissing Jacques and Carlos, spending more time on Snow.

Nika hid a smile under a twist of her mouth and looked down.

The executive looked at Benedict.

"That one," Benedict said, pointing to Nika. "Body modder who claims she's been deregistered. But you can't mistake her when you watch her work."

The stunningly handsome man turned to look at Nika. He shook his head, lip lifted in a sneer. "Nika would never use a Dietel, not even to save her own life."

The boss looked at Benedict.

"No mistake, sir."

"You have wasted my time again, Benedict."

"I haven't."

The boss flicked a hand. "Kill her."

Nika tilted her chin slightly, defiantly. Josune saw the handsome man's eyes widen.

"Wait. Nika?" Incredulous. Disbelieving.

Benedict smiled.

The boss turned to Nika. He looked her up and down, as if he didn't believe it either.

He touched his fingertips together and looked sideways at the handsome man. "That could have been a costly mistake, Alejandro. Don't get it wrong again."

Alejandro. Nika's ex-boyfriend.

He turned back to Nika and bared his teeth in a fake smile. "Nika Rik Terri. We've been looking for you."

It looked, for a moment, as if she was going to deny who she was.

"That's not Nika Rik Terri," Snow said. "That's Nika James." He looked from the company men to Nika, then looked back at the company men again. "She's Nika J—?" He shook his head. "She can't be."

Nika said nothing.

The boss smiled. He had gleaming white teeth, and looked as if he'd gone to the same modder as Benedict. "Bring her."

Nika spoke. "First, let's get this straight. I have *never* claimed to be deregistered. Second, we had a deal, Wickmore. You were to keep him away from me. What's he doing here?"

There was no doubting who *he* was.

Or the boss. Leonard Wickmore, Nika had named him.

"My dear modder. That deal became void the moment you left Lesser Sirius."

"I ran from a man who was going to kill me. One of your men, in fact."

"I kept him away from you. Perhaps you have a short memory."

"You've more thugs than just Alejandro. I wasn't staying around to die."

Alejandro's gaze narrowed.

Nika stepped back involuntarily.

Josune wished she still had Nika's laser. She had no chance with one weapon, not against Wickmore, Alejandro, Benedict, and two guards.

"We can't solve your day-to-day problems, Nika. You left. You have nothing to bargain with."

"Can't you get anyone else to fix your damaged team?"

Wickmore waved a hand. "We can always get modders. You were convenient, that was all. But Nika, you built an exchanger, and unfortunately, it's locked. Isn't that strange, don't you think?"

Nika shrugged, an unconscious imitation of Wickmore.

"We're taking you back to your studio, and you will show us how to use it."

"No."

Wickmore looked at Alejandro. "The redhead."

Alejandro was fast. He snatched at Snow through the bars,

grabbed his arm, yanked him close. Snow's head hit the metal. Alejandro twisted the arm he was holding, up, and around.

They all heard the bone crack.

Alejandro punched the arm where the bone had broken.

"Aargh." It was almost a scream.

"Wait. Stop. Yes."

Josune pulled Snow away from the bars as Alejandro aimed a punch at Snow's throat. Not fast enough. Snow went down.

"You bastard. I already capitulated."

Leonard Wickmore smiled. "So it's agreed? You'll come back to your shop and give us access to the body exchanger."

"Studio. Yes."

Snow tried to speak but couldn't.

Nika said to Josune, "Look after him. Please. And feed Roystan. He'll need constant replenishment until he builds up some reserve."

Josune nodded. There was nothing she could do right now, but that didn't mean she planned to do nothing.

Benedict unlocked the door.

Nika stepped out and he locked the door behind her.

Alejandro took out his blaster, turned, and took aim.

Leonard Wickmore pushed the nozzle to the floor.

Josune rolled Snow away. The blaster melted the bar at the bottom.

"Are you a complete idiot?" Wickmore demanded. "If she has no one to protect, she won't cooperate."

The handsome features scowled. Even the scowl was attractive. How much of that was Nika's work?

Wickmore smiled. "Alejandro will take you back to your studio." Nika's hands trembled, but that was the only outward sign. "Enjoy the journey. And Alejandro."

"Executive?"

"I want her capable of operating that machine when I get there."

"That won't be a problem, sir." Alejandro smiled at Nika.

The smile made Josune shiver. Crouched by Snow, she watched them walk out. She'd never felt so helpless.

Wickmore turned to Benedict. "Is Roystan talking yet?"

"He refuses to say anything until he sees his crew." He looked at Snow. "We should take that one to the doctor if you want Roystan to cooperate."

"We only need him long enough to tell us what he knows. I'm not happy with the time it's taking to get that information."

"We might need him longer than a few answers. Taki Feyodor was on to something. She was excited. That day on Pisces III she claimed to have the final piece she needed to lead us to the Goberling find. That piece was Roystan." Benedict looked into the cell. "Feyodor was obsessed, but she did not believe indiscriminately."

"Mmmh." Wickmore looked back at Snow. "Leave this one. It's time Roystan learned what will happen if he doesn't cooperate. Get me answers. Have them for me before I am forced to return."

Snow could breathe, at least, with difficulty. Josune knelt beside him. "What can I do?"

"She should have told me who she was." It came out as a hoarse sob. She had to listen closely to decipher it. "She let me say all those things." Snow looked up at Josune. "She knew what I thought of her."

"Snow, is your throat going to bruise anymore?" How much swelling could it take before he couldn't breathe?

"I want to die."

She bit back the urge to tell him to pull himself together. "What can I do for your arm, then?"

Snow shrugged.

"Snow."

His hoarse whisper didn't stop. "She's still crazy, you know."

"Should you be talking?" Or should he keep talking, to continue getting air into his lungs?

"She might be a genius." The whisper went high and his voice faded. She had to lip-read. "But she's still crazy."

Nika was Nika, and Snow would come to appreciate her in time.

The prison door opened. Josune moved in front of Snow to shield him.

Pol sidled in.

Some people didn't realize the best way to be furtive was to act naturally.

"They're bringing Roystan down. He won't cooperate until he sees you in person." Pol slipped a small blaster through the bars. "Be ready."

She froze as Benedict and a guard entered with Roystan. The blaster dropped from her hands. Josune caught it.

Roystan was all skeletal bones and angles. Josune wouldn't have recognized him if he hadn't smiled. That same crooked smile she knew so well.

"Gods," Carlos said.

"You're spending too much time down here, Pol." Benedict looked at the guard with him. "She gave them something. Find out what it was."

They were out of time.

Josune held the blaster out to the guard and hoped it was loaded. She wouldn't put it past Pol to set them up. She raised her other hand to her head, offering surrender. Her fingers closed around the sparker in her hair. She aimed it at Benedict. Aimed at his eye, hit his leg instead. Damn. She jumped left, blasted the guard, and aimed again for Benedict.

Benedict spun sideways, ignoring his injury. His weapon was out, aimed at Josune.

Roystan kicked Benedict's damaged leg, unbalancing him. The blast from Benedict's weapon hit the ceiling. Roystan was tossed aside. Benedict aimed again and went down as Roystan flung himself back into the fight. Benedict's blast burned the top of Josune's arm. Roystan grabbed the blaster and forced it up. Benedict shook him loose.

Josune fired at the lock and kicked the door. It opened. She exited with a rush of relief—and adrenaline—and grabbed Benedict's arm. She couldn't use her blaster. Roystan was too close.

"Behind you," Jacques yelled, and Josune swung around, pulling the sparker from her hair. Another guard. She fired. Sparker and blaster sent a molten stream of lightning the guard's way.

She swung back to Benedict, who grabbed Roystan and pulled him in front for a shield. Roystan struggled to get free, but he had no strength left. Benedict lined up his weapon again.

Josune aimed her sparker at his eye and fired. Benedict went down, hand spasming. The blaster missed Roystan by a finger's width.

She jammed the sparker into Benedict's enhanced eye, raised herself so she wouldn't be caught by the feedback, and pressed the button. Then she grabbed the hand holding the blaster and turned on him while he still convulsed. Roystan broke free. Josune turned both blaster and sparker on Benedict, until he stilled permanently.

This was for her crewmates.

"Josune," Roystan said, insistent behind her. "He's dead. And your sparker will short the whole station any moment." He sounded as if he'd said it more than once.

It was done.

Roystan put a hand on her shoulder. "Better?"

"It is, actually." The heaviness that had weighed her down since the *Hassim* had nullspaced in front of her was gone, the noise in her head, silenced. Avenged.

"Good."

"Are *you* okay?"

"I haven't felt this good in years." He glanced at the door. "We should go."

She nodded and picked up Benedict's blaster as she stood. "Jacques, Carlos, help Roystan. Snow, can you get up?"

Snow hardly seemed to realize what had happened, but after a moment he pulled himself up with his good arm.

"You can't be Josune," Pol said. "You lied to me."

Pol held a weapon. Had she picked it up from the dead guard? Pol might use it on her soon, given she'd been so keen to find Josune Arriola.

"How can we get off this station?"

"We're not trusting her," Carlos said.

Josune trusted Pol to look out for herself, and right now Pol was in as much danger as they were.

"A shuttle leaves every hour to Burnley Hub."

Snow gave a hoarse laugh. "The Hub? We'd be welcomed with open arms, I don't think."

At least, that was what Josune thought he said.

"We can still ship out from there," Roystan said. "A quick in and out. If Pol books the fares."

"No way. She's not welcome."

"After what she's done?"

Jacques and Carlos spoke together. Josune wanted to protest as well, but Roystan's plan was sound. They were wanted on the Hub.

"I can—"

She almost missed the slight shake of Roystan's head.

Pol looked at Josune, looked at her weapon. It wasn't hard to guess what she was thinking. "We'll go to Pisces III."

What did she think was there? Feyodor had left Pisces III, moved on to *The Road*. But Josune didn't care if it got them off this station.

Roystan rubbed his nose. "We could do that. Yes."

Snow mangled his words getting them out. "We have to rescue—"

"Not the direct route, though," Roystan said, over the top of him. "If Benedict talked to his boss, that's where they'll expect us to go."

"But we—"

Carlos put a hand to Snow's shoulder. There was pressure behind it, judging from Snow's wince.

"If you come along, Pol, you have to pay," Roystan said. "You took all our funds. And you're the only one not on a wanted list."

Pol looked at Josune, then looked away, her gaze sliding down to the blaster in her hand and the sparker in Josune's. "Sure."

Jacques growled, low in his chest.

Roystan waved Pol in front of him. "Lead the way." He followed her out the door, walking like a man who'd run a marathon.

Josune pocketed her sparker and pushed past Carlos and Jacques to support him, though she knew she should have been on guard. "You two, keep watch." It was good to hold him, even for a moment.

She could feel every rib. "What did Nika do to him, Snow?" He was alive. That was important.

Snow enunciated every word carefully. "She cannibalizes bodies."

Roystan's stomach growled then. Everyone looked at him. He looked back sheepishly. "I confess, I'm a little hungry right now."

37

NIKA RIK TERRI

The walk through the station to Alejandro's private yacht gave Nika time to think. To remember the first rule. Never show Alejandro how frightened she was. He liked that too much.

She glanced at a trader as they passed. He turned away, avoided eye contact. An enforcement officer approached. Alejandro raised his head, eyes narrowed. The officer nodded and turned away. No one lingered.

The yacht they boarded was nothing like Roystan's *The Road*. The passage walls were celadon blue, the carpet a luxurious light charcoal. Nika missed *The Road* already. She should have told Josune how old Roystan was. It was important, somehow.

The vibration under her feet changed subtly as the ship started to move. Not long after, they nullspaced. Nika shivered. Her friends were too far away now to help. And she was too far away to help them.

Alejandro smiled at the shiver. "Worried?"

"Cold." She wasn't. She was hot, if anything. Sweating under her pretended indifference.

The room they entered was a stark contrast to the luxury they had walked through. White walls. White light. A single white table. Two white chairs. There was no other furniture.

Nika hadn't expected an interrogation room on a luxury yacht.

Alejandro pushed her into a chair, stepped back to look at her, then came forward to wind a lock of hair around his finger.

"You must have been desperate to go so far to disguise yourself. A Dietel, no less."

Nika shrugged.

He jerked her head back by pulling on the hair. "Although— your eyes are amazing."

The whole of her had been amazing, before the Dietel.

He ran a hand over her face. A gentle caress. She'd loved it once. Now it jangled on her nerves as she waited for what was to follow.

"But then, your eyes always are."

Alejandro touched a finger to her nose. "I should have known you from that. But there are so many copies nowadays, aren't there."

He moved his hand back to her cheek, then slapped her. Hard.

"You gave Tamati *my* body."

Of course she'd shown him the design. She'd been proud of it. Still was.

"You let *him* use the exchanger, use *your* body?"

"It's not as if I had a choice."

He grabbed her arm, twisted it. "Don't get smart."

Nika wasn't going to scream. She wasn't going to beg. In the early days she had done that, to stop the pain. But that only encouraged him. "Don't forget your boss wants me to unlock the exchanger. I can't do that with a broken arm."

For a minute, she thought Alejandro would break her arm regardless. He eased off at the last minute. He always knew the breaking point. Nika was tempted to push it, to get him in trouble with his boss. But if she wasn't whole she wouldn't be able to run.

He stepped away, started to pace. His walk—the elegant, animal grace—was the first thing she'd noticed about him.

"Executive Wickmore visited your studio last week. Now I know why."

How did he know who did and didn't visit the studio? Was he watching it?

"Tamati told him about the exchanger." He turned to Nika. "You should have denied it."

As if she could have done that with a weapon in her face. "You shouldn't have told Tamati about it in the first place."

Alejandro leaned close, his beautiful eyes hard. "You put *me* in a difficult situation with the executive, because *I* hadn't mentioned it." He kicked her chair over. "If you hadn't run, no one would have known. You'd be dead and I wouldn't be out of favor, would I?"

The pendant slipped out from Nika's coverall. She closed her hand around it.

Alejandro kicked her. "Get up."

Nika got up.

"Chair."

She righted the chair, glanced at Alejandro, who was pacing again, slipped the pendant back under her coverall, and sat down.

"You instigated my disgrace."

If she took Alejandro out now, she wouldn't get out the door alive, let alone off the ship. But if by some miracle she did escape, there was still Tamati. He would wait forever. And Snow had given away her name. All that angst and planning, useless in a matter of weeks.

Roystan, Josune, and Snow were probably all dead by now. And Carlos and Jacques. Or on one of the cattle ships Snow dreaded so much.

Don't think about that. Think of a plan. What would Josune do? She'd wait to do the most damage possible. That would be when Tamati, Wickmore, and Alejandro were all together at her studio.

She could last that long. No one here knew she had a weapon. She would take out as many as she could.

The chair smashed to the floor again. Her head smacked against the table leg. Alejandro loomed over her. "You're not listening to me."

She looked up at him. She had learned—the hard way—that tuning out when Alejandro was about to teach her a lesson was the worst thing she could do.

"Thank you." Alejandro smiled. He moved his hands around her face in a gentle caress. "You shouldn't have gotten me into trouble with my boss."

38

JOSUNE ARRIOLA

They caught the shuttle with time to spare, and an hour later they were at the Hub.

"Remember," Roystan said, as Pol ordered tickets, "not the direct route. They'll be waiting for us."

Pol said, "There's one here that goes to Lesser Sirius. Then to Cambon, Achilles, and on to Pisces III."

Josune wasn't the only one frowning to hide her smile.

"I suppose it's enough delay," Roystan said.

"Good."

Pol booked a four-berth cabin for the men. "Josune and I will share."

"I think we should—"

"I'll be fine," Josune said. Not that she had any intention of staying in a room with Pol. "Let's grab some food and take it back to the boys' cabin."

There was no dining room, only a row of vending machines down one corridor. Pol certainly hadn't wasted money on luxury tickets.

Josune stopped at the vending machines, coded for purchase, and started hitting buttons randomly. "Jacques, what can Roystan eat?"

"Corasbread," Jacques said. "That grain porridge."

She hit those buttons, too.

Two noisy construction workers queued behind them. "Someone's hungry."

She hoped they were construction workers. "We won't be long."

"I know how you feel," one of the workers said. "I'm starved myself."

"I'll wait. Take the fast shuttle down to Lesser Sirius," the other said. "Get a decent meal before we have to catch the transport."

"At a hundred credits. You've got to be desperate."

"I am. I want real food and I've nothing else to spend my credits on."

Josune gathered their packages—some hot, some cold—and dumped them into Jacques's arms. "All yours."

Roystan said something quiet to the worker who wanted a better meal. She rolled her eyes. "Not me."

Every second they delayed was one more second someone could recognize them.

Roystan shared a final laugh with the worker and moved on. Josune's back itched all the way down to the cabin.

Pol came with them.

Josune wasn't the only one who heaved a sigh of relief as the door closed. Roystan leaned back and took the food package Jacques pushed toward him.

"I don't know what that modder did to you," Pol said to Roystan. "But she certainly made a mess."

"She saved his life." Snow still spoke in a hoarse whisper, but he looked to be breathing more easily.

"He doesn't look very saved," Pol said.

"You have no idea how hard that was." Snow's whisper was a cross between reverence and disbelief.

Roystan laughed. "I feel better than I have in years. My skin." He flexed his free hand, held it up. "Look. She's a miracle worker."

Josune looked at the hand. She couldn't see what he meant.

Roystan closed his fingers around hers. "And to recognize—"

He faded away. Josune thought it was discretion that silenced him.

Snow turned to Roystan. "Giwari has been dead eighty years."

"Yes, he has."

"And you're . . . what, thirty-five? Forty?"

"A bit older than that."

He had to be older, for old Jed Brown had been dead forty years and Roystan had known him.

How old was Roystan really? He'd had the Atalante run a long time, and here he was implying he was older than forty. He couldn't be much older. Modding certainly extended your life, kept you fit and active and your mind healthy far longer than a nonmodded body. But eventually your body showed age, regardless of the mod.

Snow said, "Sometimes Nika imagines things, that's all."

"I like the way her mind works. She keeps herself open to possibilities." Roystan smiled gently at the younger man. "That makes her very receptive to ideas other people wouldn't countenance."

"Some people might call her gullible."

She was Nika Rik Terri. Snow seemed to have forgotten that for the moment.

"You shouldn't encourage her," Snow told Roystan. "When she asks questions like that, be honest. Don't lie to her."

Questions like what? Was he protecting Nika now?

"I wouldn't lie to her."

"How could you know what Giwari was like?"

"Don't you think he would be like Nika? Confident, knowing he was a good modder."

Josune recognized evasion when she heard it.

What had Snow said earlier? A miracle, but no ghost, no Giwari. No old men.

What was she missing?

Realization hammered through her. Goberling was eighty years missing. If Roystan was old enough to have been modded by Giwari—which was what Nika implied, although he certainly didn't look it—he was old enough to have met Goberling.

What had Feyodor known, or suspected, that was important enough to send Josune to Roystan before she'd even found proof of what it was she'd been looking for on to Pisces III?

Giwari's studio had been on Pisces III.

Unbidden, the memory rose, of Roystan and the *Hassim*'s memory, when it had been asking for identification. Of him leaning across to thumb off the request. He never used his thumb to close a link. He flicked off.

Roystan hadn't bypassed the security that day. He'd provided it. His thumbprint.

Taki Feyodor had owned the *Hassim* for twenty years. She'd bought it new, and Josune knew every single person who had access to it, and the access they had.

The crew had access to general ship functions, and to their own specialty areas. Josune had more access than others. She could access everything except Feyodor's own special files.

One other person had the same access she did. The name in the security logs showed as Roy King. Avid Goberlingophile that Josune was, she'd recognized it as the name Goberling had adopted when he'd first tried to disappear.

"Isn't it pointless to give access to Goberling?" she'd asked Feyodor at the time. "He is dead, after all."

"He's our whole reason for being here," Feyodor had said. "We owe him some form of recognition, surely."

They were the most sentimental words Josune had ever heard from her captain, so she hadn't said anything further about it. King had remained on the security manifest, and he'd been granted the same access Josune had on any new systems they'd added.

What if the access hadn't stopped with the ship systems? What if Feyodor had coded King into her private systems as well?

If Roystan could access Feyodor's files, when only Feyodor and King had access, that meant Hammond Roystan was Roy King. Which meant Hammond Roystan was Roy Goberling.

It wasn't possible.

Was it?

She realized her mouth was open. She closed it with a snap and looked over at Roystan. He was watching her.

Josune had spent her life chasing after Goberling's lost lode of precious metals. She'd carried a model of his ship, the *Determination*, everywhere with her since she was six years old. The dream had sustained her through the long years earning her engineering degree without company backing. It had been inevitable she would eventually meet Feyodor, and the older woman would convince her to share her knowledge by offering her a berth on the *Hassim*.

She'd been chasing a dream.

She hadn't been chasing a man.

They'd been chased on the *Hassim*. It hadn't been fun, watching their backs all the time.

Roystan couldn't be Goberling.

What would they have done when Feyodor finally arrived? No matter what Roystan wanted—and it was clear that all he wanted was to continue his cargo run and live a peaceful life—she'd have forced him to come with them. At weaponpoint, if necessary.

Josune gripped the fingers of her sparker so tightly her fingers cramped. Pol could never be allowed to learn who Roystan was. Nor Leonard Wickmore's people. They would hound him until they killed him, or got what they wanted.

Roystan leaned toward her. "Are you all right?"

"All my life I've been making someone else's life a misery."

His mouth twisted into the crooked smile she was so familiar with. He kept his voice low, so only Josune could hear. "If I'd met you earlier, maybe I'd have let myself be caught."

Pol scowled at them both. "If you must talk, say it aloud so we can all hear."

"Please, no," Jacques said. "We don't want to hear their sweet nothings turning the air blue."

"What do you mean?" Carlos asked.

"Carlos, you haven't noticed they've a thing going? Sometimes I despair of you."

Roystan rubbed the back of his neck.

Josune hid a smile. Roystan had been flirting a little. At least, she hoped he had. And admitting who he was.

Pol gaped at him. "With Josune?"

Jacques and Carlos moved closer to Josune and Roystan. Even Snow, staring at nothing in the bunk above them, raised himself to look down on her.

Jacques bristled. "Why not Josune?"

Pol looked at them both, looked at Roystan, then at Josune. Shrugged. "We should get some sleep," she said to Josune, as if the atmosphere weren't tense.

Josune settled back against the wall. "I'm staying here."

"Don't be stupid."

"I've seen how you look at me. I've seen how you look at your weapon." Josune could beat Pol in a firefight, but she didn't want to have to watch her back all the time.

"I don't know—"

"We're not stupid, Pol," Roystan said. "And we're not leaving Josune alone with you."

Pol stayed in the cabin with them, and they endured her presence until Roystan stood up. "I don't know about anyone else, but I need food. Vending machine time."

He tapped Snow—who'd spent the hours staring into nothing. "Even you, Snow. If you don't move, you'll seize up."

What Snow needed more than anything, was sleep. They all did.

Jacques and Carlos dragged themselves up.

"You're stupid," Pol said. "Someone will recognize you."

"So you'll buy it for us, then," Roystan said.

"You know what I hate most about you. How manipulative you are."

"So you'll buy the food?"

"Feed yourself," Pol said. "Get caught. I don't care. I'm staying here."

"I'm hungry," Roystan said.

"You're always hungry."

"He needs food," Jacques said. "You know he does."

"He's sucked you in, Jacques, and you pander to him."

Josune helped Snow off the bunk. She wasn't going to leave him here with Pol.

"She should have told me who she was."

"I know," Josune said, soothingly. "But she was running, remember."

"You're all crazy," Pol said.

They followed Roystan out.

"Vending machine food," Carlos said. "To think it has come to this, after what we've eaten."

"I'm hungry enough to eat it, too," Roystan said, but he led them straight past the vending machines, down to the shuttle bays. "Sorry, Josune, we have to spend more of your credits."

"My pleasure." Even if she didn't know what it was for yet.

Roystan said something quiet to the cargo master on duty.

"Hundred credits each."

Josune put up the money.

The cargo master nodded at the front shuttle. "Leaving in two," she said.

They boarded the shuttle to the chimes of a public announcement. "Passengers who wish to disembark at Lesser Sirius, please ensure you have purchased a boarding pass."

Inside, Josune was unsurprised to see the contractor Roystan had spoken to earlier.

"You found it."

"Yes, thank you." Roystan smiled at his crew. "It's always good to beat the crowd."

Especially when you had someone with a blaster waiting back in your cabin to force you to stay. "It certainly is," Josune said, fervently.

39

NIKA RIK TERRI

Nika moved slowly, careful not to show how much she hurt. She needed time in her own Songyan.

Her studio was much as she'd left it, except that for the first time in its existence, the big Songyan hadn't been cleaned. The broken link had been repaired and two extra cameras were fixed to the wall. Subtly placed, but breaking the symmetry. Tamati would be along soon.

She forced her hands away from the laser pendant. No hint of what she planned to do, or Alejandro would take it from her.

"Don't think you can dupe me. I know how the exchanger works. I know what's supposed to happen."

Was Tamati watching? Should she wait until he arrived and try to kill them both? No. She couldn't even handle Alejandro on his own. Josune had reminded her that victory was half in the mind. If you already thought your enemy could beat you, then he would.

Don't think, act. That's what Josune would do. Think instead about what would happen next. Anticipate.

After she killed Alejandro she'd run. Before Tamati arrived.

If she could kill Alejandro.

She raised the laser. Please let her have understood Snow's instructions.

Alejandro turned. "Give me the codes."

She pressed the firing button and flinched as he raised his hand.

The laser passed a centimeter by Alejandro's face and cut a line down the wall.

Nika shook as she repositioned the laser. Too late. Alejandro smashed it out of her hand. She felt the bone crack.

Alejandro's fist smashed into her face. Again. And again.

Then he stopped.

Waiting to be hit was almost worse than being hit. After what seemed forever, Nika chanced a peek through the protection of her elbow.

Alejandro had picked up the laser. "Nice little toy." He swung around, finger on the button, and sliced a wide circle around her. "This could be fun." He sliced another circle two centimeters inside the other.

Nika didn't move.

"Give me the codes."

The burned wall smelled of hot sand and burned plastic.

The numbers came out. No matter that she tried to hold them back. Her body controlled her actions now, and her body had declared, *Enough*. Though she knew enough would never be enough. Alejandro would always win.

"4334-3444-" A whisper, whistling through the damaged mouth.

"I can't hear you."

She raised her voice, though it hurt. "1221-2221-2224." It was part of her own DNA, the A's, C's, G's, and T's converted to numbers.

"4334-3444-1221-2221-2224." Alejandro had always had a phenomenal memory. "Only you, Nika, would think up a code that complicated."

Only she would need to, to keep it from someone like him.

Alejandro loomed close. "I don't trust you, Nika. I don't believe you."

He never had. Not even when she'd given him everything he wanted. In a way, it was power. Her power over him, rather than his over her.

"There's only one way you'll prove it."

He knew that as well as she did, and he didn't like it.

Nika didn't laugh. Didn't even smile. She wanted to.

"If this is one of your tricks."

The knowledge grew in her, stiffened her resolve. It didn't matter what Alejandro did now. He had to trust her enough to use those codes on himself.

"You should have thought before you hit me," Nika said. "My body is weak." She finally permitted herself that smile. "You never know what I might do."

An alarm on the back door chimed softly.

There was only one person it could be.

Tamati Woden.

Alejandro ignored the alarm, probably didn't realize it was an alarm, for it didn't sound like one.

Nika kept her eyes on Alejandro, forcing herself not to look at the laser he'd put on the bench beside him, not to look toward the door.

"Try anything and I kill your body. I go back into my own body then, and you die. That's how it works, doesn't it?"

"That's how it works." Except that she wouldn't die immediately, because of the modifications she'd made to her own body to increase oxygen capacity. She would remain alive for thirty minutes, even though her brain would start to die after fifteen.

Nika, in Alejandro's body, would have time to put her—Nika's—body into the Songyan. She could set it so he didn't come out until after the twenty-four hours. Meantime, she could take Alejandro's body away from the studio.

Like Tamati all over again, except this time when their bodies swapped back, she'd be in the studio, and Alejandro would be as far away as she could physically get him.

"Good. If you try anything, that's what I'll do."

She watched him remove his jacket and place it between them.

Watched as he set up the head nets. She didn't offer to help. He knew the routine as well as she did. He placed the tiny nodes on her first. One either side of her forehead, one behind each ear, one at the top of her spine.

Then he put the nodes around his own head.

Where was Tamati? Why hadn't he come into the studio?

Alejandro hesitated at the controls. Then typed in the codes.

Nika watched the blue field form across his head, felt it doing the same to her. It tickled a little to start with. Watched as the color faded from blue, to white, to gold, then disappeared. The cap across Alejandro's head was invisible now, as was the cap above her own.

Suddenly, she was in Alejandro's body. Fit, and healthy, and feeling so much better.

Alejandro made a garbled sound that might have been a groan. He winced, fumbled for the jacket on the chair, and pulled his blaster out of a pocket. He pointed it at her. "Don't try anything."

Tamati's shadow moved in the doorway.

She held up her hands, mutely.

"Good."

Could she get to the laser?

Would it help if she could?

Alejandro used the studio link to call Leonard Wickmore.

"Alejandro here," he said, through Nika's mouth. "I've got the codes."

If Wickmore thought there was anything strange about Alejandro doing it in Nika's body, he didn't comment. "I'll be around to collect the genemod machine."

Alejandro nodded, and switched off. "I might keep you alive until—" He—Nika's body—jerked back. A knife protruded from her chest.

The body crashed to the floor.

Tamati stepped into the studio. "Kill the body and your brain reverts back to your own. What a tidy way to kill someone. Hello, Alejandro."

Nika stared at her broken body on the floor. Their bodies hadn't switched back. She was still alive. She pulled herself together, channeled her best Alejandro. "I wanted her alive until we'd moved the Songyan."

Alejandro wouldn't have said *Songyan*, he'd have said *machine*, but Tamati didn't seem to notice. She moved over to the bench where Alejandro had left the laser, and tried to make it look natural.

"She was a dead woman," Tamati said. "Be grateful I waited until you made your call. I nearly didn't."

Nika picked up the laser. "Tamati." Aimed. Pressed the fire button. The first shot sliced off his arm. "I forgot to mention." The second was a diagonal cut from shoulder to torso. If she'd been trying for symmetry, it almost matched the angle of the scar that he no longer had. "It doesn't switch back immediately anymore."

Was he dead? She didn't want to check, but she couldn't turn her back on him. She picked up Alejandro's blaster and used it on Tamati, until he had a black hole in his chest and had stopped moving.

Then she dropped the blaster and turned to the other body on the floor.

Fifteen minutes. She'd used two? Five? The net kept the brain alive for fifteen minutes after death. The machine would fix the rest. She had to get her body into the machine. Now.

She scooped up her body. Grunted at the weight. Alejandro was strong, but not strong enough to lift an adult human easily.

"Hold it right there," Josune said.

She hadn't heard the second alarm, could hear its chime now. Adrenaline rushed through Nika, froze her to the spot. Josune, Roystan, and Snow. They'd entered via the front door.

They all held weapons. Josune could kill her from here.

Carlos and Jacques pushed in behind them. They, too, held weapons. Nika nearly dropped her body, realized it was probably the only thing keeping her alive at the moment, and clutched it tight.

"Don't." Her voice came out in a shrill, un-Alejandro-like squeak.

"Move away from the body." Josune's blaster was pointed directly at Nika's—Alejandro's—head.

The other four blasters were pointed at her, too.

"Josune. It's me. Nika. Body exchanger. Remember. Don't kill me." She lowered her own body carefully.

The blaster didn't waver. "Prove it."

"You were damaged by a sparker. You went into a Dietel. You've pink patterning over your skin. Dendrites. But then you went into another machine, which ruined it." The patterning was covered today. Alejandro couldn't possibly have known. "You came from the *Hassim*."

"Spicy flatbread. Airy-fairy modder." She was babbling. She turned to Snow. "You're Bertram Snowshoe. Banjo—" She didn't finish. To Roystan. "Gino Giwari modified your genes. He did something to you. You don't look as old as you are."

"If you're Alejandro, you could have beaten that information out of Nika," Josune said. "If we find you've been lying, I'll kill you."

"I really am Nika. And please help me move my body before I go brain-dead."

Carlos sheathed his weapon. "Where to?" He shrugged at Josune. "*Airy-fairy modder* isn't something she'd tell him."

"Thank you, Carlos. Upstairs."

"Upstairs?" Snow raised his weapon again. "If you're Nika, you'd use the Songyan."

"Alejandro's boss is coming for the exchanger. He'll check both Songyans." She wouldn't have a hope. None of them would. Besides, this Songyan was already being used for the exchanger. "I've got old machines upstairs in my lab."

Snow shook his head, but Josune indicated with her weapon. "Jacques, help. Snow can't lift with his arm." She looked at Nika. "I'll watch him. Her."

Nika turned to Snow. "We've at most five minutes to keep the body alive. After that, I'm brain-dead."

"How come she's alive now? She looks dead to me."

"My mods keep the brain alive." For an extra fifteen minutes. She hoped. She'd never tested it. "The genemod machine will repair any damage to other organs."

Nika locked down the studio—including the front door—before turning to the lift. She typed in the override codes, because even the lift was protected from Alejandro. She didn't want anyone else walking in on her.

Which machine should she use? The Dekker, because she could flood it, which would save precious minutes on the startup. Plus Snow now had some experience calibrating the Dekker. Most importantly, it was on air casters, and she could plug in a portable power pack. They might escape before Wickmore arrived.

Nika turned to Josune and Roystan. "The minds will switch back after twenty-four hours. Provided there's a live body to go into."

"How many hours to go?"

"Twenty-four. Less ten minutes."

Josune nodded.

Snow stopped at the door to the lab. "It's like a museum."

At least it was a working museum. "Open the Dekker, Snow." Nika made for a cupboard and pulled out a container of mutrient.

"There are other machines here. What about the Netanyu?"

"The Dekker."

Roystan opened it for her.

Nika nodded her thanks. "You're looking better, Roystan." She started connecting inlets.

"I am better." He watched Jacques and Carlos ease the body into the tank. "What can I do to help?"

Nika had most of the basic mixes up here in the lab. Not all. "Downstairs. Dendrian salts. Third cupboard from the left in the main studio." But she'd coded them all against Alejandro, and that meant she'd coded them against everyone. "No. Wait. I'll go. You won't be able to open the cupboard."

She flooded the Dekker's chamber with stabilizing gel.

Snow gave a horrified mewl. "You can't do that. It'll kill her."

Her body was technically dead, which Snow seemed to have overlooked.

"It's the only way it'll work fast enough." She adjusted the calibration settings. "Snow, you know how to keep the calibrations steady. You can do that one-handed."

He opened his mouth to protest but moved to calibrate, because the readings were already moving off.

Nika deftly hooked up portapacks of mutrient, additional stabilizing gel, and blood plasma, and snapped them in. If she used one for dendrian salts, she had two outlets left. She thought quickly. Hooked up naolic acid, careful to place it in the outlet farthest away from the mutrient.

"Desperate times call for desperate measures," she told Snow, before he could tell her how dangerous that was. "Let the stabilizing gel drop to fifty percent and keep it at that. The mutrient at forty, and the salts at five. Keep the other three inlets at equal amounts of the five percent that's left."

She hooked up the portable power pack. "I'll get the salts and then we'll go."

Roystan kicked off the brakes. "Like old times," he said, as he pushed the Dekker toward the lift, Snow frantically calibrating as they went. Josune stayed clear, her weapon ready.

The studio bell buzzed while they were in the lift.

Nika used the manual override codes to link in and see who it was. Leonard Wickmore. Along with five suited men. Four of them were big and muscular. The fifth looked familiar, but she couldn't place him.

She didn't answer until they were out of the lift and she'd waved the others out of camera view.

"The bitch has everything manually coded. On automatic lock-down," she told Wickmore. "It takes a couple of minutes to reset."

Josune raised her weapon.

Nika closed the link. "This way he'll understand a delay." She wasn't sure if she was disappointed that Josune didn't trust her, or pleased.

She brought up the outdoor cameras. Two of Wickmore's heavies were laughing. Presumably at Alejandro's need to unlock the doors manually.

"I'll stay. Delay them. You need to get away." She stopped at the cupboard, grabbed the dendrian salts, and thrust them Josune's way. "Take my body out the back. Keep it in the machine. Snow knows what to do. Don't believe him when he tries to tell you it's hopeless. The machine should keep me alive long enough to do repairs. Alejandro and I will switch back after twenty-four hours."

She hoped. "I'll let Wickmore in the front." She hesitated, then looked at the machine. The exchanger was too dangerous to leave in Eaglehawk's hands. Think what they could do with it. "I don't suppose you brought bombs?"

Josune tossed the salts to Snow. "Of course." She reached into her bag, took out some small white boxes, and placed one under the front of the Songyan and another at the back. Among the cleaning pipes, where they couldn't be seen easily. "I'll set it to blow after twenty-four hours."

Nika was glad for Snow's anguished "It's a Songyan" to give herself time to recover. They were only machines.

But they were her machines, designed to her specifications.

She blinked. This was a stupid time to get sentimental about a box, when lives depended on those boxes being destroyed.

"We'll buy another one, Snow." She looked at Josune. "There's another Songyan in the smaller studio." She indicated the way.

"The art," Snow said, and looked as if he would follow.

"Calibrator," Nika said. "You haven't got time to sightsee."

Josune set two more explosives under the smaller Songyan, then pulled out a timer. "I'll set it for twenty-four hours." She put that timer back into her bag, pulled out another one, and handed it to Nika. The countdown on the face showed 23:59:010.

"This is an emergency trigger. In case things go wrong. It will activate the bombs immediately. Don't use it unless you absolutely have to."

Nika nodded and glanced up at the screen to where Wickmore, at the front door, was getting impatient. He said something to the heavies he had with him. Two of them turned and walked briskly back along the street.

Making for the alley.

"They'll be around that corner in no time. Go. Go."

They took the Dekker out the back door.

Nika quickly locked up after them, moved to the front room, and typed in the manual codes to open the front door.

40

JOSUNE ARRIOLA

Over the road, a man smoked outside an open door. It was the only accessible exit in the whole street. "Across there."

Roystan turned the Dekker. Snow turned too, but not as fast. "Did you really put a bomb under the Songyan?"

If that was the big black box—and Josune hoped it was—then yes.

"You can't destroy the Songyan," Snow said. "Do you know how much they cost?"

Did he understand how dangerous the exchanger would be in Eaglehawk's hands? "It's Nika's life or the Songyan," Josune said.

Snow glanced at Nika's still body and didn't say any more.

At the last minute, the smoker dived through the open door, lit kafismoke flying. Josune got to the door as he slammed it, braced her arm against the force, and pushed hard, before the smoker had time to lock it. Something crashed inside.

Josune forced the door open.

The smoker was on his back. Two large drums had fallen over. One was still rolling. They were in a storeroom. A man and a woman ran out from the kitchen. The man brandished a meat cleaver.

Maybe Jacques could swap attacking techniques with him.

"If you've hurt Amarri I'll kill you."

"Relax," Josune said. "Amarri hurt himself."

"Did not," Amarri said, from the floor. "They weren't going to stop. She's like a battering ram."

But the machete-wielding man had seen through the transparent lid into the machine. "What have you done to Nika?"

"We found her like that," Josune said. "We're trying to save her life."

"I bet it's that boyfriend again."

"He sent some goons around to the back of the studio. We had to get her out of sight." Josune helped Amarri up. "Are you all right?"

Amarri nodded, then peered into the box. "He beat her up bad this time."

"This will be the last time." Josune meant that. She might not be able to kill Alejandro immediately, but that would happen. As soon as Nika was back in her own body.

If Nika returned to her own body.

"You can go out the front." The chef hurried ahead of them, clearing the way. More of a hindrance than anything else, for he took them through the dining room, and the space between the tables was too narrow for the Dekker.

"Excuse me," the chef said. "Emergency. Coming through." He snatched a cloth off a table as he went and spread it over the top of the machine.

Josune gritted her teeth but didn't say anything, just watched the trail of destruction as he barged through.

Outside, she circled in the street and didn't relax her grip on the blaster until she was certain Wickmore's men hadn't followed them. All clear. "Thank you," she said to the chef. "We'd appreciate it if you didn't tell anyone we came through." Given that the whole restaurant had seen them, it was a stupid thing to say.

"Our lips are sealed," the chef said, pantomiming the action.

She wished he hadn't done it with the hand that held the meat cleaver, but he didn't appear to do himself any damage.

"Thanks. Nika owes you one." And Josune followed the others down the street.

41

NIKA RIK TERRI

"Took you long enough to unlock the door," Wickmore said.

Nika knew how Alejandro reacted to criticism. She didn't know whether he reacted differently to his boss. She scowled. "She's got this place locked up with so many manual locks it's a nightmare. Paranoid." She ignored the heavies as they blasted open the back door.

Wickmore's tone was dry as he stepped past Alejandro. "I wouldn't know why." He stopped as he saw Tamati's fallen body.

His voice changed. Turned as reasonable and gentle as it had been the day he'd murdered Chandra.

"Explain."

Sweat beaded Nika's forehead. She knew Wickmore saw it. She forced away her first instinct, which was to wipe her damp palms down her trousers. Alejandro would never do that. Instead, she flicked a contemptuous glance at the body, trying to channel her best Alejandro. "He was too slow to get out of the way when her friends came calling." Because she had to explain why her own body was gone.

Wickmore's eyes narrowed. "Friends?" He blinked five times, rapidly. Waited. Blinked again. Waited a moment longer. Turned to one of the heavies. "Contact Benedict. Drag him out of his interrogation, if you have to."

"Yes, sir."

Bad mistake. Wickmore hadn't known the others had escaped.

Nika controlled her breathing, indicating the room that contained themselves, the guards, and Tamati's dead body on the floor. "They came for her. No loss to us. I had the codes. I let them take her."

She tried to smile. A cold, hard-edged smile.

What had Tamati and Alejandro told Wickmore about the machine? She'd have to assume they'd talked only about what the exchanger could do, not about the timings. Wickmore hadn't taken long to get here after Alejandro's call. He knew that Alejandro had been in Nika's body.

"I was back in my body by then." She looked at the damaged wall. "They threw around some heavy artillery before leaving."

"And you managed to avoid Tamati's fate. How enterprising of you."

How could she talk her way out of this? It didn't matter, because Wickmore continued talking. "The security feed will show us what happened."

Nika's returning smile was chilly. At least she hoped it was. If he wanted to see the feed, it meant he didn't trust what she'd told him. "Of course."

Wickmore looked at the guard trying to contact Benedict. He blinked on his own link again. "We've been compromised," he told whoever answered. "Roystan and his crew are here, on Lesser Sirius. I want them found." He listened a moment. "They'll have come through the spaceport here at the capital. They didn't have time to come in another way. Go through every ship that arrived in the last two days. Check them all. Stop anyone who tries to get onto a ship." A longer pause. "I don't care if you have to shut down the spaceport. Do it."

Only the Lesser Sirius police could close the spaceport, but Nika knew the police would do whatever Eaglehawk asked. Lesser Sirius had once been a safe place to live. It wasn't anymore.

Alejandro's body had an involuntary tic in his jaw when he was nervous. Nika had never seen the tic, but she could feel it now.

Wickmore turned back to Nika. "Any other news you've omitted to tell me?" He was using his reasonable, friendly voice again.

This time she didn't care that he saw the sweat that rolled off her forehead. She shook her head.

"Good. Get me the security files."

Nika moved over to the link console near the door. Once Wickmore saw the files, he'd see her talking to Roystan and his crew, convincing them of who she really was. What had she told them? Had she given away Roystan and Josune's secrets? She couldn't let Wickmore get hold of that. He'd hunt them relentlessly forever after.

Could she destroy the file without giving herself away?

"You," Wickmore told the not-so-heavy heavy with him. "Start prepping that machine. We're moving it to a secure Eaglehawk building."

"You can't do that." The words came out unbidden. Nika bit down on her lip before she blurted out anything else. The Songyan had twenty outlets built in, with piped feeds to large vats of mutrient, stabilizing gel, and six other common ingredients. The electricals were hardwired. They'd have to turn the power off. If they did that in the next twenty-four hours they'd break the connection to the exchanger. There'd be no way for their bodies to return.

"And why not?"

Think fast.

"It's built in," Nika said. "How will you be able to put it back together the way she did?"

"Don't worry about destroying the machine. I've brought in a technical expert for that." Wickmore nodded at the man he'd earlier instructed to dismantle the machine.

"Have no fear I will destroy anything," the expert assured her.

"All our machines have override codes, and I know this particular model well."

Nika realized why he was familiar. Nikolas Comantra. One of the Songyan service engineers. Not the engineer who did the regular servicing on her own machines. That was Sinead Agutter. But Sinead had once had difficulty with the fine sensitivity on the calibrator. She'd brought two other engineers in to work on the problem. One of them had been Nikolas Comantra.

Comantra had been modded since, probably more than once, but he still retained a certain look. And he knew his product, knew it enough that he could relocate the Songyan without damage. Especially given that he thought he was moving a machine that wasn't in use.

Except that it was.

If they turned the exchanger off, what would happen to her body? The genemod machine would fix it, but whose mind would be in it?

Alejandro's?

She turned back to the console. "If you move the Songyan, you could destroy the exchanger."

Wickmore's smile was wintry. "I'm starting to think you don't want me to have this exchanger, Alejandro. Convince me why your career should last past you giving me those codes."

"Of course I want you to have the exchanger. I simply don't want to see it destroyed through not being careful enough."

"It's such a pity, Alejandro, that you choose now, of all times—right at the end of your career—to show some backbone." The smile hardened.

Was that a threat? Working for Wickmore would be like Nika waiting in her studio each day, hoping Alejandro was in a good mood.

What did she have to lose? "Don't forget that I have the codes to the exchanger."

"And I'm still waiting for that security feed."

If she wiped the feed, Wickmore would know something was wrong, whereas now he only suspected. She turned back to the console.

"Perhaps I could help," Comantra said. "Our Songyans send an aural and visual feed to the link. I have the overrides that could read it."

It was worse than Alejandro punching her in the stomach. The Songyan engineer.

She'd never buy another Songyan.

Well, she would, because there was nothing better on the market, but she'd make them work hard for the sale.

If she stayed alive long enough to buy another genemod machine. She was starting to doubt she would.

"Do it."

Nika forced down the impulse to order him away from her machine. Her fingers closed around the detonator in her pocket.

"If you destroy the exchanger—now that people know it exists—will your career survive the backlash?"

Wickmore was an executive at Eaglehawk, but executives could be sacked. It was rare, and Nika didn't think losing the exchanger would be a career-destroying blow, but she could pretend that she thought it was.

"We could work together on this. Leave the machine here, at least until someone reproduces the exchanger successfully." As if they could. "I'm interested in a long-term career. I know how it works. With my knowledge of the exchanger, we can work together."

She looked up to see Wickmore smiling at her. A true smile, something she'd never seen from him before. It changed the light on his face and dropped his apparent age by ten years. She could work with a face like that. Even with the SaStudio teeth.

"Well said, Alejandro." Then he added, more softly, "If you are indeed Alejandro."

If she was Alejandro? What had given her away?

"Let's see what happens, shall we?"

Comantra coughed. "If you're ready, I'm pushing the feed through now."

Nika bit down on what she wanted to say.

On the screen, Alejandro said, "Don't think you can dupe me."

Nika stared blindly at the feed, aware Wickmore watched with her. She was out of options. The laser was on the bench. It would take valuable seconds to get to it. Then what? There were six people in the room with her, five of them armed.

"Fascinating," Comantra murmured, as he watched Nika and Alejandro don the nets. He looked at the Songyan bed, at the controller.

Nika couldn't help her involuntary twitch.

How did she get out of this? Or did she accept that she couldn't?

"This is still connected," Comantra said.

On the screen above them, Tamati's knife entered Nika's Alejandro-controlled body.

"Kill the body and your brain reverts back to your own," Tamati said.

Wickmore moved over to the Songyan's controls. "But it didn't, did it? Nika Rik Terri in Alejandro's body. That could be interesting." He touched the controls. "What happens if I turn this off?"

Comantra pushed him away, knocking the box of nodes Nika used to link to the controller off the bench as he did so. "Don't. You could kill them both. We don't know how this works."

He realized what he'd done, choked off an apology, and dropped to the floor, scrabbling for the tiny nodes. Nika thought he might have done it to get out of Wickmore's line of fire, because the back of his neck was white.

"I have the codes," Nika reminded Wickmore. "Turn that off and you'll kill me. Alejandro's already brain-dead."

It was her and Wickmore, staring each other out, and then

Wickmore laughed. "So do I, now, modder. So do I." He glanced up at the screen, where Nika—in Alejandro's body—was frantically telling Josune not to shoot. "You said them aloud to Alejandro. We have the feed."

On the floor Comantra bumped his head as he started to stand up. She barely heard him say, "That's interesting."

Comantra used the edge of the Songyan to pull himself up. "You can't turn this machine off. She's customized everything. There's even added connections underneath. We don't know what they do." He held up one of the explosive devices.

Wickmore stilled for a second that felt like an hour. "Kill her," he ordered. "Then get out."

He ran for the door.

Yes, he knew what that add-on did.

Nika was out of ideas, and out of time.

She pressed the button as the first blaster burned a molten hole in her chest.

42

JOSUNE ARRIOLA

The docks were busier than they had been earlier.

Josune looked around. "I don't like this. Media's here, too," as reporters, surrounded by camera drones, ran past them. Headed the same direction they were—toward the ships.

She glanced at the Dekker, still shrouded with the tablecloth the chef had provided. They had to get it out of sight before anyone asked questions. "Don't like this at all."

"Me either." Roystan frowned at the genemod machine. "We need to get off the streets. Where can we take this?"

The police had their images, and probably their names. The best they could do was slip away. And cover Snow's hair, which was a distinctive color.

"Snow, lend me your sling. I need to cover your hair."

They'd be looking for a redhead. Nika would make the hair covering look as if it was designed to be fashionable. All Josune hoped was that it would buy them some time.

He handed it over.

Josune moved to tie it around his head, only to bump into two more reporters.

One of them stopped and did a double take. "Snowshoe Bertram."

Snow lost any color he'd had, and he hadn't had much to start with. "Banjo." It was more of a choke than a word.

Banjo grabbed Snow's arm. Thankfully, his good arm. "Bertram, by all that's wonderful." He dragged the shocked youth over to the other reporter. "Linnie. This is him. This is my modder."

"Doesn't look like a modder." Linnie's accent said she came from money.

Banjo reached for him again.

Snow flinched back.

"Careful." Josune softened the rebuttal with an apology. "He's hurt, took a fall. Sandrawall climbing. Broke his arm. Hasn't had time to repair it."

"Oh, you do Sandrawalling." Linnie's eyes sparkled. "I love climbing."

Josune turned away. Nika would have known if the sparkling eyes were real or a mod.

Snow muttered something that might have been "It was my first time."

"Not that Banjo doesn't look good." Linnie waved a hand dismissively. "But I told him. People like us. We look good naturally. It's only tweaks and fashion for us."

Snow and Banjo shared a look that Linnie would never, in all her years, ever comprehend.

Snow sighed, then seemed to relax. "Let me look at you." He turned to Banjo. "I didn't get a chance to see the finished you, before I had to leave."

Roystan and Josune both laughed out loud, although Roystan did clap a hand to his mouth.

"He is such a chip off the old block," Roystan said, when Linnie looked at him. "Fast learner, too."

Carlos and Jacques eased the Dekker past. Josune and Roystan stood between the machine and the reporters.

Snow walked around Banjo. "Not bad."

"Not bad," Banjo declared. "It's brilliant, and you know it."

"Maybe," Snow agreed. His eyes flicked to the box holding Nika's body.

They didn't have time for this. "Shouldn't you be over there?" Josune indicated the growing crowd over at the shuttle gates.

Banjo snorted. "Big-time media's over there. We can only hang around the fringes, won't even get close." He took Snow's arm again, carefully this time. "This is more important." He leaned close, whispered. "I kept your shop safe. Everything's there. Everything's as it was. You can fix your arm."

Josune heard him only because she was right behind Snow.

"Actually, we were just—"

An explosion deafened them all. Josune spun around. A cloud of black smoke rose above the rooftops. She knew the sound of a bomb going off. Knew where it had gone off.

Banjo watched the black cloud. "That's over toward Salamander Street. Linnie. Quick. This could be our scoop." He turned back to Snow. "Everything's there. Got to go."

The two reporters were gone, almost before Banjo had finished speaking.

"Salamander Street," Snow whispered. He started to shake.

Josune knew what he was thinking. She was thinking it herself, and she'd set the bombs. "We need to get out of sight, Snow. Where's your studio?"

"It's not far." He turned blindly and led the way. Jacques and Carlos followed with the Dekker. Josune walked with Snow, while Roystan stayed on point behind.

Roystan stopped not much later. "Snow." He put out a hand to stop Carlos, who was closest.

Snow kept walking. Josune tapped him on the shoulder. He looked up, back at the corner, at Roystan.

"Oh." He turned down the street.

The studio was four doors down.

43

JOSUNE ARRIOLA

When they finally reached the dubious haven of the studio, Roystan was ready to fall. Josune handed him another protein bar, the last of her pocket supplies.

She turned to Snow, who looked to be in shock. "Can you check Nika?" Giving him something to do might bring him out of it.

Snow's teeth chattered. "What if she's d-dead?"

Josune had no idea. They'd gotten her into the machine in time, according to Nika. She'd also said that the minds switched back after twenty-four hours, provided there was a mind to return to. She hadn't said what would happen if one of them died. Who was going to come out of the box?

If it was Alejandro, she would have to kill him. It wasn't something she looked forward to. Not while he was in Nika's body.

Josune pulled the cloth off the Dekker. "Nika knows what she's doing."

Nika's body was twitching.

Snow raised a hand to his mouth. "She's not supposed to do that."

Red dots flickered over the console controls. Josune had no idea what they meant.

"She's awake." Snow frantically pushed at the controls with his good hand. "I don't understand half these alarms. This shouldn't be happening."

The lights remained red.

"I can't get the calibrator to balance." He gave a strangled laugh. "Nika will kill me."

More likely Josune was going to kill Nika. Literally. "How long before she comes out of the machine?"

"She lost a lot of blood, but that doesn't take long to fix. It depends how far her system shut down."

Which wasn't an answer.

"She shouldn't have flooded the Dekker. It's dangerous. And stupid. She'll drown in the fluid. I need to run proper diagnostics." Snow ran over to the other genemod machine and started setting it up. "I have to move her."

"You can't. You said she's awake. And she said not to touch her."

"She'll die if I don't. Trust me on this."

Who was more likely to be right? Nika or Snow?

The Dekker pinged, then sounded a klaxon blare that could only be a warning. Snow swung around. The liquid surrounding Nika expelled onto the floor in a gurgling whoosh. The lid opened.

Nika sat up, coughing up clear liquid. She leaned over the side of the Dekker, almost fell out, and wiped her mouth with the back of her hand. "It worked."

She sounded surprised.

Josune swallowed bile and pulled out her blaster. Nika, or was it Alejandro, wasn't armed. It didn't matter. Killing someone in cold blood wasn't something she'd done before, not something she wanted to do now.

But she had to be sure.

Roystan moved to the other side of the Dekker, his own weapon out. "What worked?"

"Getting my body into a machine within fifteen minutes, so my brain survived, so I wouldn't be brain-dead." Nika waved a hand at the mess, at the Dekker, at herself. "It's not something you can test, you know." She swung her feet over the side of the mod machine and fell.

Snow closed his mouth with a snap. "How did you—?"

Josune lifted her blaster, her other hand going to the sparker hidden beneath her shirt.

"Prove who you are."

Carlos stepped carefully through the liquid. "Here. Can't have you getting cold." He wrapped the tablecloth around her.

"Thank you, Carlos. Proof. Right. Is Giwari enough?" Nika looked around the studio. "Snow, why aren't you in the Netanyu? Your arm is broken."

Josune holstered her blaster. She was Nika, all right. "How long have you been conscious?"

Nika shuddered. "Since I—when Alejandro's body—died. When we all blew up, I suppose."

"You can't get out of a genemod machine yourself," Snow said. "It's impossible."

Nika pointed to a large button set into the side. "You can in a Dekker." She looked with distaste at the machine. "If I never see another Dekker in my life I'll be happy."

After that, things quieted down. Nika insisted on supplies for the genemod machine. Jacques insisted on food. They ordered both.

Josune and Nika sat by the door, waiting for the deliveries.

"What will you do?" Nika asked. "If we get away. We can't go out looking like our wanted posters, and Snow needs time in a machine. He doesn't have enough supplies to do a good job."

Josune noticed she said *if*, not *when* they got away. She glanced at Roystan, dozing beside her, and lowered her voice. "That depends on him."

Hammond Roystan, aka Roy Goberling.

"All my life I've chased this dream. For the last eight weeks, it's been standing in front of me." She didn't know what to do anymore. "I don't know what to think, Nika."

It wasn't the running. Or the fighting. She'd spent ten years on the *Hassim* fighting. She'd followed Feyodor to find transurides. But Hammond Roystan wasn't Taki Feyodor. She'd follow Roystan because she . . . because she wanted to. Yet Roystan had said exploring was a waste of time.

"Maybe he'll go with you if you ask him."

She blinked hard. She hadn't cried for years, and she wasn't going to start now. She shook her head. She had no future with Roystan. He had no use for her. And she couldn't betray the one thing that would get Roystan hunted again. It wouldn't just be Eaglehawk after him, it would be every one of the Big Twenty-Seven, and hundreds of smaller companies, too. Roystan would be running forever.

He was so tired of running, he'd said.

"He'll never ask me. He knows what I represent."

Roystan got quietly to his feet. He hadn't been asleep. Josune's face flamed.

He went via the coffee machine and poured three coffees, then brought them over. "I don't know where it is, Josune. I don't remember."

She'd been chasing something so unimportant to him, he'd forgotten it.

"I remember who I am." Roystan sat beside her, his shoulder brushing hers. "I remember my early life. I remember Brown Combine. I remember Jed Brown."

Jed Brown and Roy Goberling had been best friends.

"I remember being hunted. Running, all the time. I remember Taki Feyodor when she was younger than you, and just as determined." He looked at Nika. "I remember Gino Giwari. I wanted it all to stop. I thought that if I had no memory of it, it would all go away. Gino said he could do that. Wipe my memory.

"I don't remember anything related to transurides. I don't remember those trips, but I know the verse on the outside of the ship.

I don't know where the ship went, but I know I had an apartment at Pisces III and I always started out from there."

The coffee was bitter on Josune's tongue.

"Selective forgetting," Nika said. "Giwari played around with that early in his career. Until it was banned as too dangerous. That's when he moved his specialty to modifying the genome."

She tapped her mug, an unconscious beat. "No one does gene-mods anymore. Even Giwari is largely discredited now. I used his techniques to fix bad mods. I came to believe he was only a technician."

Josune looked at Roystan. He wasn't looking at her, he was staring into his coffee.

"Giwari had a shop on Pisces III," Roystan said.

"Studio."

"I used to go there a lot. I don't remember why; I just remember going." He looked up. "I don't remember our first meeting."

Nika nodded. "The transurides are important. I'm sure of that. It must have cost you a fortune every time you came to Tilda."

He inclined his head.

"You're not aging. Your cells are not degrading; they're reproducing in their entirety every time. That has to be due to the mods of the telomeres at the end of your cells."

Josune was sure that meant something to Nika. It didn't to her.

The buzz at the door made them all jump.

Josune checked the exterior cameras. The delivery drone. A second drone, with the genemod supplies, arrived behind it.

They let Nika collect the packages, while Roystan and Josune stood guard, and then went over each one carefully, checking for bugs.

Josune couldn't find any.

"Snow." Nika shook him awake.

He stared at her, glassy-eyed.

"You want to set your own mod?"

He stood up, still so much asleep that Josune wondered if Nika should let him do it.

"We've fresh mutrient. Naolic acid."

Snow shivered.

"Arrat crystals, aluminum salts, dendrian salts."

"Dendrian salts?" Snow looked up with the first sign of life he'd shown. "How much did you get?" And he became more animated as he tapped on the screen.

Nika watched over his shoulder. "Don't you dare change your hair color."

"They'll be looking for someone with red hair."

"It's not red. It's red-gold. And Snow, before you do anything I want a gene read on your hair. I'll pay you for it."

"You can have it."

"Snow, don't give away gene reads and don't take anything less than a thousand credits for one."

He looked at her.

"I'm serious. Now, I'll pay you five hundred credits."

"Snow," Josune said, when Snow shrugged. "Don't you dare. Charge her a thousand."

Snow looked from Nika to Josune and back. "Three thousand," he said.

"Deal," Nika said promptly. "Add the gene read, Snow. I want it before you do anything, and don't you dare color your hair."

"It is rather distinctive," Roystan said.

"I'll make it short, then."

"That's what most people would do. They'll be looking for someone with a shaved head," Nika said. "Or short, red hair."

"Red-gold," Josune and Roystan said together, and shared a smile.

"Red-gold," Nika agreed. "Make your hair longer, Snow. Extend it to halfway down your back."

"Halfway?" Snow looked doubtfully at his design. He shook his head. "We can extend hair a centimeter, maybe two, but it breaks after that."

"Hair is a protein," Nika said. "You just have to ensure that it extrudes smoothly and doesn't break." She touched the screen. "Here's where it's going to break. How are you going to stop that?"

Roystan collected Josune's empty coffee mug. "Snow will be fine."

At least someone would.

"Josune. I'm sorry. I—"

Josune looked away. He had nothing to be sorry about.

"You don't need me to find things for you. You were doing better on your own. Fourteen worlds. I only ever found one."

But the *Hassim* had never found transurides.

Roystan's hand moved under her chin and turned her gently to face him. "But maybe I could help you look." There was a pause that seemed to last forever. "If you'd have me."

She leaned her head against his chest to hide the sudden tears that welled. "Maybe you're right. Maybe it's time I stopped chasing something someone already found. Maybe it's time to settle." A home with Roystan. She could fit in with that. Even if it was out on the edge of the legal zone.

He moved his arm across her back and drew her close. "Don't give up on your dream, Josune. We could work through what information we have, what Feyodor had."

"I'm not the only one with dreams."

"Maybe some of us had stopped dreaming. Maybe it's time we started again."

Josune stayed in the circle of his arm. He was like a sparrow in her arms. She gave a choked laugh. "You need to eat more." She was going to carry protein bars around in her pocket. Then she wouldn't have to move.

Snow was in the machine. Carlos was asleep. Jacques was cooking. Nika frowned at a DNA sequence on the nearest wall screen.

"Is that Snow?" Josune asked. "What's wrong?" Snow was competent enough to do his own mod, so what was Nika's expression for?

"Not Snow. Roystan. This is a typical Giwari cell mod." Nika tapped the screen. "See, here. And here." She put her finger on the end of the cell. "He never touches the telomeres. I studied him. He wasn't a modest man. He documented everything.

"In his early life he played around with memories, worked with them until it became illegal. The rest of his life was devoted to modifying DNA. There was nothing in his notes, in his life—in his work—about reducing cell senescence."

"What's that?" If they traveled long with Nika they'd learn a whole new language.

"Cells deteriorating with age." Nika turned back to the image again. "Nothing about modding telomeres either. Do you know what I think?"

"What?"

"Your longevity"—with a nod to Roystan—"is a by-product of something else he did."

"Longevity. That's an intriguing way of putting it."

"It is intriguing." Nika turned around. As if she was looking for answers. She stopped suddenly. "Of course." She swung back to Roystan. "Giwari wasn't stupid. And you had access to one thing no one else did."

Josune felt like clapping a hand to her own forehead. Of course. "The location of the transurides."

"Exactly." Nika's finger was strong enough to push Roystan back. "You're his client. One day, you might regret what you did. You might come back and ask him to reverse it. If I were Giwari, I'd have a backup plan for that. People change their minds."

"Are you saying he programmed the coordinates into my genes?"

"Of course not. You wouldn't tell him where it was."

"So what—"

"Your memory of it."

"So he put my memories into my genes? Can you do that?"

"Of course not. It's a key. He put the code for unlocking your memory into your genes."

Roystan scratched his head.

Josune tried not to hope. She wasn't an explorer anymore. She'd retired. But was it possible? "Do you know how to use the key?"

"Not yet. But I'll work it out." Typical Nika, with no room for doubt or false modesty. "I bet whatever he did took a massive chunk of transurides. Otherwise it wouldn't have taken."

"That, I do remember." Roystan held his cupped hand, palm up.

"I wish I had my Songyan. You have the most fascinating body I've ever had a chance to work with."

Roystan made a deprecating movement with his hands. "My body. All yours." His stomach rumbled. "Provided you feed it at intervals."

He made for Jacques, in Snow's kitchen. "I'm starved."

44

NIKA RIK TERRI

Two days later the police and company men had dispersed. According to their own personal news source—Banjo, who visited on the second day to see if Snow needed anything—the criminals had slipped past the cordon and were long gone.

Nika stayed in the shop front with Snow when Banjo arrived, dusting their fast-dwindling modding supplies. Ready if Snow needed help. The rest of them went into the back room, out of sight, but watching and listening.

Banjo glanced at Nika, then took Snow to one side to talk. He wouldn't have known her for the same woman he'd met the other day. Wouldn't have known any of them, except for Roystan—whom even Nika wasn't prepared to touch for the moment. Quick, cosmetic changes—a couple of hours in a genemod machine—but enough to last until they got off-world. Which they planned to do immediately after Banjo's unanticipated visit.

Carlos's markings had been enhanced and enlarged. Nika had inked them by hand. They'd wear off, but in the meantime, he looked truly fearsome. Jacques—under protest—had lost half his size.

"You'll get it back," Nika had told him. "After all, Roystan can eat different foods now. Lots to experiment on."

"Surely you can leave me with the one thing that belongs to me."

"For your own safety, Jacques," Roystan said. "And ours."

He'd muttered under his breath but hadn't argued any more.

Josune's skin was now a single color, her head shaved. Nika

mourned the loss of the dendritic markings. That had been a good mod.

She had left her own Dietel-patched skin, although it hurt her soul to do so. No one would look for Nika Rik Terri with obviously patched skin. Even Leonard Wickmore would expect her to change it as soon as she could.

The criminals apparently—according to Banjo again—"had a decoy ship here at the spaceport. Kept the police here at the docks while they escaped overland."

Banjo couldn't fail to know that one of the "criminals" was a red-headed man. Or to notice that same redhead now wore his much-longer hair—darkened with oil—in small plaits all over his head. Or that he'd lost ten years in age. Nika suspected that was the reason for the very slight emphasis on the *apparently*.

"Someone tried to assassinate Eaglehawk's Executive Wickmore while he was at the body modder's. Nika Rik Terri's, no less. He lost an arm, half a leg, and an eye."

It couldn't have happened to a more deserving person. That sort of damage took time to repair, and some eye replacements didn't take well. The pity was that he hadn't died.

"He'll be in a tank for months."

"What happened to Rik Terri?" Snow asked.

"Rumor has it her boyfriend did away with her. That's why Executive Wickmore was there. She did work for him on occasion, and she went missing a couple of weeks ago. Parts of the boyfriend were found. Five other bodies were identified too, one being Nikolas Comantra, a specialist engineer from Songyan Company. There was a sixth body. Currently unidentified. The police are still trying to work out what happened." Banjo leaned close, and Nika strained to hear. "I don't want to see you go, but if you need transport, I might know someone."

This was the man who'd tried to extort credits from Snow mere weeks ago.

"I'd appreciate that."

Banjo opened a link and brought up a contact. "Tell them I sent you."

"Thank you." Snow hesitated. "Look, about your mod. I'm—"

"I love my mod. People look at me now and smile. I don't hurt anymore."

"That was because you went to a bad modder to start with."

Nika smiled. You couldn't keep Snow's personality down for long.

"Make sure you go to a good one next time."

"Maybe you'll be back by then."

"You've got two years before you need another mod."

"You're a good man, Bertram." Banjo finally turned to go. "If you ever need help, you know who to call."

"Thank you." Snow stood up too, and walked with him to the door. He stood staring in the direction Banjo had gone, until Nika joined him. "It's like you gave him a different personality when you changed his looks."

Nika said, "Sometimes your personality is defined by your looks. That's what a good modder does, Snow. It gives the client the confidence to be themselves. It makes them happy."

Behind them, Josune checked out the contact Banjo had left.

"What will you do?" Snow asked, as they stared into the street together.

Where could she go? Leonard Wickmore would hunt her down and destroy her.

Josune joined them at the door, Roystan at her back.

"Come with us," Josune said. "We're hunting transurides. And new worlds. There's safety in numbers, and we'll be a long way from Eaglehawk."

"Besides," Carlos called, from inside. "Who's going to fix Roystan when he needs it if you don't come?"

To finish the work Giwari didn't even know he'd created; to

perfect the mod that finally made the genemod machine live up to its name.

"What about you, Snow?" He didn't have anywhere to go either, but it wasn't the time to point that out. She owed Snow a studio. And some training.

"I am your apprentice, aren't I? Don't I have to go where you go?"

Nika nodded, and took it as the tacit okay Snow meant it to be.

"Why not," she said to Josune. It would be nice to be part of a team; to have friends. "Let's go mod the galaxy, Snow, with these crazy explorers."

Roystan put a hand on her shoulder, a hand on Snow's. "Welcome to the crew."

"You do understand," Snow said, as they turned back inside. "I want a Songyan of my own."

There'd be a lot of modding—from both of them—before he was ready for that.

Nika looked forward to it.

ACKNOWLEDGMENTS

Thanks once again to our agent, Caitlin Blasdell, and our editor, Anne Sowards, both of whom provided invaluable input to the early drafts and made the book so much better, as they always do.

To our copyeditor, Amy J. Schneider. To Judith Lagerman, who designed the book cover.

To everyone else at Ace who turned this into a book for us.

Our beta readers, Jenny and Arthur. (Sorry we got the book to you so late, Arthur.) Thanks for reading the book and for your feedback.

Our family, who are there for us always.

And to you, our readers, who add a whole new dimension to writing a novel.

S. K. Dunstall is the pseudonym for a writing team of two sisters. Together they are the national bestselling authors of *Confluence*, *Alliance*, and *Linesman*. They live in Melbourne, Australia. Visit them on the Web at skdunstall.com.

Ready to find
your next great read?

Let us help.

Visit prh.com/nextread

Penguin
Random
House